PENGUIN BOOKS

Stick or Twist

Eleanor Moran is an executive producer for TV drama at the BBC, where her credits include *Rome*, *Hotel Babylon* and *New Tricks*. This is her first novel.

Stick or Twist

ELEANOR MORAN

PENGUIN BOOKS

PENGUIN BOOKS

Published by the Penguin Group
Penguin Books Ltd, 80 Strand, London WC2R ORL, England
Penguin Group (USA), Inc., 375 Hudson Street, New York, New York 10014, USA
Penguin Group (Canada), 90 Eglinton Avenue East, Suite 700, Toronto, Ontario, Canada M4P 2Y3
(a division of Pearson Penguin Canada Inc.)
Penguin Ireland, 25 St Stephen's Green, Dublin 2, Ireland (a division of Penguin Books Ltd)
Penguin Group (Australia), 250 Camberwell Road, Camberwell, Victoria 3124, Australia
(a division of Pearson Australia Group Pty Ltd)
Penguin Books India Pvt Ltd, 11 Community Centre, Panchsheel Park, New Delhi – 110 017, India
Penguin Group (NZ), 67 Apollo Drive, Rosedale, North Shore 0632, New Zealand
(a division of Pearson New Zealand Ltd)
Penguin Books (South Africa) (Pty) Ltd, 24 Sturdee Avenue,
Rosebank, Johannesburg 2196, South Africa

Penguin Books Ltd, Registered Offices: 80 Strand, London WC2R ORL, England

www.penguin.com

First published 2009
1

Copyright © Eleanor Moran, 2009
All rights reserved

The moral right of the author has been asserted

Lyrics from 'The Lion Sleeps Tonight' (Weiss/Creatore/Peretti)
© Courtesy of Memory Lane Music Ltd.
Reproduced by permission

Set in Monotype Garamond
Typeset by Rowland Phototypesetting Ltd, Bury St Edmunds, Suffolk
Printed in England by Clays Ltd, St Ives plc

Except in the United States of America, this book is sold subject
to the condition that it shall not, by way of trade or otherwise, be lent,
re-sold, hired out, or otherwise circulated without the publisher's
prior consent in any form of binding or cover other than that in
which it is published and without a similar condition including this
condition being imposed on the subsequent purchaser

ISBN: 978-0-141-03646-5

www.greenpenguin.co.uk

Penguin Books is committed to a sustainable future
for our business, our readers and our planet.
The book in your hands is made from paper
certified by the Forest Stewardship Council.

For my mother, Stephanie

Was I happy? You be the judge. Here was my nightly routine: fight my way home from the office through grid-locked London traffic, cursing and swearing in tandem with the 'wind-down zone' on Suicidal FM. Tramp up the stairs in perilously high fuck-me shoes, pour myself a bucket of red wine and sink into a glazed stupor in front of *CSI*. Communication between Adam and I was largely limited to one or other of us grunting that we needed a refill. Collapse into bed in profoundly unflattering night-wear, sharing a chaste kiss and a mechanical 'I love you' before disappearing into muzzy catatonia.

I guess I never really stopped to ask myself the question, because I was too scared of the answer. While I frequently whinged about my sixty-hour working weeks, if I'd been truly honest with myself, I'd have admitted I was grateful for the anaesthesia they provided. Besides, how could I not be happy? My job was kind of glamorous, my friends were unbeatable and my boyfriend was unbastardly.

But life's never that simple.

I

Saturday mornings are the most menacing time. Teeth brushed and genitals soaped, this is the moment when 'monogamous man' stalks his prey.

I can hear Adam going about his business – whistling as he snatches the overfed Saturday paper from the door-mat, chatting away to Hector as though he might suddenly confound science and reply. All those little habits and traits which add up to him are so utterly familiar that they're almost part of me. Not having him in my life is unimaginably awful: it would be like cutting out a chunk of myself with a kitchen knife. He's my best friend, the person who's on my team no matter what – but an evil, anarchistic part of me is starting to wonder if that's enough.

Monogamy and monotony are worryingly similar words, don't you think? When the sex first began its inevitable decline, I tried my best to claw it back. I'd wear uncomfortable thong knickers that felt like cheese wire, and send Adam self-consciously sexy emails at work. Eventually I had to gracefully accept defeat. It became clear that it's almost impossible to feel truly erotic about someone who you also have to trudge round a super-market with discussing the ply of your loo roll. Quilted?

Recycled? None of these knotty dilemmas make me feel particularly hot.

But of course it's not just about sex, it's about who we've become to one another. I'll quite happily clip my toenails in front of *EastEnders*, while he's all too prone to tunnelling down his ears in search of waxy lumps. There's something comforting and familial about how intimate we can be, but there's not much novelty or mystery left in its wake. And I'm terrified that the arrival of children would increase the domestic tedium tenfold. Right now I feel way too immature to sign up to a life of carrot pureeing and vomit wiping, but who am I trying to kid? My days as a hard-bodied twenty-something are well and truly behind me (if they ever existed). Maybe it's time to get with the programme and sign up for stage two.

Adam and I are so good for each other in a million different ways, but I still can't help longing for something exciting to happen. I don't know what exactly, because the idea of an affair appals me, and the thought of throwing away what's an almost ten-year commitment is frankly terrifying. But the suspicion that most of the adventures are already behind me, at the grand old age of thirty-two, depresses me beyond measure.

Now he's bounding up the stairs and through the bedroom door, all expectation and nerves.

'Morning, beautiful girl.'

My vain little heart jumps, hopefully. Could I be having one of those days where it miraculously comes together? You know the ones I mean — where it's not about how much make-up you've got on, or what you're wearing, you've just somehow 'got it'. But then I catch sight of myself in the wardrobe door and it becomes crushingly clear he's lying. My blondey-brown curls are looking distinctly mouse and my eyes look Honey Monster puffy. At least I'm not a chubber, although the pay-off is Britain's smallest breasts.

It's so hard to judge one's own physical charms objectively, even though we're relentlessly judgemental of each other's. Women are hopelessly competitive, whether or not they choose to admit it. If another girl's walking past me I'm like Rain Man with my split-second calculations: *great face, fat arse, lank hair*. Or it could go *amazing eyes, perfect figure but, joy of joys, hairy arms*. I do scrub up quite well, I know that, but I'm no natural beauty. I definitely have to work at it.

Adam flops into bed beside me like an eager Labrador, his hand snaking its way beneath my manky pyjamas.

'I really want to be inside you right now.'

Oh God, not the sub-standard porn dialogue. I stroke his thick, dark hair. 'I love you,' I whisper, which is achingly true. I want so much to want this, yet every fibre of my being longs to flee. He's as handsome as he ever was – stubbly and dark with sinuous rower's legs – but it somehow doesn't register any more.

As his hand slips lower, I try to lose myself in imagination. But, disastrously, I've got fantasist's block. I take hold of his cock, working it between my palms. At first he responds, moaning softly and reaching for me. But then he suddenly tenses up, sensing my dislocation. He jerks away, angry and hurt.

3

'What's the problem here? Jesus, why do you have to make it so hard for me?'

'Don't be cross with me,' I plead, feeling hot, self-hating tears springing to my eyes. 'I'm just so tired.'

But we both know I'm lying.

Adam's struggling into his jeans now, looking painfully undignified. Rage has destroyed any vestige of co-ordination. I try again, desperate to soothe his wounded pride.

'Please don't leave like this, just come back to bed.'

But is that really what I want? He takes the stairs, two at a time. The door slams and he's gone. I feel like a witch, but I'm a witch with a lunch date so there's no time to wallow.

Half an hour later I'm in the gastro pub round the corner (you know the score: over-cooked, over-priced slabs of leathery meat, swimming in 'jus') waiting for my two best girlfriends. They always make me feel like the best possible version of myself, which right now is what I desperately need. Adam is refusing to take my calls.

Susie's first through the door, all long limbs and apologies. She's one of life's eternal optimists, always searching for the good in people. Maybe George Bush has a point, perhaps Saddam Hussein had a really bad childhood – you get my drift. It can be intensely annoying if all you're looking for is a partner in slander, and yet it also makes life seem less bleak. But professional Susie is a different animal entirely: a ball-breaking building inspector who makes hairy-arsed labourers stand to attention. Dark hair piled under an unflattering hard hat,

4

high heels lying forlorn in the boot – femininity thrown aside in favour of authority. She, more than any of us, splits herself in two in order to survive. Polly turns up soon after, and now the whole sorry mess that's been my Saturday is tumbling out. It was Polly who got me and Adam together, so I feel perversely guilty for the fact that I'm having doubts. They're old university mates; I think they even had a drunken fumble at a student party, unimaginable though it now is.

'But, Anna, you're so good together!' pleads Susie. 'You just need to make more time for each other.'

'It's gone beyond that,' I tell her emphatically. 'There are no surprises left.' I grope for the right way to express my frustration. 'I wish I inspired him to invent cures for crippling diseases or ... I don't know, scale uncharted mountain ranges.'

Pretty much the most surprising thing I've done this month is nearly take his eyebrow off with the unexpected velocity of my big toenail. That said, I can tell from Polly's expression that I'm sounding spoilt. It's not that I expect endless thrills and spills, rollercoasters make me hurl, but I wish we could still expect the unexpected. Sometimes it feels like we've had every conversation we're meant to have, exposed every crack and crevice. I'm just not sure where's left to go. Polly sighs.

'Don't even think about getting out unless you know you can handle it. Dating in your thirties really isn't pretty.'

She should know. Despite having curves I'd sell my grandmother for, combined with the kind of translucent

Irish skin that never looks anything short of perfect, she's a total romantic disaster zone.

Polly's latest disaster was Matt. Matt is one of the worst breed of men you can stumble upon in the thirty-plus dating jungle – 'the bolter'. He stalks his prey with ruthless efficiency; having met you once, he'll call and text obsessively. He might even resort to a poem, maybe one which rhymes 'lovely' with 'hump me'. You're really not interested and at first it's irritating. But then your fragile ego kicks in and you start to believe the hype. Perhaps he really hasn't felt like this in ages, perhaps you really are that unforgettable; why not give him a chance? It's not like there's a queue of single men beating down the door. Still not sure, you hold off from tumbling straight into bed. He is, of course, a total gentleman. He wants to wait too, because you're worth it.

Five dates in, having convinced yourself against your better judgement that he's almost husband material (Matt's eyes were no longer like tiny piss holes in the snow, they were 'intense'), you finally succumb to his dubious charms. And, as if by magic, the texts and calls immediately peter out. You can't believe it at first. Surely he wouldn't have gone to all that trouble if he wasn't really, really keen? But the bolter's proved his point – he can get whomever he chooses into bed by sheer force of personality – and he's ready to move on. Besides, he wonders, why are you getting so upset? You were only 'seeing each other' after all; it's not like he was your boyfriend.

Polly's still smarting.

'I drove past him the other day and I couldn't help myself. I shouted "You pin-eyed wanker," thinking he wouldn't hear me, but the sun roof was open. So now he'll be telling all his friends I'm a bunny boiler.'

Poor Pol, I really feel for her, but it's also starting to sober me up.

'Adam loves you so much, Anna,' says Susie. 'He'd never screw around, he'll be a great dad and he makes you laugh. Do you really want to chuck that away?'

She's right of course. If my single self could hear me now she would give me a sharp pinch and tell me to pull myself together. Why am I so incapable of counting my blessings? Surely if I try harder I can find a way back to him?

'But,' Polly counters, 'if you really can't face having sex with him any more, where does that leave you? If you can't fix it, you owe it to yourself to get out.'

Maybe sex always dwindles, sooner or later. Are any couples really at it like rabbits on their ruby wedding anniversaries? Being with someone is about so much more than lust, after all, and constancy is a much under-rated commodity.

'You could always try and pull a few tricks out of the bag,' smiles Susie, looking at me suggestively.

The idea of going home with a bag of hideous plastic 'love toys' is so horrendous. Besides, I know Adam would laugh uproariously, and who could blame him?

'OK, maybe not,' says Susie, clocking my expression.

The image of Adam peering, baffled, at a 'cock ring' or

7

whatever they're called, suddenly reminds me of why he's so utterly adorable.

'No, you're right. I've got to put more effort in, in every sense. I can't just chuck this away, not after all this time.'

Besides, the very thought of leaving kicks my evil inner calculator into overdrive. An Adam-free life is an agonizing prospect, so it would take me at least a year before I could begin to contemplate the idea of someone else. At this moment in time, I've got scant interest in children. However, if I then get struck by the earth mother thunderbolt, I'll want at least two childless years with the father, which makes me thirty-five and a half before it's even a possibility. And, as I explain to the girls, by that time there's every chance my womb might've decided to punish me for my lack of interest by shrivelling right up like a malicious old prune.

'Stop it, Anna!' wails Polly. 'I can't bear it. I don't want to think about this stuff.'

A chill runs through me as I resolve even more firmly to make it work. 'We're still in denial,' I say, 'but it's coming to us all. We're on the cusp of Botox. Not there yet, but fast approaching the moment where we'll secretly start to wonder if it's worth it.'

'The Cusp of Botox,' says Susie dreamily. 'That sounds kind of inviting, like some fantastic Mediterranean island.'

'Maybe to you!' says Polly.

Susie starts gathering up her things. 'I've got to go.

Friends of Martin's from work are coming over tonight, and I'm roasting a sea bass.'

Polly nudges me and I try to ignore her. Martin is possibly the wettest man in north London, so cooking him a fish is highly appropriate. But Susie's actually married him, so it's imperative that we don't convey to her what we really think. I wonder if they still do it; sex with Martin conjures up such a repellent image that I can't bear to ask. I bet he calls it 'making love' and insists on holding her for ages afterwards, even though the pressure of his spindly arm makes it impossible to get a decent night's sleep.

Polly and I soon follow, and I let myself back into the silent flat, wondering how it would be if this really was it. Just me and a solitary cat, hurtling towards spinster-hood. Perhaps I could teach Hector to do tricks, so I'll have something to talk about at work when the mothers' mafia cast me pitying glances while discussing their toddlers' bowel movements. 'But can Alfie swing from a trapeze?' I'll pipe up. 'Or walk a tightrope? Hector's just as advanced.'

Suddenly there's a crash from the kitchen. Adam's in there, pulling the scales down from the top cupboard. He's got Nigella's *How To Be A Domestic Goddess* propped open at a lethal-looking chocolate cake recipe and is lightly dusted with flour. One of Adam's many sterling qualities is that he can bake. He can also braise, sauté and fricassee.

'Anna!' he cries, with a sheepish grin. 'I'm so glad

you're home. I'm sorry I was such a prick this morning. I was trying to surprise you.'

'I can see that. Nice apron.' His mum brought it back from somewhere, and it has two fried eggs for breasts. As do I, come to think of it.

'Yeah, nice hat.' I'm wearing a black cashmere beanie, which he always says makes me look like a lesbian cat burglar. I go over and hug him, squeezing him tightly and drinking in his smell. There is nowhere in the world I feel safer than here.

'Are we friends again?' he asks, stroking my face.

'Of course we're friends,' I say, overwhelmed with affection. What I should probably do now is snog him passionately, but instead I just nuzzle his chest.

'Thank God for that. I can't bear it when we row.'

'No, me neither,' I say, desperate to repair us. 'In fact I've got a surprise for you too.'

'Have you?' he says, sounding genuinely excited.

And I hear myself promising him an amazing weekend away for our tenth anniversary, which I internally resolve to fill with passion and excitement and fireworks and … blah, blah, blah. It can be right again, can't it?

2

'Why are you wriggling around like that?'

'Wriggling around like what? I don't know what you're talking about.'

Of course I know exactly what Adam's talking about. I can barely sit down, which is making driving something of a challenge. Yesterday I went to see Renee, the merciless beautician across the road from work, and had my muff waxed to within an inch of its life. She kept viciously tearing great swathes off it, snarling, 'I need you to relax now, please!' I was aiming for my first ever Brazilian, but I couldn't ultimately last the distance. Instead I'm looking sort of piebald, like some kind of battered furry mammal from a rescue shelter. Not so erotic I fear.

Our weekend away has officially begun, and the signs are good. For example, rather than us arguing bitterly about what music to put on, failing to find a compromise and driving along in stony silence, Adam has agreed to listen to Joni Mitchell, my all-time favourite recording artist. He hasn't even said it's 'menstruation music' like he normally does. And he's poured his heart and soul into making us a picnic so elaborate that it's worthy of the glorious spreads the downtrodden cook used to make the Famous Five.

'Look, there's your boyfriend,' pipes up Adam, 'why don't you offer him a lift?'

Please don't get the idea that I've been holding out on you, and we're actually swingers. The 'your boyfriend' game is the singly most childish and entertaining thing you can play on a long car journey. It blows I-spy right out of the water. Adam is subtly pointing at a gnome-like man with a Friar Tuck haircut. He's got huge headphones on, and is wheeling a pull-along trolley, while mouthing along to a song. He is the last man on earth I would ever want to go out with, which is the whole point of the game. Polly and I have played it since school, but one particularly rainy and tedious holiday I broke and taught it to Adam, even though he's the wrong sex.

'We've actually finished. He's left me for your girl-friend, who's just over there.'

I'm not going to bother to describe her, as none of this reflects well on us, but it gets the journey off to an amusing start. We zip out of London, clearly blessed by the traffic gods, and tootle through the countryside. I've booked a rural hotel from one of those smug couple guides, which means that it's going to be stuffed with other stressed-out urbanites, desperately trying to reignite their flagging sex lives. Oh God, I can't go there right now. It will be good, it will be good.

'I'm sure we take the left-hand exit,' he says, as I approach a particularly menacing-looking roundabout.

'No, we definitely don't come off until Chichester.'

'Anna, trust me on this. It's hardly like directions are your strong point.'

Maybe they're not, but I studied the map obsessively before we left, desperate for every aspect of our trip to be perfect. Still, as I can't handle bickering and driving (I took six tests, I swear they passed me out of pity), I do as he says.

After an hour-long detour down muddy, smelly country lanes we finally arrive at the stucco-fronted hotel. I congratulate myself on my restraint – not a single complaint about the duff directions has passed my lips – as I park our ancient Punto amongst the Mercedes and BMWs that litter the car park. We're shown straight up to our intimidatingly gorgeous room. It's all chocolate brown and taupe, with a velvet chaise longue and an enormous four-poster. There's a free-standing bath in the corner, so you can playfully soap each other before tumbling gaily into bed. I drink it all in, slightly goggle-eyed, while Adam tips the retreating porter.

'Thank you, sir. And may I offer you my congratulations.'

'Congratulations? What's that supposed to mean?'

Adam looks pleased with himself. 'Oh, I kind of upgraded us. I think he thinks it's our honeymoon.'

I can't believe it. We're in the actual honeymoon suite. So no pressure then! I briefly surf a wave of irritation at his inability to leave me in charge of my own surprise, but I know that he's only trying to make it special. By now Adam's keenly eyeing the plasma screen in the corner, and before I know it Bolton Wanderers versus Southampton is blaring out through the surround sound speakers. I wish I was one of those women who could loyally learn to love football, imparting the offside rule with girlish pleasure. Instead I hate it, hate it, hate it. To me, footballers are just a bunch of overpaid, uncouth tossers watched by hordes of underpaid, uncouth tossers. Thank God this isn't my actual honeymoon.

I think I've slightly missed the boat on that one. Adam and I met in our early twenties, when it would have seemed almost perverse to have got married. No one else was doing it, so why would we? It's only been in the last two or three years that people have started marching up the aisle in droves, and now it feels slightly too late. Surely you've got to be madly in love when you marry, rather than reassuringly comfortable? Maybe we'll do it in our dotage for tax reasons.

I must not complain, football makes him happy and this weekend is all about happiness.

'I'm going to go downstairs and check out the spa. Do you want to come?'

'No, I'm going to watch to the end of the first half.' He pats the bed encouragingly. 'Come and join me.'

'Think I'll skip it. Bolton Wanderers are so last season.'

I give him a slightly forced smile, and head to the basement. It's full of jolly, well-groomed women in bathrobes; I so don't want to talk to strangers today. I try to simultaneously exude friendly and aloof, which is as impossible as it sounds, and climb into the jacuzzi. As the hot water seeps through my bikini, I yelp with pain.

'Ow, ow, ow! Oh my God, that hurt!'

'Are you OK? What happened?' asks a concerned yummy mummy type.

'I'll be fine, honestly.'

I vault out of the jacuzzi and beat a hasty retreat. My nether regions literally feel like they're on fire. I vaguely remember Renee saying something about hot showers, but there were no warnings about jacuzzis. Could my muff feel any more unloved? Convinced everyone's staring at me, I decide to curtail the spa experience and go for a walk in the grounds. I wander around, trying to feel excited about being in this beautiful place with Adam. I'm so lucky, and yet I feel so flat. Does familiarity always breed, if not contempt, then a certain sense of resignation? Oh, pull yourself together, Anna! This is not the time to start coming over all Sylvia Plath.

I head back upstairs to the room. Adam's looking livid.

'Where were you? There were only twenty minutes left, but when I came to find you, you'd totally disappeared.'

I look at my watch and realize I've been aimlessly walking for forty-five minutes. I try to explain, but it sounds fairly lame.

'I don't understand why you didn't just come upstairs and get me. We could've had a walk together.'

He's right, of course. I'm a thoughtless, selfish baggage. I go and put my arms round his neck.

'Why don't we open our lovely honeymoon champagne?'

'Why do you have to take the piss out of everything? Anyway, I wanted to save it till after dinner.'

'I wasn't taking the piss. I thought it would be nice. We can get some more later if you like. I'm paying, for God's sake.'

'Fine, we'll open it then.'

Could it be more romantic? He angrily twists the cork out and it hits the light fitting. Both of us stubbornly refuse to laugh. We chink glasses moodily, and I think about saying 'to us' but I can't get the words out. Adam looks at his watch.

'We should go down to dinner soon.'

'But it's only six thirty! I wanted to watch *X Factor* in the bath.'

'You haven't got time. I booked the seven-course tasting menu, and we need to dress for dinner.'

So it's relaxing as well as romantic.

'Let's have a nice time tonight,' I say, reaching up to kiss him, before remembering what bad breath champagne gives you. Which has always made its status as the world's most romantic drink a total mystery to me.

'Yeah, obviously,' he says, still sounding hurt.

We head down to the almost empty dining room. I feel incredibly self-conscious, like all the waiters are staring at us, thinking how alienated we look. I really need to get a grip. How hard can it be to connect with my very best friend? We haven't had much time together in the last week, so I earnestly question him about the minutiae of work. Adam does a computing job, the details of which I've never been able to grasp. He always says he hates it, but insists it's too late in the day to switch horses. My enquiries are so dull that I'm boring myself. *Look how much I care!* is what I'm trying to say, but it comes over more like I'm the kind of dreary maiden aunt you body swerve at weddings. He reaches for my hand.

'Are you OK, Anna? You don't really seem like yourself at the moment.'

'No, I'm fine,' I tell him brightly, unable to find the words, even for myself. 'It's lovely here, isn't it?'

'Yeah, it is. I'm glad we came. Thanks for organizing it.'

'That's OK,' I tell him, feeling choked. There's a longish pause, during which I dig my fingernails into my palms, forcing myself not to well up.

'I didn't know your boyfriend was serving the vegetables.'

There's a callow youth with terrible acne and gel-ridden spiky ginger hair crossing to our table. I try my hardest not to laugh.

'He's a demon in the sack. What can I say?' I mutter under my breath.

That's the thing about a long-term relationship. You can always fall back on those stupid shared intimacies that you build up over years. Soon we're chatting away, gossiping about our friends and assigning personalities to the various couples around the room. When we get to pudding, I start to feel butterflies in my stomach. Not good butterflies, more moths of doom. How long is it since we did it? About four weeks ago I came home from a drunken hen night and sort of straddled him, inelegantly. Maybe what I need is a tequila slammer, but this really isn't the right establishment.

'Shall we get some more champagne sent up?' he asks.

'There's quite a bit left in the bottle, surely?'

'Yeah, but won't it be flat?'

'I'm sure it'll be fine, Adam.'

We head upstairs. He pours us another glass of the distinctly unfizzy champagne and we sit on the chaise longue, sipping it primly. I wonder if he's going to put on the *Match of the Day* highlights, and if he does, whether I'll mind. Oh God, let's get this show on the road. I turn round and kiss him, trying to bat away my fear of having pooey breath. He kisses me back, and pushes me flat on to the chaise longue. We carry on kissing for a bit, and then he starts trying to pull my skirt off. I wish men realized how important all the other bits are. You know: one's neck, one's shoulders, one's back. Even the best lovers are so crotch-centric. I wonder if lesbians are different? When I'm naked he looks at my poor, beleaguered pudenda with something akin to disgust.

'What's happened? I was going to ... you know, but perhaps I'll skip it.'

'Oh, OK,' I mutter, instantly wanting to curl away from him.

But instead I force myself to step up to the plate: the stakes have got too high for me to shirk my responsibilities. I try to imagine how I'd be behaving if this was the first time, the effort I'd make, and I do manage to pull a few tricks out of the bag. I can tell he's trying too, and it's definitely better than it's been for a while, but there's a sense we're concentrating more than we're connecting. Once we're actually having sex, the distance between us seems to expand into infinity. I'm looking away, slightly wishing it was over, when I realize that tears are rolling down my cheeks. I can't let him see, he'd be so upset.

Instead I make some appropriate noises, trying to hasten things along.

'Did you enjoy that?' he asks afterwards, stroking my hair.

'Yes, it was great,' I lie.

All those bloody relationship gurus go on about how critical honesty is, but I refuse to believe they don't lie to their partners every bit as much as the next person. No relationship could survive unvarnished truth.

'I love you,' he says.

'I love you too,' I whisper back.

We try to sleep all intertwined, but it's far too uncomfortable and we both roll away after a decent interval. I lie in the darkness, listening to his breathing, trying to imagine a life without it. It's almost too painful to contemplate, but maybe this kind of slow drip pain is even worse. Like Chinese water torture versus beheading. Oh, stop being such a drama queen!

Eventually I get to sleep, and when I wake up Adam's not in the bed. Oh God, has he reviewed last night in the cold light of day and left in disgust? I stand under the shower, reassuring myself that he's probably just gone to breakfast. As I'm drying myself I hear a noise from next door.

'Adam?'

Nothing. I hate it when they start cleaning the room when you're still virtually comatose. I wrap a towel round myself and venture out, which is when I get the shock of my life. The room is strewn with flowers and Adam is standing by the window.

'Anna, I know this weekend's not been perfect, but I can't let our anniversary go by without doing this. Will you marry me?' And with that he's down on one knee with a ring.

I feel frozen, catatonic, incapable of speech.

'Anna?'

'Adam, I just don't know . . .'

He gets up, looking like I've stabbed him. 'What do you mean, you don't know? For fuck's sake, if you can't marry me now, after ten years, there's something seriously wrong.'

Oh God, I don't want to lose him like this. I feel totally ambushed. I really wasn't ready for it all to become so black and white. I'm shaking with sobs, trying to grope my way through it.

'Adam, I love being your girlfriend. Maybe I'm just not a marrying kind of a person. I love you so much . . .'

'Don't fucking patronize me. If you don't feel the same way, then at least be honest about it.'

And I cry more, and tell him time and time again how much I love him, but I know now that it's no longer enough. It's way too late for that.

3

It's 6.30 a.m. when there's a knock on my door. While Polly tries to evict Horst, her German lodger, I've temporarily holed up at my grandmother's mansion flat, in deepest St John's Wood. Why do old people get up so early? If I was old, I'd sleep till noon and then sit around all day in my pyjamas eating Maltesers and watching black and white films.

'Good morning, my darling,' she says, spryly crossing the room to fling open the curtains. 'I've brought you a nice cup of tea. Look what a divine day it is!'

It is a beautiful day, sunny and clear. Even so, I can't help wishing that it was stormy and wet. Selfish though it is, I want my frustration and pain to be reflected outside of myself. 'Thanks, Gran,' I say, reaching for it, my irritation at the alarm call swiftly subsumed by affection for her. I'm much closer to her than my mum, who's utterly different from me. Gran's got enormous spirit, regularly cleaning up at the local bridge club, and always ready with a story from her floozyish days during the war. When we were kids, my little brother and I were regularly sent to stay with our grandparents while our activist parents went off to fight for some cause far more deserving than us. Dan and I used to love the normality they provided, the perfect antidote to the radicalism of our home life, which invariably rendered us the school freaks. Like the time we came back from the Christmas holidays and innocently told our classmates that our dad's gift to our mum was a dinky pair of padded handcuffs. We knew it was just to make being chained to the perimeter fence of Greenham Common that bit more comfortable, but the world at large thought we were the progeny of sex perverts. In those days, our outcast status bonded us, but since Dan's set about reinventing himself as *Daily Mail* man, complete with the world's most dreary wife and some disturbingly fascistic views on the benefit system, we've lost that connection.

Gran leaves, and I lie in bed for a while, trying to summon up the strength to face the day. I feel utterly desolate right now. I really can't work out what I've gained by leaving; instead there's just an enormous Adam-shaped hole blown through the centre of my life. But how could I have said yes, feeling like I do? And once marriage got slapped on the table, there was no discernable route back to where we were before.

I try to cheer myself up by working out what I've learnt from the situation:

1. If your break-up is sudden, think very carefully about what you take with you. Pack in haste, repent at leisure. Adam abandoned me at the hotel, leaving me with only my weekend bag. As I can't yet face the prospect of seeing him, all I have in the world right now is some agonizing lacy knickers, a pair of wellington boots, an evening dress and a copy of *The*

Kite Runner. I know I should read it, but I just don't want to.

2. Which brings me to point two. You may think that a copy of *Hello* will cheer you up, but when Ulrika Jonsson's love life starts looking more successful than your own you know you've hit rock bottom.

3. Do not, under any circs, tune the radio to Melancholic FM. If you're sobbing along to Phil Collins and Marilyn Martin singing 'Separate Lives', applauding the profundity of the lyrics, you've definitely tipped over the edge.

I eventually force myself out of bed, arriving at the office to be greeted by an enormous bouquet of roses. I work on what might be the least glamorous magazine this side of *Rodent Weekly*. *Casual Chic* is written for a very specific kind of woman. She's too old to read *Elle*, too mumsy to read *Vogue* and too self-deluded and aspirational to admit that what she'd really like to buy is *Heat*. Within its glossy pages she will find 'Fifty ways with a cherry tomato' juxtaposed with 'Impotence: why no marriage is safe'. Originally I wanted to be a foreign correspondent, but I took a wrong turning somewhere around 1999.

The office is ruthlessly commanded by the mothers' mafia: without offspring you count for nothing around here. Right now they're circling the extravagant flowers like curious orcs. Jocasta – mother to Percy and Agnes –

is the leader of the pack (since when did it become compulsory for all middle-class children to sound like octogenarians?).

'Oh, Anna, they're beautiful,' she coos. 'He's going to propose any minute now, I can feel it in my bones!'

I haven't yet found the strength to tell them. And the stream of flowers that Adam's been sending have provided a pretty great red herring.

'Fingers crossed!' I stutter nervously.

I can't bear to either suffer the sympathy or do battle with their world view. After all, why wouldn't the pinnacle of achievement be eliciting a proposal from someone, anyone?

'Is there something you're not telling us, Anna?' asks Tabitha, a whey-faced mother of twins who edits the interiors section. Oh God, is it that obvious I'm lying? Perhaps I should just come clean.

'No, I mean . . .'

Jocasta can hardly contain her excitement. 'He's already asked, hasn't he? I can tell!'

'Sort of . . .' I can't bear this. I feel like I'm going to start blubbing, right here in the middle of the office. 'Look, I can't talk about it right now, but as soon as there's any more news you'll be the first to know.'

And with that, I feign blushing embarrassment and cross to my desk. Luckily I haven't got to endure their scrutiny for too long as I'm spending the week out of the office supervising make-overs. Bored, obese housewives from Huddersfield are whisked down to London to be transformed by a highly dubious 'team of experts'.

I call Adam from the taxi, en route to the studio.

'Adam, please, I know you're hurting, but I can't bear this. It's making it even harder than it already is.'

'I'm not going to just stand by and let you throw ten years away like it was meaningless.'

'Of course it's not meaningless! When did I say it was meaningless?'

'Why can't you appreciate what we've got? Other people would kill to have a relationship like ours.'

'But there's something wrong, Adam, something that's just not there any more.'

I hate my own vagueness. So much of what I feel is indefinable, and what isn't would crush him to nothing.

'You're making a mistake, Anna, a pretty fucking monumental mistake actually. You might think you're going to meet this magical man, who's going to sweep you off your feet and make everything suddenly brilliant, but you're wrong. Nothing will ever be good enough for you, it's just the way you are.'

This is even worse than I thought it would be.

'I'm going to go – this isn't helping either of us.'

'This can't be it, Anna, I'm telling you that right now.'

I hang up, shaking. I can't bear how much pain I've inflicted on him, the snarling monster I've turned him into. And what if he's right? What if some part of me is too bitter and gnarled to open myself up to making a real connection with someone? I take a drag on an imaginary stress-busting cigarette (it's been five years, a girl can dream) and force myself not to spiral into panic. I have to stay calm and keep believing that I'm going to find something that feels more right in the dim and distant future when I'm ready.

The 'experts' (or rather the hags, as I affectionately call them) are already gathered in the studio when I arrive. All three of them are fiftyish and Northern, with deep, unnatural tans and smoker's coughs. They are the last people on earth you would entrust your physical appearance to if you had any common sense. Doreen, the chief hag, immediately starts tugging at my bedraggled curls, very much the worse for wear after four days without my hair straighteners.

'What's happened to you, love? You're all tangled up!'

That is so exactly how I feel, all tangled and knotted and chaotic, that I immediately well up. Soon she and Michael (the fag hag) are plying me with HobNobs and prising the whole sorry tale out of me. The tea and sympathy does the trick as, professionally speaking, the day's an unqualified success. The willing victims are put in hideously unflattering outfits and plastered with so much make-up that they wouldn't look out of place in the *Rocky Horror Picture Show*. Nevertheless, they all seem bizarrely delighted with the results and I return to north London with something close to a spring in my step.

Gran's got an inevitable gin and tonic on the go, and immediately sets about mixing one for me. She shakes some Twiglets into a bowl, laying them on the table with a jaunty flourish.

'Karen's been on the phone, but I said I'd let you tell her all the gory details yourself.'

Our parents never let us call them mum and dad: they considered it far too hierarchical. Instead they were good old 'Karen and Greg', a couple of mates who just happened to have conceived us. This was actually more weird than fun. I found myself secretly wondering if they actually wanted to be parents, or were just making the best of an unfortunate accident.

'Did she? I'll ring her back,' I say vaguely. I love Karen, but talking to her always makes me feel like I'm failing at some invisible test I don't yet know the rules to. 'Have you heard from Henry today?' I ask.

Henry is eighty-six, an old codger in Gran's book. Four years makes a big difference in your eighties, kind of like it does when you're a teenager. Then you're worried that they'll pressurize you for sex, whereas by Gran's age you're worried they'll pressurize you for 24-hour nursing care.

'Not a peep. I must admit I'm frightfully relieved.'

Henry lived near Granny and Grandpa when they were in their thirties and had young families. Granddad died four years ago, at which point Henry called up out of the blue. Now he's claiming that he's been in love with Gran since the 1950s, despite having had a perfectly good wife for most of the intervening years. It's entirely understandable – with a little help from a bottle, her hair remains the same ash blonde it's always been, and her outfits are nothing short of immaculate – but she's determined that her romantic days are long since over. Luckily Henry's far too decrepit to get down on one knee, so thus far he's been spared the heartbreak of rejection.

We have our dinner, eaten at the table with actual silver, and settle down in front of *24*. Having been in the Intelligence Corps in the war, Gran's got oddly macho taste in television. She'd rather poke her eyes out with a stick than watch *Last of the Summer Wine*. 'What do you think he does when he needs to spend a penny?' she asks matter-of-factly as Jack Bauer scales a skyscraper in search of a particularly murderous terrorist.

All in all this isn't so bad. Maybe I should just stay here, living the urban high life with my crazy geriatric flatmate. But of course she can't resist picking the scab.

'Darling,' she starts.

'Yes,' I mutter, knowing what's coming.

'Are you absolutely sure about this? You know I love having you here, but you really need to think about what you want in the long term. By your age I was married, I'd had three children. I know it's different for your generation, with your smart jobs and your flexible mortgages, but it won't stop you being lonely.'

Oh God, the L word. She's on a roll now.

'You're thirty-two, Anna. Please don't leave it too late. If you don't marry this chap, you have to think seriously about who's left.'

'Don't say it like that, Gran. When I feel ready to start dating, there'll be plenty of men around.' Yeah, right. Who am I trying to kid?

'Yes, but what kind of men? By now, all that's available are divorcees. Or I suppose you could have a child with a gay. I believe that's what a lot of career women do these days.'

'A gay?! What kind of statement is that? I really, really don't need this.'

'Please don't get angry with me, Anna.' She sounds almost stern now. 'I understand far more of what you're going through than you realize. But when I was your age we didn't question all the time, we just accepted what we had.'

By now the stress of the last few days, or months, is flooding through my system and my face is an attractive mass of snot and tears.

'Gran, sometimes there comes a point where you have to choose whether to stick or twist. Well, this is me twisting, and maybe that's wrong, but it's what I've decided.'

She softens a little, puts her arm round me.

'Anna, darling, don't be offended, but do you think it might be an idea for me to freeze your eggs for Christmas? I've been reading up on it, and it's really quite a straightforward procedure.'

I'm weirdly touched, but as gifts go, it sounds even less festive than the handcuffs. And anyway, it's clearly the wrong religious festival. At least if it was Easter there'd be some kind of twisted logic to it.

I know she means well, but I also know that this isn't going to work out. So I swiftly retreat to my room, where I pack my bags in preparation for throwing myself on Polly's mercy.

4

Lying in bed that night, totally incapable of sleep, I start obsessing about how me and Adam started out. In those days I swear he thought he was the South Coast's answer to Liam Gallagher. It was the height of Brit pop, and he had straggly, collar-length hair, an earring and some highly dubious round glasses. He used to take loads of 'E's and dance like a monkey, sweating profusely. The fact that he was an economics student from the mean streets of Surrey kind of ruined the effect, but he clearly thought he was pretty cool.

He shared the same student house as Polly, so I used to see him whenever I took refuge from all the sloanes at Exeter. Brighton was a very different kind of town, lined with trendy clubs and bars, and I gradually found myself heading down there most weekends. Adam would always be hanging around their greasy kitchen, nursing a hangover and listening to guitar-based rock through tinny portable speakers.

We soon developed a weird intimacy via our constant mutual piss-taking. I would tell him that in ten years he'd be back in the stockbroker belt with a Stepford wife and a job in the city. He'd say I was clearly a social outcast: why else would I keep trekking cross-country to seek out my only friend? Looking back I think that Polly found our banter kind of excluding, so maybe the fact that she snogged Adam on one particularly loved-up night was her way to try and get a piece of the action. Although I urged her to go for it – she'd been single for ages, as per normal – I definitely felt odd about it. But I swiftly dismissed my feelings: how could I possibly fancy him? It just wasn't what our relationship was about.

Not long after that I started seeing a much older man, and my visits to Brighton became less frequent. Jerome was a work-obsessed chef who drank far more than was good for him. I was kind of in awe of him – the fact I hardly ever saw him added to his mystique – and never stopped to question how little he had to give. He called me 'angel' and cupped my face in his hands when he kissed me, and I felt like I was starring in my very own romantic melodrama. I was so eager to impress him, to prove that I could be mature and sophisticated enough to hold his interest, but I don't think he ever thought of me as a serious prospect. When he unceremoniously dumped me on the way back from a sex-sodden weekend away, I was gutted. But once the jagged agony had subsided, it was kind of a relief. No more energy wasted desperately willing him to call: he just wouldn't.

By this time we were nearing the end of our final year. Polly and Adam hadn't worked out – she said she just didn't feel it – but luckily they'd stayed friends. As soon as I got back into the habit of making my regular weekend pilgrimages, I realized how much I'd missed him. After my bruising interlude with Jerome, I so appreciated our easy familiarity. I no longer had to permanently hold my stomach in and fake a sophistication that wasn't truly mine.

One weekend the unthinkable happened: Adam asked if he could visit me. Polly gave me her blessing, and I spent three days in a state of perpetual nerves. What if it just felt weird? We hadn't even kissed yet; it could all turn out to be a total disaster. What if, even worse, I'd totally misunderstood his intentions and he just possessed a burning desire to see the sights of Exeter? No worries on that score: he snogged me the second he got off the train and, with that, the transition from friends to something more had effortlessly materialized. Perhaps the very fact that it was so painless was ominous. All those years later, it felt frighteningly easy to step back through the romantic looking glass and find I was gazing at a lovely, goofy friend.

5

As I'm rushing off to work, I'm stopped in my tracks by Horst's idea of a tasty breakfast. He's spooning gherkins direct from the jar into his enormous German mouth, burping with satisfaction between bites.

'So was Adam not good guy? He seem like good guy to Horst.'

Horst has been sent over from Stuttgart by his architectural firm. He and Polly have a slightly love/hate relationship, but she desperately needs his rent. What she doesn't need is his taste in German soft rock, his table manners or his stream of bleached blonde one-night stands. This morning is no exception: there's a pair of leopard-skin stilettos tossed casually aside at his bedroom door. While Polly's plucking up the courage to give him notice, I'm camped out on the sofa bed.

I smile ruefully. 'You're right, Horst, Adam's a totally great guy. Some lucky cow is going to be thrilled she's snapped him up.'

With that, I'm out the door, wondering how many more variations of this conversation I'm doomed to have. Sitting on the bus, I send a stilted text to Adam. I desperately need more clothes, but I can't face seeing him yet. If I actually lay eyes on him, I'm not sure I'll be able to hold out. Right now I'm having to ruthlessly focus on everything that was wrong in order to avoid getting swept right back to where I started.

When I get to the office, Jocasta's looking thunderous.

'Roger's asked you to go straight to his office. He needs to speak to you urgently.'

Oh my God. Can I be sacked for lying about my romantic status? Surely not. Roger's far too nice to sack me anyway. More 'The Cherub Wears Top Man' than 'The Devil Wears Prada'. *Casual Chic* is so low rent.

Roger's looking harassed, uselessly brushing away the croissant crumbs which are cascading down his too-tight cashmere hoodie. His picture of Graham, his unfeasibly good-looking boyfriend, is turned face down on the desk, which is a very bad sign. Graham's what's known as an 'A-Gay' – handsome, popular and scarily confident – while Roger's more of a B/C. Roger lives life under a ghostly neon sign, constantly flashing 'Must Try Harder'.

'Anna, thanks for coming down. I've got something to ask you. A favour, really.'

'Sure, Roger, whatever you need,' I tell him, hoping to God it's not overseeing the 'Light Up Your Love-Making' supplement Jocasta's sadistically conceived for the Valentine's issue. Trying to write about sex toys in the language of *Casual Chic* is not a challenge I relish ('Let the Rabbit get you hopping mad with desire, but make sure you don't leave it anywhere the kids might find it!')

'The word's come down from on high that we're not connecting with our readership enough. *Elle*'s got the style awards, *Vogue* throw all those poncey soirées in biscuit factories, and all we've got is one pathetic little stand at the Ideal Home Show.'

'You do your best, Roger. What more do they want?'

'They want us to make a noise, and grab younger readers by the jugular. Find a way to define the brand and pull in the advertisers.'

He's obviously just come downstairs from a bollocking. His eyes are wild and manic and he's got no idea what he's talking about.

'So what are you thinking?' I ask, in as soothing a voice as I can muster.

'A bridal show, but a bridal show like no other! A bridal show for funky young brides who thought they were too cool for convention, but are too in love to resist. We're going to have a huge catwalk show and an enormous party. And it's going to be stuffed with real celebrities, not those conceptual artists and weirdo aristos that *Vogue* love so much.'

As you may have guessed, Roger got sacked by *Vogue* for not being, well, *Vogue* enough.

'It's a great idea,' I tell him, as a feeling of cold dread starts to seep through me. Could there be anything in life more alien to me right now? I scrabble for a get-out clause. 'But do you really want me to coordinate it? Don't you need someone more senior?'

'Well, it was sort of Jocasta's idea, but between you and me, I worry about how much time she has. She's a very devoted mother.'

You can say that again.

'Besides, Anna, don't be coy. You must be able to guess why you're the ideal candidate!'

I've got a horrible feeling I can.

'Nothing gets past me! Who better to road-test bridal fashion than an almost bride-to-be? You'll bring your own unique perspective to bear on every aspect of our event. Have you set the date?'

I'm going to have to fess up. But just as I'm plucking up the courage, Roger leaps on to another train of thought.

'You'll be needing a pay rise, obviously. And a change of title. This is a major step up for you.'

And I start to think about my credit card bills, and the hell of trying to extract my half of the equity from the flat. And how even if I do, it'll probably only fund a damp shoebox above 'Finger Lickin' Chicken' in Plumstead. And before I know it, I'm thanking Roger profusely and sashaying out of his office with the kind of joyful spring in my step that any bride-to-be must surely have.

As I cross the room, I can sense Jocasta giving me the death stare. Although she's the bane of my working life, my sense of *schadenfreude* is tinged by sympathy. It was her idea after all.

'So Roger's told you then? Are you going to do it?'

'I couldn't really say no, Jocasta. It's such a brilliant concept you've come up with.'

She gives me a rictus grin. 'Yes, well, there's no way I'd've had time to run it myself. Percy's sitting his common entrance and Agnes's grade six lute exam is coming up in a matter of months. I simply don't have your kind of freedom.'

God, I hate her.

I spend the rest of the day glued to the Internet, trying to think about concepts that will make this event feel sparkly and glamorous. The more I burrow into the world of weddings, the more incomprehensible it feels. Did other little girls really dream about their 'special day' right from when they were sitting in their Wendy houses? The fact that Karen would never have let me hang out in something as blatantly patriarchal as a Wendy house is perhaps why I'm back in the land of microwave meals for one, with no ring on my finger. Feeling downcast, I call up the most married person I know and ask her out for dinner.

What I love about Susie is that, despite being the most married person I know, she's also the least smug. Although she counselled caution, since I left Adam she hasn't once destroyed my fragile mental equilibrium with 'what ifs'.

'Of course you're not a freak, Anna! How could you say yes if it didn't feel right? You can't say vows like that if you don't mean them.'

She's covered in a light smattering of brick dust, but still manages to look poised. Even so, I can't help noticing the dark rings that are etched under her eyes.

'But I'm not sure I ever will. How can you guarantee that it's not going to get mind-numbingly mundane? That the way that they gargle their mouthwash or sneakily pick their nose during the rugby won't overwhelm everything you first felt? Or is that just horribly shallow?'

She considers me for a minute. 'You don't sound shallow, you sound scared.'

Maybe there's some small nugget of truth in there, but I can't even begin to digest it. Besides, I am talking to someone who, lovely though she is, thinks Martin's 'the one'.

'So,' I ask her, trying not to sound acidic, 'did you "just know" when you met Martin?'

'I really don't want to sound patronizing, Anna. I'm just saying that love is always a risk. You end up with a lot to lose.'

I feel her words hit me right in the gut. Sometimes I'm almost relieved when something precious has gone, from a person right down to a favourite pair of gloves, because at least I no longer have to negotiate my fear of it being taken from me.

'Look, whatever your granny thinks, you've been incredibly brave. So many people would've said yes just because it was the easy option.'

I smile at her gratefully. 'But there is no easy option, is there? Getting married when you're not sure would be hideous, but at least I wouldn't be sitting around awaiting the arrival of perky girl.'

'Perky girl?'

'Oh, you know, the perfect replacement girlfriend. She'll appreciate everything about him and give the best blow jobs in human history. Then I'll be reduced to a distant blot on the landscape.'

Susie laughs. 'But it never stays that way, does it? We're all perky girl at the beginning. You just have to hope that when you stop being perky girl they love you for your rubbish bits too.' She pauses, grabbing my hand. 'Besides, however bloody perky she is, he'll always adore you.'

I look at the table, fighting back tears, wondering if she's right. It's not like I want him to remain pickled in romantic aspic, unable to love anyone else, but I still find the idea of him meeting someone unbearably hard. I grit my teeth, determined we won't spend our entire evening poring over my pain. Instead we talk about Susie's wedding, laughing about the thirty-stone slob-o-gram that Polly and I booked for her hen night. Somehow I don't think that Roger would appreciate me hiring him for the big day.

'Did you feel like you were leaving a lot behind when you were standing up there?' I ask her.

'In a way, but it felt like it was time. I think those stages of life are there for a reason, and you're just lucky if they work out for you.'

Suddenly she looks sad, and I start to wonder why she turned down a glass of wine, despite the fact that dinner's 'research' and is going straight on my expenses.

'Susie, you're not up the duff are you?'

She's welling up.

'What is it? What's wrong?'

'We've been trying for ages, but it's just not happening. I didn't want to talk about it in case it jinxed us. We're about to start these horrible tests. This time next week they'll be sticking metal probes up me and telling me I'm barren.'

'Oh God, I'm so sorry. But you know they might say

that everything's fine and you just need to relax. Or it could be Martin's problem.'

I bet it is. I bet his sperm are tiny, ineffectual sprats who can't even swim without armbands.

'I'm trying to be positive, I really am. I'm just so frightened. I wasn't even that bothered until I started to think maybe I couldn't have them. Now I'm turning into a weird pram stalker, staring at babies as though they're some kind of exotic species.'

I grab her hand across the table. 'I'm so sorry. I wish you'd told us. I know it's a cliché, but if there's anything I can do, I will.'

Flash forward to me bearing Wet Martin's child, in some kind of hideous surrogacy arrangement. Surely that could never happen?

When we hug goodbye I feel overwhelmed with sadness. In comparison to living in a war zone, these trials are obviously trivial. But when I look around at our lives, it suddenly all seems insanely complicated. So many random elements need to miraculously fuse in order to deliver happiness. And even then there are no guarantees.

As I hail a cab, my phone beeps. Adam's sent me an incredibly terse text. 'Get stuff Sunday. Will not be here.' How can ten years of intimacy have been reduced to monosyllabic messaging in a matter of days? And despite the fact that it's me who's walked away, I find myself wondering where he'll be. Sunday is a restricted zone: the day when couples hibernate or go to the in-laws, while single people struggle through their hangovers in front of the *EastEnders* omnibus. He couldn't have a date already, could he? The idea is as searingly painful as it is inevitable. Even if it's not this weekend, or next, he will eventually start to look elsewhere. And of course that's what I should logically wish for him, but the very idea of it makes me want to howl.

6

I've got a late morning meeting, so I decide to grab the opportunity to take Polly out for breakfast. I'm feeling pretty bad about the fact that I've turned her living room into a shrine to shoes, and wondering if it's really tenable for me to stay, but she's typically good-natured about it.

'Don't worry about it, Anna, it's such a relief to have a girl around. You're kind of neutralizing Horst. You've no idea what listening to his one-night stands is doing to me.'

The snarling waitress is suddenly looming over us. 'Ready to order?' she snaps. We've had the menus for approximately twenty seconds.

We've come to the Polish deli round the corner. The food's delicious and organic, and we're your typical urban hypocrites, who don't mind drinking our livers into oblivion or even taking the occasional drug, but insist on knowing exactly which Wiltshire farm the pig in our sandwich snuffled his last in. The downside of this place is that they seem to import the waitresses from some kind of Stalinist work camp in the Eastern Bloc. The idea of service with a smile is an anathema to them, and they always behave like they've never laid eyes on us before, despite the fact that we come here every single week.

'Can we have a few minutes?' asks Polly timidly. The

waitress gives an incomprehensible snort and stomps off.

'Are you feeling better about Pin-Eyed Matt?' I ask her, painfully aware that most of our conversations have revolved around me recently.

'Yeah, I mean it was obviously never going to work out. And anyway, someone else asked me on a date yesterday!'

The good thing about Polly is that she always bounces back quickly. The bad thing is that she never seems to learn from her mistakes.

'Who is he?' I ask warily.

'Michael.'

'Michael who?'

'Michael the plumber.'

'What, the guy who ripped out the cistern? I thought you said he did a really bad job and it flooded downstairs.'

'I know, but he was so apologetic. And he came out and fixed it himself, even though he runs the whole company. Besides, he's not just a plumber, he's also a trained hypnotist. He's stopped all his employees from smoking.'

She's clutching at straws here, but if it's going to stop her smarting over Matt, I guess it's harmless.

'When are you going out then?' I ask her.

'Tonight. He's going to come round and look over the bathroom first. He says if I need any more work done he'll knock off the VAT.'

'How romantic.'

By now we've been waiting ten minutes for our waitress to come back. Since we initially turned her down, communist rules mean she's now boycotting our table.

43

As we flag her down, I fill Polly in on what Susie told me.

'Oh God, I hope she manages it,' she says. 'Though it'd be so weird, one of us crossing the line. It's never the same afterwards.'

'We thought that when she got married though, and she's still Susie.'

'But she's not just Susie any more, is she?' says Polly. 'There's always the danger we'll have to factor in Martin, even though he's the world's biggest drone.'

'Did you feel like that with me and Adam?'

'No, I love Adam and I loved seeing you together.' She pauses awkwardly. 'Sorry, that's probably not that helpful right now.'

'It's fine,' I tell her, feeling a little internal wobble. 'Do you think you'll be able to tell Horst soon?' I'm desperate to change the subject, and also desperate to start living in an actual bedroom. If I was brave I'd get one of those awful studios, but the prospect of it is just too depressing.

'I will, I promise. It's just that he doesn't know anybody. Even though we've got absolutely nothing in common, he seems to think that I'm his best friend in England. Which I guess I probably am.'

One bacon sandwich later, I suddenly realize how late I am. When the bill arrives we're plunged into our eternal dilemma about service. Should we register our dissatisfaction by refusing to tip, or will that just land us with gobbed-in eggs next time we visit? Of course we end up chickening out and leaving about thirty per cent in the vain hope that they'll start to like us.

I jump on the tube and head into town. Despite the fact

that it's hitting a nerve, I'm actually starting to get into the swing of this event. It's giving me a chance to pour all my frustration and confusion into creating something that's uniquely mine. And most crucially, it's keeping me out of Jocasta's air space, averting the inevitable moment when I'll have to admit to being back on the scrap heap. In office politics' terms, it's far better to be a divorcee than single. It gives you an understanding of marriage and a certain painful mystique. And it proves that you at least succeeded in snaring a man once, even if it did go horribly wrong.

Right now, I'm searching desperately for a venue. I have such a strong sense of what it should be like – sort of eccentric and atmospheric – and I'm convinced it's out there somewhere waiting for me. I've managed to make the lack of location an intriguing mystery on the invitations, but time is running out. I meet with the caterers and then hook up with the director I've hired for the catwalk show. I'm trying desperately to sprinkle some magic dust on the whole thing, so that despite the *Casual Chic* association it acquires a modicum of cool. With this in mind, I've kicked off a competition amongst London's most pretentious fashion colleges to design a wedding dress for the show. The winner gets a year's sponsorship from the magazine, as well as the dress being photographed in the pages of *Casual Chic* (and if that doesn't kill their career then nothing will).

But however sophisticated the event is, the issue itself has got to have the cosy, unthreatening feel that our readers have come to rely on. I've decided to follow three completely different couples in the run-up to their big day. The idea is that they share their hopes, dreams and 'hilarious catastrophes' over the course of the preparations. Our relentlessly keen research assistant, Ruby, has been lining them up, and I haven't even had time to look at the notes. This afternoon I'm meeting the first couple, Arthur and Hilda. Arthur and Hilda? They're either four years old or seventy-five, and I'm guessing it's the latter. What was she thinking? This really isn't what I'm after.

A car's been sent to take me to deepest Essex, and soon I'm knocking on the front door of their modest bungalow. A white-haired man hobbles to the door, leaning painfully on a walking stick. He talks to me through a metal chain.

'Miss Christie? We'd started to think you weren't coming.'

I'm five minutes late.

'I'm so sorry, at least I'm here now! You must be Arthur.'

'Mr Mullins, if you don't mind,' he replies, grudgingly opening the door.

Luckily, Hilda's a much easier nut to crack. She's small and trim, with odd, purple-tinged hair. She tells me that she was widowed in her sixties and never thought she'd meet another man.

'My kids were all grown up, so then it was just me, stuck on my own, watching the telly.'

'So how did you meet?' I ask encouragingly, trying to knock back the weak, sweet tea that they've given me.

Arthur starts to mellow. 'I'd never been the marrying

kind. I think some people thought I was a woofter!' They smile at each other and he reaches for her hand. 'I used to get my clothes at that charity shop down the high street.'

Hilda jumps in. 'I'd got myself some volunteering work there, just to get out of the house.'

'When I clapped eyes on her, I suddenly knew why I'd waited so long.'

Weirdly, I understand what he means. Despite being in her seventies, there's something rather sexy about Hilda. Not in an age-defying, surgery-ridden, Joan Rivers kind of a way. It's more an innate confidence and poise that's oddly sensual. In her presence, Arthur's transformed from a grumpy old curmudgeon to a lovesick softie.

'I took some persuading though!' Hilda says, laughing. 'I'd got used to my life the way it was.'

'So where was your first date?'

'This won't sound very romantic to a youngster like you,' she says.

I'm so glad they're old enough to think that I'm young. Of course these days it's all about your reproductive age, and I'm refusing to go there.

'I drove him to his hospital appointment.'

Arthur jumps in. 'We stopped off at the Little Chef on the way back for a cup of tea and I proposed.'

That sounds even less successful than Adam's proposal. Please God, if I ever do get married, may it not begin over a Happy Meal.

'I said no, of course.'

What a relief! I think even *Casual Chic* readers would baulk at that particular romantic fantasy.

'But a few weeks later we went down to my son's caravan in Canvey Island for the day. It was so sunny and beautiful, and when he asked me again I didn't have the heart to refuse!'

She's smiling coyly at him now. It's plain to see that they're madly in love. I wonder if they actually do it? Come to think of it, they've probably had way more sex in the last year than me.

'So what do you think the secret is to lasting commitment?' Could this be my moment of revelation?

'Really wanting that person to be the last thing you see at night, and the first thing you see in the morning,' says Hilda simply.

'And not being a fly-by-night,' pipes up Arthur. 'Some of these young people don't know the meaning of sticking it out.' He's peering at me myopically. 'Are you married?'

Obviously it's none of his business, and there's no way I should risk the awful truth getting relayed back to the office. Even so, his beady stare somehow demands a response.

'Not quite yet,' I gabble nervously, 'but it's looking like it might be on the cards.'

Hilda immediately starts clucking over me, assuring me it'll all work out. I give her my hopeful but modest act, thinking how much less painful the lie is than the truth. There's two months to go before their wedding, so I arrange to come back in two weeks with the hags and a photographer. Arthur harrumphs a bit, but Hilda looks genuinely excited. She's so lovely, and I feel terrible about deceiving her, but I can't take the risk of being found out. Would Roger take the supplement off me if he knew the truth?

On the journey back to London I start to worry that Arthur's my bad-tempered alter ego. Obviously I don't have a stick, or an elasticated waistband, but perhaps I'm the kind of person who's so picky that they don't find their life partner till they've lost their teeth. How depressing would that be? I distract myself by calling Ruby, who definitely needs some redirection.

'Ruby, why did you pick out those crocks for me to interview? I want it to feel glam, not drab.'

'Sorry, Anna, I just thought you wanted a range of couples.'

'Yeah, a range of types, not ages ranging from twenty to a hundred. Now I've interviewed them we'll have to keep them, but I want to sit down and select the rest of them with you.'

'OK,' she says in a small voice and I immediately feel guilty for being so minty with her.

'Look, don't worry about it now – just talk me through the RSVPs. Has Sam Taylor-Wood come back to us?' I've targeted the most fashionable people I can think of, and designed a beautiful gold-leaf invitation.

'No, not yet.'

'Stella McCartney?'

'No, nothing,' she says anxiously. 'And when I called her PR I got cut off.'

I'm starting to feel a bit panicky. 'Surely we must have at least one star in the bag by now?'

'Well, I don't know how you'll feel about this, Anna,' she says hesitantly, 'but Dean Gaffney's agent's been on the phone to say he's desperate to come.'

Dean Gaffney! Is this truly the level we're looking at? I've really got to up my game. I'm secretly hoping that this event will finally deliver me from writing about hair removal creams and land me the job of my dreams. Maybe *Vanity Fair* will be so impressed by the kind of stars I attract that they'll make me their London correspondent. Soon I'll be lying on a bed in George Clooney's suite at Claridge's commiserating with him about the demise of his pot-bellied pig. We'll fall in love and travel to war zones together, and I'll write searingly intelligent polemics while he gets the UN on side. That'll be in between all the hot sex of course. But none of this is going to happen if my crowning achievement is netting Dean Gaffney.

Combing through my BlackBerry I remember that I've been invited to a photography exhibition tonight. It's in one of those super trendy galleries in Hoxton, all exposed pipes and unpainted walls, and I was planning to give it a miss, but now I'm wondering if it might somehow bear fruit. I touch up my make-up and redirect the car.

I toil my way up a wrought iron spiral staircase, arriving at the top bright red and panting. My outfit is so inappropriate: I wore a neat jacket and skirt for the interview, and the entire room is full of arty types in bizarre get-ups. I swear one girl has come dressed as a jockey, complete with jodhpurs and a peaked cap. Worst of all, I don't recognize a single person. I think about doing a runner – I've got a dinner party to get to on the other side of London – but can't face the stairs without rehydrating. Luckily I spy a waiter.

'Excuse me, is there any way you could find me a glass of water? I'm dying of thirst here!'

'Sure, I'd love to,' he twinkles, making no move to do so. He's blond and angular, with eyes so strikingly blue that the squarish glasses he wears seem to frame them, like they're pictures.

'Um, thanks,' I say. Is he actually going to get it? I'm quite happy to stay here, gazing dumbly at his gorgeous profile, but it could start to get awkward soon.

'I'm not actually a waiter, but I can try and find one for you.'

Oh no, I'm such a fool, I've totally misread his outfit. Whilst most of the men are wearing spray-on jeans and lurid tank tops, he's wearing a beautifully cut black suit with a crisp white shirt.

'Oh God, I'm so embarrassed. I just thought . . . You look lovely, by the way.' Why did I say that? I can feel myself going even redder, if that's possible.

'You don't have to lie, I probably look like my mum dressed me. I just can't get the hang of this whole Hoxton vibe,' he says, casting a look around the room with a slyly disparaging smile.

He looks young enough that his mum really might've dressed him. 'I know, it's all a bit try hard, isn't it?'

'Isn't it just?' He laughs.

'So considering how scary it is, what's actually lured you here?'

'I've got some of my photos on display. That's one of mine.' He's pointing to a black and white nude portrait of an up-and-coming American indie actor. In fact, I'm sure I've seen that very shot in the Oscars special in this month's *Vogue*.

'You're not Harry Langham, are you?'

'I am, yes. Have you heard of me?' he says, looking bashful.

'Of course I have. You've been doing such amazing shoots!'

'I've just been lucky really. You get one of those kind of gigs, and it starts to snowball.'

The snowball effect, that's what my event needs. Once I start to get guests like him, PRs will offer up their coolest clients at a rate of knots. I start to hesitantly describe it, getting more enthusiastic as I lay out how I'd like it to be.

'I'm really hoping the design competition will give it a bit of excitement, so that it's not just a boring old fashion show. In fact . . . no, you're probably too busy.'

'Go on, try me,' he says, with another melting smile.

'Would you think about being a judge? I haven't put the panel together yet, but if you were on it, it would instantaneously become a cool thing to do.'

'You're such a flatterer.' He's laughing at me now, he's clearly not going to dirty his hands with *Casual Chic*. 'I might be shooting a campaign that week, but I'll speak to my agent and come back to you.'

Yeah right, if that's not a kiss-off I don't know what is.

'Thanks,' I say, feeling humiliated all over again.

There's an awkward silence, which seems to go on forever. I can't stand it any longer.

'Look, Harry, it was lovely meeting you, but I've got to run.' I gather up my bag and make to leave.

'Aren't you going to give me your card?' he asks.

'Of course.'

I clumsily scrabble around my handbag for it, feeling sure he'll discard it in the nearest ashtray as soon as I leave. I'm too embarrassed to initiate a goodbye kiss, but he unexpectedly leans in. When his lips touch my cheek I feel a definite tremor, but I bat it away. As if this vision of precocious success would give a second thought to a thirty-something, world-weary hack like me. But as I start my interminable climb down the stairs, I sneak a look back. He's staring after me, smiling. 'I'll call you,' he mouths, and I feel my tummy turn over. But I won't be holding my breath ...

7

I enter Mark and Amy's flat with fresh eyes. They're old university friends, and I can't actually remember the last time I saw them as a single entity. Coming here without Adam casts the whole environment in an entirely new light. The school pictures that litter the mantelpiece, Freddie's random splotches of paint that are reverentially stuck to the fridge and optimistically described as pictures – all these touches make me feel as though I've entered a foreign country. I suppose I always assumed that I was heading for the same place, and now that I've lost that certainty I suddenly feel almost mocked by them. How egotistical is that? I pull myself together and head for the fridge.

Obviously if you have dinner with parents, there's no guarantee you'll actually get to see them. There's bath time and poo routines and incessant stories to take into consideration. I try not to swig my wine too fast, in case the dreaded request to read him his bedtime story comes floating down the stairs. I can just imagine the look of woeful judgement he'll cast up at me as I breathe booze fumes all over his precious blond head. Freddie's my god-son, and I do love him, albeit in a slightly hypothetical way. But making conversation is definitely a struggle: we're just not on the same wavelength yet.

Eventually Mark comes downstairs, covered in bath foam and looking harassed.

'Sorry, Anna, Freddie's been having a really stressful time at nursery recently, so Jodie's asked us to ensure we give him as much reassurance as possible at bedtime.'

'Who's Jodie?'

'His play therapist,' he says matter-of-factly.

He's suffering from stress? He's got a therapist? The child is four years old! Have his shares in Tonka toys taken a nose dive? Has he been overlooked for promotion to owl class in favour of Tarquin?

'Poor little thing,' I murmur.

'Anyway, there's a great bunch of guys coming over tonight, and don't worry, you're not the only single person. Oh God, I'm sorry, I didn't mean that how it sounded.'

'What, like it's a terminal illness?'

Too harsh, too harsh! I laugh, trying to take the edge off the situation. Mark's an incredibly straightforward bloke, and I know he didn't mean it badly, but I'm sick of feeling like I have to constantly defend what I've done. 'We had sex once a month!' I feel like screaming. But then I remember that Mark's a parent, so for him that probably counts as a rampant shagathon.

Gradually the other people start to file in. I vaguely recognize a few of their guests, but not well enough to strike up a conversation.

'Anna, this is Gerry, you must remember each other! Gerry did Ancient History. And Chrissie, his wife.'

Never laid eyes on him in my life. But I don't want to

embarrass Mark, particularly having been so snappy when I arrived.

'Hi, Gerry, yeah, I'm sure I remember seeing you around the place.'

'Oh, do you? I can't quite place you, but then it was all such a drunken haze!'

By now his wife is eyeballing me suspiciously. She probably thinks I spent three years lusting after her luscious husband, while he never gave me a second glance because he was holding out for her. Gerry is 5 foot 5 and plump. He's wearing a tight polo neck, which makes him look as though his chubby face is being squeezed out of a tube. How am I going to get through this?

'So, Chrissie, what do you do? Have you come from far?' I wish I could stop overcompensating. Who knew my social skills were so inextricably bound up in my couple status?

She gives me a look of faint disdain. 'I'm a solicitor and we've come from Barnes.'

'I love Barnes,' I tell her inanely.

And with that earth-shattering observation ringing in my ears, I duck out in search of more alcohol. Luckily not everyone is as frosty as Chrissie. There are a couple of nice teacher colleagues of Amy's, as well as Mark's older brother Tom, whom I met a few times at university. He always seemed terribly grown up and sophisticated then, having both a proper job and a fiancée. Not so much now. His tablecloth-like checked shirt is tucked into his unflattering jeans, and his straggly dark hair sticks up randomly like the bristles of a broom. He's toweringly

tall and there's a real chance there's a good body lurking
beneath the ill-fitting clothes, but he's a man in desperate
need of a make-over. Maybe I could hand him over to
the hags? Going by his appearance, it's no surprise to
discover that he's my fellow sufferer – and how he's
suffering. He's going through a divorce that is the stuff
of nightmares, where his wife has run off with another
man but is squeezing him for every last penny. Rather
than simply living with his children, he now has to enter-
tain them, taking them on more and more elaborate
outings in order to ensure he stays uppermost in their
thoughts. I'm not sure if we're being fixed up or not,
but, even if I did fancy him, acting on it would be like
combing through a car wreck for cash.

I hope I'll be able to sit with the jolly teachers, but
unfortunately there's a table plan. Mark's delusional idea
that Gerry and I are old mates means we're next to each
other, with Tom seated to my left. Chrissie's chair is
on her husband's other side, from where she continues to
cast me beady glances. Conversation swiftly turns to the
fascinating topic of school catchment areas, a subject I
know almost nothing about.

'Do you have children, Anna?' asks Chrissie with a
malicious smirk, even though my lack of input makes the
answer utterly self-evident.

I try for icy nonchalance. 'No, none at all. I'm not sure
I could handle the sleep deprivation.'

There's a shocked silence. Even the teachers hate
me now. Can't they see what she was doing? Now I look
like a psychopath.

'But of course I don't think that when I see Freddie! Spending time with him is an utter joy.'

There's a sense of palpable relief around the table.

'You probably haven't met the right man yet!' pipes up a presumptuous earth mother, whom I literally haven't exchanged a word with.

Why do these womb Nazis assume that they're party to some mystical secret that us childless types are too naive and deluded to appreciate? I'm clearly on the back foot here, so I give her a non-committal half smile and try to turn back to Tom. But Chrissie hasn't finished with me yet. With a triumphant smile she leans across Gerry and starts to regale me with how much of a shock she found motherhood, so much more demanding than a career, but how now she's done it she wouldn't swap it for the world. I've heard this particular lecture so many times I'm virtually mouthing along with her. However, from the extravagant boasts she makes about her work I can well imagine what the real story is. She works an eighty-hour week and barely recognizes her children when they dash past her en route to their Suzuki violin lessons. But no matter, she's won! She's proved that she's superhuman, that she can have it all, and us little people must trail in her wake.

By now the starters are on the table, spears of asparagus with big jugs of hollandaise. As Gerry's doughy paw reaches out for the sauce, Chrissie slaps his wrist, hissing, 'No, Gerry, hollandaise is for fattipuffs!' Instantly cowed, he timidly withdraws and starts to tuck in to his dry vegetables. I think about licking his neck just to see what she'd do. Instead I turn to Tom, and hear how he's been reduced to living in his childhood bedroom because his ex has used their joint account to hire Princess Diana's divorce lawyers. Looking round this table, marriage really does feel like the triumph of hope over experience.

The rest of the evening passes in an inebriated haze. Once I've got Tom off his suicidal divorce jag, he turns out to be quite good fun, regaling me with stories of his upmarket gardening business.

'You're lucky you've got such a good job. You wouldn't believe what these women get driven to when they're stuck at home,' he tells me conspiratorially.

'What like?'

'No, you won't believe me.'

'Why wouldn't I believe you?'

'Because I'm not one of those sexy, earthy types, like Monty Don. But I honestly do get offered a bunk-up in lieu of payment at least once a month.'

'Don't put yourself down, Tom!' I tell him, laughing. 'Although the use of the phrase bunk-up isn't particularly sexy, it has to be said.'

Chrissie's now glaring at us for being too raucous, and I've really had enough. I turn to Gerry, smiling sweetly.

'Do you ever get offered sexual favours in exchange for conveyancing, Gerry?'

'Not so far, Anna, no,' he titters. Chrissie looks utterly disgusted with me and suggests they leave soon after. Despite the pathetically early hour, it rapidly turns into a stampede, as people rush to get home and relieve their babysitters. I decide it's time to cut my losses and call a cab. Tom insists on seeing me into it, and I'm about to give him a kiss on the cheek when he grabs my wrist.

'I really enjoyed tonight, Anna. The last few months have been fairly rough, and I know I'm not the best company, but if you fancied doing it again some time, I'd love to take you out.'

'Tom, I'm really flattered . . .'

But as I'm trying to give him the gentle brush-off, he swoops in. His stature means I'm suddenly faced with a huge expanse of tongue and teeth, bearing down menacingly from a great height. I feel like a lowly pre-historic creature, hunted mercilessly by a Tyrannosaurus Rex. I swerve, panicked, and our noses crash into each other painfully.

'Oh Christ, I'm such a twat. I'm totally out of practice at this stuff. Fuck, fuck.'

I feel terrible for him. I should've just gone with it.

'No, you're not, not at all. I had a great time too.' And then I hear myself uttering the fateful words, 'You should call me, obviously.' What am I saying? Tom's looking hugely relieved, like I've just handed him his balls back, and the cab driver's hooting his horn monotonously.

'OK! I really felt a connection tonight, Anna. Oh God, shut up, Tom, stop talking.' He's beaming at me. 'See you soon. Very, very soon.'

I give him a weak smile and hurl myself into the cab. What have I done? I really don't fancy him, which is bad enough, but he's also my friend's brother. Mark's going to hate me for leading him on when he's clearly deranged on

60

divorce hormones. Meanly, I'm also slightly horrified by how gauche and clumsy he was. He's clearly no dummy, and yet he totally misread the signs. Is that what happens to you once you've been off the horse for a decade? Will I be as blundering myself? I'm not sure I can take the risk. I've got to get back in the game sharpish, before my pulling skills ossify and I'm propositioning traffic wardens. Besides, however much I try to dismiss it, there is an undeniable time pressure. Even if my maternal urge remains in hiding, men get gradually more frightened of you as you creep up your thirties and your window of opportunity narrows. They become utterly convinced that you're an unhinged sperm bandit, determined to plunder their seed at any cost. Oh God, what a luxury it was to not have to engage with any of these uncomfortable truths. However much I'm missing Adam, there's no time to be lost. I'm going to force myself to go out on a date, even if it's just for practice.

The cabbie's one of those maniacs who averages a speed of about a hundred miles an hour all the way back to Polly's, screeching to a halt behind a badly parked car. A car that looks oddly familiar and is filled with over-flowing bin bags. Overwhelmed with panic, I distractedly thrust a twenty into the driver's hand and rush through the open front door.

8

Adam's in the hallway, struggling with a CD rack. When he sees me he almost recoils in shock.

'Anna! Polly didn't think you'd be back till one at least.'

'What are you doing here? I said I'd come round on Sunday.'

I'm trying to hold it together, but I can hardly get my words out. It's partly such a relief to lay eyes on him again, but also so agonizing. What are the rules now? I want so much to hug him, and yet to do so seems utterly inappropriate.

'I can't stand living in the middle of all your things. I had to get them out of the flat.' He determinedly turns his back on me, yanking another box in from the front porch.

'I'm really sorry, Adam, but it's not fair to just ambush me. I feel hideous about what's happened. Please don't think I'm not in bits as well.'

'You're in bits?' He sounds incandescent with rage. 'You've got no idea what I'm going through here. I thought girls were meant to crave all this commitment stuff. Or is it just that you want it with someone who isn't me?'

I'm groping for the right words. 'Maybe I don't want it

with anyone, Adam. I don't know what it is if I'm honest. But I know I couldn't marry you.'

'So basically I've just wasted the last ten years on a relationship with no long-term potential? Nice work, Anna. Thanks for ruining both of our lives.'

He's white with fury, heading for the door. I grab his arm, padlocking myself around him.

'Please don't leave, please don't leave,' I beg him, tears streaming down my face. 'I wish I could make this go away.'

I feel the fight go out of him. 'I'm being such a girl about all of this,' he says sadly. 'I'm ready for the whole deal. I want babies, I want a proper house, I wouldn't even say no to a Labrador. I suppose you were right all along, underneath it all I'm just a suburban throwback. Oh my God, I'm Bree!'

What I've always loved about Adam is that he can take the piss out of himself, and the idea that he's the most uptight of the *Desperate Housewives* really makes me laugh. Before I know it we're hugging each other, and I'm crying, and he's stroking my hair and it's all feeling so familiar and comfortable.

'Just come home, Anna,' he mutters into my hair. 'What are you doing living on Polly's sofa bed? It's ridiculous.'

I pull away and look him in the face. 'I can't come back. I just can't.'

'You're having some kind of weird brainstorm which eventually you'll snap out of. I'm just going to have to wait it out.'

There are never any mind games with him. The concept of playing hard to get has obviously completely passed him by.

'It's more than that, Adam, it really is.'

And with that I give him another squeeze and start to unload more things from the car. I feel utterly wretched, and if I'm honest I don't want him to go. Being with him still feels as natural as breathing, but it doesn't mean that it's enough – for either of us. As I'm ferrying stuff into the house, Polly pokes her head out of the kitchen.

'I tried to call you but your phone was on silent. Is it OK now?'

'Yeah. It's worryingly nice to see him, but I'm staying here.'

'Can we ask him to stay for a drink?' she asks me hesitantly. 'Or will that just be too weird?'

I pause for a moment, reluctant to open the wound any further, but longing to grasp hold of whatever remaining time I can legitimately spend with him.

'Of course we can, he's your friend as much as he's my ex.'

And he does stay, and we all get even drunker together. Being with these two is partly so easy and fun: it's almost like we're twenty-somethings again. But the fact that Adam is no longer mine infuses everything with sadness. Right now he's still gazing at me with uncomplicated love, denying to himself that I'm not coming back. But as the truth starts to seep in, the tangible reality of his feelings for me will melt away and disappear into the ether. He'll no longer be my champion or my protector:

he'll just be my ex. And once perky girl pitches up, I'll probably be rubbed out completely. I wish so profoundly that I believed we'd have a happy marriage, but I don't. Even so, I have to summon up all my willpower not to get into the car with him at the end of the night.

'Can we at least have dinner next week?' he asks me, when we're out on the pavement.

'I would love that so much, but seeing you makes it too hard.'

He stares down at me. 'Do you know how boring other men are? Just to warn you. I've spent quite a lot of time with them this last couple of weeks, and they really don't cut it conversationally.'

He reaches out, slipping his hand round the back of my neck and pulling me towards him. I stretch towards him like a cat, leaning into his touch, viscerally aware of how much I've missed the feel of skin on skin. Even so, I force myself to pull away.

'Adam, you need to back off a bit.' I sound sharper than I mean to, just because the effort is so great.

'All right, Anna, I get the message. Jesus!' And with that he leaps into the car, slamming the door and hurtling off.

After he's gone I stand there for a few minutes looking at where the car was. I'm hurting him, I'm hurting me, and for what? Despite all my misgivings, the loveliest night I've had since we've broken up has been spent with him.

When I get back inside, Polly's looking anxious, and I jump right in before she can speak.

'Please don't ask me if I'm sure, I really can't go there.'

'I won't, I promise. But,' she says pleadingly, 'we had such a lovely time with him, you must admit.'

'I know, Pol, but it's been so lonely for so long. And if I'm honest, I just don't think I fancy him any more. I wish it didn't matter, but ...'

'I think he's got better-looking with age, I really do.'

'Polly! Do you? You don't ...'

'No, of course I don't!' she says, outraged. 'But I tell you something for nothing, he's a much better catch than most of the losers out there.'

I'm desperate to change the subject. 'So you didn't let Michael inspect your pipes then? Tinker with your plumbing?'

'Yeah, yeah, very funny. It was horrific, Anna. He turned up in a bootlace tie, you know, like Billy Ray Cyrus.'

'Nice!'

'And then he just talked about himself in a monologue. How he's got some special plumbing award, and how all his employees worship him. Every time I tried to speak he'd say "Can I just finish?" like he was my headmaster.'

'Where did you go?' I ask her, laughing.

'Nando's! I don't mean to be snobby, but I just couldn't stop thinking about what those poor little chickens must've been through. At least it was "Chicks' Night", so they pretty much gave me an intravenous drip of free sangria.'

I tell her about my horrific dinner party, and how

Chrissie tried to make me feel about three inches tall all evening because I was on my own.

'Yes, that was the worst bit! He asked me why I was still single, so I was trying to explain how hard it is to meet anyone remotely decent, and he gave me all this cod psychology about how it was down to my negative conditioning about men. Then he offered to hypnotize it out of me!'

'Yeah, right,' I say. 'Look into my eyes: you WILL give me a blow job in the car park.'

'Exactly! Then I asked for the bill and he made such a song and dance about paying, like he was King Chivalrous. I really wanted to pay half, but he just wasn't having any of it and I ended up feeling kind of obligated to kiss him goodbye. Does that make me like a really, really low-rent hooker?' she says, looking perturbed.

'Of course it doesn't,' I tell her, and then fill her in about my awful near-snog with Tom.

'At least he sounds funny,' she says. 'Since Michael dropped me home he's been plaguing me with these awful texts.'

She shows me her phone. 'Thanx for nice evening. Home now.' Then 'Staying up watching *Top Gear*.' The next one reads 'Have brushed teeth and am in bed.' By the time I get to 'Can't sleep, reading *Nuts*,' I'm losing the will to live.

'I'm thinking about taking a rain check on the whole business,' she says, looking crestfallen. 'I mean, all these bloody women,' she gestures to the swathe of self-help books lining her shelves, 'say you have to be open to the unexpected, give everyone a try. But they never warn you about how disappointing it is.'

'I know what you mean,' I tell her, 'and Cistern Man's clearly a tosser, but there's a flipside to that argument. If so many men are a waste of space, maybe we have to resign ourselves to working our way through a load of no-hopers en route to finding someone loveable.'

'What, like rootling through rubbish in the sales till you find the perfect pair of shoes?' she says hopefully.

'Exactly!' I say, warming to my theme. 'We can't give up, it's not an option, so we'll just have to toughen up.'

'So are you going to give this Tom bloke a proper go?' she asks.

'Life's way too short. But I am going to force myself to go on a date. I'm determined. We've got to start taking charge of the situation rather than just sitting around waiting for the wrinkles to kick in.'

'Are you sure you're ready to start up again?' she asks doubtfully. 'I swear to you, Anna, it's way worse than you think.'

'No, I'm probably not, but how will I ever be if I just sit around thinking about Adam? I've got to start living the rest of my life.'

I'm sounding way more bullish than I actually feel. The prospect of a real date fills me with naked terror, let alone the thought of actually getting naked. But now I've thrown down the gauntlet there's no turning back.

9

As I walk into the office I can hear my phone going. It's an officious-sounding Roger.

'Anna, can I see you in my room, please? Victor's going to be joining us.'

This sounds bad: if Victor the Vulcan's coming downstairs it can only bode ill. I rush through, trying not to look thrown by the unnaturally early meeting. I bet Victor sleeps upside down in his office, hanging from the door jamb by his toes. He's as grey as February, with a cruel, pinched face. His sharp, pointed nose juts out ferociously above his thin sliver of a mouth. No warmth or good humour has ever been known to emerge from that particular orifice. If there was any justice he'd have pointy ears, but to say that he does would be a blatant lie.

'Anna,' he says mechanically, shaking my hand like an automaton. 'Sorry to ambush you. I'm just looking for an update on the event so I can brief the other directors.'

He stands back, giving me a thin smile. Rog, meanwhile, is looking terrified, and seems to be trying to signal something with his eyes. I hope he got clearance to give me this gig: I don't get the feeling that Victor's remotely impressed with his choice. Feeling like both of our heads are on the block, I launch into an extravagant description of the competition, trying to make it sound like the next Alexander McQueen will be bought and paid for by *Casual Chic*. Then I move on to the show itself, enthusiastically talking up the catering, but grinding to a crashing halt as I get to the lack of RSVPs, panel and – indeed – venue. Oh my God, what am I doing?

'Hmm, it sounds like there are quite a few blanks to fill in, wouldn't you say? It's vital that this event repositions the brand, and shows those top-end advertisers what we can do for them. If it's unachievable I'd prefer we pull the plug now.'

I can't bear to be the person who single-handedly destroyed Roger's career. It's time the gloves came off.

'The reason the panel's still work in progress is because there are so many high-quality judges jockeying for position.' He looks at me through narrowed eyes, as I blunder on. 'As we speak, Harry Langham is clearing his diary just so he can come on board.'

'Harry Langham?' he says, showing a brief flicker of interest. 'That's absolutely the kind of person we'd like to have associated with the magazine. But it doesn't address our lack of venue.'

'I'm very close to securing a site that will answer all your concerns, but I'm afraid I can't divulge it until the deal's been done.'

'I'm sorry, but I'll need more than that,' he says brusquely. 'How, for example, does it conjure up the spirit of the event?'

I'm rapidly running out of ideas. My mouth takes hold before my brain has time to protest.

'I don't know if Roger's told you, but I'm actually getting married myself.'

'Congratulations,' he says, in a tone that implies *who gives a fuck?*

'So in searching for a wedding venue, I came to realize that the ideal location had to be a church. Other than the obvious associations, a church also gives us a huge sense of British tradition. But by throwing a decadent party right in the heart of the institution, we make it deliciously subversive.'

I'm actually starting to sound like him.

'I fail to see how we capitalize on that if no one knows where it is.'

'If we keep it under wraps, it'll automatically intrigue those jaded party-goers who've seen it all before. It'll become a cool underground event that only a chosen few can access.'

Roger gives me a discreet thumbs-up sign, which brings to mind Simon Bates presenting *Top of the Pops*. There's an interminable pause.

'You've offered me some reassurance, Anna, but I'll be continuing to closely monitor your efforts. An investment of this size needs to deliver significant tangible benefits.'

As Victor vaporizes, Roger crosses the room to clutch me to him.

'Anna, you were amazing. Thank God for the wedding. It seems to give you such an innate understanding of what this event needs to be!'

'I'm doing my best,' I tell him, inwardly squirming.

'And I'm thrilled that you've found somewhere for it.

Whatever anyone else said, I knew you were the right person to do this.'

Great, so now I know for sure that the knives are out for me. And, even worse, Roger fell for my lie. I'd hoped he knew I was bluffing but would be so grateful that I'd pulled us back from the brink that he'd help me find a brilliant solution. I'm on my own on so many levels right now. If I don't manage to deliver a spectacular venue and a Harry-based panel my job can just get added to the long list of life elements that are going down the tubes.

'How long can you keep this up, Anna?' says Susie, whose tubes are a far more pressing concern than my own. We're sitting on ugly orange chairs in the fertility clinic waiting room. Martin's supposedly got an essential meeting, so I'm holding Susie's hand at her second appointment.

'I mean, what are you going to do, buy yourself an engagement ring?'

'Yeah, great, so I either shell out three grand on a stupid rock, or have the orcs say Adam's cheap.'

'Let's not worry about that now,' she says comfortingly. 'What you need to concentrate on is finding a venue.'

'Really? You think?' I say, feeling slightly hysterical. 'I can't engage with it today, you're the priority here.'

'I'm fine, really,' she says brightly. 'Now I'm getting the help I need I'm sure it's all going to work out for us.'

I can hear the dismal IVF statistics rattling round my brain like a pinball.

'Yeah, I'm sure it will too,' I say, awkwardly patting her hand.

'Anyway, I want to hear all about your first pull in ten years!'

'What, Tom? That so doesn't qualify.'

And I tell her all about the teeth clunking and my determination to get back out there pronto. Soon she's scrolling down her mobile, determined to come up with someone suitable.

'Robert: he's not bad. He works with Martin.'

'Why does he call himself Robert? It's so formal! What's wrong with Rob? Or even Bobby?'

'OK, calm down, he's off the list. How about Gordon? He's actually Martin's cousin. If you got married, we'd be related!'

The idea of having sex with a blood relation of Wet Martin's is just too hideous to contemplate. We're still trawling through by the time Susie's in stirrups. I'm trying to avert my eyes, pleading with her to take a break.

'No, no – I'm about to find the perfect person. How about Eddie? He's slightly lame, but he's ever so funny.'

'So what's lame about him?'

'One of his legs is significantly shorter than the other. Ow!'

'Sorry, Mrs Barton,' says the doctor, 'I really need you to relax.'

'I am relaxed,' says Susie snappishly. 'There's always David . . .'

'Susie,' I say, squeezing her hand.

After a bit more inelegant prodding, the doctor declares she's done. I make to leave, so they can have the chat in private, but Susie holds on to me for dear life. The doctor's a gentle Indian woman who is obviously painfully aware how frightened Susie is.

'Firstly I want to reassure you that the fact that you are so young makes your chances of conceiving extremely high.'

Now that has to be cheering. There aren't many scenarios left in which we're still deemed young.

'My assessment is that the most likely cause of your infertility is hostile cervical mucus.'

'Hostile mucus?' says Susie, looking slightly nauseous.

The doctor explains how the mucus has to clear out of the way in order to let Martin's horrid seed flood past and make her pregnant. Personally I can sympathize with the mucus's position, but I force that uncharitable thought aside. She tells her how she's going to have to go through a hormonal menopause, before her poor exhausted ovaries are ambushed with even more drugs in order to trigger mass egg production. By now Susie's looking fairly shell-shocked.

'Why don't you take a few days to think it through?' the doctor asks, smiling kindly.

Back at the house, Susie shakily pours us each a vat of wine.

'If I'm really going to sign up for this hell, I'm going to drink like a fish till they force me to stop. Cheers!'

'It's really unfair, Suse. I'm so sorry.'

'I don't know,' she says, tearily looking out of the window, 'it probably serves me right.'

'What are you talking about?' I ask her incredulously.

'I know you always say I'm not smug, but maybe I am a bit. You know, once you've found someone you really want to be with, you just assume it's all going to be straightforward.'

Only if you're Susie. If I finally met someone I wanted to marry I'm sure I'd just start wondering if they were going to be killed in a freak accident or give me deformed children.

'Why is my mucus so damn hostile anyway?' she says, laughing jaggedly. 'What have I ever done to offend it?' She sinks back into a chair. 'I wish we were still young enough for none of this stuff to matter.'

The problem being that when you are young enough for none of it to matter, the very fact that it doesn't means that you get no added value from your mental freedom. Besides, me being me, I simply invented a whole alternative subsection of worries to keep me busy.

I stay until Susie's calmer, and Martin's arrival home has become worryingly imminent. As she hugs me goodbye she suddenly shrieks, 'Giles!'

'Who's Giles?' I ask her suspiciously. 'Just cut to the chase and tell me what's wrong with him.'

'Nothing. He's incredibly high-powered, which means that he never has time to meet women. I think you might really hit it off.'

'Job?'

'Finance, but he's not a stuffed shirt.' I look at her doubtfully. 'For God's sake, Anna, take a leap of faith for once in your life!'

'I'll think about it,' I tell her, sticking my arm out for

a passing cab. Once ensconced, I check my mobile for about the hundredth time, vainly hoping that either Harry or his agent might've called me back. He's apparently shooting abroad, but from his agent's tone earlier, it's obvious that she can't imagine anything less likely than him wanting to judge my competition. The only way to come back from this is to find panel members even more dazzling than him, unlikely though it is.

I let myself into Polly's empty flat feeling distinctly gloomy. It's a bank holiday Friday night and I've got absolutely nothing to do. I toyed with the idea of visiting friends out of London, as Polly's done, but ultimately decided I couldn't face it. As a result the next three days are looking decidedly holey. Still, I think, at least it gives me a chance to trawl the Internet for a venue. I distract-edly shovel gluey pasta into my mouth as I try out various search options. Horrifically, wedding sites seem like the best way to track down vaguely religious locations (I've decided that I can interpret the term 'church' loosely if I have to). I get increasingly misanthropic towards the stream of bovine brides, skipping round rural locations in their hideous white concoctions. *'You're a virgin, are you?'* I sneer at one, who's clearly pushing fifty. Once I've got to the point of muttering divorce statistics at them, I decide it's time to log off.

I retreat to the sofa and try to enjoy an episode of *Friends* that I'm sure I've seen at least twice. It's one of the unfunny later ones, and I find myself obsessing about how much older they all look than when it started. It's as though they've been put through a distorting mirror; the men have expanded into middle-aged spread, whilst the women have stretched out into emaciated lollipops. I suddenly wish so much that Adam was there beside me, sharing the joke. Knowing how fatal this train of thought can be, I decide it's time to give up on Friday. I grumpily yank out the sofa, straining my shoulder in the process: it's the perfect end to the perfect evening.

When I wake up there's still no sign of Horst. He must've pulled, yet again; perhaps I should ask him for some tips. I decide to go out for coffee, which brings to mind one of my most hated self-help witches. She insists that you have to eat breakfast out every day, wearing a perky cap with a French slogan on it. Apparently it's the perfect way to lure your future husband into making conversation with you. I think about winding my pillowcase into a turban and scrawling *merde* on it, but I'm not sure it'll create the desired effect.

After coffee I set off on a long walk. I put my iPod on, and treat myself to a torrent of cheese. The Carpenters, Chicago, the Eagles: no band is too uncool for my state of mind. I walk right the way across Hampstead Heath to Highgate, and think about how I used to crave solitude when I was with Adam. When he had the occasional work trip, the time I had alone in the flat felt like the most delicious luxury. Solitude and loneliness might look the same from the outside, but from the inside there's a world of difference.

I get back to the flat early evening to find it's filled with billowing clouds of smoke. Horst is home, and for the first time ever, I'm delighted to see him. He's grilling huge sausages and crooning along to the Scorpions, Germany's worst musical export. He sticks a couple more sausages on and tells me about his latest conquest, a sloany temp who's been working in his office.

'I am doing the wrong thing it seems,' he says sadly. 'Maybe I have lovemaking with them too soon. They never want to take another date with me.'

'Oh, Horst, I thought that was what you wanted! Sowing your wild oats.'

'Oats? I don't see about the oats,' he says, looking perplexed.

I can't be bothered to explain. 'You're probably just meeting the wrong women. Loads of girls would love to find someone like you.'

'Maybe I go back to Stuttgart soon. You Londoners are hard to get to know. You could have my bedroom also.'

I've been absolutely longing for this moment to arrive all the time Polly's been chickening out of telling him. Even so, now it's finally happening, I can't bear to make him feel more rejected. Instead I find myself geeing him up, promising it'll get better, and resolving to invite him out with us more.

'I am trying to meet more people, however. Tomorrow I am to be seen for a part in an English play, *The Importance of Being Arnold*.'

'Arnold? I'm sure you mean Earnest.'

'Yes, quite so. To learn the English words is very hard for me.'

The production's being mounted by an appalling

sounding am dram group, who are holding open auditions the next morning. Horst is up to play the butler, but I'm not holding out much hope. I decide I've got to step in.

'A Miss Furr-fax has recently called to see Mr Woorthing on the most important of business.'

'No, Horst, it's Fairfax. And you say it Wurthing.'

We stay up till one working on his lines, although I'm not sure that we make any real progress. I collapse into bed, but when his alarm shrills at 8 a.m., I realize that there's no chance of getting back to sleep.

'So, Horst, repeat after me: Fairfax.'

'Fur-facts. Oh, Anna, I am so terrible at this, maybe I will not go.'

'You've got to go! You've worked so hard. And, anyway, you're not terrible.'

And, weirdly, he isn't. There's something genuinely charming about his mannerisms, it's just the heavy German accent that lets him down. Before I know it, I've agreed to come in the car so that we can carry on practising right up to the wire. The audition's somewhere in Bloomsbury, and he drives us there, veering around the road as he tries to multi-task.

'Shall I lay the tea here as is the usual, Miss?'

'No, it's just *as is usual.*'

We arrive in a beautiful Georgian square, lined with blossoming trees.

'So where's the hall?'

'It is here, attached to the church, I think,' he says, white with nerves.

And, just like that, I've found my venue. It's a beautiful, Gothic-looking church which has fallen into a state of disrepair. There's a 'for sale' sign erected outside it: it's obviously in line to be turned into luxury apartments. As I peer through the dusty windows at its ornate interior, I'm determined to make sure it's mine.

When Horst comes out we're as excited as each other.

'I think my reading of the part was mostly a success! They said they will call me by the end of the week.'

I'm not holding out much hope, but I'm thrilled to see how much happier he is. Horst agrees the church is perfect and we head home, buying ourselves a celebratory bottle of Cava en route. Finally the clouds of bank holiday gloom feel like they're lifting.

As we come up the path I notice a large parcel that's been left on the doorstep. 'Anna's First Aid Kit' reads the label, and it has a big red cross on it. I rip it open, pulling out a copy of my all-time favourite weepie *Love Story*. It stars a whiny but gorgeous Ali MacGraw and a devastatingly handsome Ryan O'Neal. When she dies at the end I always weep buckets, even though I've seen it at least thirty times. There's something about the way that their hard-won happiness is cruelly snatched away that really gets to me. A certain someone has seen this reaction many, many times and has thoughtfully stuck a packet of Kleenex in the parcel. There's a Post-it note on the DVD on which he's scrawled 'Love is never having to say you're sorry', one of Ali's most irritating mantras. If you ask me, love is about learning to force yourself to say you're sorry when you know you're in the wrong, even if your misplaced pride can barely stand it. Crying in earnest now, and thus availing myself of the Kleenex, I pull out a copy of Jilly Cooper's *Riders*, my all-time favourite bonkbuster. There's also a big bar of Green and Black's with another Post-it on it: 'Bank holidays suck, no? Missing you more than ever, if it's possible.'

I'm incredibly touched, but also kind of gutted. He so knows which buttons to press. How will it be possible to build up this kind of intimacy with someone else? Will I ever stop loving him as much as I do?

I've got a big choice to make here. I can either give up now and force myself to make it work, whatever the price, or push forward, refusing to look back. It's time, once again, to stick or twist.

10

Why did I ever agree to this? I'm not remotely ready
and, even if I was, this man is a friend of Wet Martin's.
Who in their right mind would specifically select Wet
Martin to be their friend? Oh God, I bet this is him.
Thinning gingery hair, which I'm sure he'll describe as
'strawberry blond', a horrid striped date shirt and a brief-
case. Is it too late to make a break for freedom? Oh no,
he's spotted me.

'Anna?'

Horrid teeth too. Why am I so superficial?

'Giles? Hi. Susie didn't tell me you were so, um, tall.'

What a ludicrous opening gambit. Now he'll think
I'm a one-woman egg factory, desperate for a strapping
Aryan to impregnate me at any cost. Spying the waiter,
I maniacally flag him down.

'Do you want a drink, Giles? I know I do.'

Now I sound even more desperate. A desperate
alcoholic with withering ovaries. Luckily he's too distracted to notice, browbeating the wine waiter with his
encyclopaedic knowledge.

'Is the Cabernet ninety-eight or ninety-nine? For my
money, ninety-nine was a very disappointing year.'

'Come on, Giles, it's Friday. Let's have cocktails. I'll
have a cosmopolitan.'

He gives me an unimpressed stare, but decides to go with it. 'Oh, OK. I'll have a pina colada.'

A pina colada? This man clearly hasn't been on a date since the mid 1980s.

'So, I hear you're a fashionista.'

I haven't got the heart to tell him that, until recently, I spent most of my time writing about the relative thread count of pillowcases. Hell, I can be whoever I want to be. I'm never going to see him again.

'Oh yes. I go to all the shows. I just came back from shooting with Mario Testino in New York last week.' What if he checks? Then he'll think I'm a delusional, alcoholic, nut job egg box.

'Who?'

What a lucky escape.

'I travel constantly,' he continues. Last week was Bogatá, and I'm off to Japan on Friday. You're lucky to catch me!'

This is delivered with a jokey snort (which is every bit as attractive as it sounds), but is imbued with much meaning. A) He thinks I'm lucky to have snared a Friday night date with him, considering that he's got a smorgasbord of honeys in their mid twenties queuing round the block. B) If I'm looking for a husband I can forget it. His life is far too busy for commitment. But the snort's designed to tell me that, if I play my cards right, I might get lucky and at least get a shag. And what a treat that would be.

Have I really left a man who adored me, wanted to marry me and was desperate to father my children for this? Right now I would so much prefer to be slumped on the sofa with Adam, swilling wine and watching *Entourage*. I didn't realize quite how much of a chilling game of Snakes and Ladders it is out here. And single women in their thirties are right at the bottom of the board.

But I'm still too chicken to make a run for it, so instead I try to drink my way out of jail. Giles tells me in great detail about the world of trading. It turns out that he's marvellous at it, possibly the most marvellous trader who ever lived. He's not sure that women can cut it on the floor, particularly after they've had kids, but insists he's no chauvinist. Perversely, I kind of agree with him, sick as I am of staying till 9 p.m. working on a page layout because Percy's got toothache and Jocasta's raced home. I tell him all about the iron rule of the mothers' mafia, eliciting another snorty laugh in the process.

Three cosmopolitans down the road it occurs to me that I'm almost enjoying myself. The fact that none of it matters is making me feel peculiarly liberated. In fact I find myself flirting with him, just to see what it feels like. Maybe I can still cut it out here in the big bad world.

'Do you realize this is my first date this century?' Oh no, big mistake. I can see him physically curling away in his chair. 'No, no. I just finished with my boyfriend. I'd been with him for ten years.'

'Oh I see. Right.'

He's visibly brightening, eagerly anticipating the potential for no-strings rebound sex, and I suddenly find myself wondering if he's got a point. He's not all that bad when you get to know him. Perhaps I could use him to get back in the game, so that when I meet someone who isn't ginger and I really like, I won't feel so terrified about getting my kit off. Or is that really slutty? Or is the twenty-first century the post-slut age, where anything goes? I wish I'd quizzed Polly more thoroughly about the rules of engagement before agreeing to this.

When we're out on the street he hails a cab and asks which way I'm going, and before I know it I've agreed to call a cab from his place. As the cab pulls away, he makes his move. He kisses like an over-eager cocker spaniel – sort of sloppy and enthusiastic – but I force myself to stick with it all the way back to Fulham. His flat's most definitely the lair of the 'bachelor playboy'. The fridge is bare, but for two bottles of Laurent-Perrier, and a mouldering lump of Tesco's Finest cheddar. The bathroom is chrome and characterless, with some slightly dubious stains. A single toothbrush hangs proud and aloof in its stand. There is an enormous plasma screen, and a shelf full of testosterone-fuelled box sets. It's a flat which screams, 'You are here for one night only. I will not be committing!' Which is absolutely fine by me.

As I nosily peer into the fridge, he pops open the champagne with a flourish. We chink overflowing glasses as he fixes me with an intense stare.

'I want you,' he mutters gutturally, and I struggle not to laugh.

'Thanks,' I reply stupidly, and then jerkily lean forward to kiss him in a transparent attempt to mask my romantic ineptitude.

Once I've done that, there's no stopping him. He's pawing at my clothes, snaking an eager hand up my skirt. I feel myself start to panic at the unexpected sensation of a strange man's hand on my skin, but it feels too late to turn back. In fact I start to find that, if I keep my eyes shut, there's something oddly gratifying about the bodily contact. I feel like I'm in character – a lusty drunk girl who never over-analyses – and before I know it I've let him drag me into the bedroom.

As we start having sex I feel a wave of shock go through me. Despite my inebriation, I'm still corrosively aware that the contours of his form are not Adam's. It's kind of enjoyable, but only in the way that a Big Mac is. Sort of momentarily satisfying, but ultimately slightly distasteful. Afterwards he rolls away, but thinks better of it and rolls back. There's a toe-curling pause while we both search for the right post-coital conversation.

'Mmm, that was delicious,' is what he finally musters up.

'Yes it was, thanks, Giles,' I say, trying to squash the revulsion out of my voice.

'That's all right,' he replies smugly. I can almost see the thought bubble floating above his head: *another satisfied customer*. He shifts around, trying to find a way to wrap his clammy body around mine.

'It's OK, don't worry. I'm not much of a cuddly sleeper.'

Clearly relieved, he rolls over and drops straight off, leaving me to sober up in solitude. And that's when the grief really starts to kick in. I feel bizarrely violated, even though I was a willing participant. What am I doing lying next to this snoring stranger? And what's Adam doing right now? Is he having casual sex to try and erase me from his mind? Or worse still, waiting until he falls passionately in love with someone really special who he can provide with scores of perfect offspring?

Once Giles's rugby ball alarm clock hits 4 a.m., I realize that I have to get out. But what to do? Leave a note? 'Thanks for the shag. Sorry, I'm an insomniac. See you around.' What's the form here? In the end I settle for 'Nice to meet you, Anna', with a single x, and hope that he won't think that it's code for 'I can't believe you fell asleep. If you ever do that when we're married I won't let you see your children. I LOVE YOU!' Stepping out on to the Fulham Road, I start to retch. What's the root cause – alcohol, anguish, or a bit of both? As I stumble up the road, with black cabs sailing past, unwilling to stop, I wonder if this really is the lowest I can go.

11

I crawl back into the office on Monday, still smarting from my humiliating experience with Giles. How could I possibly have thought that was a good idea? I feel woefully under-qualified for life right now.

After some seriously hardcore negotiations, I've managed to persuade the developers who are buying the church to hire it out to me prior to the renovations. But even though I've got the venue I've still got no panel, and there's been no word from the elusive Harry.

Jocasta's hanging round my desk, desperately searching for a conversational opener, but I'm stubbornly refusing to engage.

'Oh, how eye-catching!' she says, picking up one of the invitations. 'Surely these must've blown most of the budget straight away?' She beckons over a couple of other members of her coven to revel in how extravagant I've been.

'I cut quite a good deal with the printers actually,' I tell her with a tense smile. 'You know how it is with these events, it's all about contacts.'

'Yes, it is, isn't it? Though I hear from Ruby that the responses are still more of a trickle than a flood.'

I'm going to have to get Ruby to sign a confidentiality clause and drum up some A-list confirmations pronto.

'If I can be any help at all, I'd be very happy to stay on board,' she says. 'I gather from Roger that you were worried you might be a teensy bit junior to coordinate such a big bash.'

'Thanks, but it's all under control,' I tell her, trying to turn back to my computer, but she won't let it lie.

'In fact, I hope you don't mind, but I've been chatting to Roger about it while you've been out and about. You know, throwing a few ideas in the pot.'

This sounds ominous. 'Oh?'

'Don't worry, Anna, you're going to love this!' squeals Tabitha, who's dressed like she's been sucked up and spat out by the Boden catalogue.

'It's clear for all to see that Adam's on the brink of popping the question,' says Jocasta.

I make a non-committal noise, while Tabitha emits a high-pitched yelp and does some odd noiseless clapping.

'It's very much the reason why you've been put in charge,' she adds cattily. 'So why not allow the readers to enjoy your personal story? You could even start it now, share your nerves and anticipation about when he's finally going to make it official. After all, every woman's been there.'

'Yeah, maybe.'

'It's not really a question of maybe, Anna. Roger's mentioned it to Victor, and he thinks it's an excellent idea.'

How to play this? Could this week get any worse? It's vital they don't find out that I've lied through my teeth. I really could lose everything here and be stuck writing about wrinkle creams for the rest of my natural life. May God (and Adam) forgive me for what I'm about to do.

'There's something I haven't told you.' My voice is conveniently wobbling all over the place.

'What is it, Anna?' says Jocasta. They're looming over me now, longing for scandal.

'We're not getting married.' Saying this out loud genuinely makes me feel teary. I blunder on. 'He's – he's broken up with me.'

'No!' says Jocasta. 'I can't believe it. How could he? It's not as though you've got time to waste.'

It's taken her less than a minute to allude to my ovaries.

'But why?' pipes up Tabitha.

Oh God, I haven't really thought out an answer to this one.

'He said … he said, he just didn't feel the same any more. That he loved me, but he wasn't sure if that was enough.'

Saying the words out loud again immediately makes me choke up. My gruesome sexual escapade seems to have set me back at least a month. Jocasta and Tabitha are casting each other significant glances.

'Anna, I don't want to make this any more painful for you, but I think you might need to hear a few home truths about men. Are you sure there's no one else involved? It seems like a very sudden change of heart.'

'Men can be such hounds,' agrees Tabitha solemnly.

'No, no. It's nothing like that.' But is my story water-tight enough? 'At least, I hope it isn't. I really couldn't bear it.'

'Only time will tell,' says Jocasta sagely. 'You poor, poor girl. I want you to know that we're all here for you, every step of the way.'

I hate that expression. What does it actually mean?

'Thanks. I really appreciate your support.'

Now I'm a hypocrite as well as a liar. I just want it to be over, but the two of them stand there expectantly, waiting for the next revelation. This is clearly the most exciting thing that's happened since Percy's first unaided visit to the lavatory. Luckily at that precise moment my mobile starts ringing. Jocasta's eyes swivel to the caller ID.

'If it's him, you mustn't answer. Playing hard to get has saved many a relationship in crisis.'

Oh my God, now she thinks she's got carte blanche to comment on my personal life. This could end badly.

'It's not. I'd better take it.'

They slide off, disappointed, but keen to spread the news.

'Is this Anna?' says an unfamiliar male voice.

I hope it's not Tom. I've already dumped two of his calls because I don't know what the hell to say. 'Yes, who's this?'

'It's Harry, you know, from the opening.'

Harry, the most gorgeous man in London Harry?

'Thanks so much for calling me back!' I squeak. 'How was the rest of the party?'

'Actually, it took a real nosedive after you disappeared.'

91

'Yeah, that's what tends to happen when I leave. Sorry about that.' Are we actually flirting?

'So I've been seriously considering your offer, but I think I'd need more convincing to get involved.'

I knew it! Why would someone as hot as him want to have anything to do with such a lame publication? In fact, why am I wasting my time trying to make this event something it can never be?

'Oh. OK then,' I say, trying not to sound sulky.

'Don't you want to give it a go? Have dinner with me and try to talk me round?'

'Oh!' This totally throws me. 'Yeah, I guess.'

'No need to sound so enthusiastic,' he says, sounding amused. 'Are you free Saturday night?'

Obviously I should lie. All the self-help witches say you can only agree to a mid-week date, six months hence, until you're actually married. Fuck it: I'm from Harlesden, not Manhattan.

'Totally, I'd love to.'

'Great. I'll book somewhere and call you back. See you then.'

And with that he's hung up, leaving me feeling ridiculously excited. Jocasta comes sailing past, casting me a sympathetic smile.

'You're looking a little brighter. Good news on the Adam front?'

'No, no. It was just Harry Langham calling about the party,' I tell her, hurriedly trying to readjust my features into an expression of abject misery.

'It's all material, Anna. You could maybe write a diary,

charting your progress as you bounce back from the brink of matrimony. It'd be a fascinating contrast to all those happy couples, tripping up the aisle.'

I grit my teeth. 'Thanks, Jocasta, I'll give it some thought.'

I have to get out. Luckily it's nearly lunchtime, so I've got an excuse. The self-doubt has started to kick in now: will it still feel totally wrong to be with someone who isn't Adam, however sexy they are? Is it callous to even try? Perhaps the fact that Giles was such a disaster proves that it's way too soon. I'm dying to talk to someone about it, so I call Polly and blurt it all out.

'Yeah, that's great, Anna,' she says flatly.

'You don't sound very excited for me. Google him, he's unbelievably gorgeous.'

'I just feel bad for Adam. He rang me the other day, he still sounds terrible. But you don't seem bothered about him at all.'

'Of course I'm bothered! But I can't mope around indefinitely, and nor will he. I bet he's got loads of girls offering to love his pain away.'

Saying it out loud sends a jolt of pain through my solar plexus. I'm suddenly feeling distinctly uncertain about my date with Harry and horrible about slandering Adam to save my arse. Polly mustn't find out.

. 'Look, Pol, I don't mean to sound harsh. Let's talk about it tonight.'

She pauses. 'I'm actually going out tonight.'

'Oh, OK. What are you doing?'

'I'm having dinner with a friend from work.'

Polly hates her job. She does market research, which mainly seems to involve asking halfwits what they like best about Jaffa Cakes. Normally she tries to avoid having anything to do with it when she's not there.

'Who's that?'

'You don't know her, she's new.' She pauses again. 'Barbara. Anyway, I've got to go.'

She hangs up, still sounding distinctly frosty. Am I being brutal? Perhaps I am, but I'm too intoxicated by Harry to let the chance to see him again slip through my fingers. It's been so long since I felt this kind of fizzy anticipation. Even if it turns out to be a disaster, I'm determined to savour every last feverish minute. However artificial the shot of adrenalin is, I'm pathetically grateful to have escaped the pervasive gloom.

I spend the whole afternoon on tenterhooks, willing Harry to call me back. I get Ruby in and try to subtly impress on her how much we need to keep the details under wraps. Then I make a series of furious calls, desperate to pull in panel members as impressive as Harry. When I work on the basis that he's doing it, doors suddenly start to open. Soon I've got an angular beanpole of a supermodel looking likely, as well as a shoemaker to the stars. I'm still obsessing, so when a withheld number call comes up, I answer it within a single ring.

'Anna?'

It's Mark. I try my best not to sound disappointed.

'Tom's been busting a gut trying to get hold of you. It sounds like your party's keeping you totally tied up.'

'Oh God, how rude of me. I'll call him today, I promise.'

'Do. I know he's my brother and I'm biased, but he's a fantastic bloke.'

A sudden image of Harry kissing the back of my neck burns its way into my brain. I could never, ever feel this turned on by the thought of Tom.

'Anyway, that wasn't what I was calling for. Amy and I were really touched by what you said about Freddie when you came over.'

'I meant every word!' What the hell did I say?

'So we thought we should make an effort to create more quality time for the two of you. You are his god-mother after all.'

Oh no. I am so hopeless with kids.

'Great. What were you thinking?'

'Well, the two of you have actually got a surprising interest in common.'

What? Drinking cosmopolitans? Classic Woody Allen films?

'Freddie loves his baby yoga class, and we wondered if you'd like to take him along on Saturday. It'd really help us out actually – Amy's mum's ill and we need to drive up there.'

'Oh, um . . . sure. I'd love to.'

'Fantastic, we'll drop him off at nine thirty.'

Nine thirty! God is truly punishing me for the lies. At least if I start early I should have enough hours left to reverse the ravages of time before my date with Harry. If he ever calls me, that is.

I get back to the flat to find Horst engrossed in *A Matter of Life and Death*, repeating the dialogue to himself as he goes along.

'Anna! I have most wonderful news! The actors are going to take me into their band. They say my talent is raw but it can be natured.'

Are they insane?

'That's brilliant, Horst, well done.'

'It is all up to you, of course. I am very thankful.'

I chuck myself down on the sofa and settle down to watch the film with him. For once in my life I'm staying firmly focused on the positives. I'm off the hook with my pseudo-engagement, and the venue and panel seem to be shaping up nicely. If Harry's also set to land in my lap, life might just be too good to be true.

12

The rest of the week passes in a frenzy of anticipation. The day after my hideous deceit I come back from lunch to find a basket of muffins on my desk with a sinister-looking teddy bear balloon tied to the handle. This is such an un-Adam gift: I know he'd find the bear nauseating, and anyway I haven't heard from him since he tore off in the car. I go to call him, but as his phone starts to ring I find a card that's slipped underneath the muffin mountain. 'Sorry you're blue, the only way is up! Love from Jocasta, Tabitha and all at *Casual Chic*.' The perfect gift for a wheat intolerant compulsive liar.

I hurriedly go to hang up, but Adam beats me to it, dumping my call mid ring. It's illogically hurtful, but also kind of a relief. He's obviously not pining anywhere near as much as Polly thinks. I glance up to find Roger looking over expectantly. I give him an awkward smile.

'Were you part of this, Roger? It's a really sweet thing.'

'We just want you to know we're thinking about you. If Graham just upped and left . . .' He gives an involuntary shudder. Poor Rog, he's so in denial. I bet Graham's banged every single member of the gay water polo team he captains.

'Anyway, if you need to take any time off, you just have

to ask. I'm sure Jocasta will be only too pleased to step into the breach.'

Wouldn't she just. I give him an awkward smile. 'Thanks, Roger but, you know, it's good to keep busy.'

'Yes, well, I know you'll have a rather different take on it all now, which is obviously something of a worry, but I'm sure you're far too much of a professional to let that get in the way.'

Is there a veiled threat in there? I can see Jocasta peering over keenly, but I try my best not to let the paranoia kick in. Instead I gush more guilty thanks, before offloading the Judas-muffins double quick. Luckily the fact that *Casual Chic*'s hardly a style bible means it's staffed by women who actually eat.

Harry still hasn't rung back, but I'm forcing myself not to contact him. Every time my hand wriggles towards my phone I get a vision of my inner self-help witch wagging her finger and intoning 'She's a caller!' Instead I'm distracting myself with the huge amount of coordination the event requires. I get Ruby to take me through the other couples that she's shortlisted for the feature.

'I thought it was important we got a mix of ages,' she says, gingerly pushing some Polaroids over the desk. The first photo is of a plump, middle-aged couple with a large brood of children. 'So I wondered if a blended family would be good. It's second time round for both of these two, and they've got six kids between them.'

What a nightmare! I can't imagine anything worse than taking on a tribe of someone else's offspring. Ruby's looking at me anxiously.

'Yeah, maybe,' I say unenthusiastically. 'Who are the other candidates?'

She takes me through various other options. I toy with an arranged marriage, wondering if it'll give the feature a breadth of experience, but I'm unable to find another couple who really capture my imagination. I want to inject the article with at least a smidgen of the glamour that the event's got, which means finding a pair who are very different from our average reader profile. I ask Ruby to keep looking and she slinks off, looking crushed.

'Ruby?' I call after her.

'Yes?'

'Thanks for your help. And . . . and for the muffins.'

'No problem,' she says, brightening a little.

Saturday arrives and there's still no word from Harry. If he's disappeared again it'll be such a disaster in so many ways. I want to ask Polly if she thinks I should give up on him, but I'm frightened she'll bite my head off. Instead I decide to concentrate on being number-one godmother. I leap out of bed and rootle through my clothes. Do you wear actual yoga clothes to baby yoga? Will I be able to join in, or will I just have to sit around, making inane cooing sounds? And how advanced is Freddie? Can he wind his chubby legs into the lotus position? I can't believe I'm feeling competitive with a four-year-old. Horst comes lumbering through on his way to the kitchen and I ask him if I should just bite the bullet and call Harry.

'Oh, Anna, the not so easy to get stuff seems no good

to me. If you want to speak with him, just dial his tele-phone.'

'So it doesn't put you off when a girl seems keen?' I ask him hopefully.

'No, I love it!' he says, beaming.

I can hear Polly emerging from the shower, so I swiftly change the subject. Anyway, I'm decided. If Harry hasn't called by midday I'm going to ring him. What's the worst that can happen?

Mark and Amy turn up on the dot. Amy stays in the car, looking stressed, while Mark thrusts Freddie towards me.

'I'm sorry not to have time to stop. Amy's mum's had these tests this week, and we still don't know how serious it is.'

Freddie's clinging to his leg, bleating, 'Daddy, Daddy!' I weakly pat his head, eliciting a blood-curdling snarl.

'Bye-bye, noodle,' says Mark, smiling beatifically at this raging midget. It's like people literally lose their powers of perception when they become parents. 'Be a good boy for Auntie Anna!'

I struggle to control my rising panic.

'He'll be fine! Everything you need is in this bag. We'll see you at five.'

Mark starts off down the path, while Freddie bursts forth with a wail of anguish. As the car drives off, his cries reach a crescendo, and I have a sudden flashback to me standing in the same spot, watching Adam's car recede into the distance. I feel a wave of sympathy for him.

'Let's go inside, Freddie. Maybe I can wangle a packet of Monster Munch off Horst.'

I'm relying on the fact that Mark and Amy's idea of a treat is a carob flapjack, but bribery just won't wash. 'Nooooo,' he screeches, lying face down on the ground.

I try to pick him up, but his body is rigor mortis stiff. Reasoning with him has no effect and my attempt to be stern makes him weep all the harder. I find myself wondering, not for the first time, why the hell Susie's moving heaven and earth to add a child into the mix. Eventually Horst appears on the scene. He crouches down on the ground next to him.

'Hello, little man. Why is there all the crying?'

'Want . . . want my daddy!'

Horst strokes his blond head and promises him faithfully that his parents will be coming back. Freddie soon casts him a look of blind devotion and obediently trots inside. I grab Horst's arm.

'Thank you so, so much. I really owe you one. How the hell did you manage that?'

'Owe me one what?' he asks. 'Is OK, I have four smaller sisters, it's not so hard for me.'

Ten minutes later Freddie's watching cartoons with a bowl of cornflakes as if none of it ever happened. I, meanwhile, am a gibbering wreck, seriously contemplating taking up smoking again. Then it's time to set off for yoga, so we spend half an hour gathering together all of his essential items (a wooden truck, a manky square of fleece) and trying to work out whether or not he needs to do a 'number two'. Is it a prerequisite of parenthood that you start using these twee analogies for bodily functions? We both plead with Horst to come with us, but he's having none of it. All the faffing around means we just miss the bus, and have to stand in the cold for ten minutes, struggling to make conversation. It's like the worst date ever.

'So, Freddie, do you like it at school?'

'It's OK. Why isn't Horse coming to my club?'

Obviously we arrive late, so I try to strip Freddie of his coat as quickly as possible. He insists that he be the one to unzip it, but it's jammed. We end up in a bad-tempered tussle, each yanking at it, until he pulls out his trump card and starts wailing again. The class is already in full flow, so all the perfectly groomed mummies have to crane their long necks to stare, aghast, through the glass studio wall. All the yummy mummies ... and one very ungainly dad, who's now dashing across the room to rescue me.

'Uncle Tom!' shouts Freddie with unbridled joy. Why does he love everyone else and hate me? A mixture of relief and embarrassment cascades through me as Tom deftly removes the offending anorak and ushers us in. An adorable little moppet of a girl sits beside him, who looks uncannily like Freddie. Soon we're clapping encouragingly as the children bend their ludicrously flexible bodies into various poses. I mutter my thanks to Tom, wondering if he's pissed off with me, but he seems genuinely warm. I gradually start to get into the swing of it, helping an excitable Freddie into his downward dog, but just as he's holding the pose my mobile starts up. Why did I ever choose 'Goldfinger' as my ringtone? The yummies all stare disapprovingly as I race out of the studio to shut it off. It's the first time this week I haven't been focusing on whether or not it's Harry, and now of course it is. Though I know I shouldn't, I can't resist answering, just in case he disappears back into the black hole from whence he came. I try for cool nonchalance, which is almost impossible to achieve when you're whispering.

'Hi, Harry, how are things?'

'God, I can hardly hear you. Are we still meeting later?'

Is there a mysterious and intriguing way to answer this faintly dismissive question? If there is, it's passed me by. Instead I find myself blindly falling in with his plans, which involve worryingly early drinks, followed by a friend's party. The fact that I have to mutter inaudibly makes it almost impossible to negotiate. If Mark and Amy aren't pretty darn punctual they'll find Freddie and me sipping Martinis on the other side of London.

I try to slip unobtrusively back into the class, but the teacher fixes me with a death stare. These yogi types always try to pretend they're so serene and spiritual, when really they're the most controlling old crones out.

'Are you with us for good now? This is the part of class where the lucky mums and dads get a chance to have their turn. Everyone find a partner.'

Oh no. I'm wearing the world's rattiest tracksuit bottoms and feeling far too jittery to hold a pose. I can see a shy-looking mum casting a hopeful glance at Tom, but he's much too kind to abandon me.

'Looks like it's you and me then, Anna.'

'Great!'

'This week it's headstands,' she says, staring over. 'Do you think you'll be able to keep up?'

I should just say no – I've never been much cop at yoga, it's just a cunning means of avoiding the gym – but she's got my back up now. Soon we're laying out neck supports, eagerly assisted by Freddie and Belle. I start trying to push my chunky calves upwards, but keep collapsing sideways in an inelegant heap. The teacher zeroes in on my woeful efforts.

'That's why we've got partners, Anna! Tom, grab her legs and help to pull her upwards. That's it!'

So now he's literally grappling with my thighs, getting a bird's-eye view of my lycra-clad arse desperately trying to steady itself.

'Anna looks funny!' says Freddie gleefully.

'No she doesn't, Freddie, she's doing very well. Look, she's all the way up, let's give her a clap!'

The three of them applaud, while I force my legs to stay vertical, despite the fact that my neck's virtually breaking. After that the class is mercifully over, and Tom suggests we take the children for lunch. Is this a set-up? Either way, I'm too desperate to avoid any more one-on-one time with Freddie to turn him down. As we walk out of the centre I make myself address the white elephant in the room.

'I'm sorry we haven't managed to speak this week. I've just been crazy busy. I tried you, but ...' Yeah, once, at 7 a.m. on a Friday, which I figured was the most unlikely time in the week for him to answer.

'Don't worry, I know how hectic it all is.' He gives me

a faintly knowing smile: it must be so obvious I've been avoiding him. 'Seeing you here's an unexpected bonus.'

'Thanks again for making it all OK. I'm such a loser with kids.'

'You're not! I didn't have a clue till I had my own. When it stops being scary, it's honestly got its compensations.'

He might have a point: I was momentarily enjoying myself before my mobile rang. There was something oddly gratifying about Freddie's total trust in me. We walk to one of those family friendly places that I studiously avoid, littered with pots of crayons and paper tablecloths you can draw on. There's soon a bacchanalian circle of children dancing in the centre of the room, while waitresses swerve to avoid them. I can't remember ever having felt that kind of abandon when I was small. We were always weighed down with worry about whether or not there'd be a nuclear war, or if whales would be hunted to extinction. I feel a sudden wave of sadness, but I bat it away.

'So, are you a yoga regular then?' I ask him, sneakily trying to establish whether Mark's engineered our chance meeting.

'Me and Mark always tried to take Freddie and Belle, but since I only have her every second week I just come when I can. And now Joe's a teenager all I can do is try and fit round his packed social schedule.'

He's trying for irony but it's patently obvious that he's absolutely gutted. Filled with a sudden surge of compassion I fight an urge to grab his hand. Worried it counts as leading him on, I settle for leaving it hovering ineffectually over his fajitas.

'Oh get me, Mr Maudlin. I'm so self-obsessed. Tell me about all the glamorous things you've been up to, Anna.'

So I tell him about all the couples, and how the panel's coming together since Harry agreed to join it. I'm trying to keep our date under wraps, but the fact that I'm kind of lying by omission makes me go stupidly red. There's something so open about Tom: he's like a one-man truth drug.

'He sounds like a real catch. Well done.'

'He's not a catch, catch! He's very young and sort of gangly.'

'I didn't mean that, it just sounds like it's a real coup to've got him on board.'

'Oh, right. Thanks.'

There's an awkward silence which is broken by the children dashing over at the sight of their burgers arriving. I copy Mark's parental modus operandi, cutting up Freddie's food and bargaining with him over the salad. When lunch is over, I decide it's time to take him home, which fills me with another wave of panic.

'I know this sounds stupid, Tom, but what do I actually do with him? I'll feel guilty about sticking him in front of the TV, but I don't really know what else.'

He actually laughs at me. 'You'll be fine! He's having a great time with you. Stage some crashes with his trucks maybe. Let him win, that's my top tip. I'd suggest you come back with us, but my mum lives in Hammersmith.'

Even though it's wholly understandable, I'm struck by

how terminally unsexy it is for a grown man to live with his mother.

'So, see you soon,' I say limply.

'Yeah, hope so,' he replies, having clearly got the message. I feel bad, but how can I arrange another meeting when I'm sexually obsessed with another man? I give him a platonic hug, trying to convey in its fervency how much I like him as a person, before setting off with Freddie.

I hoped that lunch would've oiled the wheels, but I still can't think of a single thing to talk to him about. Everything I say either seems inappropriately adult or painfully patronizing. When I discover that Horst is still at home I almost cry with relief.

'Horse!' cries Freddie, hurling himself towards him. Horst swings him round and round, and then sets to work building ramps for his trucks out of sofa cushions.

'Will you be OK if I start getting ready for tonight?' I ask him.

'Oh yes, Anna. It is fun for me.'

So I set to work, plucking my eyebrows and painting my hoof-like toenails a seductive shade of scarlet. Freddie bursts into the bathroom whilst I'm slathering on a violently green face mask.

'Anna looks funny again!'

Why does this child take such delight in humiliating me?

'Anna is just trying to make herself even more prettier,' says Horst, leading him out. 'We will let her continue with this.'

Time's ticking by now: it's only half an hour till Mark and Amy are due to arrive. I can't believe how draining a few hours of proxy parenting have been! How does anyone do it day in, day out? Horst comes to find me and I jump up guiltily from Polly's bed, which I've been lounging on with a book.

'Anna? I have to go now. I am going to Guildford to see a funky band and I believe the journey will take some time.'

'Thanks again, but I should be fine now. His parents are coming any minute.'

Horst gives me a cheery salute and is out the door. As it slams behind him, the phone starts ringing.

'Me answer it, me answer it!' screams Freddie, grabbing it. Please let it not be Harry calling to cancel. 'Daddy!' he shrieks, swiftly launching into a stream of consciousness about our day. I try to manoeuvre the phone off him, but he clutches it to his ear, kicking at me. Eventually I wrest it away, to hear that Amy's mum is much worse than they thought.

'We really hoped we'd have been able to leave by now, but Amy doesn't want to go till her sister gets here. Is there any way you can hang on to Freddie for another hour or so?'

What to do? I can hardly say that my first date takes precedence over Amy's trauma. Instead I meekly agree and immediately start trying to contact Harry. To my horror, his phone goes straight to voicemail. 'Hi, Harry, it's Anna. I'm definitely coming, but I need to meet you a bit later. Something's come up. Er, call me!' What an idiot message: how did I manage to say 'come' twice in the space of fifteen seconds?

I try to throw myself into playing with Freddie's trucks, but my heart really isn't in it. Half an hour passes and there's still no word from Harry. I can't bear the idea of him sitting in the bar and me just not turning up, particularly if he doesn't have his phone. If he gives up on me and heads straight for the party I'll never catch up with him. I wanted this date so much, not just for the sake of my loins but also so that I could seal the deal on him joining the panel. I can't let it slip through my fingers.

Mark's 'hour or so' passes, and still no sign of him, just a text promising that they're doing their best. Freddie's getting tired and fractious, so I distractedly make him some beans on toast. As I'm stirring them, I wrack my brain for a solution. I wish Polly was here, but she's disappeared off somewhere mysterious.

Then I have a sudden thought. Would it be so outrageous to drop Freddie off with Tom and then double back to Holland Park in a cab? Is my need great enough to justify such mercenary behaviour? Kidding myself that it's for the sake of *Casual Chic*, I call him up.

'It's this work meeting, Tom, I just have to go. And I can't possibly hurry Mark and Amy up.'

'You're very devoted to this job, aren't you?' Is he mocking me? Is it patently obvious it's a date? 'Of course, it's no problem. Just bring him round.'

I bundle Freddie into a cab and speed over there.

'We must stop meeting like this,' I tell him. How unfunny am I?

109

'Must we?'

'Er, yes. No, I mean, it's been lovely seeing you today, but I've got to run.'

This time I go for a peck on the cheek and race back into the cab. I check my breath and touch up my lipstick. If the traffic's good I'll only be ten minutes late. Surely the self-help witches have made that pretty much compulsory anyway?

13

So of course when I get there, there's no sign of Harry. To call or not to call? I decide to have a coffee martini and wait it out. Twenty minutes later, and one more cocktail down the road, he finally ambles through the door.

'Sorry, Anna! I got your message and I figured you'd be at least half an hour late.'

So why the hell didn't you call me back, I feel like demanding, before getting painfully distracted by how perfectly aquiline his profile is. I look downwards, taking in how his tight black T-shirt shows off his buff, muscular arms and his expensive imported jeans hug his gorgeous arse. What's with the lechery? Since when did I metamorphose into north London's answer to Hugh Hefner?

'Don't worry about it,' I tell him, 'I only just arrived myself.'

As he kisses me hello I forgive him everything, lost in the sensation of his stubble brushing against my face. I'm starting to feel like a 14-year-old trapped in a 32-year-old's body – which might actually provide the perfect median age for this relationship.

'So what's your week been like?' he asks me. 'Have you conquered the world?'

'Hardly,' I say, feeling a sudden wave of guilt over my

lie about Adam. The very thought of him makes me feel irrationally treacherous for desiring Harry quite as much as I do. How could I ever go back now? I give him a brief overview of my day with Freddie, cutting out all mention of Tom.

'That sounds really hardcore. Pretty much none of my friends have got kids yet.'

'You wait, suddenly they start mushrooming like fungus. Before you know it, non-parents have become this freakish minority.' Shut up, Anna. Could I make the age difference sound any more significant?

'Thanks for the warning,' he says, smiling. 'I guess if anyone's in line to break first it's Becky and Lucas.'

'Who?'

'They're the couple whose party it is tonight. They've just got engaged.'

'Oh great.'

As I could barely hear him this morning, I missed this vital piece of information. Oh God, am I going to have to meet a whole shoal of his shiny, judgemental friends? I wish we were just having dinner.

'Anna, how rude of me, what are you drinking?'

Obviously I can't admit that I'm already at the bottom of my second. I should really take a break and have a sparkling water, but I don't want to seem square. Instead we have another round of coffee martinis, which leaves me feeling both tipsy and wired. I ask him about the pictures he did for *Vogue*, which featured an actor with a truly diva-ish reputation.

'He was pretty gruesome, but having to pretend you're

straight every day would make any self-respecting homo fairly edgy.'

'Oh come on, he's not gay! He's married!'

'And you struck me as a woman of the world!' he says, laughing. 'Does the term "lavender" mean nothing to you?'

'I can't believe it! He was my back-up celebrity just in case me and Clooney didn't work out. I suppose if he's horrible anyway . . .'

'It was a bit like lion-taming. Anyway, you must have to deal with some pretty tricky celebs in your job.'

'Oh yeah, Lorraine Kelly's demands can get really out of control. And as for Gabby Logan, just don't go there.'

'I know you're exaggerating, because if your magazine really was like that, someone like you wouldn't be there.'

I decide it's time to seize my chance.

'So, Harry, level with me now. Are you going to do the panel? I don't want to demean myself, but I will if I have to.'

He gives me a blatantly appraising look. 'That sounds promising.'

It's kind of sleazy, but I can feel myself melting. I hold his gaze.

'Of course I'll do it. As long as you're not going to bail out of our night now you've got what you wanted. I hate to be used and abused.'

'Oh fantastic! I'm so pleased. I've already told loads of people you are doing it, so . . .'

He looks understandably perturbed, and glances at his watch.

'We ought to shoot. Are you ready?'

I dismount from my stool shakily. There'd better be canapés at this party or it could get ugly. He hails a cab, holding the door open for me. Climbing in beside me, he slips an arm round my shoulders. What do I do: lean in? Too unsure, I sit there rigid, wondering if he's going to kiss me. Even if he is, the fact that I'm staring straight ahead, babbling about the evils of yoga instructors, makes it almost impossible. We arrive outside an elegant apartment block in Battersea, from which I can hear emanating the kind of painfully cool dance music which makes me long to blast out Dolly Parton's '9 to 5' full volume. As I'm struggling to quell my mounting dread, Harry suddenly thrusts me against the door and kisses me, hard. When I've got over the shock, I find myself feverishly kissing him back, grabbing at him greedily. I hope he'll decide, like me, that the party's way too much trouble, but he pushes the buzzer as we're mid snog, announcing us as he's slipping his hand under my shirt.

As we walk in I'm still feeling dazed with lust. It's an amazing open-plan loft, filled to the rafters with un-naturally poised and attractive guests. I want to squeeze Harry's hand, but it feels way too proprietorial a gesture. A curvy blonde detaches herself from the throng, flinging her arms round his neck.

'Harry! Thank God you're here, it didn't feel like a real party without you.'

My gaze immediately fixes on her left hand, which is weighed down by an ostentatiously gorgeous diamond. It perfectly complements her luxuriant beauty; loose curls are artfully pinned up just so they can cascade back down, thick black liner accentuates the enormity of her grey-green eyes. She feels somehow expensive, as though she's been finished in gold. Thank God she's the bride-to-be. If we were competing for Harry I wouldn't stand a chance.

'Becky, this is Anna, the girl I told you about.'

'Hello, darling, how lovely to meet you. I was so excited when Harry said he was bringing a date.'

I hate it when people I don't know call me 'darling'. How can I possibly be in any way darling to her when she only clapped eyes on me twenty seconds ago? I also feel like exhibit A: what's he said about me? Of course I don't share any of this: instead I compliment her on her ring, her flat and her hair, stopping just shy of her choice of bathroom tissue. Soon her fiancé, Lucas, comes sidling up. Handsome in a feral way, he radiates the same sense of total self-belief that Becky has.

'Cool necklace,' he says, gesturing to the pendant I agonized over, along with the rest of my outfit. 'Is that part of it?'

I reach up to find that one of Freddie's congealed baked beans has welded itself to my décolletage. How could I possibly have missed it? Has Harry been fixating on it all evening? I decide that honesty's the only way to go, and tell them all about my lamentable efforts at childcare. It somehow breaks the ice and I suddenly find myself slipping back inside myself, relaxing into the evening. Lucas tells me all about the screenplay he's trying, and failing, to get off the ground and we bond about what depths you have to plumb in order to get by as a writer. She's an interior designer, hence the fabulous flat, and describes the truly hideous ideas she's forced to make flesh by tasteless clients. Eventually they move off to talk to their other guests, and Harry leans in and kisses me.

'I feel like I could take you anywhere and you'd be the belle of the ball,' he says, smiling down at me. 'We could be at George W's birthday dinner and you'd have Dick Cheney inviting us skiing in a matter of minutes.'

I can't believe I've pulled it off! Does he really think that I've got the kind of effortless confidence that these people possess?

'Not at all. I just really like them.'

'I'm glad you do. Maybe you could be my wedding date.'

'When's the wedding?'

'I don't know, sometime next summer.'

And I try to force myself not to project forward and imagine the rest of our lives together. The fabulous trips I'll take with him as he photographs the great and the good. The beautiful, artistic, tantrum-free children we'll have. Could it really be this easy? Are the love gods rewarding me for my bravery by delivering the perfect man right into my lap? We retreat to a sofa, where we lock lips like adolescents. I sort of lose myself in kissing him. I don't care if we're making a spectacle of ourselves because I've drifted off into a parallel universe that I've been denied entry to for so long.

'Can we just cut to the chase and go home to bed?' he says, stroking my thigh.

I pause, staring at him, trying to assess the situation with my head rather than my crotch.

'Sorry, Anna, was that incredibly presumptuous of me?'

'No, no. Not at all,' I say, running my hand over his stubble. 'I just think it's maybe too soon.'

That sounded so unbelievably geeky. And I want this so much. But then an image of Giles floats past me whilst his 'Mmm, that was delicious' rings in my ears. I can't risk it quite yet. I want to keep this feeling of infinite possibility alive for as long as I possibly can.

'I really would respect you in the morning,' says Harry, subtly tugging at the back of my hair in a way which tells me just how sordid and exciting the sex is going to be. 'In fact I'd probably respect you even more than I do now.'

'I'm decided, Harry. Tonight is not the night.'

'Okay,' he says, wryly smiling at me. 'I'm not going to pester you. You're obviously not as over-heated as me.'

'Obviously,' I say, thinking how pleased the self-help witches would be with me.

Now what? The party's starting to thin out, so Harry gives me a tour of the flat, stopping to kiss me in all the dark corners. We're virtually the last to leave – I'm not going to let myself go home with him, but I can't bear to say goodbye. Eventually it's just the four of us, and Lucas and Becky roll up a joint and pour out some whiskies. I can't bear spliffs – they make me choke horribly – and I decide that the potential inelegance outweighs seeming like a party pooper. Soon they're all talking through a muzzy haze, which gives me a certain social advantage.

'So are we going to see much, much more of you?' says Becky, grabbing my hand while looking at Harry.

'You definitely will, if I've got any kind of say in the matter,' he says, pushing my fringe out of my face.

'Oh good! It's been ages since Harry had a proper girl-friend. We can all go off to the country and stride around in our wellies like old buffers.'

Is that a good sign or a bad sign? Am I the girl who's finally managed to capture his imagination or is it just that he's one of life's bolters? It's so much easier to see the wood for the trees when it's not your forest.

'To Anna,' says Lucas, raising his glass unsteadily. As they toast me, I look round their faces, trying to keep the uncertainty out of my expression. Should I let myself fall into this unexpected embrace, or keep a part of myself back in case? Oh shut up, Anna, stop thinking and start living.

'I've got something I'd love to ask you,' I hear myself saying, and before I know it I'm persuading this utterly radiant twosome to be my final couple.

'Now you won't be able to escape our clutches even if you want to!' says Becky, laughing so hard that she falls backwards off her pouffe. As we lean in to clink glasses, with the sun starting to stream in through the blinds, I find myself suffused with a feeling of utter rightness. Maybe today really is the first day of the rest of my life.

14

Oh God, I'm going to be sick. I force myself into an upright position and dash into the bathroom, where Horst is vigorously cleaning his teeth.

'Horst, please, I've got to . . .'

But by now it's too late: I'm violently spewing up into the bowl. It's the height of elegance and sophistication.

'Oh my, poor Anna. Can I take you some water?'

'It's OK, I'll be fine. Honestly.'

And now I've expelled approximately ten martinis from my battered system I actually do feel a bit better. I curl up on one of the kitchen chairs and let Horst work his sausage magic while he tells me about his top night out in Guildford. Of course I'm not actually absorbing a word of it, as I'm lost in a Harry-based reverie, wondering how soon it's decent to have sex with him. Maybe he'll call any minute now and say he can't bear to wait a moment longer. Then what do I do?

Polly comes tumbling out of bed next, looking just as hungover as I feel.

'Ah, Polly is here also,' says Horst. 'She too had a date last night I believe.'

He's totally blown my cover. Hoping she's not going to give me another ticking-off about Adam, I swiftly try to deflect the attention off me.

'You didn't tell me that! Who'd you go out with Pol?'

She looks incredibly embarrassed.

'Don't give me a hard time when I tell you.'

'Who? Come on, just spill it.'

There's another long pause.

'Michael. You know, the plumber.'

'What! Cistern man? But what about those awful texts?'

'I know, I know. But he kept calling and I thought maybe I was being a bit judgemental.'

'And were you?'

She actually looks a bit love-struck. This is bad. From her last account he sounded even worse than Wet Martin.

'Yeah, I think I was actually. He's quite sweet when you get to know him.'

'So did you have another hot night out at Nando's then?' I've got to be more supportive. 'Um ... what I mean is – where did you go?'

'Er ...' she says, looking flustered, 'we went to a late opening of that Renoir exhibition and then had sushi.'

'Really? Has he undergone a total personality transplant since your last date?'

'Kind of,' she says sheepishly. 'Anyway, tell me what you got up to.'

Horst's been following our conversation like it's a ping-pong match. 'Yes, Anna, what of your date with the Harry man?'

I start out tentatively, but as Polly keeps on smiling I gradually give way to my elation, telling them all about our amazing night.

'I just can't wait to see him again. I really, really want to text him but I shouldn't, should I?'

'No way! Let him do the running. I'm totally thrilled for you, Anna, really.' And she does look genuinely happy for me, relieved even, and doesn't go near the subject of Adam. I feel very warm to her right now.

I retreat back to the sofa for a bit, trying to block out the knowledge that I've got to go to my parents' for lunch. Looking healthy is going to require an inordinate amount of make-up: I can't bear to be on the receiving end of a binge-drinking lecture from Dan. I watch *Hollyoaks* for a bit, painfully aware of the fact that I'm about double the age of their target audience, before stumbling off to the tube.

'Hello, petal!' says Greg, opening the door with a roll-up stuck rakishly behind his ear. As usual, I'm momentarily shocked that he doesn't look like his eighties' incarnation, the dad of my teenage years. His shaggy beard provides a grey frame for his weathered face, skin gnarled like it needs sanding down.

'Hi, Greg, lunch smells delicious! Is Dan here yet?'

'He's running a bit late. Church and so on.'

He starts to raise his eyes to the heavens, but thinks better of it, and concentrates on taking my coat. I weave my way past their battered bicycles and seek out Karen in the kitchen. I was lying about lunch: it smells like the kind of vegetarian sludge that's always served up by our parents. When we were kids we used to long for a roast chicken, and occasionally they'd give in, but the fact that they'd remind us of its suffering by clucking while we ate it kind of took the pleasure away.

Karen's stood by the sink, chiselling thick mud off some organic carrots. Her face is twisted up with the effort and her hands look painfully raw. She pushes her long red-grey mane out of her face, smearing herself with grime in the process.

'Anna, darling, I'm so glad you could make it this time.'

I body swerve the guilt trip, and ask her how her week's been. Karen works for a refugee charity, and is capable of describing the minutiae of the suffering she encounters for hours on end. She rambles on for a while about people I've never heard of, but eventually pauses to take a good look at me.

'You're looking pretty bright-eyed and bushy-tailed all things considered. We've been worrying so much about you and Adam, but the single life obviously suits you.'

Have they really? I always feel like any trauma I encounter can't possibly compare with her latest Sudanese orphan, and then end up feeling terrible for having such uncharitable thoughts.

'Yeah, I'm doing OK with it,' I tell her, grinning away. Obviously the real reason I'm looking this way is my newfound Harry obsession, but I feel like I'll jinx it if I let on. What is it with those girls who tell their mothers their most intimate secrets? Instead we chat about Gran, and I tell her about getting Horst through his audition.

'You should bring him round for supper sometime,' she says earnestly. 'It sounds like he needs to establish stronger roots here.'

Typical: Karen can sniff out needy at two hundred paces. I'm unreasonably irritated by it – he's from Stuttgart, not Kurdistan.

As we're prising creepy-crawlies out of the lettuce, Dan finally pitches up. He's wearing a hard-collared shirt under a tank top, looking every inch the young fogey. There's something endearingly vulnerable about his choices – it's like a suit of armour, designed to ward off the chaotic influence of home – but when I try to convey my understanding via a sisterly hug, I feel him tense up. God, I wish he'd get over his extended teenage rebellion and go back to being my funny, gregarious little brother.

'Hello, Mum,' he says stiffly, and I derive some guilty enjoyment of Karen's obvious disgust at being addressed like that. She's far too non-confrontational to take him to task, and busies herself instead with pouring him a glass of wine.

'So Julia's staying with her parents, is she?' she says brightly, papering over the enmity that exists between our parents and Dan's wife.

'Yeah, she is. They've gone rambling in the Chilterns together.'

His tone's positively reverential, filled with wonder at this vision of parental normality. Dan's managed to hook up with the most conventional woman in Peterborough, quite a feat by anyone's standards.

Karen starts spooning vegetable sludge out of the casserole dish, dispatching me to the basement to retrieve Greg. If they tarted this place up it'd probably be worth a fortune by now, but the peeling walls and vague whiff of damp seriously overwhelm its charms. Greg's watching the cricket in a fug of dope smoke, his beard rendered still greyer by a light sprinkling of ash. He creates an unhappy contrast to last night's stoners. He sits up hurriedly, stubbing his joint out clumsily in a plant pot.

'Are you OK, Greg? Lunch is on the table.'

'Oh, sorry, darling. I was just, you know . . .'

'Yeah, sure,' I say awkwardly, unable to work out what the correct response is. A lecture on carcinogens? He heaves himself up and we troop back upstairs to tuck into Karen's wholesome stew.

'So what's with you and Adam?' says Dan. 'I can't believe you chucked him!'

'I wouldn't expect you to understand.'

'Try me.'

'I didn't feel right about marrying him, and once I'd said no there was nowhere left for us to go.'

'Oh, come off it, Anna, there's absolutely nothing wrong with him.'

'I didn't say there was!'

'You're too bloody picky. You shouldn't knock marriage when you haven't even tried it.'

An irritating little brother is still an irritating little brother, even when they're thirty. Spotting how incensed I look, Greg tries to butt in.

'Dan, your sister's probably feeling very sensitive . . .'

'I'm not feeling sensitive,' I burst out, 'I'm feeling hungover and excited because I spent last night with someone amazing. At least I'm still having fun, rather than living like a fifty-year-old.'

'Don't be so ageist,' says Karen.

Oh my God, does anyone have a family as irritating as mine?

'All right, Anna, calm down,' says Dan. 'I was just saying that I liked Adam.'

He so wasn't, but I can't be bothered with a full-scale row. It was much better when he was small enough to be barricaded into his bedroom.

'So who's the lucky man?' says Greg, trying to placate me.

And I tell them a bit about Harry, feeling vaguely self-conscious about how young and glossy he is. No one seems particularly impressed. I'm sure my parents would much rather I was going out with someone called Grant from Peckham CND but they're in for a long wait. Is it possible I was switched at birth?

After lunch we play a game of Trivial Pursuit although my concentration's blighted by my compulsion to check my phone every three minutes in case Harry's been in touch. Although Dan can't resist making a couple of jibes about it, the fact that we play in a team against our parents can't help but conjure up a sense of that heartening solidarity which we always felt as kids.

At seven I decide it's acceptable to start making tracks, and Dan can't wait to hurl himself on the bandwagon.

'I'll give you a lift, Anna, you shouldn't be walking to the tube in the dark on your own.'

My parents make dismissive noises, obviously feeling that he's casting aspersions about the neighbourhood.

We hug them goodbye, waving to them as we drive off. Greg's got a hairy paw clamped protectively round Karen's shoulder, but it looks to me almost like she's straining away from him.

'Do you think they're happy?' I ask Dan.

'Dunno really. I never bother to think about it.'

Much as they infuriate me, there's something intensely grating about his lack of engagement.

'What about you then?' I ask waspishly. 'Are you and Julia still blissful?'

He visibly bristles. 'Yeah, we are actually. She's incredible.'

Incredibly dull more like. Luckily I'm distracted from making any more inappropriate remarks by the shrill ring of my phone. I dive into my bag to retrieve it.

'Anna?'

'Tom, hi,' I say, trying not to sound gutted.

'Did you have a fun night?'

'Amazing, thanks. I mean obviously it was all about work,' I say, backtracking, 'but it was good.'

'I'm glad,' he says. 'Look, I'm calling on Mark's behalf. He wanted me to say thank you for what you did yesterday. Freddie can't stop talking about funny Anna. He had a real blast with you.'

How is that possible? Surely he's got me mixed up with Horst.

'I'm always glad to help. He's such a sweetie.'

'That's the thing. I think we all might need to help out these next few weeks. Amy's mum's worse than they thought. It looks like lung cancer.'

'Oh God, poor Amy,' I say, feeling flooded by shock. 'I'm around for whatever needs to happen.'

'Thanks so much, I knew you'd say that. I'll pass it on to Mark.'

Lung cancer's bad: I know for a fact it's almost always incurable. I feel terrible for Amy, and guilty about how grumpy Karen made me feel. Knowing your mum's going to leave you behind must be the worst feeling in the world.

'What's up?' asks Dan as I hang up the phone, and I tell him about Amy's bad news.

'Shit, what a nightmare,' he says sympathetically.

'Isn't it? I know they can be naked hell, but I can't imagine Karen and Greg not being around.'

'Yeah, I know,' he replies vaguely.

I wonder if his in-laws feel more like his family than we do? I think about telling him about Greg's spliff-smoking, but I don't know if it'll make him laugh or drive him even further away from us. He pulls up outside the flat.

'You should come and stay with us some time. I know you pretty much shrivel up and die if you leave London, but there are some nice pubs near us.'

He does a weird shrivelly thing with his face as he says it, like the Wicked Witch of the West melting, and I can't help but laugh. We used to love *The Wizard of Oz* when we were kids, although Dan was always too scared to come out from behind the sofa when the witches appeared.

'Yeah, no, I will,' I say non-committally. 'It'd be fun. It was really nice to see you.' I try to give him a hug, but he doesn't turn his body round quite enough for it to take hold.

'Yeah, you too,' he says, slightly coldly. 'See you soon.'

I wave goodbye from the doorstep, feeling saddened by the thought that I've hurt his feelings. I know I should make the trip, but our moments of connection feel too intermittent for me to take the risk. Right now I feel way more comfortable in my bizarre new domestic set-up than I ever seem to feel with my own family.

I come through the door to find Horst lying prone on the sofa, weeping with laughter at a *One Foot in the Grave* repeat. How much more dad-like is that than the furtive drug-smoking that was going down in Harlesden? He sits up, patting the cushion next to him invitingly.

'Oh, Anna, the Meldrew man is so filled with fury!'

As I settle down beside him, Harry finally sends me a text: 'Away this week, but want to see you Friday. Meet me at Heathrow at 7 p.m. Don't forget your passport.'

In an instant, everything else gets swept away by my all-consuming euphoria. Could this relationship get any more glorious?

15

'How could you possibly know that fast?'

I'm sitting in the lobby of a smart London hotel, buttering a scone and getting to know my third couple. Oliver had lived with a woman for seven years, and had two kids, when he met Steve on a work trip. Nine months later they're getting married.

'I suppose when you've been in something that feels wrong for so long, the contrast you get when something feels right hits you extra hard.'

Don't I know it.

'You can tell me to back off if this is too personal a question, but I can't help wondering if the guilt always gets in the way.' I correct myself, feeling flustered. 'I mean would get in the way.'

This week's round of obsessing has been severely marred by Adam. Not by anything he's done, but by my feeling that, with every step I take towards Harry, I move an extra mile away from him. I want so much to call him, but what would I say? I don't want him back, but nor do I want him to just dematerialize from my life like it never was. We're going to have to start talking about the practicalities soon, and although the prospect's painful, I'm kind of relieved that there's still something binding us together.

'No, don't worry, it's a good question.'

Oliver gives me a rueful smile, and I sense he's been spun through some of the same emotional cycle. He's incredibly handsome, in an over-groomed kind of a way. His blond hair is highlighted to perfection, and blow-dried to within an inch of its life. Much as I love a blond, I find it hard to take men with highlights seriously. I can't help imagining them in the hairdresser, with wispy tufts poking out through those ridiculous holey caps. It destroys David Beckham's dwindling appeal pretty fast, don't you think? Oliver's high maintenance routine extends downwards. His gorgeous skin looks like it's submitted to bi-weekly facials, and is topped by perfectly plucked eyebrows. Even his lips look suspiciously plump. How could his girlfriend ever have thought he batted for our team?

'Yeah, it did make it hard.' He smiles at Steve, holding his gaze. 'You don't mind me saying that, do you?' Steve nods his assent. 'But what can you do? If something's not right you owe it to the other person to be honest. They deserve the chance to meet someone who's going to treasure them.'

They grin at each other, merrily treasuring, and I feel weirdly comforted. I wonder if Harry could ever look at me like that? Their openness totally emboldens me.

'How was it for you, Steve? Did you worry that he was only flirting with being gay?'

'Don't spare the horses!' he says, laughing. 'I was more worried that I was flirting with being monogamous, because that had definitely never happened before. But it really just felt completely different from anything else either of us had ever experienced. I know I'm sounding like a Mills and Boon, but I don't know how else to explain it. Do you understand what I mean?'

I don't know if I do, in all honesty, but I smile knowingly and encourage him to carry on. They tell me all about their Ibizan wedding, and Oliver proudly shows me pictures of his kids, who are all set to be bridesmaids. Even his ex-girlfriend is coming along for the ride. It all sounds suspiciously harmonious: could she be coming along solely for the purpose of committing hara-kiri during the ceremony? Even though I walked away, I can imagine few things more painful than watching Adam pledge himself to someone else. I'd be the one at the back, heckling: '*I didn't know your fiancée had piggy little trotters.*'

Enough talk of Adam. Today is the day of days: Friday! Harry's sent me some joyfully naughty texts this week, but I haven't actually spoken to him. I've been agonizing over my weekend wardrobe, not least because I don't know where the hell I'm going. I've ultimately decided to concentrate my efforts on good underwear and a shed load of grooming products, which has surely got to pay dividends.

But before I go I've got to endure four more monotonous hours in the office. I lug my weekend bag down the corridor, and try to surreptitiously stow it under my desk. Unfortunately Ruby's looking straight at me, desperate to demonstrate how keen she is.

'Hi, Anna, how did it go today? Ooh, are you going away?'

My brain freezes over. Obviously there's a million perfectly good answers but none of them are coming to me right now.

'Yeah, I'm going to my parents.'

'Are you? I thought they lived in London?'

'Yes they do, but . . .'

By now Jocasta's ear-wigging.

'You don't need to explain, Anna. In difficult times the bosom of one's family often represents a safe haven. I hope that Percy and Agnes will always feel my door is open, even in their mid thirties.'

I'm not in my mid bloody thirties. I'm thirty-two! Although thirty-three is creeping up frighteningly fast.

'Er, yes, quite. Ruby, shall we catch up on the RSVPs?'

'How are your RSVPs going, girls? Are the eager party-goers finally starting to roll up?'

One of the many things I hate about Jocasta is the way in which she speaks like a minor aristocrat from the 1940s. 'Eager party-goers'?! Doesn't she realize rationing ended more than sixty years ago?

'We've actually had to stop giving out plus ones,' shoots back Ruby, with surprising feistiness. 'We're almost at capacity.'

Jocasta looks momentarily put out, but swiftly recovers herself. 'It sounds like the venue you've picked might be rather too small, Anna. It does pay to think through all the eventualities.'

I haven't got the energy today.

'Who knew? I think that once Harry Langham signed up it automatically became a hot ticket.' I'm slightly overstating his importance, but I'm lost in that phase where all roads lead back to the object of your affection. Jocasta's slyly studying me: let's hope she's not cottoned on.

'You definitely look like you're on the road to recovery, Anna, which is marvellous to see. Anyway, I must get on. Don't forget, my door is always open.'

'What are you working on?' asks Ruby, trying to alleviate the palpable tension.

'I'm constructing a supernatural pull-out. How seances can perk up your sex life, that kind of thing. It's early days.'

I'm desperate to ask how they do, but I know I won't be able to keep a straight face. I pull Ruby into a meeting room where we both collapse with laughter.

'I can't believe the things she comes up with!' she says, aghast. 'I'm so glad I'm working on this, rather than ringing up creepy mediums asking if they'll conjure up dead studs from beyond the grave.'

'Are you really glad you're working on this?' I ask her, surprised. I haven't exactly been boss of the year.

'Yes, totally.'

'I'm really pleased,' I say, beaming. I want to apologize for allowing my panic to make me sharp, but I can't quite get the words out. Instead I concentrate on the list of RSVPs, which is looking gratifyingly healthy. I vow to get Ruby more involved in the fun stuff, and charge her with taking next week's meetings with the venue designer. The afternoon zips past, and I suddenly realize that I'm in danger of being late.

'Oh hell, I've got to go.'

'Are your parents very formal about dinner?'

I have a sudden image of Karen and Greg dressed up smartly, starched napkins at the ready. It's the most ludicrous idea in the world.

'Yeah, Mum will've gone to loads of trouble. I mustn't be late.' *Mum.* I so wish she was *mum* and that she really would've gone to a lot of trouble. There's only so much stew one can eat in a single lifetime. But then I guess a prim and proper super-mummy would have presented a whole heap of alternative traumas. Agnes will probably end up a drug-crazed sex fiend, hell-bent on rebellion.

'No problem. I can finish the calls up.'

'Thanks, Ruby,' I gratefully reply, inwardly lamenting the fact that my work life is built on a tissue of lies. I jump in a cab, toying with calling Harry en route to Paddington. I'm still working on the principle that I can't initiate contact, so I sit on my hands and try to control my nerves. I'm pretty sure these are the good butterflies, but I do feel like I've drunk five double espressos.

I get to the terminal about ten to seven, and try to concentrate on taking deep breaths. I go to the loo and touch up my lipstick, then blot most of it off so it doesn't attach itself to my teeth. I start practising my smile for when he arrives, but it seems to come out like Jack Nicholson as The Joker. I go back out at five past – late is surely cooler than early – but he's still not there. By quarter past I'm starting to worry, particularly as I don't know where we're going. How fine is he cutting it? His phone's off, as per, so all I can do is stand around anxiously. At 7.25 he finally pitches up, looking sexily harassed.

'I'm so sorry, Anna. I had to come from East London and it took forever.'

Don't display irritation, don't display irritation.

'It's fine, don't worry about it.'

'Christ, you look amazing. I love your hair up like that.' He reaches out, cupping my bare neck, and lightly kissing my lips.

'Thanks, so do you,' I stupidly reply. I never know how to take a compliment. I suppose one's meant to just give an enigmatic smile of acceptance.

He picks up my bag. 'Come on, we'd better check in.'

'Check in for where, Harry?'

'Follow me.'

He grabs my hand, grinning, and steers the trolley to the check-in for – Stockholm. Yes, not New York, Paris or Rome, but Stockholm. I try my best not to look wrong-footed.

'Anna, I promise you're going to love this,' he says.

I look at him, luxuriating in the jolt of lust that I get, and realize that a weekend at the Slough Travel Lodge would have its compensations.

Queuing for security and passport control feels oddly intimate. As I try to avoid him seeing my frizzy-haired mugshot I'm reminded how much of a novelty my relationship with Adam was when it was taken. Suddenly all the holidays we ever took concertina up in my memory, and I have to fight down an unexpected wave of tears. Who knew that feeling so high would involve feeling so low?

We perch at the champagne bar in the terminal and

chink glasses. 'To us,' he says, and I wonder if he's being ironic. When he leans in to kiss me I stop caring.

'You're so fucking sexy,' he mutters in my ear and I let my fingers slip under his shirt, exploring his warm flesh. Even though breath anxiety means I'm only sipping, I feel like the champagne's going straight to my head.

I can't resist buying trashy magazines for the flight, and we spend the journey flicking through *OK*, laughing about the essential pointlessness of various WAGs. I mean, what do they do all day? At least Paris Hilton's got her perfume to administer.

Eventually I shove the magazine in the seat pocket. 'There's nothing exciting in there. Can't you treat me to some properly salacious gossip?'

'No way, you're a journo. I told you too much last time.'

'Don't you trust me?'

'Not yet,' he says, caressing the inside of my knee through my break-the-bank Wolford stockings. 'It's kind of fun.'

Stockholm is bone-freezingly cold, and my skimpy outfit offers little in the way of insulation. I'm dreaming of a warm fire and a glass of wine when Harry breaks the devastating news that we're taking a connecting flight. I'm gutted although the plane turns out to be intriguingly tiny, and it's a mercifully short flight. We're picked up from an obscure airport and driven into a snowy wilderness. It's like I've stepped through the wardrobe and pitched up in Narnia. We get out of the car and I pull my scarf around my ears.

'It's an ice hotel,' says Harry. 'I shot here last year and I've been longing to find someone who'd love it like I do.'

Oh God, I hope I do love it. We collect deeply un-flattering thermal clothing and go for a cocktail in the ice bar. I'm almost too overwhelmed to speak, but we stare and stare at each other, squeezing hands. The level of anticipation is getting absurd: I so hope I'm going to be able to live up to it.

I'm gratified to find that we're not sleeping in an actual ice bed, that's tomorrow night's adventure, and instead we retreat to a cosy log cabin. As we get through the door Harry manoeuvres me over to the sofa and starts kissing my neck.

'I know you're terribly well brought up, but please tell me tonight's the night. I don't think I can handle it if it isn't.'

I pull back, looking directly at him. 'Tonight is definitely the night, yes.'

'Good,' he says, tracing my collarbone with kisses. 'I know I've been a bit full on but I'm hopelessly obsessed.' He looks up at me questioningly.

'I'm totally obsessed,' I tell him, grabbing a handful of his blond curls. A finger-wagging self-help witch pops up, and I accidentally mutter 'Oh fuck off' under my breath.

'What did you say?' asks Harry, puzzled.

'Nothing,' I say, flustered, and try to distract him with kisses.

What's so divine about it is that he doesn't rush things. We stay clothed for a deliciously long time before he finally peels my slutty top off. I feel kind of self-conscious about my mini-mammaries, but when he peels off my bra and starts to kiss them my anxiety instantly melts away. I'm no longer thinking about what's happening, I'm just enjoying it. Sex has been so loaded for so long, and being able to abandon myself to it is pure joy. I don't exactly howl like a hyena, but it all feels pretty animal.

Afterwards we lie in the bath, end to end, and I soap his toes.

'Did I cut it?' he asks, and I wonder if the self-doubt is for real. 'I feel like if you've been with someone for ten years I've got a lot to live up to.'

I think about telling him about my hideous interim shag with Giles, but I'm worried he'll think I've got no standards.

'Don't be crazy, that was amazing.' What a relief to say it and mean it.

'Great,' he says, stroking my breasts with his toes. 'Do you miss him? I don't know if it's the time to ask but I want to know where you're at.'

He looks at me questioningly and I wonder if it's possible he feels as vulnerable as I do. 'Yeah, I do miss him,' I say, feeling my gut clench, 'but it was definitely over.' I can't afford to think about Adam right now. 'What about you? Surely you must get loads of models flinging their tiny little knickers at you?'

He laughs. 'I think you really overestimate me. Anyway, they're always mind-numbingly dull.'

'So who, then? You've clearly done this before.'

'Had sex? Yeah, couple of times. Whisked a woman I barely know to a sub-zero shag pad? Definitely a first.'

'Harry . . .'

'I've had a couple of serious girlfriends, but nothing like a ten-yearer.'

And my inner calculator goes into overdrive. Of course not, ten years ago he'd have been seventeen. Not even old enough to buy a Campari at the bar (an unlikely scenario, but you get my drift). This is never going to work.

'Are you OK, Anna? Or have you frozen over?'

'Yes, I'm fine,' I say in a stiff voice. How soon is it polite to retreat from the bath?

'Have I done something wrong?' he says, sliding round the bath. 'Come and jump in the sauna with me.'

I contemplate him for a minute, whether I should treat him to a whistle-stop tour of my insecurities, but obviously I scrub that idea. The sauna leads to the bedroom, and by the time we're ready to sleep it's 3 a.m.

'I'm having an amazing time with you,' he says, wrapping me up in a big gangly embrace.

'Me too,' I say, trying to feel safe there.

And some part of me obviously does, as I fall sound asleep right there on his chest. After that slightly scratchy start, I force myself to let go and truly enjoy being with him. We go on a ridiculous sleigh ride through the forest, and struggle to sleep through the night in the ice bed. I don't yet feel a profound connection with him, but I'm laughing more than I have in months and right now that's good enough.

The fact that the landscape feels so unfamiliar makes me feel utterly free. I realize how every shred of my life in London evokes my relationship with Adam: every street, every restaurant, every tube stop contains a trace of our life together. Here it's just Harry and me, writing a brand new page. I'm relishing every second, but I can't help but wonder if the bubble's going to burst when I'm back on home ground.

16

I arrive back on Sunday night, feeling shagged out and blissful. We kiss goodbye at Paddington, doing all that nauseating new couple 'you go, no you go' stuff. Eventually I wrest myself away and hop in a cab, although the entire journey is punctuated by frenzied texting. Harry's no plumber; his messages are sexy and eloquent and intoxicating. Why the hell is Polly continuing to put up with the cistern king? Surely it can't be for the sake of new taps.

I get back to the flat to find Horst hunched over the computer. He shields the screen guiltily as I get through the door.

'What is it, Horst? You can tell me.'

'Oh, Anna, I think that with this play I will meet ladies who are suitable for dating. But the persons are all very much older than me. I see how much happiness you and Polly are encountering so I start to think that maybe the interweb is the answer.'

Internet dating. I know I'm a Luddite, but the very idea fills me with cold dread.

'Yeah, why not? You probably need to widen your options.'

'That is the very problem, Anna, there are so many options. How to know which one to pick? Some places appear to be just for people who want to get on with the lovemaking right away, while other places seem to encourage friendship. For me I need a little of both.'

'So have you narrowed it down?'

'The ladies on this site seem very agreeable. They have good jobs and wear smart outfits in their pictures.'

'Show me,' I say, pulling a chair over. Oh sweet Jesus; how did he manage to alight on JDate?

'Horst, you do realize what this is, don't you? I really don't think these girls are going to go for you.'

Horst looks horribly crushed. 'Am I too ugly for them? Must I lower my reach more, Anna? Are you to be cruel to be kind?'

'No, Horst, it's a Jewish site. You're not only a gentile but you're an actual German. I'm not sure they'll have got over that whole Holocaust business.'

Although he makes it abundantly clear his family played no part, he sees my point and we settle on Guardian Soulmates. Nice muesli-munching liberals with dreary jobs and firm moral opinions. I'm sure Karen and Greg would love me to husband-surf it. But no matter now I've got my gorgeously glossy sex puppy. I'm locked in a Harry-based reverie when Polly comes through the door.

'How was it!' she asks.

Seeing her unexpectedly brings Adam to mind, and I feel myself deflate.

'It was great, it really was.'

'So why . . .'

'I don't know . . . I guess I didn't know how much

being with someone else would bring it all back up. It's so final somehow.'

Polly gives me an inscrutable look. I guess she thinks I'm being spoilt and greedy. It's not like she's ever had much romantic good fortune, while I somehow seem to be skipping from one man to the next. It's nowhere near that easy, but it probably looks like it is from where she's standing.

'Have you seen him, Pol?' I ask her haltingly. I'm almost afraid of the answer. 'How is he?'

'No, I haven't,' she says hesitantly. 'He's been a bit off-radar the last few weeks.'

'Really? He's stopped calling me, but I didn't realize he wasn't calling you either. Oh God, you don't think . . .'

Now I know I'm being unreasonable. He's got every right to have a new girlfriend: it should be positively desirable. But the very idea makes me rigid with fear.

'What, that he's met someone else? No, not yet. But he will, you do realize that, don't you?'

'Obviously!' I snap.

'You're just going to have to start getting used to the idea, Anna,' she fires back, exiting the room.

Polly and I have always had our spats, mainly because she's the closest thing I've got to a sister. I give her a few minutes and then follow her with a peace-making glass of wine. She's in her bedroom, unpacking an overnight bag.

'Sorry, Pol, I didn't mean to be a brat. You've been incredible, and I'm sure it's been horrible feeling stuck between us.'

'Don't say that!' she bursts out, crossing the room to

143

hug me. It all seems a bit excessive for such a minor tiff, and I start to wonder if she knows more about his love life than she's letting on. What's she not telling me?

'Hey, calm down,' I say, soothingly stroking her back and trying to extricate myself. 'I want to hear all about your weekend. Have you had full sex yet?' Full sex has been one of our favourite expressions ever since our bearded biology teacher, the appropriately named Mr Grubb, used it the week we hit the reproduction chapter. Even so, Polly's oddly quiet.

'Come on, Pol, full sex or just heavy petting? Or did he hypnotize you, so it's all an erotic blur?'

She looks incredibly awkward. 'Yeah, we did.'

'Was it good?' She gives a barely perceptible nod. 'Fantastic! Don't look so embarrassed, I'm sorry if I was a cow when you first said you were seeing him. Do you *like* him, like him?'

She grabs my hand, looking almost beseeching. 'Yeah, Anna, I do. I really do.'

'Well, that's great!' I say, squeezing her hand, desperately trying to convey to her that I don't disapprove. Or if I do, that it really doesn't matter. Why's she being so weird about this?

'So do you think it'll be time for us to go on a double date soon? Like that time we went to Burger King in Wembley with those fifth-formers.'

We groan about the abject horror of our teenage outfits, but it's clear she's not in a rush to repeat the experience. From her original description I can't imagine Michael and Harry having much in common, but I'm intrigued to see what the appeal is. I can't remember the last time she was this smitten.

I turf Horst off the computer so I can check my email. There's a message from Tom.

Hello, Anna, went to yoga today and wished you were there to advise me on my downward dog, which was more like a downward frog. Belle wished you and Freddie were there too. Perhaps we could remedy it soon? Meanwhile Mark and Amy have asked whether you could help out with Freddie next Sunday. Hope you can, though sadly I won't be around. Love from Tom xx.

Damn, damn, damn! I really wanted to spend the day in bed with Harry. I immediately cast my selfish carnal desires aside, and fire back an email committing myself. I hope to God I'll be able to rope Horst in: perhaps I can barter in hot single gentiles. Not that I know any now Polly's off the market.

That's not strictly true. I do know 'the crones', a group of women about five years older than us who are really in the last chance saloon, ovaries wise. They're actually perfectly attractive, but the way they hang around Soho House chain-smoking Marlboro Lights and scanning the room for prey kills their appeal stone dead. *The crones: a warning from future history.* God, I hope I'm not wasting my remaining window on a pointless fling. Is it possible for a man in his mid twenties to be husband material? And does it even matter? I comfort myself with thoughts of

Demi Moore and the divine Ashton Kutcher, although the fact that I'm so not in her league makes the comparison fairly meaningless.

I'm not due to see Harry till Wednesday, but I've got my first meeting with Becky and Lucas the day before, which will at least give me an excuse to talk about him. I'd also love to find out more about his romantic history, even though I know it's a Pandora's box I should steer well clear of. I just feel like if I had more of a road map of his past I could attempt some predictions about our future. Anyway, I don't get the chance because Harry calls to tell me he can't bear to wait till Wednesday (hurrah!) and that as he was meant to see Becky and Lucas too, we should all have dinner together on Tuesday night (boo).

So basically it's a double date. I'm not sure I'm ready for it, but I can't see an elegant way to refuse. We meet at Julie's in Holland Park, a restaurant beloved of all stick-thin West London blondes. They love to sit outside guzzling over-priced white wine and refusing to eat. Embarrassingly I get there first, swiftly followed by Lucas.

'Hi, darling!' he says, kissing me enthusiastically. 'Are you all set to grill me? I've been looking forward to it all week.'

I'm not very good at harmless flirtation. I always end up either coming over incredibly prim, or saying something wildly inappropriate like 'I've been thinking of nothing but your enormous cock all week.' So I just smile demurely and ask him what we should order. We settle down with a bottle of wine and wait for the other two to arrive. I'm used to Harry's unpunctuality by now, but Becky also seems to be taking her time.

'Oh, I think she was picking up Harry on her way. Knowing those two, he's probably insisted on playing her some obscure record he's got from Japan and they've forgotten the time.'

'Oh right,' I say, painfully aware of how little I yet know about him. 'Does he have decks?'

'Have you not been to Austin Powers Towers yet?' says Lucas, and I wonder if the implication is that he has a constant stream of pneumatic lovelies trooping through his leopard-skin bedroom.

'No, we did way better than that,' I say defensively. 'Did he tell you about Sweden?' And I regale him with stories about the fantastic time we had, before deciding I should really use our window to get down to some proper questioning.

'I know it's an obvious place to start, but how did you two meet?'

'Has Harry not told you this?' I wish he'd stop answering questions in such a way as to make me feel like we've got nowhere. 'He's the one who introduced us. Becky's an ancient ex of his.' Oh God, I'm not sure I can handle this. Lucas obviously clocks my expression. 'From school, Anna, it was years ago! And he and I were at uni together. We only started dating last year though, after I broke up from a long stretch with this Brazilian girl.'

'So it's all been pretty quick?'

'Yeah, but you know ... anyway, Becky didn't want to leave it too long. She says she wants to make sure she still looks shaggable in her wedding pictures.' He gives a dirty laugh. 'Which she will.'

Won't she just: she's absolutely gorgeous. I'm so depressed she's an ex of Harry's, however long past. I'm going to have to step up my grooming routine and try to attain some of that effortless-seeming polish. Perhaps the hags could help? Cut to me with a shaggy mid-nineties' 'Rachel' cut and pencil-thin arched eyebrows. What am I thinking!

I really want to change the subject, so I ask Lucas about his screenplay writing.

'Are any of them looking likely to happen?'

'None of them are dead certs, but in a way it doesn't matter because I love writing them so much. It's so important to get that buzz from what you do, isn't it?'

He's right of course. I'm kind of in awe of his dogged determination to follow his dream. You'd never catch him crafting a double-page spread on the magic of mushrooms.

Becky and Harry finally roll up, and I find myself fruitlessly studying their body language. Does he still fancy her? Not judging by the fervent kiss he gives me: I have to kick this unattractive insecurity into touch. Becky is charm itself, and I scold myself for my underlying desire to find fault. Determined to overcome it, I find myself asking her if she wants to come to (non-baby) yoga with me.

'I'd love to! How sweet of you to ask. Let's do it next week.'

Harry smiles at me approvingly, and I'm filled with

pride at my own maturity. I even manage to bring up the circumstances of their introduction without displaying any beadiness.

'Oh God, did Lucas tell you that?' she says, playfully smacking his hand. 'Me and Harry were the worst couple! We went out for literally two weeks in the sixth form. Harry got sent in amongst all these hordes of girls and we all got terribly over-excited, but it was not to be.'

'I was a bit of a bastard, Becky, let's not fudge the issue.'

Hmm, interesting. Becky laughs gaily.

'Yes, he dumped me for the captain of the netball team!'

'Too athletic to resist, hey, Harry?' says Lucas, as Harry gives a *mea culpa* kind of smile. I try to laugh along, struggling with both what it says about Harry and the eternal dilemma of how familiar one should be with a new partner's intimates. I remember a brief university squeeze of Adam's who used to come round and cook them couply dinners in their student kitchen. She'd jealously guard the stove like a rabid squirrel, zealously disposing of any food that had passed its date stamp and doling out uninvited relationship advice. Polly and I absolutely loathed her.

Anyway, Harry's giving my arm a comforting caress, obviously aware that hearing about his sexual escapades might not be my top choice of a third date. 'I was an infant,' he whispers, and I try to prevent my inner calculator from piping up with how old I would've been at the time.

'Shall we order?' he says, fussing over what I should have, while keeping a tight grip on my free hand. Becky also makes a huge effort, asking me all about life at *Casual Chic*. I try not to be as disparaging as I normally am, desperate to keep them hooked into the feature.

'Anyway, Becky, I'm meant to be doing the interviewing here! I know you'd known each other for years, but how did you finally get together?'

'I was a bit of a party girl,' she says, giggling and making doe eyes at Lucas. 'But I knew it was time to slow down. I was coming back from Italy on the plane, feeling sad there'd be no one there to meet me at the airport, and I thought rather than whinging I should do something about it. I'd always wanted kids too, you see, even in the midst of all the frantic socializing.'

'Step away from the Bugaboo,' says a nervous-looking Lucas.

'You'll love it, Luke, you really will,' she replies, smiling at him. 'Anyway, I decided to make a list of all the traits I wanted in my ideal man. I'd got the idea out of one of those books, you know?'

Oh my God, she's a self-help witch aficionado. How many times have I helped a sobbing Polly put together one of those husband templates? They're always so pointlessly general too: '*My husband will be handsome, kind, funny and intelligent.*' Really? But surely you're looking for a gnomic, humourless moron to father your children? Maybe I'm a cynic and she really did put '*Billy Ray Cyrus lookalike with practical abilities and a sideline in circus trickery*' on the last list. But somehow I doubt it.

'Oh yes, I know all about them,' I laugh. 'So did the universe instantly deliver you your heart's desire?'

'Not immediately, no,' she says, 'but here's the evidence it works!'

Lucas smiles back at her with genuine warmth. 'Things were really on the rocks with the Brazilian, and I'd always liked Becks.'

I wonder if 'the Brazilian' has an actual name. Every time he calls her that I have an unpleasant flashback to my mutilated muff the weekend of me and Adam's break-up. I don't want to go there for so many reasons.

'It was the final push I needed to get out,' he continues. I'm on the verge of asking if they had an affair, but it feels too nosy.

'How did she take it?' I ask.

Lucas shrugs. 'I think she was pretty relieved, truth be told. One of us needed to put that relationship out of its misery.'

There's a brief pause, like we've just mentioned a dead person, and then they start telling me how blissful their time together has been. The wedding's taking place at Becky's parents' place in Gloucestershire and sounds unbelievably lavish.

'But you'll be there to see it of course,' says Becky excitedly.

'She certainly will!' says Harry. 'I need her to go halves on my fabulous wedding present.'

Everyone laughs, and this time I join in for real. The rest of the night sails past in a haze of alcohol and sexual tension. I'm so glad it's easy with Becky and Lucas, but I can't wait to be alone with Harry. We kiss our good-byes, with promises of yoga and further interviews, and jump in a cab bound for Harry's flat. I'm fascinated but apprehensive. Someone's home reveals so much about them: what if it totally turns me off? Perhaps it'll be all chrome and sterile, with his last girlfriend's head perfectly preserved in his top of the range Smeg fridge. Or covered in framed T-shirts from his favourite heavy metal gigs, complemented by gold discs he's bid for on eBay.

Luckily it's neither Hard Rock Café nor American Psycho. It's definitely a bachelor pad, but it's artfully decorated, with a charmingly chaotic roof terrace, festooned with fairy lights.

'Did Becky deck this out by any chance?'

'Is it that obvious?'

I hope I don't sound jealous. I can't help but like her, even if they have had full sex. Not that there's any proof they have. Can I ask, or will I just sound like a jealous freak? We brush our teeth in tandem, and then climb the stairs to his anally tidy bedroom. A huge king-size bed dominates the space, but there's nothing to be seen on any of the surfaces. No photos, no books, nothing that offers any kind of clue to his nocturnal habits.

'Wow! You run a tight ship.' What corner of my psyche did that phrase pop up from?

He smiles bashfully. 'I cleared up, in your honour. I didn't want you to think I was a slob, but perhaps I went a bit too far.'

In that moment, I find him almost unbearably endearing. I love the idea that he was in here, without me, trying to second guess how I'd feel in this very moment. Isn't it strange how it's those subtle moments of consideration, rather than the showy gestures, which make you love a person? LOVE! Anna, you may not yet use the L word, even to yourself.

'It's lovely,' I say, smiling up at him. Lovely doesn't count by the way. 'It's so nice to see where you live.'

'It's lovely having you,' he says, with a naughty twinkle.

And then of course he does, a number of times over the course of the night, leaving me to struggle into work bleary-eyed but love-struck. I mean affection-struck. Healthy-regard-struck. Oh, who cares: it's going well, by anyone's standards.

17

So of course when Sunday comes I'm left cursing myself for ever agreeing to look after Mark and Amy's bundle of joy. Horst has an all-day rehearsal, and I'm too proud to ask Harry to help. I'm worried he'll think I'm a psychotic wannabe mother, determined to force him to play happy families so he'll appreciate how PERFECT IT'S ALL GOING TO BE! Instead I overcompensate wildly, banging on about how useless I am with kids and how much I'm dreading an entire day with Freddie. I leave him dozing in his enormous bed, probably asking himself why he's hooked up with such a hard-hearted harridan.

I've decided it'll be easier to connect with Freddie in his natural habitat, so I take the tube over to their house in Chiswick. Amy opens the door looking grey and strained, and I immediately feel glad I've agreed to do the decent thing, however grudgingly. Her mum's been given a matter of months, and she's trying to spend every possible moment with her. Despite all that she's going through, she's still managed to prepare a smorgasbord of organic vegetables and dips for Freddie's lunch. I consider telling her the truth about what this kind of diet does to a child. How Curly Wurly's and Monster Munch were like crack cocaine to Dan and me, reducing us to stealing money from our sleeping parents like the craven addicts we were. But I decide she doesn't need any more bad news.

'Hello, Freddie!' I trill, in my yucky 'loving godmother' voice. He sees straight through me of course, dragging his eyes away from the *Teletubbies* for all of two seconds to emit a meaningless grunt.

'Aah, he's been looking forward to seeing you all week!' says his deluded dad, pulling out nappies from under the bath. 'Now if you take him to the cinema, one of these might be a good idea.' His voice drops to a stage whisper. 'But whatever you do, don't say it's a nappy. They're his night-time knickers.'

'But it's not night time. And they're definitely not knickers.' I wonder how Harry would feel if I turned up in a pair of these babies later?

'That's not the point, Anna. He simply won't put it on if you call it a nappy.'

Parenthood is such an enduring mystery to me. It's like they're living under the rule of a particularly capricious dictator, with all this whispering in corridors and strategizing about how best to appease him. I try not to roll my eyes, and wonder how on earth I'm going to sit through another hour of Tubby-time.

Flicking through *Grazia* makes it just about bearable, and my inspired 'choo choo train' game means that Freddie eats at least half of his carrot batons. By the time we set off for the cinema, 'night-time knickers' successfully donned, I'm feeling rather pleased with myself. The film will take out two whole hours, and once we get back I'll be on the home straight. When I say he can have a

Magnum, he almost does a victory lap round the foyer. 'Thank-yooo, Anna,' he says sweetly, and I'm hit by an unexpected wave of affection for him. I grab him and swing him round me, like dads do in the park, paying for my sentimentality via the large lump of Magnum which slides down my cleavage.

The film's plot is staggeringly inane. A tadpole has got separated from its frog family, and has to swim the Atlantic, dodging the attentions of a number of misunderstood sharks and piranhas before being reunited with his relieved mother. They then sing a sickening ballad together, accompanied by a backing band of crabs and turtles. *Battleship Potemkin* it ain't, but Freddie seems to love it.

When we set off home he proffers a sticky little hand, and doesn't let go till we get back. I ask him what he'd like to do next and he shouts, 'Hide and seek! Hide and seek!' jumping up and down with excitement. His version doesn't involve much give and take, it's all about him hiding himself somewhere completely obvious (such as directly in my eye line under the kitchen table) while I look in ridiculous places, wondering aloud about what ingenious spot he's concealed himself in. When I have a go at hiding, just behind the kitchen door, he's reduced to a whimpering wreck until a well-judged cough allows him to triumphantly reveal me.

Three rounds in I'm getting mightily sick of it, but Freddie won't let up. Still, at least he's getting more inventive, and when he tears upstairs to find a tougher hiding place I seize my chance to call Harry.

'What are you up to?' I ask, suddenly realizing I haven't got anything of interest to say.

'Oh, you know, nothing much,' he says, with a lazy yawn. 'Just trying to while away the Anna-free hours.'

'You must be doing something.'

'I'm actually going to head over to the studio. I want to sort out the layout for my shoot tomorrow.' I love how driven he is. I'm sure I had that kind of zeal once upon a time, but somehow it faded. 'In fact, I hope you don't mind, but I was looking at those proofs you had in your bag.'

I've just got the initial hag-shots of Arthur and Hilda back, which are much as you'd expect. A lovely pastel backdrop, and an explosion of purple feathered eyeshadow. Hilda actually looks older than she is: no mean feat.

'They're not great, are they? But they're kind of what I expected.'

'Not great? Anna, you should ask for more than that! Look, if you want me to, I could probably shoot them for you. I've photographed Becky before, so I'm sure she'd be quite relieved.' In what circumstances, I want to demand, remembering some misjudged naked Polaroids I once let my older man snap. 'I could make the rest of the couples look way better than anything your team's going to produce. Sorry, I don't mean to sound arrogant, but . . .'

'No, no. It's an incredible offer.' And it is: Victor's Vulcan-like toes would probably curl up in delight at the prospect of Harry Langham shooting for *Casual Chic*. Even so, my own toes curl in horror at the idea of how crestfallen the hags would be if I told them they were being kicked off. But perhaps I need to get in touch with my inner career bitch to ensure this project really delivers. As I'm tossing it around, I hear a blood-curdling scream coming from upstairs.

'Harry, I've got to go.'

'What's up?'

'Nothing, I hope,' I say, hurriedly dumping the call.

Freddie's in the bathroom, blood pouring from a gaping wound in the centre of his forehead. He's used a footstool to climb into the sink, and then fallen forward into the medicine cabinet.

'Freddie!' I say, scooping him up in my arms and pulling him down on to the floor. Oh God, how do I stop the bleeding? I'm trying to staunch the flow with a flannel, but it just keeps on coming.

'Want mummy, want my daddy,' screams Freddie, as I try to calm him down. What the hell should I do? I can't bear to call poor Amy at the hospital to tell her that her son's pouring blood. Even if they rush straight back, they're a good two hours away.

'Shh, Freddie, it'll be OK.' Does he need to go to hospital? If he does, I can hardly call an ambulance, and I don't have a car. Freddie's hysterical now, and nothing I do seems to make any difference. I try to get him to sip some water while scrabbling around for my mobile. How could I have been so irresponsible? I'm not fit to take sole charge of a goldfish.

'Tom?' I say, over the sound of Freddie's wails. 'Ssh, Freddie darling.'

'Anna?' he says, over the sound of chinking glassware. 'What's wrong?'

'I'm so sorry to bother you, I know you're busy today, but I just didn't know who else to call.'

And I blurt out the whole sorry mess, starting to sob as the guilt and panic really start to kick in.

'Christ, Anna,' he says angrily, 'why was he left alone long enough to do that?'

'I know, I know. I'm an idiot. I'm so sorry.'

I can hear the rising anxiety in his voice, but he swiftly gathers himself together.

'Hopefully it looks worse than it is. Even so, I'm going to come and pick you both up so we can take him to casualty.'

'Are you sure you're able to?'

'Can you think of a better option? Just hang on for me.'

'Thanks for being so kind,' I snuffle. I take Freddie downstairs and cradle him in my arms in front of the *Teletubbies*, who suddenly seem strangely soothing. I can't bear the idea I've let him do this to himself. Luckily the bleeding gradually subsides, and by the time Tom tips up Freddie's settled down. However, as soon as he sets eyes on him, he gives another enormous wail, well aware how much sympathy he's due. Tom cuddles him back to calmness and deftly slips him into the car seat. He drives one of those big, boring dad cars, littered with nursery rhyme compilations. My heart lurches when Freddie's frightened little whimpers start up again, but Tom simply sticks a CD in the stereo, and leads us all in a chorus of

'The Wheels on the Bus'. I can't help noticing that Tom's tone deaf, but it's not the time to mock.

We rush up to the reception desk where a doctor takes an initial look at the wound. He shines a light in each of his eyes.

'Look at me, Freddie, not at Mummy and Daddy.'

'We're not actually his . . .'

Tom lays a gentle hand on my arm, silently reminding me that there's no point getting into it with them. He fills in all the forms, politely but firmly refusing to accept a three-hour wait. The injury's not serious, but Freddie's still going to need a couple of stitches. When they tell us, I'm knocked sideways by a fresh wave of guilt, and find myself unconsciously leaning into Tom's burly frame. He puts a comforting arm round my shoulders.

'It's going to be all right now, Anna, I promise.'

We're tucked away in a cubicle, waiting for a nurse. Freddie's exhausted by now, and stretches out across our laps for an afternoon snooze. I sit stock still, determined to provide him with the world's best knee pillow.

'I'm so sorry I've ruined your day.'

'Don't worry about it. I'd have been a pretty shoddy uncle if I hadn't stepped up.'

I want to ask him what he was up to, but it seems too damn nosy. Freddie sleepily rolls over, and Tom automatically sticks out a hand to prevent him tumbling off us. I wonder if Karen and Greg ever displayed that kind of instinctive nurturing. Maybe the parenting chip's simply absent from my DNA.

'You're so good at it, Tom,' I say wistfully.

'You will be too. I mean, if you ever decide you want them.' I hope he's not referring to the defensive nonsense I came out with at the dinner party. 'Besides, I'm just a boring old uncle. You're the fun godmother who takes him on adventures.'

'That depends if you consider Charing Cross Hospital an adventure.'

He laughs. 'I was crap at it at first, anyway. When Joe was born I used to go out and get drunk all the time. I was in complete denial. I'm not sure Maggie ever really forgave me for that.'

I'm pulled up short by this. Somehow I imagine him like an enormous, dependable oak, with rings of responsibility running right through to the core of his being. But then I remember a distant student party where he turned up and handed out speed bombs to Mark's friends like they were Polo mints. I'd never taken it before, and after twenty-four hours without sleep, vowed never to take it again.

'Did I really do that?' he says, laughing. 'I can't believe the stupid things I used to do in those days.'

'You were such a laugh that night. All those pompous boys in their cricket jumpers. You really livened things up.'

'Yeah, but I shouldn't have been giving out drugs to my little brother's mates, however much they needed them. God, it feels like a lifetime ago.'

'It was a public service, honestly. But then that scary blonde you turned up with dragged you off home.'

'The one before Maggie! She's the real reason I'm in

this sorry mess. She dumped me, and I got together with Maggie on the rebound.'

'It didn't look like that from the outside. Not that I knew you very well, but . . .'

'It's not that I didn't love her, it's just that marriage is such a bloody big decision. I wasn't remotely ready.' His eyes are far away, like he's driving round and round his own cul-de-sac of sadness. 'I didn't think it through properly. You're much more rational than me.'

I mentally try on 'rational' for size, but it doesn't really fit. Besides, can it ever really be a compliment outside of a science symposium? I think I'm more cowardly than rational. If I don't let things get too messy, I never have to deal with a major clean-up operation. Although it's hurt like hell, the fact that Adam and I never got married, never had kids, has stopped the separation becoming gruesomely complicated. If I'm honest, the naughty child inside of me is gleefully running away, crowing about not getting caught. But how much longer will it be till the grown-ups capture me and force me to admit I'm one of them?

'Yeah, I'm pretty much a cyborg,' I say hollowly. 'I've got oil running through my veins, not blood.'

'I didn't mean . . .' starts Tom, but then the nurse bustles up, ready to administer a local anaesthetic to Freddie's head. His bottom lip immediately starts to go, and I find myself jumping in.

'Shall we sing our special song again, Freddie? The wheels on the bus . . .'

'Go round and round,' he joins in delightedly.

'Round and round,' booms Tom, in his wobbly baritone.

The nurse quickly adheres a couple of stitches, and then it's time to go home. When we get back, Tom offers to take over, but I'm determined to see my babysitting duties through.

'Don't you trust me?' I ask him. 'Not that I'd blame you.'

'It's not that, I just thought you might have something you wanted to get back to.'

I don't know why, but I can't bear to tell him about Harry. I'm sure he's long since over his crush – rebounds are clearly his Achilles heel – but it still feels inappropriate.

'What about you? What did I drag you away from anyway?'

'Oh, it was nothing ... I was just having lunch with someone.'

I want to ask who, but of course I can't. 'Were you anywhere nice?'

'Yes, it was pretty nice actually.' And he mentions a wildly fancy fish restaurant that I've always longed to go to, but never found a suitably significant occasion to justify it.

'Oh God, I'm so sorry. Was it totally delicious?'

'Um, well, I think so – we only got as far as starters. In fact I had two prawns. I could hardly chow down on my main while Freddie gushed blood from a head wound.'

'I can't believe I dragged you away.'

'It's all right. She was a nice woman, but I don't think

163

she's the second Mrs Thomas Linklater.' He laughs. 'Well, she certainly isn't now.'

I can't help thinking I'm romantic Black Death for this man. First I brutally refuse to date him myself, and then I blithely destroy his attempt to date someone else.

'Thanks, Tom. I really, really owe you.'

'Good, I'll hold you to that.'

The three of us play interminable games of Snakes and Ladders until Mark and Amy finally get home. Still tortured by guilt, I refrain from busting Freddie for nudging the dice towards a six. He gives me a sly smile, and I wonder if it'll be my fault if he ends up a master criminal. After the initial shock, Mark and Amy are incredibly understanding about my appalling misdemeanour. The fact that Freddie's wearing his stitches with pride, and bragging about how brave he was, helps to make it all feel less catastrophic.

I promise to look after him again soon, and leave the house wracking my brains for a way to repay Tom. Although judging by my current form, the biggest favour I could offer would be to steer well clear.

18

When Monday comes, I take a long, hard look at the pictures and decide I've got to take Harry up on his offer. I'm sickened by what it's going to do to the hags, so I try to force Ruby to come to the same conclusion.

'Look at the way Arthur's holding his chin and swivelling towards the camera. He looks like Lionel Blair playing the child catcher.'

She laughs. 'They're not great, I agree. But, Anna ...' She looks at me imploringly. 'Doreen loves working with you, I'm sure she'd re-shoot them.'

'It's Harry Langham, Ruby!'

She looks at me askance. 'So have you actually shown them to him? Surely the photos only came in on Friday night.'

'I didn't see him as such, I more spoke to him.' She stares silently, gimlet-eyed. She's a better journalist than I thought. 'On Saturday morning. About work.'

I don't know why I'm being so shifty. I'm absolutely entitled to have a new boyfriend, particularly if I really had been dumped en route to the altar. I think the guilt's more about Adam himself than deceiving my colleagues: the man I've made him out to be is so far from the truth of who he is. It's his birthday later in the week, and the idea of not acknowledging it claws at my heart. Should I send him a card, or am I the last person he wants to hear from? Will he wake up alone? And, most importantly, when will it cease to matter?

Luckily I've got a night with Susie and Polly booked in, so at least I'll have a captive audience for my mental contortions. Obviously I can't share any of it with Harry. Every time a wave of it hits me, I fix a Stepford grin on my face and force myself to act like everything's marvellous.

'But is it stopping you from falling for him?' says Susie, talking through a mouthful of Scampi Fries. We're sitting in the garden of a pub at the end of her road. It's not really warm enough to justify the alfresco vibe, but her IVF-induced hot flushes have rendered it a necessity. Polly's cried off with a last-minute work crisis.

'No, no it's not. How can you eat those things?' I ask her, distracted by the odour of synthetic fish.

'It's these steroids. I swear they're making me crave MSG. If I ever do get pregnant I'll probably have one of those twenty-stone junk food monsters who get forcibly removed from their parents.'

I contemplate her birdlike frame, unable to imagine it. 'So?'

'Harry? No, that's the weird thing. I love being with him; he makes me laugh, he's thoughtful and you have to admit he's totally hot.'

'Isn't he just?'

'I suppose I kind of admire him too. Adam and I drifted along, but Harry just goes after what he wants.'

'But you're still obsessing about Adam?'

Perhaps this is how two-timing is. It's not something I've ever tried, but this feeling of intoxicating novelty mingled with a sense of betrayal is how I imagine it might be. It's like there's a ghost lodged somewhere in the machine.

'I want to be with Harry, I really do. It's just that it doesn't mean I don't love Adam any more. Not that he seems particularly bothered.'

'Just because he's not calling . . .'

'It's probably for the best anyway. It's just that we're gonna have to sort something out about the flat soon. I can't stay at Polly's forever, and once I move I won't be able to keep paying my share of the mortgage.'

Just then, Susie emits a long, low fart. She blushes almost purple.

'I'm so sorry. Thank God we're outside. I wouldn't wish IVF on my worst enemy, Anna. It's a nightmare.'

And she tells me more about its hideous indignities. The internal exploration she's been subjected to, the creeping weight gain, the constipation.

'I'm getting so moody too! I bollocked this plasterer so badly that he actually welled up.'

'I don't believe you.'

'He did! I just hope it's worth it, Anna, I really do.'

'It will be,' I promise, meaninglessly. I hate that there's so little I can do.

'You and Pol have been amazing,' says Susie un-expectedly. 'Martin tries to be understanding but it's so hard for him to know what it's like.' She gives a guilty laugh. 'Sometimes I wish they'd stick a long metal spike up his willy, just so he could get a proper insight.'

Oh no, I've gone visual. I can't bear the idea of Martin's limp, white penis. I bet it flops around flaccidly like a dead mollusc.

'Why didn't Polly just finish what she could and come out with us?' asks Susie. 'I really wanted to see her.'

'I dunno. She's so hard to pin down right now. She seems completely obsessed with this plumber guy, even though he sounds like a total numpty to me.'

'The plumber? She hasn't even mentioned him to me.'

'Really? Oh God, it's probably because I was so awful about him. I've been such a crap friend recently. And now I bet she can't bring herself to tell me she needs her living room back. I've got to work something out about the flat.'

And I find myself taking a mental tour of it, thinking about how excited we were when we'd finally saved up enough for a bath with feet. Adam's always been quite 'Queer Eye' about interior design: he knows exactly what he likes. We invested so much of ourselves in that place, emotionally and financially. Maybe my refusal to engage with extracting my equity is more selfish than I'm making out. Once we've lost our shared space, our separation will be writ in stone.

I think about him constantly on his birthday, wanting so much to at least send a text. But knowing Adam's temper, if I follow it up later in the week with the conversation we urgently need to have about the practicalities, he'll assume I was simply smoothing the path. Besides, it'll cut me to the quick if he doesn't bother to even acknowledge my message. I find myself obsessing about his last birthday, and how I sent my overdraft into freefall by taking him to Nobu, his very favourite restaurant. As I slide into sentimentality, I force myself to remember the waves of sadness I felt as I waded through my raw fish. I knew there was something wrong with my lack of interest in making a commitment, and tied myself in knots wondering if it was down to the relationship itself, or the fact that Karen and Greg remain resolutely unmarried.

Today is also Arthur and Hilda day. I need to interview them again, and I also want to break the news that we're going to have to re-shoot their first batch of photos. Hilda's tending to her garden, watering the bright pots of flowers that line the path. Arthur's stomped out for the morning, so we settle down for a relaxed cup of tea in the sunshine. When I tell her about the change of plan with the photos I see a flash of humiliation cross her face.

'It's not a reflection on you, Hilda, please don't think that.'

'No, love, I understand,' she says, giving a fake laugh. 'You have to make a bit more effort by my age.'

'Don't say that! You look amazing for your age. I mean, for any age. They just didn't do you justice.'

I hope I'm making the right call: Doreen sounded absolutely gutted when I rang her this morning. I'm not sure my new power bitch mentality really suits me, but I've got to hold my nerve.

'The thing is, dear, if you believe that's what you need

to do, then I trust you. All my friends can't wait to see me in the magazine, so I need to look my best.'

'Thanks, Hilda,' I tell her gratefully. 'I promise you you're going to look amazing. The photographer who's doing it works with supermodels most of the time.'

'Elle Macpherson to Arthur! Are you sure he's going to want to do this?'

'It's a favour,' I say, blushing. 'So, let's get going with some questions.'

What I'm hoping Hilda can give us is a sense of perspective. Her second marriage is taking place nearly sixty years after her first, in a world that's almost transformed. I ask her about the challenges the post-war marriage brought, how much scrimping and saving she had to do to create a stable home for her family. Although she lived a much more materially deprived life than my granny, I can detect some of that same steeliness. That determination to cope with whatever life throws at you.

'Did you lose anyone during the war?' I ask her, wondering what it is that makes their generation so stoical. As I'm thinking about it I find myself bitterly regretting how judgemental I was about Gran's lack of understanding.

'Oh yes, dear. My brother got shot down and my cousin died in an air raid. It's not like we didn't mourn them,' she adds defensively, 'but you had to carry on.'

'Of course,' I say, suddenly struck by how comparatively intangible the threats to our generation are. We bleat on about terrorism, or the environment, but we've never had to live with that stark daily knowledge of our own mortality.

'Tell me more about Gerald. Did it feel very different first time round?'

'Of course it did. This won't sound very romantic, but it was a bit like starting a business. You invest in your kids, in your home. There wasn't much time for having fun.'

She's not really selling domesticity to me. In my more cynical moments I've felt that procreation is like a precarious endowment policy that you take out in the hope of dodging a lonely old age.

'And with Arthur?'

'Ooh well, I've got selfish, haven't I? I've been on my own so long. Not had to do things out of duty. It's like I'm treating myself to a husband, I don't actually need one.'

It's hard to imagine that prickly old stick being a treat, but hell; some people eat Brussels sprouts for pleasure.

'So it's all about fun now, is it?'

'In a way. It's not like I didn't love Gerald, and I still miss him sometimes. But I need something different these days.'

Listening to her I feel strangely comforted. Maybe loving someone new doesn't mean you have to exorcize the last person from your psyche. It's like I'm on a particularly vicious detox, trying to flush Adam out of my system, but perhaps he can live alongside Harry for a while. I've felt like such a villain for deserting him, but it might be that needing something different doesn't invalidate what we once had. A person who'll push me forward, rather than someone to wrap around me like a comfort blanket.

I realize I've been slightly sidestepping Harry this week, scared my confusion will poison things. Every time I see him my feelings bubble up like delicious lava, and I resolve to start enjoying the sensation again. I call him up to ask if he's free Saturday night.

'I'm sorry I've been a bit distracted this week,' I tell him awkwardly. 'You know, work and . . .'

'Have you?'

Now I feel like an idiot. Why would he notice? I really should get over myself.

'Look, Anna, I'm going to be working all day Saturday, but I'd love to see you Saturday night. I'll be knackered though, so shall we just stay in?'

I feel a little shock of pleasure go through me. A night in on a Saturday is gloriously intimate. I'm thrilled I won't have to negotiate my way through another social minefield too.

'Great, what time shall I come over?'

'Why don't I come to you for once? I'd like to see where you live.'

'My home is a sofa bed, Harry, you do realize that.'

'Well then, for one night only it'll be my home too.'

Could he be more adorable? I say yes immediately, although I know I'll have to run it past Polly. However chilled out she's being, I'm not sure she'll want to actively harbour Adam's replacement. But when I call her she's incredible about it. The fact that the plumber is taking her away for the weekend might be why, but I'm not complaining. Displaying his newfound great taste, he's spiriting her away to a luxurious rural hotel in the South of France. Determined to let her know how grateful I am for everything, I splash out on an ultra-slinky pair of shortie pyjamas for her to take with her. Polly has a tendency to wear the kind of voluminous nighties most often seen in Victorian mental asylums so I figure she could do with some help.

'Oh, Anna,' she says, ripping off the paper, 'I really, really wish you hadn't done this.' She actually looks on the verge of tears.

'Calm down, Pol, I can afford them! I just wanted to say thank you properly. And now I've given you actual sex wear, you must know I'm really pleased about you and Michael.'

That's it; she's reduced to a sobbing wreck. How premenstrual can she be?

'You're an amazing friend, Anna, you really are,' she says, hanging round my neck like a rhesus monkey. She suddenly breaks away. 'I need to go and hang them up.'

'Glad you like them,' I shout after her retreating back. I'm bemused: whoever heard of hanging up pyjamas?

I spend Saturday agonizing over my menu. Adam did pretty much all the cooking which means that my culinary skills are decidedly rusty. As I'm poring over Delia Smith, wondering who convinced her that a pudding-bowl haircut was a good idea, Horst comes lumbering in. I explain my dilemma, immediately realizing that I'm now duty bound to ask him to join us.

'I would enjoy that very much, but I do not wish to impose.' Performing in an Oscar Wilde play has left Horst sounding increasingly like my granny. Maybe I should set them up.

'You wouldn't be,' I say through gritted teeth, hoping he'll get the hint.

'I was meant to be seeing a lady tonight, but maybe to stay in would thrill her as much as to go out.'

So Harry's not only going to see that I'm a loser who dosses on a pull-out bed, but also be exposed to the madness of Horst's love life. I really hope our fledgling relationship can survive this. Horst rootles around in his room till he finds a well-thumbed Bavarian recipe book. I outlaw any sausage or cabbage-based dishes – which cuts out at least half of his suggestions – but reluctantly agree to let him cook some curious sponge dumplings for dessert. I settle on roast lamb for the main (how wrong can it go?) and we head off to Tesco for the ingredients.

As we wheel our trolley down the aisles Horst tells me about tonight's mystery guest, a banker called Jenny.

'She is so successful. I am surprised that she does not have many, many boyfriends. But she says that my accent is highly erotic.'

Great: I absolutely hate bankers. Giles was a terrible aberration. Why the hell did I allow good manners to overwhelm good sense? This is just another reminder that I have to extract my equity from the flat and find a place of my own. I bat away the images of the kind of slum half an Archway maisonette will fund, and power on to the organic meat section. Horst comes scuttling after me with a Toblerone.

'You seem a little not yourself, Anna; will this make you more pleased?'

I take it from him, forcing myself to remember how well-meaning he is.

'Thanks, Horst.'

I bite into it beadily, and shove some mint sauce in the trolley. Horst piles it high with food I would never go near – Hula Hoops, Pot Noodle, Sugar Puffs – as well as the ingredients for his crazy German pudding.

Once home, I decide I need to bite the bullet and call Adam. My whole body shakes as I scroll down to his number, but I force myself to go through with it. I immediately start fantasizing about where he might be: preparing for some fabulous birthday party with his 25-year-old girlfriend perhaps. As his phone starts to ring, the tone is that unmistakeable long drone you get when a person's abroad. I'm frozen with dread: if he's away on his birthday weekend surely he must have a new girl-friend? Oh God, where could they have gone? Has this totally trumped me taking him to Nobu? Angry, irrational tears course down my cheeks as I hurriedly hang up. It all seems so irrevocable now. It's not even that I want to go back, but the idea that the door has slammed shut so hard behind me makes me feel terribly alone. Adam's love for me was such a given for so many years, and the fact that I've wilfully destroyed it suddenly fills me with self-disgust.

I concentrate fiercely on cooking the world's most amazing dinner. I've got a new relationship too, and I bet it's more wonderful than his. I send Harry a determined stream of flirty texts, although every time I pick up my phone the shock of my call to Adam reverberates back through me. I want so much to call Polly, but I don't think it's fair to intrude on her romantic weekend away. I put the dish for the meat on the hob, trying to heat up the fat to baste the potatoes.

'Anna, shortly I will need the gas area in order to whisk the fluid for my dumplings.'

'Can't you just back off, Horst!' I snap back, immediately regretting my tone when I see how crushed he looks. 'I'm sorry, I'm sorry, I'm sorry,' I say, starting to cry.

Horst turns out to be an amazing surrogate girl, listening to my tedious anguish for hours, and moving seamlessly from tea-making to aperitif-mixing. It emerges that he finished with his university girlfriend, Helga, only for her to marry his room-mate, Olaf, within a year. Even though he'd ended the relationship he had to move away from Bavaria just to recover from the trauma.

'In a certain way the dampfnudel form a tribute to her,' he says, with a faraway look in his eye.

'The dampfnudel! Come on, Horst, we've got to get on. We're seriously behind.'

It's wrong I know, but the vodka muzziness definitely gets me through. We chop and whisk in tandem with Horst's A-Ha album, having discovered we were both teenage fans during our bonding session. We sing into our spoons, and do funny eighties' dancing round the tiny kitchen. I open the door to Harry flushed and giggly.

'What's with you?' he says, laughing.

I fail to get him excited about 'Take On Me' – he was a mere infant when it came out – but he's soon chatting away to Horst about rock anthems like they're the oldest of friends.

Jenny turns out to be quite a strange creature. She arrives in a beige velvet trouser suit, as though she's closing a business deal in the mid eighties. There's something terribly disciplinarian about her; her hair has been brutally clipped down like an unruly lawn and she peers out suspiciously from behind severe, black-rimmed glasses. Questions are sharply batted back with the minimum of detail. Can you chain drink? If so, she does: non-stop Campari from the bottle that she's brought for that express purpose. Doesn't she realize it tastes like earwax? Despite her peculiarities, Horst seems utterly entranced. 'She is full of charm, Anna, don't you believe?' he asks me in a booming whisper.

'Yeah, well done, mate,' says a valiant Harry, clocking that I'm struggling for an appropriate response. Horst beams with pride.

My lamb is almost a triumph, but the lumpen gravy lets it down. And let's not even discuss the roast potatoes, which are more like roasted rocks. How did Adam ever learn to cook so well? I've never been able to pull off that mysterious alchemy you need, however conscientiously I follow a recipe. As I gaze gratefully at Harry I kick myself under the table. Why do all roads stubbornly insist on leading back to Adam?

'A round of applause for the chef,' he declares, raising his glass aloft, and I'm suddenly glad that dinner's fatally flawed. If he's learning to love my foibles, then he's halfway to loving me. And if he loved me, maybe I could start to relax.

'I tend to use caterers when I throw a dinner party,' pipes up Jenny, and I bristle with righteous indignation. She takes another swig of Campari, giving a brittle little laugh. 'Though since my divorce I haven't had much call to.'

Oh God, why do we all have so much baggage? Harry and Horst both look a bit lost for words, so I jump in and ask her about it. It starts out informational, but as she spills, she starts to defrost. It doesn't sound as bloody as Tom's, but she's lost the inevitable popularity contest and has been abandoned by most of their mutual friends. No wonder she's scouring the Internet for lovelorn Germans.

'I know what you need!' I tell her, and share my discovery about the healing power of A-Ha. It turns out she hates them, but I'm stuck in an eighties' vibe now, and decide to drag out Polly's *Now* albums from the box under her bed.

'Oh no, Anna, no more cheese, I'm begging you,' says Harry, determinedly attaching his iPod to the stereo. The room's instantly filled with some screeching dance music which just sounds like noise, and propels me straight into Polly's bedroom on a rescue mission.

'Come back!' says Harry, grabbing my legs. We have a distracting roll around on the floor, but then I return to the job in hand. There they are, lined up in their cassette boxes, with the picture of the leather-clad pig on the covers.

'Look at all these songs. "The Safety Dance", "Wouldn't It Be Good". I can't wait to play these.'

'I don't know what you're talking about,' says Harry, but by now I'm distracted. Also nestling under the bed is a folder of computer print-outs, clearly relating to Polly's weekend away. But the copy of the itinerary doesn't include any mention of a lothario plumber. Instead her travel companion appears to be someone I know very well: a certain Adam Bradshaw.

19

'So what was the hotel like, Pol?'

'Oh, you know, lovely.'

'Big bed? For all that first flush of love shagging?'

My voice is shaking with suppressed rage. I wish I could be philosophical, but I'm murderous. At least she's got the good grace to look tormented. As I take in her obvious distress, I feel an unexpected wave of pity. I wish so much that we could step backward and undo this – be Polly and Anna again – but instead her treachery's reduced us to these puppet versions of ourselves.

'Actually, Anna, I think I'm going to go and unpack. You know, jet lag and everything.'

'What, has that hour time difference really knocked you for six?' I shoot back sarcastically.

'It's just been a long trip,' she says uncertainly, trying to back away.

'Don't go: I want to hear more. Did Michael get obsessive about the French plumbing? Or was he on more of a hypnotism jag this weekend? What is it that you love most about him, Polly?'

By now I'm red in the face, quivering with anger. I can't bear to think about all those little intimacies she'll be party to now. How Adam's such a sensitive flower that he has to sleep in an eye mask all summer. His funny, wheezy snoring. Has she teased him about all this stuff, just like I did? Am I the biggest joke of all to the pair of them? Or do they just feel sorry for me?

'Anna, what's wrong?'

'You know perfectly fucking well what's wrong. Just stop lying to me.'

She visibly crumples, falling backward on to the arm of the chair. She's struggling to speak, but I don't let her get a word in edgeways.

'All that time, were you just waiting? Hoping we'd break up so you could get your claws into him? No wonder you told me not to settle.'

She's sobbing now, but I'm too furious to care. 'Of course I wasn't. You know I wasn't.'

'Not good enough. Were you really that desperate to find someone that you didn't care who it was? What the price was?'

Her eyes flash back at me. 'I'm sorry, Anna, I really am, but I'm sick of you patronizing me. I'm not this fucking desperado. You've got no idea how hard it is being alone. You dipped your toe in for about a fortnight, and whinged on about it like you were dying. You don't know what it's like to come home to an empty flat for month after month, because no one's ever right. I waited and waited and waited, and then the person I fall in love with is the wrong person. And I'm so sorry for that, but I can't help it. You dumped him!'

'It doesn't mean I don't love him!'

'Well what use is that to anyone? You don't want to be with him and I do. And he wants to be with me. And I'm so sorry that we've hurt you, but you can't expect us to throw it away just to save your pride.'

The use of the phrase 'us' makes me feel physically sick. I yank my bag down from the top of Polly's wardrobe and start throwing my possessions in it. Seeing how it's been wedged there, destroying any vestige of order, provides a stab of realization about how much she's sacrificed to put me up. My shoes are blithely sprinkled around the living room, my clothes hang from an intrusive plastic rail. I harden my heart again: maybe she did it just so that I'd be indebted to her when her two-faced behaviour was revealed.

I pack as much as I can and slam out of the house, scouring the road for a cab. But where to go? I can't bear to throw myself on Harry's mercy like some pathetic damsel in distress. I couldn't bring myself to tell him what I'd found straight off the bat, so I'd shoved the folder back under the bed and tried to pretend I was fine. Luckily Horst and Jenny were desperate to rip each other's clothes off, so dinner wrapped up fairly fast. We tried to clear up, but the sound of Horst's lusty German exhortations was too distracting. Harry couldn't control his laughter, but listening to him just made me obsess about what Polly and Adam were doing, right there and then, and my tears started trickling into the washing-up bowl. I haltingly told him what I'd found and he did his best to be sympathetic, but I could tell that he thought that as I'd ended it I couldn't be all that gutted. I didn't want to overplay how painful it was, in case it made him feel insecure. Instead I forced myself to have creaky, uncomfortable sofa-bed sex, but for the first time it felt as flat and unmeant as the kind that Adam and I ended up with.

I punch a furious text to him into my phone: 'I know I hurt you, but you destroyed me today. I need my share of the flat.' Looking at it, I start to sob. How many more people do I stand to lose? It's unthinkable that Polly and I could be permanently estranged, but I don't know if I'll ever be able to bear seeing her with Adam. It's not just the relationship itself: it's the thought of all the conniving they must've done to keep the truth from me.

Blinded by tears, I decide that I should bite the bullet and head for Karen and Greg's. At least I've got an actual bedroom there, even if my Nik Kershaw posters have long since been ripped down and replaced with War on Want ones.

'Darling, what happened?' says Karen, as I tumble through the door, and I wonder if she might actually understand why I hurt so much. She does try her best, but her bleeding heart liberalism will not allow her to condone my rage.

'Anna, I think you need to close your eyes and envision Polly in a beautiful garden. Let your red hot anger surround her, and then blow into it from your heart and turn that anger into love. Can you see her there?'

'No, Karen, I can't. I really can't.'

'You're shivering, darling, let me get you a cardigan.'

I'm actually back to shaking with rage – the first bit of the visioning went a little too well – but I let her drape a rainbow-striped woollen monstrosity around my shoulders.

'Thanks and everything, but do you mind if I take the badge off?' It's got a picture of a toothsome rat drawn on it, paws aloft. The lettering above it declares 'Rats Have Rights'.

'I mean I do think they've got rights and everything, but . . .'

'Do you really?' she says earnestly. 'Do you really think rats have rights?'

I'm not sure how long I'm going to be able to stick it out here.

'I'm just going to go and call Harry, it was all a bit weird this morning. I want to check he's OK.'

'Oh yes, Barry,' she says distractedly. Trust her to try and make his name more egalitarian. 'Why don't you invite him over for supper? We're having dhal.'

Harry + Karen + Greg + lentils = relationship cyanide. I'm not going to be doing that any time soon.

'Yeah, I'll see if he's free,' I say vaguely, wandering upstairs with my mobile.

Harry's sweet, but distracted. He's wandering round Selfridges with a stylist, looking at clothes for a shoot he's got coming up. I'm suddenly glad it's not a video phone: I'm sure she'd throw her hands up in horror if she could see my moth-eaten cardigan. I pull it more tightly round me, realizing how bone-chillingly cold I feel. The familiar smell of Karen's super-natural soap suddenly seems incredibly comforting. What is home right now? Maybe it's here.

'I'm sorry if last night was weird.'

'No, no. It was fine. Horst's brilliant, even if that Jenny girl's a bit of a freak.'

'No, I don't mean that.' Oh God, maybe I'm making too much of a song and dance about all of this. He really doesn't get it. I tell him that I've moved out of Polly's, although I'm not sure how much he hears over the insistent, jarring beat that's ringing out in the background. I bet the stylist's a razor-thin 24-year-old: perhaps they'll jump up on a podium in the middle of the shop floor and start spontaneously dirty dancing to the tuneless drone. I hope I never have to dance in front of him – I literally shuffle back and forth on the spot like I've got hooves. Adam and I had a silent agreement to sit on the sidelines at weddings, soberly contemplating those people foolhardy enough to hurl themselves around the floor to 'Waterloo'. If we'd ever made it up the aisle our first dance would've been a national emergency.

I hate having to paper over all my cracks again, vainly hoping that I'll be able to gradually peel back the layers and re-expose myself. When you don't know someone terribly well it's hard to know what will seem repellent to them. And I'm no better: I'm relentlessly watchful at the beginning of a relationship, constantly searching for clues. At least when you're a few years in there's not much that can shake your fundamental belief in the other person. They might irritate you, or anger you, but your love for each other is pretty much a given. The tragedy is that it's not necessarily enough.

Harry suggests I come over to his flat later, and I

gratefully agree. Then I sit on the bed wondering how I can distract myself. There's a pile of *New Statesman*'s lying on the side table, but one hand-wringing article on inner-city deprivation is all I can stomach. My lack of interest throws me into brief existential despair: maybe I really am too shallow to write about anything but hand cream. I think about calling Susie, but I figure she's got enough on her plate right now, and Polly's comment about me 'whinging on' has lodged itself in my psyche. I go downstairs to seek out Karen and Greg, but they're donning their anoraks in preparation for heading off.

'Are you going for a walk?' I ask them hopefully. Until today I'd forgotten how much I hate my own company.

'No,' says Karen, smiling kindly. 'We're actually going to do our shift outside the Chinese embassy. The whole Tibetan situation goes from bad to worse.'

'Why don't you come?' adds Greg, struggling to free his beard from the zip. 'It's been ages since we spent any proper time with you.'

Welcome to the nightmare of my parents. Their idea of quality time is three hours standing on a windy kerbside, waving a placard. Being united in a common cause is the ultimate in familial intimacy for them. I'm in complete agreement with them about the Tibetans, but I'm also frustrated. Could they not spend the afternoon actually talking to me, rather than shouting slogans at a locked door? I'm sure Dan and I learnt to chant 'Maggie, Maggie, Maggie, Out, Out, Out' long before 'Baa Baa Black Sheep'.

I let them leave, grumpily informing them I won't be in

for dinner, and settle down in front of a repeat of *The Sound of Music*. Not only do they not have cable, they don't even have Freeview. Once Julie Andrews skips off the screen, the best I can hope for is *Songs of Praise*. It's almost as if the last sixteen years haven't happened, and I'm back at home revising for my GCSEs and rolling my eyes at my parents' eccentricities. But at least then I had Polly to share the joke with.

I wander around the house, moodily chewing on an earth-laden stick of celery. The cork noticeboard downstairs is papered with the normal campaigning flyers, but I also notice that Karen's got a hospital appointment. It suddenly brings to mind Amy's mum, and I feel an unwarranted wave of dread. I really don't know where they're at in life. I can see the broad brush strokes, but beyond the rats and the Tibetans it's hard to know what's truly important to them. If Karen was going through a medical scare I'd have no idea. I resolve to use the time I've got at home to get past my irritation and force them to connect with me. Maybe there's a reason why I've come back.

Thinking about Amy makes me realize I owe her a call. However disastrous my last attempt at childcare was, I want her to know I'm available. Harry's texted me: 'Hope you're having a relaxing Sunday. Can you pick up a bottle of wine?' Relaxing? He so doesn't get it. Perhaps he's in denial because he's so insanely infatuated with me. Right now he might be beating his naked chest in the Selfridges food hall, declaiming 'A life without Anna Christie is a life without meaning!' But it's unlikely.

I can't get hold of Mark or Amy so I decide to try Tom. 'Hi, Anna,' he says, and then disappears. The phone gives forth some strange rumbling sounds, before he comes back on line.

'Sorry, I'm in this tank full of plastic balls and I dropped the phone.'

'I see. Do you have company?'

'No, I just love the sensation of round plastic against my naked flesh.'

'Yuck!'

I ask him if he's got Freddie with him, but it's just him and Belle, living it up on a Sunday afternoon. Treasure that she is, I can't help thinking that it sounds pretty mind-numbing. But who am I to talk? I'm spending Sunday with a stick of celery.

'So are you having a roast dinner with your parents?'

I laugh hollowly. 'No, not exactly. They've gone out.'

'So why are you . . .'

And with that, hot tears spring back to my eyes. I didn't realize how much I'd come to value my peculiar set-up with Polly and Horst, however uncomfortable the sleeping arrangements were. My relationship with Harry feels like a blessing, but he's certainly not a safe haven. That sense of crushing aloneness I felt directly after the break-up is flooding back in, full force.

'Anna, are you OK? Have I upset you?'

Without meaning to, I find myself telling him all about the last twenty-four hours. How much I want to be mature about Polly and Adam, but how violated I feel by her betrayal. How even though it's me who left, I can't stand the idea of Adam loving someone else. How I'd expect it to be the idea of the sex that would kill me, but instead it's the idea of the times when they don't have sex. The times when they lie intertwined in bed, just talking.

'It's pathetic, isn't it? I wish I was a better person than the one I am.'

'No, not at all. We forget, don't we, at the start of a relationship, how bad the end can be.' He laughs. 'If we didn't, the human race would've died out years ago.'

'It is worth it though, isn't it?'

'I reckon it is. But only if you really, really want to be with the person. It's not worth going through all this shit for something which doesn't even matter.'

He's a braver man than me I think. A kind, solvent divorcee is worth a fortune on the second time lucky merry-go-round, but he's refusing to rush back in.

'Anna, I'm sorry, I've got to go. My friend Louisa's just appeared, and we're going to take the kids for lunch.'

Oh: maybe I'm being presumptuous. Perhaps his new-found authority comes from having finally found someone who actually is worth it.

As indeed have I. It's early evening now and I decide it's time to pillage my make-up bag: my dry cheeks are ravaged by tears, and my eyes look like puffy little raisins. I splash out on a bottle of pink champagne (after all, my mortgage payments are most definitely suspended) and head over to Harry's.

'Hello, sexy,' he says as he opens the door, and I give him a lingering, emphatic kiss. He cooks dinner while

I perch on the counter, and we chat about his day. I'm trying to be as light as possible about what's gone on, and the industrial-strength foundation I shovelled on to my face is covering over the outward signs of trauma.

'You seem pretty OK, Anna, are you sure you have to move out?'

'Yes, yes I do. And anyway,' I add hastily, 'it'll be good to have some time with my parents.' I don't want him to think I'm trying to move in by stealth.

'They sound like a laugh.'

It's hard to explain why they're not a laugh unless they're your parents. In principle the idea of parents who let it all hang out is a hoot, but in practice it's downright weird. There's only one way for him to understand.

'You should come over for supper and meet them. In fact my mum suggested it only today.'

'Yeah, that sounds good,' he says vaguely, chopping away at some tomatoes. 'We should arrange something.'

'Just don't come on lentil night. Or marrow night. In fact, I'll try and talk them into ordering a takeaway.' I'm babbling, thrown by my uncertainty about whether it's a step he wants to take at all. He looks over, laughing.

'You're really loveable, you know that?'

I'm lost for words. Does he mean that he actually loves me, or that I'm hypothetically loveable? I consider asking, but it's probably the least romantic question that's ever been formulated. As I'm groping for the right response, I suddenly realize that I'm as unsure of myself with him as I was with my older man. Like Jerome, he's living a different stage of life from me – one for which I don't possess the rule book. Harry says all the right things, but it's easy to be open-hearted when you've got so much time to play with. I worry that for him relationships are like shooting stars, burning short and bright: gloriously intense but inherently brief. Or is that pure paranoia? He's mentioned quite a few women in passing, but he always seems to say that it was just a fling, or it didn't mean much. Is that what he'll say about me a few months hence? I want so much to jump off the precipice, but I'm still stubbornly clinging to the ledge.

I give up on finding a prescient reply, and kiss him instead, grabbing a handful of his hair and pulling my body up close to his. I love the feel of him, the heat that's generated between us. It's so basic, this feeling, but so vital. My mobile starts to ring, but I ignore it. However, as soon as it's rung out it starts right back up again. Is this going to be Polly? She's sent me a couple of apologetic texts, but I deleted them immediately. I break away to look at the display: Karen.

'Oh darling, I'm so glad you picked up. We've been arrested! I think I can only make one call.'

'Oh God, what did you do?'

'Well, it all felt so pointless, you know, the Chinese don't listen to a word we say. So Greg thought we should step things up a gear.'

It turns out that they chained themselves to the railings of the embassy and started blasting out 'Give Peace a Chance' through their ancient tape player. After being subjected to a full hour of Yoko Ono's tuneless wailing, the Chinese understandably decided it was time to ring the police.

'We didn't want to bother you, but because it's Greg's third offence they're taking it all quite seriously. We were hoping you could find us a solicitor.'

I briefly précis the call to Harry, who looks understandably perplexed. He offers to come with me, but as he's got to fly to Italy first thing, I tell him not to bother. Mark's a solicitor, so I call him for a recommendation (fortunately it's not hen-pecked Gerry) and within a couple of hours I've sprung them. They want to take the bus back, but I insist we take a cab, and they sit in sullen silence like chastened teenagers. It turns out that Greg's got an outstanding ASBO, so he's probably going to have to go to court. He might even get sent down, although hopefully his age means he'll get away with a fine. Looking at the grey streaks that run through his beard, I'm horrified by the idea of how vulnerable he'd be inside. Why can't they look after themselves better?

'Please don't tell Dan!' pleads Karen.

'Of course not,' I snap back, thinking how much pleasure his hateful in-laws would garner from the whole debacle.

We arrive back in Harlesden, and I try to reconnect with all the good intentions I had earlier in the day. It's hopeless: I'm too infuriated with them right now. 'You will stay for a few weeks, won't you?' says Karen needily. Greg's already shuffled upstairs, having grunted a gruff goodnight. I'm as vague as possible, newly determined to hatch an escape plan. But knowing how much I hate to be alone, I'm fast running out of options. How long will it be before I can finally shut the door on somewhere that truly feels like home?

20

Karen spends the following week trying to make up for the whole Chinese embassy disaster. I think she's still terrified I'll bust them to Dan, but she also seems desperate to persuade me to extend my stay. Every morning she makes me a disgusting bowl of millet porridge accompanied by a cleansing nettle tea. She even does my washing, despite the fact that such blatant home-making goes against all her feminist principles. Unfortunately her eco-friendly washing liquid, combined with her refusal to waste power by using a tumble-dryer, means I give off a permanent whiff of mildew. Luckily Harry seems quite happy that I use his place as a bolt-hole, which is giving me a whole new insight into the intricacies of his life. How he likes to read Raymond Carver short stories in the bath, the sneaky roll-up he smokes on the roof, looking across to the Gherkin, before he goes to bed. Often I find myself simply observing him, drinking in what it is that he adds up to.

But it's not just me that wants a piece of him. On Tuesday Roger summons me up to Victor's office, providing me with another heart-stopping lift journey in which I'm convinced I'm going to be sacked. As the doors open, he's waiting to pounce on me.

'Victor's thrilled about Harry Langham signing up for

the photos,' he hisses. 'We've got to capitalize on it. Do you have a relationship with him?'

I feel myself blush, remembering the feeling of his hands all over my body as I woke up. 'Yes, in a sense.'

'Fantastic!' he says, hurrying me down the corridor. 'You've really come through for us on this one.'

Even Victor summons up something akin to enthusiasm.

'If we were able to consolidate this relationship, and use it to attract other high profile talent, we'd be able to attract an entirely different calibre of advertiser.' There's a deathly pause. 'Less casual, more chic.' There's another pause, and then a wheezy hissing sound, which turns out to be Victor's own special version of laughter. Roger gives forth with the kind of fake mirth you hear on laughter tracks on seventies' sitcoms.

'Quite, Victor, quite.'

Victor fixes him with an icy stare. 'So what I'm thinking is that we need to undertake a charm offensive.'

Could there be anyone in the world less charming than Victor?

'I suggest a celebratory dinner, in a suitably stylish venue. Nobu perhaps.'

I feel a stab of anguish in the pit of my stomach. I still haven't spoken to Polly and I've ignored three messages from Adam. I can't bear that it's only now, under such hideous circumstances, that we've resumed any kind of contact. I know we need to sort out the flat, but right now I'm burying my head under the blanket of my relationship with Harry.

I snap back into focus. 'So who'd be on the guest list?'

'Yourself, myself, Roger, Harry and Martha.'

'Martha?' I try to keep the shock out of my voice. Martha is the director of the entire publishing stable. I'm so lowly that she doesn't even deign to make eye contact with me. This could either be a very good career move or a very bad one.

'Should we ask Jocasta?' adds Roger nervously. 'The event was originally her idea, and I know she's keen to stay involved.'

To my great relief, Victor shoots him down in flames. 'There's absolutely no need to dilute this. It's an intimate supper for a small group of close colleagues.'

I hate this kind of faux friendliness: we all know it's about profit margins.

'So,' continues Victor, standing up dismissively, 'shall I ask my assistant to contact Langham's agent?'

'Um, I could just ask him myself.'

Victor gives me a patronizing smile. 'I think it's high time we formalized the relationship, don't you?'

It's a bit late for that, I think, backing out of the room as fast as I can. It's a delicate balancing act, this one. They mustn't know that Harry's only taking the shots because we're shagging, so they need to think that he's doing it for the love of the work. But I really can't see him wanting to come back to *Casual Chic* any time soon. I hope he's up to this level of deception: I've become something of a master these last few months.

When we get downstairs, Jocasta looks up expectantly. But after ten minutes in Roger's office she returns to her desk looking green. I bet she was longing for face time with Martha, who's one of those terrifying superwomen types who balance a high-powered job with rearing a small nation of children. I'm so glad Victor took her out of the equation, but I fear she'll make me pay for it. I call a horrified Harry and tell him what's on the agenda.

'They're not really expecting me to come back? No offence, Anna, but shooting blue rinses isn't really what I came into the business for.'

'Of course, you've met Arthur and Hilda now. I know she's not as glamorous as you're used to, but she's a real sweetie.'

'Oh definitely, I'm not dissing Hilda. In fact, I think I've got a really good concept for their story.'

Listening to him talking about the shoot, I feel completely vindicated. The hags would never have thought in terms of a 'story'. I wish I'd gone to the initial meeting with him, but I thought that canny old Hilda would suss out our relationship from a mile off. He reluctantly agrees to the dinner and, before I know it, it's been timetabled for a few days hence.

I miss Polly horribly, but I cannot bring myself to call. The initial shock of cutting off from Adam was bad, but in a way this is just as painful. I didn't have that intensity of contact with Polly, but the steady heartbeat of our friendship has underpinned all of my adult life. I try for one degree of separation by having lunch with Horst.

'For me, a house without Anna is less of a home,' he says sadly, taking an enormous bite out of his salami sandwich. His sausage intake is obviously diversifying.

'I miss you too, Horst. We had a laugh. But you've got Jenny now.'

'Oh no, Jenny tells me that her feelings for me burn too strong and she must return to a life alone.'

'Really? I mean, I see.'

'She says that the ink is still quite moist on her divorce, and until it is dry she is doomed to a lonely life. So again I am solo. And Polly is there very little.' He stops abruptly. 'Oh, Anna, so often I choose the wrong words.'

I laugh it off, but my imagination immediately goes into overdrive. Adam's messages are getting increasingly irritable – the general thrust is that as I asked to divide up the spoils, I can't now refuse to engage – and of course he's right. But the idea of having to have cold, practical discussions about finance is almost too much to bear. He hasn't even mentioned the Polly situation, but judging by how angry he sounds, I don't think he's going to have much sympathy for my position.

As Horst walks me back to the office, we run into Ruby on a coffee run. She stops to ask if I want one and I make the introductions.

'En-charnted to meet you,' says Horst, projecting his voice unnervingly.

'Yeah, you too,' she replies bemusedly, hurrying on. Ruby's got that radiant, well-scrubbed beauty that some girls effortlessly exude, and I'm not surprised to catch Horst casting a longing glance after her. Oh God, he wouldn't stand a chance.

The event's only six weeks away now, so she and I are increasingly swamped by the arrangements. My newfound bravery means that I'm pushing the tenor of it as far as it can go. The décor is dark and moody, the music will be loud and underground. Even the food is as outré as possible. It's not very *Casual Chic*, but I'm hoping that that's the brief.

I'm actually quite grateful for my crushing workload as it makes it easier to blank out Polly and Adam. Susie's almost as upset as me, as she can't bear the way our threesome's been fractured.

'She should've told you, Anna, I know she should've, but surely this can't be it? You two have been friends for forever.'

It's the night of the dinner, and I've called her from outside Harry's flat. I'm pacing up and down waiting for him to get back. I wish I had keys, but it seems way too presumptuous to ask.

'I just don't know if I'd ever be able to trust her again. And the thought of seeing them together . . .'

'Poor you!' says Susie. 'If me and Martin got divorced and you two suddenly started a passionate affair it would completely destroy me.'

You couldn't bear it?! I'm paralysed by a disgusting image of a naked Martin wandering out of the bathroom, glistening with post-coital sweat. His pipe-cleaner limbs, his funny, pea-shaped head.

'I promise you faithfully I will never, ever have sex with Martin.'

'I'm so sorry, Anna, I can't believe how badly she's behaved.'

At that very moment Harry appears, meaning I can

hang up and avoid exploring me and Martin's red hot passion in greater depth. He's all ruffled and flustered – one of his sexiest looks – and my irritation swiftly melts. But now I'm low on grooming time, so I race around the flat trying to pull it all together. Harry spends the sum total of five minutes changing into one of his beautiful suits, and settles down to wait in front of his *Twin Peaks* box set. I love how eclectic his viewing habits are: it's a far cry from Adam's obsession with Sky Sports. If some cabbage-eared men were chasing a ball, Adam was happy, but Harry needs something more meaningful. I sit down next to him to pull on my tights, but the fact that I'm rushing means I immediately ladder them. And because I don't live here, or indeed live anywhere, I don't even have a spare pair. I'm almost screaming with frustration, trying to stop the run with clear nail varnish. 'What on earth are you doing?' says Harry, looking at the loaded brush, wobbling over the nylon. He simply takes my leg in his muscular hand, and very delicately dabs a spot on. I smile at him, struck by the way in which he combines delicacy and masculinity. He's an artist in the true sense of the word. We hold each other's gaze.

'You are lovely,' I tell him, suffused with a sudden rush of affection. These last few weeks would have been so much more perilous without him to catch my fall. I force myself to look away, aware of how moon-faced and dappy I must look.

'I love you too,' he says, grinning. Now that was un-expected. Did he think that was what I was trying to say, or was he just looking for an excuse to drop it in? Or is he just being ironic? 'Good,' I say, simply, and lean in for a kiss. I'm not going to expose the useless, relentless whirring of my fevered brain. I'm sure his meaning will become clear. And I do love him, I think, scary though it is to contemplate. After a bit more ardent snogging we head out in search of a cab. I feel as if I'm in a bubble, like I'm floating above us. I'm trying to inhabit the idea of us being in love. I'm so excited, so gratified, but also overwhelmed.

The immediate priority is concealing that we have any feelings for each other whatsoever. We decide to arrive separately, so I leave Harry to take the cab once round the block. When I get to the table, Roger's sweating like a pig, snuffling around at the far end while Martha and Victor talk amongst themselves. Martha's extremely gracious, but there's a slight sense of *noblesse oblige*. It's as though she's decided to descend from her ivory tower to give the little people a chance to learn from her. However, the moment Harry arrives, I feel her reserve start to slip. And who can blame her? His navy blue suit sets his eyes off to perfection, and his self-deprecation about being late immediately puts the table at its ease.

Martha ensures that he sits next to her, leaving me trapped between Victor and Roger. It's a pretty ropey social sandwich, but I'm feeling too proud to care. No heads turned when Adam crossed this dining room: Polly's welcome to his paunchy form.

'So what made you decide to get involved?' says Martha, one hundred per cent focused on Harry.

'Oh, it's all down to Anna,' he replies, momentarily

casting his gaze my way. He laughs. 'She wouldn't stop chasing me.'

He gives me a half smile, but I look away. I hope that's not really what he thinks. The self-help witches hate nothing more than a woman who pursues her man. He loves you, I remind myself, and then fight to control the enormous grin that creeps across my face.

'Good work, Anna!' says Roger uselessly.

'Let's hope this is the foundation for a long and fruitful association,' drones Victor, mechanically raising his glass.

Harry refuses to take the bait, turning back to Martha in order to sidestep the issue. At least I hope that's why. They're getting on rather too well for my liking, and she's got definite Mrs Robinson-ocity. When she excuses herself to go to the bathroom I find myself wondering if she employed a surrogate to pop out her multitude of offspring. She's wearing a diaphanous green shift dress which clings to every curve. Her buttocks are high and toned, and her breasts remain firm and pert. God, I've got to stop thinking like a murderous lesbian.

Dinner's divine, but my anxiety means I end up drinking far more than I intended. I'm trying so hard not to betray our relationship that I've lost any vestige of charm. As I chomp away monosyllabically, Martha hurls herself into the gap, controlling the table with her effortless confidence. The only gratifying moment is when Harry inadvertently tries to play footsie with Victor.

'So it sounds like Anna's very much your key contact on the project,' says Martha, casting an unimpressed look in my direction.

'Yeah, she's my girl Friday,' replies Harry, looking over. 'It's all going rather well, isn't it?' he adds with a secret smile.

'Indeed it is,' I say, sounding like Paul Daniels. Then I dry up.

'But now you've met the senior team I'm hopeful you'll also feel able to come direct to me with any concerns.' And with that, she lays a jewel-encrusted hand on his arm.

He doesn't make any move to pull away. 'I'd love that,' he says, looking straight at her and treating her to one of his most heart-melting smiles.

'It's a deal,' says Martha, a flirtatious smile playing around her perfectly painted lips. Harry holds her gaze, topping up her wine glass without being asked. He's basking in the sunshine of her admiration like a well-fed tom cat.

I can't watch any more. I spend the rest of the evening forcing myself to engage in gay banter with Victor and Roger. I'm so doggedly upbeat that I actually succeed in making Victor laugh twice. It's like there's a line down the centre of the table and Harry and I are on separate halves. Eventually the whole sorry affair draws to a close and we're back in a cab.

'How did I do?' he says, grinning away.

'Oh great, Harry, really great,' I snarl sarcastically. 'You made me feel like such a fucking idiot.'

'What are you talking about?' he snaps back angrily.

'Oh, Martha, you're so powerful. Oh, Martha, I'd love to shoot for you all the time. I might as well have stayed at home. It was like I wasn't even there.'

'What more do you want from me, Anna? I'm doing all of this for you, and it's still not good enough.'

I can't believe we're having our first row on the night we've declared love to one another. And I hate how his words echo Adam's. Will I never be satisfied with what I have? I should back off before I say something I can't withdraw.

'I'm sorry, I'm being a total psycho. Ignore me.' Maybe the sense of exclusion I feel from Polly and Adam's two-man canoe is making me ultra sensitive.

'I gave her what she wanted, Anna, I told her what she needed to hear. And look at how happy she was.' He smirks to himself. 'Do you think she'll be dreaming about me next time her fat old husband's pounding away on top of her?'

I laugh uncertainly and decide to let it go. It's a long time since I felt that kind of visceral sexual jealousy, and all I want is for it to retreat back into the darker reaches of my mind. Besides, I seem to be the only one who found our evening wanting. The next day Martha goes so far as to send me flowers, and Victor writes an email that borders on effusive. I'm not sure they'll be quite as happy when Harry turns their work offers down flat, but at least it'll keep me in good odour for the event. Jocasta comes over to inspect the bouquet's card, and then proceeds to presumptuously beat the stems with a pair of scissors. I bet she's wishing they were my head.

'It's been quite a while since you've had flowers at work, hasn't it, Anna?' she says, busily replacing them in the vase.

'It has, yes,' I say, pointedly turning back to my computer.

'How's the recovery process progressing? I can imagine the scars of Adam's betrayal will take quite some time to heal.'

Why today, of all days? I can't bear to have to think about Adam, and all that it entails. He sent me yet another email this morning, demanding a response. I can feel my voice starting to crack as I hurry out in search of coffee.

'I'm trying my best, Jocasta, that's all I can do.'

For once I'm telling her the truth. The murky chaos of my break-up with Adam is slyly encroaching on the springy freshness of my relationship with Harry. Of course we'll row, but the fact that the cycle's begun reminds me just how hard you have to work. That love-struck idolization can only ever be a mirage: you just have to hope that what grows in its place is worth tending to. I drink my latte in the scrubby square round the back of the office, trying to force myself to snap out of my morose mood. Harry loves me, for God's sake! And I love him. Why am I such a lazy cow? If love wasn't such hard graft it wouldn't be worth it. I'm suddenly reminded of how I only ever got one badge at the Brownies because I was too damn inert for all that pointless sewing and orienteering. But picturing my naked brown smock just brings to mind Polly's badge-laden version. She's always been so determined to be good, to apply herself. She concentrated as hard on the self-help books as she did on the Brownie handbook, nearly driving herself mad in the process. No wonder she's finally given up and abandoned herself to an outrageous short cut.

I waste half an hour I don't have before reluctantly forcing myself back upstairs. As the lift ascends, I feel a flutter in my stomach from the moths of doom, but I dismiss it. I'm golden girl today after all.

Oh. There's Jocasta, gesticulating at Adam, who's somehow managed to bypass security and pitch up at my desk. For one insane moment I'm transfixed, filled with crazy pleasure that he's right there in front of me. By the time I've remembered that it's a total disaster I've lost vital seconds.

'Will you just tell me where Anna is? She's refusing to speak to me.'

Jocasta's in her melodramatic element. She raises herself up to her full height, puffed up with indignation like an angry swan.

'It's hardly surprising, considering your despicable behaviour. If she's left on the shelf, it will be entirely down to your unspeakable betrayal.'

'My betrayal?'

By the time I've crossed the room, Adam's made it absolutely clear who did the dumping. He turns to me, eyes flashing.

'You're unbelievable, you know that? You're the one who started shagging that photographer. You get a solicitor, you sort out the flat and then you email me. I never want to speak to you again.'

21

Karma – it's a bitch. Obviously I should never have lied about Adam to save my arse, and now I'm well and truly paying the price. Jocasta was thrilled I'd been exposed in such a gloriously public way. She immediately told Roger, who's asked to see me this afternoon. Meanwhile, the rest of the office has pretty much sent me to Coventry. It's like being at one of those posh boarding schools that Karen and Greg never would've countenanced. I look across the room at Jocasta, who is spooning the foam off her latte and flicking it into the bin, desperately trying to avoid the scourge of calorific milk. Beneath all that earth mother crap lies the soul of a control freak dictator. She meets my gaze, shooting me a look that combines betrayal with pity. Thank God for Ruby – kind, loyal Ruby – who is carrying on as if nothing's happened. We're off to interview my gay couple soon, which will at least give me a couple of hours out of this hellhole prior to my summit with Roger.

But work is the least of my problems. Polly sent me the most damning email, telling me exactly what she thought of me trying to take the high ground while trashing Adam in such a spectacular way. Even Susie seems distant. I'd kind of fudged how I'd got out of the whole fake engagement scenario at work, and I'm sure she thinks I deceived her. I feel like a naughty child, knowing I've sinned but unsure when I'll be forgiven. It reminds me of the time I got busted for stealing change from Karen's purse. Our parents always had such a strong sense of moral certitude, which stretched right from the Tory government's treatment of the miners to me and Dan's childish indiscretions. When she came upon me, guiltily rootling through her purse in the garden shed, she looked at me as though she didn't even know me, as if I was part of the evil capitalist conspiracy which was destroying all that was pure in the world. 'Wicked' was what she called me, and I felt it, right in the very core of myself. I feel as wrong now as I did then. This stupid wedding event means nothing in comparison to the preciousness of my friendships, but I've somehow let it eat them whole.

'I don't want to be nosy, but are you really seeing Harry Langham? Cos if you are, then total respect. He's so fit.'

Ruby and I are in the cab, heading for Selfridges to meet Oliver and Steve.

'I know!' I smile gratefully at her: at least she's not dwelling on the ill-gotten muffins the office sent me. And it reminds me of what I've gained in amongst what I've lost. Since we declared love, our relationship has definitely stepped up a gear. I've been there almost every night this week, and this weekend we're heading off to Becky's country pile.

'Why don't I ever meet anyone like that at work? They're all gay, or gay and in denial.'

'Are you single?' I ask her, surprised.

'Yeah, like for forever.'

'I just assumed a girl like you would have some devoted man-slave hanging around at home.'

'I wish! I literally never meet anyone.'

I can't understand it, but then I guess I could never understand it with Polly. Although Polly did slightly scream desperation, whereas Ruby's got the kind of sunny disposition that surely attracts the good things in life.

Oliver and Steve are being measured up for their suits.

'What's up with you?' says Steve, giving me an effusive hug. 'You look mucho gloomy.'

'Well,' I tell him, 'I've been exposed as a pathological liar at work and my ex-boyfriend, who I co-own my one worldly asset with, says he never wants to speak to me again. But otherwise it's all going swimmingly.'

'Fuck!' says Oliver. 'We should all go for champagne.'

And we do, once their inside legs have been measured. They're wearing matching grey suits for the wedding, which sounds a bit Tweedledum and Tweedledee, but the fact that they're so beautifully cut means it looks rather marvellous. Oliver insists we go to the oyster bar on the ground floor, where we perch on high stools. When I tell them my nightmarish meeting with Roger means I can only have half a glass, Oliver defiantly fills it to the brim.

'You're going to need it, darling, let's face it!'

Ruby and I try to pose some questions, but the boys are desperate for scandal, and I find myself spilling the whole sorry tale, right from the top. Ruby listens, open-mouthed.

'Oh Christ, Anna, don't worry about it,' says Oliver.

'It'll all blow over. The one thing I've learnt from the mess that's my personal life is that you have to chase happiness. That's what your mate's doing, that's what you're doing. Life doesn't come knocking, you have to go after it.'

He's right of course, and the fact that Harry does exactly that is one of the things I love most about him. Even so, while this rallying talk is very cheering, I'm not sure that Polly and Adam are going to be forgiving me any time soon. And even if they did, I'm still nauseated by the idea of seeing them as a couple. How can Oliver be so blasé about the stinking mess that love's disintegration creates?

'Because I had to be. I was the devil as far as most of me and Julie's friends were concerned, and who wants to live like that? I spent six months drinking too much and feeling sorry for myself, and then I realized I was going to lose Steve too unless I pulled myself together.' I bet he wasn't. Steve gazes at him constantly, like a benevolent stalker.

'It's true, Anna,' adds Steve. 'You've got to have a laugh. Are you having fun with this new bloke?'

Ruby's giggling at the very thought of how gorgeous Harry is. She's way closer to him in age: I'm not sure I'm going to be introducing them any time soon. Meanwhile I'm finding I have to think about it. Yes, I am having fun, but I've allowed the whole relationship to be blighted by my anxieties. Perhaps it's now, when the shit really has hit the fan, that I can start living the vida loca. After all, I've got nothing left to lose.

Or have I? I get back to *Casual Chic* to find Roger hunting for me, looking more sombre than I've ever seen him. I'm not sure if he's faking, but it certainly kills my champagne bounce stone dead. We take the lift up to his office in deathly silence.

'Sit down, Anna,' he says, gesturing limply at the chair as though he's in pain. I jump in there quick, hoping my recent head girl status will win him round.

'Roger, can I just say how sorry I am? I never intended to lie to anyone.' I pause, continuing lamely, 'It all just got a bit out of hand.'

There's an ominous pause.

'Life, Anna, is all about trust.' Oh my God, he's enjoying this! It's the first time he's ever displayed any natural authority: he clearly missed his true calling as a rural headmaster. 'My trust in Graham,' yeah, good luck with that one Roger, 'Jocasta's trust in me, and indeed the trust we put in you. We've allowed you to have free reign over this event, despite your relative inexperience.'

'And you must admit, Roger, I've delivered.'

'Yes, apparently. But you've only ever given us the sketchiest of details.'

'But you won't be disappointed.'

'That remains to be seen.' He stops dramatically, like he's Sir Alan gearing up to fire someone. He wouldn't, surely. 'But in order to be sure, Jocasta has very generously agreed to take a supervisory role on the project.' Oh my God, this might actually be worse than being fired. 'I'm sure we'll all benefit from having her exemplary organizational skills steering the ship.'

I sit there staring at him, unable to wipe the sullen disgust off my face. 'Roger,' I say, my voice rising, 'I promise you, Ruby and I have got it covered.'

'If you hadn't made so many strides, with Harry Langham for example,' here he casts me a significant look, 'we'd take you off entirely. This is my compromise position.'

I get out of his office as fast as I can, stomping down the corridor in a rage. What havoc can she wreak? I'm almost crying with frustration; I want to punch something. I walk twice round the block, trying to get through to Harry, but his phone just rings out. When I get back upstairs, Ruby's in a meeting room with Jocasta, printouts strewn across the table.

'Anna,' says Jocasta, with a crocodile smile, 'we were wondering where you'd got to. Ruby's been taking me through all your plans.'

'And?' I say, trying and failing to keep the naked hostility out of my voice.

'There's a great deal to applaud, but also areas that I feel are a teensy bit weak.'

'Oh?'

'Catering for example. Sushi seems a little outlandish to me. Not to mention the risk of food poisoning. Don't you think that something simpler, prawn vol-au-vents say, might be a more reliable choice?'

Prawn vol-au-vents? Does she actually think we're organizing a tea party in a vicarage?

'In fact I thought I'd contact the caterers who looked after Percy's christening.' She smiles fondly, basking in the happy glow of motherhood. 'They put on such a lovely spread.'

I seriously contemplate resigning, right here and now, but obviously I can't. Ruby valiantly helps me try to combat her worst excesses, but she still manages to chip away at all the arrangements I worked so hard to perfect. She's threatening to replace the DJ set with some horrible 'light jazz' and is seriously contemplating asking Dr Fox to join the panel. When I point out that he's neither a doctor nor a fashion expert she actually tells me to 'shush'.

To make matters worse, I'm facing a night in with Karen and Greg. I haven't been able to bring myself to tell Karen what's happened – I'm worried it'll confirm all her worst fears about the weaknesses in my character – so instead I've been moping around the house like a moody teenager, telling her there's nothing wrong. Sticking with the whole teenage vibe, I get back and shut myself in my bedroom to call Susie. I can't stand being on bad terms with her too. She sounds distinctly frosty, and I jump into a long and garbled apology.

'Basically I was ashamed of myself,' I tell her, running out of steam. 'I didn't want to own up, even to you. Adam was never anything but kind to me, and I hated what I'd done.'

'Do you know what, Anna? I understand how it happened, I really do. I just don't know how you can give Polly a hard time for being dishonest when you've told so many lies.'

She's so steely, so unlike my lovely friend. I suddenly believe she could make a plasterer weep. I bleat on a bit more, but there's a reserve I can't penetrate. It turns out that she'd given Pol a real rocket for what she'd done to me, and now feels she's been completely compromised.

'Can we stop talking about this, Suse? I'm so sorry, I don't know what else to say. Tell me about how your treatment's going. Are they going to do the egg transfer soon?'

'Do you even care?'

'Of course I care. How can you even ask me that question?'

I'm sobbing like a plasterer by now. I can't believe how personally she's taking it all. Am I really as untouchable as everyone seems to think? Thank God for Harry and his lovely, welcoming friends. I'm going to go away this weekend and try not to think about any of this for forty-eight hours. I get off the phone as fast as I can, and go downstairs to make myself a sandwich. Greg's still at the sixth form college where he teaches, but Karen's at the kitchen table reading the *Guardian*.

'Do you have *any idea* how intelligent monkeys are?' she says, apropos of nothing.

'No, not really,' I say, trying to feign interest.

'These scientists have taught a troupe sign language, and it turns out they're so intellectually adept that they can blame each other for crimes that other monkeys have committed.'

Great, I'm basically on the same moral level as an ape. The only advantage I've got is slightly less body hair.

'In a hundred years, all those medical researchers who experimented on them will be vilified for their cruelty.

When we've finally realized that the monkeys are our brothers.'

Her face is contorted with outrage at the poor treatment that's been meted out to generations of monkeys. Adam thought my parents were hilarious, and used to laugh me out of my frustration with his sly, affectionate impressions. Without him to offer a buffer, I'm slightly at a loss.

The rest of my week is taken up with trying to prevent Jocasta from taking the event apart, brick by brick. Because Ruby's so unthreateningly junior, Jocasta foolishly believes she'll doggedly do her bidding. We cancel nothing – not the make-up team, not the DJ, not the raw fish – blindly hoping that we'll either win her round to the sophisticated vibe, or prise her off the project altogether. I leave a message for Dr Fox's agent which is so dismissive that he'd have to be truly desperate in order to call back. My personal life may be in meltdown, but I'm refusing to allow my work life to go down with it.

But meltdown is too strong a word, because it fails to acknowledge the joy that is Harry. When I climb into his mini on Friday night I feel a wave of relief flood through me. 'We're on an actual mini break!' I say, clapping with delight and rootling through his CDs. Who are these bands? They're all called things like 'The Crashing Bores' and 'Klutz'. I wonder what he'd say if I put on *Carpenters Gold*? I decide not to risk it, and suffer the clanging guitars all the way up the M25, uncomplainingly feeding him grapes. Monkeys would never display such altruism. So far I've downplayed the chaos that's kicked off, partly because I'm ashamed, partly because I don't want him to think I'm less trustworthy than a gibbon. But despite the fact that we lark around all the way to Cherwell services, he obviously senses that it's getting to me.

'Don't think you can't talk to me about this stuff, Anna, I'm not some kind of jealous monster.'

'I know you're not,' I tell him, reaching across to stroke his cheek as my heart squishes up with love. 'It's not just Adam,' I say hesitantly. 'I suppose I don't want you to think less of me.'

'Less of you?'

'You know, when you just see the worst side of your own nature? I find it hard enough to contemplate myself, let alone show you.'

'Yeah, like I'm always late.'

'No, not like that. I mean the dark bits of one's personality. The horrible, crap bits that you never want to acknowledge.'

'Right,' he says, a bit uncomprehendingly.

I was expecting Becky's family's house to be big, but not the full-on stately home that it turns out to be. I stay in the car, glued to my seat, taking in the mellow golden Cotswold stone which seems to stretch into infinity. We're not in Harlesden any more, Toto. Becky comes tearing out of the door and gives me a fulsome hug.

'I'm so excited you're in the country – it's a whole new phase in our relationship!'

'Isn't it just?' I reply, hugging her back.

'Harry,' she says, with a slightly minxy smile.

'Becky,' he says, slinging an arm round my shoulders.

We step through the door into a draughty entrance hall which is easily the size of Polly's entire flat. 'You're in the top red bedroom,' says Becky, gesturing into the ether, which obviously makes total sense to Harry. As he lugs our bags up the stairs, Becky drags me off to the kitchen for a gin and tonic. I'm longing for a reaction moment with him, but it seems too rude to extricate myself from her eager clutches.

'So how's it going?' she says, giving my arm a chummy squeeze. She's being so lovely, but it just makes me miss Polly and Susie all the more. Friendships are like any relationship: it takes years to build that worn-in grain.

'Oh, you know, really good,' I tell her, smiling brightly.

'Harry's such a doll.'

'Yes, yes he is.'

There's a slightly awkward pause which I break with some twittery questions about her job. She's in the midst of designing the interior of a ritzy boutique for a ghastly It-girl type. The frequent temper tantrums make it a real ordeal, and I find myself wondering why she bothers. If her family have got a house like this behind them surely she doesn't have to work?

Lucas wanders in, yawning widely like a lazy lion.

'So was it worth fighting your way through the Friday exodus for?' he asks, a cheeky smile playing round his lips.

'Absolutely,' I say. 'This house is incredible.' I hope I don't sound too much like a poor little church mouse who can't quite believe where she's landed. My middle-class tones conceal the fact that we really didn't have much growing up. Refugee-saving and teaching don't pay mega bucks, and most of our clothes either came from Oxfam or the CND catalogue. Going to school with 'Nuclear Power No Thanks' emblazoned across my chest never won me many points in the fashion stakes.

As well as being a natural beauty, Becky's also a fabulous cook. She's made a melt in the mouth duck cassoulet with gratin potatoes on the side. Is there any aspect of her that lacks this kind of effortless polish? Still, now Harry and I are more of an established couple, I've lost my pathetic paranoia about being the new kid on the block. He and I have brought down a case of wildly expensive red wine, so we all get pleasantly merry and have a drunken game of charades. It's boys versus girls, and when it's Harry's turn he tells us it's a film with two words and points at me.

'*Anna Karenina*,' says Lucas, but Harry shakes his head. '*Sexy Beast*,' is his next guess, delivered with a smirk. Harry shakes more emphatically, and Becky gives him a playful punch. Harry clutches his heart, giving me puppy eyes, but Lucas doesn't get it.

'*Love Actually*,' says Harry, after their two minutes are up. 'Wasn't it obvious?'

'Of course!' says Becky, clapping her perfect paws together.

I grin dopily, thinking how relentlessly sweet he is. How did I get this lucky? I can't wait to drag him off to bed, but I worry that my rather drunken advances might collapse the ancient-looking four-poster we've been assigned. A pee in the night is an even worse ordeal. I tiptoe down the ancient corridors, unable to find a light switch, and accidentally try to climb into a musty wardrobe. I collapse back into bed, giggling, and roll Harry-ward again.

Breakfast is a relaxed affair, with tons of coffee and papers. Unfortunately my rural idyll is short-lived as it swiftly emerges that we're going to spend the day on a bracing hike. A short ramble's OK, but people who find hardcore exercise pleasurable totally mystify me. The fact that I don't have the right footwear is no kind of get-out clause. Becky immediately whips out some hideous wellies that belong to her 'Aunt Miffy': why do posh people have such ludicrous nicknames? Or is she actually christened Miffy?

Becky's beautiful face is sans make-up, but I'm loath to go au naturel in front of Harry. Big mistake: the biting wind that's buffeting the hills immediately gives me streaming panda eyes. Not Becky though: the country air gives her the kind of perfect rosy glow that you could never get from a bottle.

We have a brief rest stop for a pasty (nothing would entice me to eat a pasty in London) and then continue on the hundred-mile march. Mark and Amy text to ask if I can babysit on Sunday night, but I guiltily tell them I won't be back in time.

'Are you all right?' says Harry, noticing I'm dragging my feet.

'Absolutely,' I trill. 'Isn't it lovely here?'

'Are you not the country sort, Anna?' asks Becky, with

a sympathetic smile. 'I've been marched up these hills since I was tiny, so it's second nature, but you must say if you want to turn back.'

'No, no,' I say, a little too emphatically. 'It's great.'

'I could always give you a piggyback,' says Lucas.

'Really, I'm fine.'

And we walk and walk and walk. Obviously there's a torrential downpour, but we all shelter under a tree and laugh gaily about it. Becky peers out cutely from inside the hood of her cosy parka. I have no hood, and thus look like I'm in Black Sabbath, what with the black make-up pouring down my face and the dripping hair. When the walk's finally reaching its conclusion, the others decide we should stop in a pub. All I want is a hot bath, but I don't want to seem churlish. Becky goes up to buy drinks, and I offer to help carry them.

'I think yours and Harry's comes to about four pounds fifty,' she says casually, as the barman puts them down.

I'm completely taken aback.

'Just because obviously we won't be doing rounds.'

'Yes, of course,' I say, slapping a fiver down. I'd forgotten the phenomenon of how tight rich people are. It's why they're all so damn rich. One of Polly's worst ever boyfriends was the sexually deviant, multimillionaire son of a famous music producer. When she dumped him, shortly after Christmas, he made her pay him back for the diamond earrings he'd got her. In instalments. I tick myself off for being so uncharitable. Becky shouldn't have been buying a round in the first place considering she's sharing her lovely house. I must be a better guest.

My first step is offering to help cook supper, which means that Harry and I hardly get a moment alone together.

'Are you sure you haven't got five minutes?' he says, pulling me backward towards the bed.

'Now there's an offer,' I laugh, reluctantly dragging myself out of the room.

'There's nothing wrong with premature ejaculation,' he shouts after me, knowing the vastness of the house means there'll be no one in earshot.

Becky gushes about how 'adorable' I am to help, and immediately sets me to work peeling a hundredweight of potatoes. She's put on a figure-hugging red top, which allows her generous bosoms to hover magnificently above the Aga like ripening fruit. Yet to change, I'm in tracksuit bottoms and a promotional T-shirt from Activa probiotic yoghurts.

'Do you not tend to cook much?' she asks, clocking my inept efforts with the peeler. 'I bet with a job like yours you don't have much time to.'

'I don't know. I guess my ex was such a good cook, I just got out of practice.' Why did I mention Adam?

'Oh, do tell me about him,' she says keenly. 'Harry said you'd been together for centuries.'

'I'm not that old!' I shoot back, and then curse myself for sounding so defensive. I sketch Adam with the minimum of detail, kind of like how you'd describe yourself to a French pen pal when you're twelve. It feels wrong to bring him into this set-up, particularly considering how he feels about me right now. When I tell her a bit about the break-up, she stops what she's doing and listens intently.

'I'm sorry, Anna. How utterly grotty.'

'You know how it is. If you really love someone, breaking up is always going to be hellish, no matter who casts the final blow.'

'I'm sure you're right, but I'm lucky in a way. I've never felt like this about anyone before Lucas, and now I'm marrying him!'

It's sweet really. She seems so untouched by the oily underside of life. I give her an impromptu hug and head off to lay the table.

Despite my lacklustre assistance, Becky produces another spectacular feast, after which we retreat to the cavernous drawing room. It's dotted with dusty oil paintings of stern-looking aristocrats.

'Are they your actual ancestors?' I ask her.

'Can you see the resemblance?' she giggles, pointing to a hair-lipped old goat in a ruff.

We chat companionably for a while, before Lucas disappears from the room. Five minutes later he's back, with four thick lines of coke laid out on a CD case.

'Ta da!' he says, looking incredibly pleased with himself.

Oh no. I really don't want to seem like a maiden aunt, but I don't think I can face it. Not only does coke turn me into a self-obsessed dullard, but it also makes me sneeze compulsively for days. The way things are going, Jocasta will probably spot my snivelling and decide to introduce random drug tests. It's never been my thing, but on the odd occasion in my twenties when I did fall prey it was because I desperately needed a boost to get through a scary social event. I'm only too glad to have left those days behind.

Lucas snorts his gleefully and passes it on to Becky. I look at the moist twenty-pound note and feel repelled. Can I refuse on hygiene grounds? Harry looks to me questioningly, and I give a noncommittal shrug. 'If I must,' he grins, leaning down to hoover his up. Now it's just me and an enormous wiggly worm of powder. I hate the idea of all the rubbish it's been cut with, and the lives that have been ruined in its production; if someone could find a way to manufacture organic, fair-trade cocaine they'd clean up with hedonistic hand-wringers like me. I compromise by snorting a tiny amount, leaving the other three to leap on my leftovers like hungry jackals. Big mistake: I should've either gone the whole hog or passed altogether. Now I'm feeling twitchy and irritable, but not gloriously high. Having swiftly taken another line, the other three are starting to look glassy-eyed and manic.

'Isn't Anna great?' says Harry.

'Yeah, she's great!' says Becky. 'I'm so enjoying having you here.' She's chain-smoking fags and necking white wine like there's a world shortage.

'It's great to be here,' I say, with a forced smile.

'I really think we're going to be next,' says Harry.

'Next?' I ask.

'Up the aisle. I could really see us getting married. Couldn't you?'

I hate it when people profess undying love on Class A drugs. Note to self: never go to Ibiza with Jocasta.

'Um, yeah.'

'But Anna's already been asked once, Harry,' says Becky, leaning over to cheekily tug his hair. 'By the man who cooks like Gordon Ramsay. What makes you think you're so special?'

Oh God, please, please can we not talk about Adam? I look at Harry, worried his feelings will be bruised, but he looks perfectly happy.

'But I am special!' he says emphatically.

'Let's have some more, let's have some more,' says Lucas, shaking some more drugs out of the wrap. They're all being so annoying: how rude would it be to go to bed and read *Grazia*? 'Come on, Anna,' says Lucas, 'get with the programme.' They all look at me expectantly.

'I think I might have a bit of a cold coming on.' I gesture uselessly at my nose. 'You know, with the rain and everything.'

'The rain!' cries Becky. 'Poor Anna, it was all a bit wild out there. Promise me you're glad you came.'

'I promise,' I tell her dully.

'Let's play a game!' she shrieks, patently unable to control her verbal diarrhoea. 'Let's say what we thought of each other when we first met.'

The fascinating news emerges that Becky thought Lucas was 'sexy' and Harry was 'handsome' on first en-counter. She thought I 'seemed kind' and 'unusual' which doesn't strike me as particularly flattering. Harry's as drunk as a skunk by now, and clamours to go next.

'Foxy!' he says, pointing unsteadily at Becky, who giggles naughtily.

'Clever,' he says, smiling at me. Oh great. 'And gorgeous, obviously!' Then, pointing at Lucas, 'My best mate.'

'Cheers, Harry,' says Lucas, all drug-sincere. 'You're my best mate too.' They bear hug, leaving attractive sweat patches on each other's clothing. I'm praying they'll leave me out, but no such luck.

'Becky seemed really –' I pause, trying and failing to think of a vaguely interesting way to answer the question – 'glam.' She looks at me expectantly, desperate for more validation. 'And pretty, and welcoming.' Now I really have run out of steam. I look at Harry next, thinking how much I don't want to boil my feelings down to a sound bite. I sort of fudge it, blandly saying how gorgeous he looked when I spied him across the room. My first impression seems so irrelevant now. Then it's Lucas; louche, unpredictable Lucas. 'Sophisticated,' I say, 'and driven.'

He smirks at me. 'Give me more, Anna, give me more!'

My brain freezes over. How did Becky play this? 'Well, sexy of course,' I gabble nervously, although it's the last thing I mean.

By now it's almost 3 a.m. and I'm flagging. I ask if anyone would mind if I went to bed, and they all implore me to stay up. But I'm determined and give them each a hug in turn.

'I'm so glad I met you,' slurs Becky. 'I feel like you're one of my best friends.'

'Yeah, me too,' I say awkwardly, feeling a stab of anguish about Polly.

'I'll be up soon,' says Harry, as I kiss his smoky mouth.

Lucas follows me out, needing a pee, and offers to put the top hall lights on for me. I'm kind of grateful, as the long corridors make me feel like I'm in a gothic potboiler, but he follows a little too closely for my liking. When we reach the top he snakes his arms round my waist.

'Aren't you going to give me a goodnight kiss?'

'I did, didn't I?'

'Not a proper one, not a really friendly one.'

I sort of twist my face away, and try to step backward, but I'm met with wall. What do I do? If I scream I'll seem like an idiot, and anyway, I doubt anyone will hear.

'Don't be like that, Anna. You've always thought I'm sexy, you said so yourself, and I know you'd be really filthy.'

That really pisses me off. I try to shove my way out of his unwelcome embrace, but it just seems to excite him.

'Ooh, wriggly. I like it.' He pushes his sour-tasting mouth against mine and tries to force his tongue in. I feel a wave of panic rise up, which finally gives me the guts to knee him in the groin. While he's doubled over in pain I race off down the dark corridor.

'I'm going to pretend that didn't just happen,' I shout, blood pounding in my ears.

'I was only having a laugh with you,' he snarls. 'Jesus!'

I toss and turn in the creaky bed, wondering what the hell to do. Should I tell Harry? Nothing much happened, and Lucas *was* completely off his face. Is it worth the potential heartbreak it could cause Becky – not to mention how upset Harry might be. Oh God, what if Lucas says I'm lying? Or says I kissed him? They've all known each other for so long – I couldn't handle it if it turned into a 'my word against his' situation. I wish so much that I could share the whole sorry mess with the girls. Nothing ever seemed as cataclysmic when there were three of us sharing the load.

Five a.m. comes and goes and there's still no sign of Harry. He arrives when the sun's coming up, and immediately tries to get frisky, but luckily the drugs and booze have taken their toll and he's soon comatose. I eventually manage to drop off, waking at 8.30 with a terrible hangover and a guilty conscience. Was it my fault for saying he was sexy? Have I given him any reason to think I was up for it?

I pad down to the silent kitchen and make myself a cup of tea. Mark's texted back to say they're struggling to find anyone at all, so even a late shift would help them out. My brain starts whirring as I think about how much they need my help and how much I'm dreading today. I head out the back door and wander around the never-ending grounds, chancing upon the ivy-covered folly where Becky and Lucas are due to tie the knot. Would I want to know if I was her?

Once it hits midday, and there's still no sign of life, I decide to take my chances. I tell a groggy Harry that Mark and Amy have had a crisis and desperately need my help. He's too half asleep to take on board that I'm leaving, but I decide that it's kinder to desert him like this, rather than muddling through the consequences of what's just happened.

Pulling away in a cab, I cast a final look at the glorious house, wondering if it's the last time I'll lay eyes on it.

22

'MERKIN. That's twelve points, and with the double word score it's twenty-four.'

'Merkin?'

'Yes.' I pause, slightly embarrassed. 'It's a pubic wig.'

The Sunday train service meant it took me hours to get back from the country, so by the time I got to Mark and Amy's they'd already left for her mum's. Tom was holding the fort, but rather than disappearing off, he cracked open a bottle of wine for us to share. So here we are, playing Scrabble, Freddie long since in bed. What I didn't warn him about is that the Christie family didn't get a television until 1984. And even then it was a tiny little black and white affair, with a set-top aerial and the fuzziest picture known to man. With nothing else to do, we played endless board games, hence the fact that I'm insanely good at Scrabble. No one outside my immediate family can beat me: my knowledge of obscure words is second to none. Poor old Tom, he doesn't stand a chance. He's peering hopelessly at his letters, distractedly pushing his straggly dark hair out of his face and straining for inspiration.

'TRAIN. That's five, but the N's making NO so that's seven.'

'Hopeless,' I say, bossily reaching for his stand. 'Can I look at your letters?'

'Er, no!' He pulls it away from me. 'It kind of defeats the purpose.'

I find myself pulling on his sleeve, trying to get a better look, but then I draw back sharply. After my hideous encounter with Lucas I'm feeling über-sensitive. What did he mean about me being filthy? The idea that Harry's been sharing graphic sexual details is bad enough, but if I'm exuding some kind of lascivious musk that I don't know about that's even worse. Surely I'm not that kind of girl?

'OK then. Seven points. Which gives you a generous total of nineteen.'

'What have you got?'

'Fifty-six.'

'Fuck! All right.' He turns his stand, hands thrown up in defeat. 'Do your worst.'

I pore over his letters for all of ten seconds. 'Tom, you've got a seven letter! With the C and the G you can do TRACING. So with your extra fifty points, and the C on the double, you've got sixty-five.'

'God, I'm good. Are you getting nervous?'

'Oh yeah, I'm really nervous.'

He seems happier somehow, so much less raw than he was at that terrible dinner, and I find myself wondering why. Is it simply the passage of time, or is there someone new on the scene? As he crosses the room to get me a refill the question pops out of my mouth.

'Christ, no. Maybe I should just cut my losses and start

using the Internet. Try to find a way to say that I'm "scruffy and fat" which isn't "scruffy and fat".'

'You're not fat!' I say, which is true. He's got one of those big, burly bodies that makes you feel like he could wrestle an alligator. 'How about physically imposing and sartorially creative?'

'You're good.'

'You bet I'm good,' I say, putting down VULVA on the triple for forty-one points.

'What is wrong with you?' asks Tom, and I blush scarlet. Maybe this is what Lucas picked up on: am I sex-obsessed? Tom gives me a sideways smile, clocking my embarrassment. 'I'm joking, Anna!'

Still, I make sure the rest of my words are incredibly tame. Things like 'saucer' and 'cloud'. Tame or not, I romp home with a clear hundred-point margin.

'Good game,' he says, shaking my hand solemnly. 'I'm glad I let you win.' He gently asks whether the Polly and Adam situation's improved and I feel myself start to wobble. I consider blurting out the whole sorry tale of my weekend, but it seems disloyal to tell him about Lucas when I haven't even told Harry. Not that Harry sounds like he wants to hear from me at all right now. When I called from the train he didn't sound remotely impressed by my excuse.

'Hey, I'm sorry, I didn't mean to pry.'

'No, no. It's all still completely screwy, since you ask.'

'It's none of my business, and I know you've got this Harry character now, but you look like someone who could do with having their mates around.'

'What, you mean I look uggers?'

'No, you look ... lovely.' There's a slightly awkward pause. I hope he doesn't think I was fishing for a compliment. 'You just seem a bit like a woman on the verge of a nervous breakdown.' He grins. 'I don't mean that literally, but maybe you need to just call Polly? It might not be as bad as you think.'

But of course it's more complicated than that. I take a deep breath and tell him all about my bare-faced lying, testing out how horrified he'll be. To my surprise he roars with laughter.

'I fucking hate those control freak alpha mummies. No wonder you lied to her. They're the worst thing about the school playground.'

I'm insanely comforted by the fact that he doesn't recoil in disgust. He seems so bloody decent, and yet he's seen me injure Freddie horribly and heard about my treachery without dropping me like a stone.

'Who do you miss most: her or him?'

What a sad question, and yet what a brilliant one.

'I miss them differently I suppose. I miss the fact that now Adam and I are over there's no one there who remembers all the little, boring things we did together as well as the big events. I mean if I recounted all those small details to anyone else they'd die of boredom, but they were the texture of our life. And as for Polly, I'm still in denial.' Can I stop talking about myself for one second? He must think I'm so self-obsessed. 'What about Maggie?' I ask him.

'It was so horrible by the end that it's hard to miss her.'

I'm suddenly reminded of the strapping fitness instructor who spirited her away. No wonder he feels fat. 'But when I look at the kids it's like they're a living reminder of what was good between us. I could never regret marrying her.'

'But what if you'd met someone who you would've gone the distance with? Had kids with them instead?'

'But they wouldn't be Belle and Joe. They'd be these hypothetical brats who wouldn't be as good. That's the awful thing about parenthood. However much you try to avoid being smug, you always think your kids are the best in the world.'

Maybe there's no such thing as a mistake, just a decision you haven't re-framed yet.

'You'll meet someone else anyway, I'm sure,' I say, and then, thinking how horribly patronizing I sound, blunder into faux irony. 'You're a hot ticket!'

'Yeah, maybe I will, but the kids have to be my number-one priority.' He laughs. 'Between them and the business there's not much time left for cruising for chicks. Let alone chicks who can handle sharing me with them every second weekend.'

I suddenly realize how late it is. I've lost myself in the world according to Tom, avoiding the inevitable moment where I have to speak to Harry. He's dumped a couple of my calls, and although it bodes ill for his mood, I've been quietly relieved. Despite current form, I'm the worst liar in the whole wide world and I'm panicking about him instantly divining that something's up.

He's on the motorway, which means that I'm stuck on crackly loudspeaker.

'Nice of you to call,' he snaps sarcastically, displaying a sulkiness I've never witnessed before.

'I'm really sorry, but Mark and Amy were totally desperate. She's having such a hideous time . . .'

'Yeah well, I thought you'd told them you had commitments.'

I fight down a wave of irritation at his petulance.

'Why don't you come by on your way back? You'll pretty much drive past my parents if you go on the North Circular.' I try for minxy: we've always had sex in our favour. 'I'll make it up to you.'

'I've got to get up at six. There's no way I can do that.'

Infuriating though my parents are, his subtle resistance to seeing me on home turf is starting to get to me.

'I'll come to you then.'

'Don't bother, Anna. Let's just see each other when I get back.'

He's shooting in New York this week, so I won't see him till at least Thursday. Partly I'm relieved to gain a few days' grace, but I'm also left bereft at the thought of leaving it like this. How dare Lucas put me in this position?

'I'll miss you.'

'Yeah, clearly,' he replies tersely, pretty much hanging up on me.

That night I can't sleep a wink. I'm tossing and turning, worrying about whether or not to expose Lucas for the snake he is. As a result I'm outrageously late for work on Monday morning. I try to sneak into the office incognito,

234

but eagle-eyed Jocasta spots me emerging from the lift.

'Good news,' she cries, sailing across the floor. 'Dr Neil Fox has been in touch to say that he'd be thrilled to sit on the panel.'

'He's not called Dr Neil Fox, Jocasta. He's not a doctor anyway, it's a nickname.' My voice rises with irrational rage. 'It's just Dr Fox. Or plain old Neil Fox.'

'Quite. Anyway, I'm planning to take him for lunch tomorrow. As you've so amply demonstrated, the personal touch can work wonders.'

I give her a chilly smile, and head for my desk to order a hundredweight more raw fish. Hopefully she'll be struck down with mercury poisoning. This event is mutating into a hideous amalgamation of me and Jocasta's clashing concepts, which can only spell disaster.

I can't stop obsessing about what I should do. I keep picturing Harry and Lucas's fervent hugging, thinking how much I want to preserve the friendship: losing your bosom buddy is no laughing matter. Not to mention the potential devastation it'll cause Becky. I get the feeling that the worst thing that's ever happened to her is the Fendi baguette bag selling out before she got her hands on one, and I'm not too keen on being the person who introduces her to the school of hard knocks.

I'm shaken out of my reverie by the shrill ring of my phone. It's Steve, calling to tell me how hot Harry is.

'You've well and truly pulled.' He stops to think. 'I mean that in the nicest possible way.'

I laugh. 'So the shoot went well then?'

'Yeah, he's kind of wild, isn't he?'

'What, do you mean by wild?'

'Well, I think the photos will be quite outré.'

'Outré how?'

'Oh, you should probably talk to him,' he says hurriedly. 'He's obviously got a vision for it all.'

I must ask Harry to show me some proofs. He says he wants to finish the staggered shoots and then assemble them as a story, but perhaps I need to force his hand. Come to think of it, he's doing another set of shots with Becky and Lucas on Friday: perhaps I can see those. Let's hope there's no unavoidable social arrangement in place for the evening. Either way, I won't be able to postpone my next interview with them much longer. There's no way this situation's going to disappear without trace.

Poring over my diary for potential excuses, I realize that I've marked Friday as an egg transfer day for Susie. She scrawled them all in, hoping it would give us an excuse to go for afternoon tea – the world's most civilized meal – on the days prior. I'm suddenly struck by the ridiculousness of this whole situation. I don't want to get sucked up whole by Harry's life, and lose hold of my own in the process. I need to claw it back with my bare hands, rather than pathetically watching it walk out the door. Tom's right, I should just call. I'll start with Suse and then try to swallow my useless, misplaced pride and ring Polly. I'm steeling myself as I wait for it to ring, remembering how fearsome she was last time we spoke. Maybe I should've withheld my number in case she dumps my call. Quite the opposite: she snatches it up on the first ring.

'Anna?' she says, audibly choked.

'What is it?'

'Thanks . . . thanks for ringing.' And with that she gives in to a bout of hysterical sobs. Hearing Susie, easily the calmest person I know, break down like that sends a wave of panic through me.

'Tell me what happened,' I urgently demand.

It turns out that two of the embryos implanted on the first transfer, and she had two heart-stopping weeks of pregnancy. She sat around at home sipping herbal tea and willing them to make themselves at home.

'And then I just started bleeding.' She starts sobbing again, but at least I can give her a hug now. I feigned a migraine and jumped in a cab, and now we're huddled together on her sofa. 'And they're gone, like it never happened. I mean what's the point?' Her eyes flash with anger, and I detect a bitterness in her that's never been there before.

'Of course there's a point: at least you know now that you can get pregnant. Lots of people never even get that far.'

'But if you never get that far you never have to go through this, feel this hopeless.'

'You can't think like that,' I counter, suddenly feeling a sense of role reversal. Who's Pollyanna now? 'You managed it once, and you'll manage it again.' I pause: what right do I have to tell her how she should feel? 'You're being incredibly brave.'

'What, better to have loved and lost you mean?' she says, smiling sadly.

'Exactly,' I agree, and then wonder if I live my own advice. 'Oh God, what do I know? I've never had to go through anything this bad.'

Susie's suddenly weeping again, apologizing for being so narky last time we spoke. It seems so irrelevant now. Sitting next to her like this I know that I have to mend it with Polly, whatever it takes. I wish she was here beside me right now. She's way better in a crisis.

'Sorry, Suse, I'm so bloody inadequate.'

'You're not inadequate,' protests Susie, scrunching up yet another Kleenex.

'I feel like I haven't lived enough to know what you're going through, that's all. I'm such an infant. No one's ever died, or even left me.'

'I'm the infant here, Anna. I've always been so bloody simplistic. You know, good girls get rewarded. If you floss your teeth and return your library books on time then it'll all work out. Newsflash –' she lobs a balled-up tissue into the bin like she's Michael Jordan shooting hoops – 'it's total bollocks!'

I look at her in slight disbelief. How could she ever believe that when she's navigating her way through a world as jagged and unpredictable as this? And, more importantly, how can she think that Wet Martin's any kind of reward? But it's patently the wrong moment to engender an existential crisis.

'Tell me fun things, Anna. Things that won't make my nose run.'

And I tell her about the curse of Dr Fox and the prawn vol-au-vents. When she asks if Harry's getting me through, the whole sorry Lucas mess comes tumbling out. It's such a relief to finally get it off my chest. To my surprise she tells me to keep schtum, that coming clean will cause too much grief. New Susie is way more cynical.

'Are we going to get to meet Harry on your birthday?'

'Oh, don't even go there.' I'm hanging on to thirty-two by my fingernails: only ten days to go. 'It's such a nothing one, and everything's so weird. I'm not sure if I can face it.'

'Please, Anna, for me. I'm desperate for an excuse to go out and forget about everything. Anyway, I bet I know what you're secretly longing to do.'

And she does of course: karaoke, my all-time favourite leisure activity. A karaoke booth is the only place I know where it's socially acceptable to love Bonnie Tyler. Maybe a night of unbridled wailing is the perfect way to say goodbye to the sticky mess of my thirty-second year.

23

So I'm back on the doorstep of Becky's palatial apartment block, thinking how much has happened since Harry first jammed me up against the wall and snogged me senseless. He's spent today taking more shots of the golden couple and, as I had feared, there was no way out of us spending the evening together. Besides, as far as he's concerned I've got a lot of making up to do. I'm gratified to hear Becky's friendly sounding tone through the intercom, but how different would she be if she knew the truth?

'I'm so sorry,' I tell her, thrusting a bottle of pink champagne into her hands.

'Oh, don't worry about it, darling,' she says, giving me one of her all-enveloping hugs. I start out stiff and rigid, but then I find myself melting into her pillowy embrace. I've got such chest envy: there's something almost mystical about those magnificent bazookas. Maybe if I whispered the truth about Lucas into the depths of her cleavage it would rise up into her subconscious and she'd spontaneously chuck him without me having to take the rap.

Last night I borrowed Greg's ancient Morris Traveller to surprise Harry at the airport. The fact that I'd taken my life into my own hands by puttering down the M4 at forty miles an hour, being cut up by furious Porsche drivers, went some way to convincing him that I was remorseful. I waited outside arrivals with a bunch of balloons, and covered his face in kisses. I stuck to my guns with my excuse, and he seems pretty much over it, but I'm still on my best behaviour.

'Hello, Anna,' says Lucas, giving me one of those cold double kisses and I see Harry raise his eyebrows at me. Oh God: do I have to? 'I'm so sorry I rushed off like that,' I say mechanically, trying to give him a private death stare, 'but there was a bit of a crisis.' I'm hoping he'll be suitably mortified, but the cheeky bastard seems to be enjoying it. Maybe it's his idea of verbal S and M.

He looks faux downcast. 'That's OK, Anna. We were very disappointed though.'

'Oh, Luke, don't be such a drama queen!' pipes up Becky, giving him one of her coquettish little smacks. 'Duty called, and Anna had to respond.' I fix my eyes on a point on the wall, unable to look at anyone. Unfortunately my gaze hits some kind of trendy nude sculpture, which probably gives Lucas even more reason to think I'm a sex-crazed dilettante. I blush red and look away, managing to lock eyes with him.

'Are you hot?' he smirks.

'No,' I snap, 'I'm absolutely fine,' buttoning my cardigan up to the neck and excusing myself for an unnecessary pee.

Becky's achieved the impossible: making lentils interesting. She's constructed some incredibly healthy and delicious puy lentil salad and we all sit round her big kitchen table tucking in. To a fly on the wall it would look like the perfect urban fairy tale, but from where I'm sitting it's pure torture. What I really wanted to do tonight was get screamingly drunk with Polly. We met for coffee on Wednesday, and started to grope our way back to normality. As soon as she came through the door, so nervous and so familiar, I knew in my gut that I had to try to forgive her. In that moment I knew that a future without her in it would be infinitely bleaker than a future without either Adam or Harry. Does that make me a commitment-phobe fuck-up? I don't know. Either way, it's definitely time to seal the deal with an old-fashioned night of cocktails and girlish chit-chat – though I'm not sure I can process too much information about her and Adam. However much of an irrelevancy our sex life became – or perhaps because it did – the idea of hearing about their lusty antics is too much to bear. I've decided to deal with it all in one hit by inviting them to my birthday karaoke as a couple. I'm hoping my supreme maturity will curry favour with Adam, and the alcoholic haze will power me through the weirdness of us spending my birthday with our new partners. Polly promises me he's calmed down, and the fact that I've found a solicitor and promised to cover the legal fees has hopefully mollified him.

'Earth to Anna,' says Harry, clocking how disengaged I am. 'Becky's asking you when their next interview is.'

'Oh, soon,' I say, waving my hands vaguely. 'Week after next?'

I really can't afford to put it off that long. The copy will need to be processed in a fortnight, and I urgently need to put all three sets of interviews to bed, but I just can't face it yet. 'So shall we look at the proofs then?' I say hurriedly, avoiding Lucas's covert eyeballing. I'm using their curiosity about their photos as an excuse to overcome Harry's caginess. Steve's comment about him being 'outré' has been quietly panicking me. When he lays them out on the table I'm immediately filled with remorse. He's shot three sets, all in black and white. Each shoot pastiches a different classic film. The first one is *Brief Encounter*, the next takes off the classic still from *Gone With the Wind* and the photos he took today are inspired by *It Happened One Night*. There are only Polaroids for those ones, but they show a perfectly coiffed Becky hanging out of a classic car. Needless to say, she looks stunning in every shot, and the monochrome somehow manages to filter away Lucas's slightly sleazy quality. Becky's moved to tears, and flings her arms round Harry, as per normal.

'Thank you so much. Promise me you'll take my wedding photos.'

'Yeah, of course I will,' says Harry, obviously gratified by our reactions.

'Now it's definitely going to be perfect!' she says, gazing adoringly at both men. I'm suddenly struck by a horrible possibility: maybe they're all swingers and I'm the sad square in the corner. Oh, don't be so ridiculous, Anna.

'Of course it's going to be perfect,' says Lucas, stroking Becky's face.

As long as the angel of doom doesn't destroy it, I

think, feeling even more convinced that exposing the truth would achieve nothing.

Harry opens his mouth in a way that could be perceived as a yawn, and I immediately insist that he needs to get home and sleep off his jet lag. 'Can't wait to get you into bed, mate,' says Lucas, raising his horrible furry brows lasciviously. He's like some kind of evil woodland creature. A stoat maybe.

'But we'll be seeing you next weekend, won't we?' says Harry, as he hugs Becky goodbye.

'Ooh, I hope so. What's the plan?'

You're so not my best friends! I feel like screaming. It's like being trapped in one of those unfunny eighties' sitcoms where the annoying neighbours constantly turn up uninvited.

'Anna's karaoke party.'

Oh no. No, no, no.

'Karaoke! I love karaoke,' squeals Becky, actually jumping up and down on the spot with excitement.

'See you there, birthday girl,' says Lucas, giving me a final, unnecessary squeeze.

So obviously there's no getting out of that one. Now I'm going to be spending my birthday night trapped in a tiny, sweaty little karaoke booth with that wandering-handed tosser. I'm seething with rage for the entire cab journey, trying my hardest to keep my mouth shut. Harry leans back contentedly.

'That was fun, wasn't it?'

'Yes,' replies little Miss Monosyllable.

'They think you're brilliant.'

'Yeah, they're great,' I say, through gritted teeth.

'You and Becky really should have a night out on your own some time. She doesn't have that many girlfriends. I dunno why really.'

I'm deeply suspicious of women who don't have female friends. What's wrong with them? Obviously women are the superior sex. Once you've got past the inevitable internal investigation into where you stand in the pecking order, there's nothing more reassuring than the accepting gaze of a woman you respect.

I don't say any of that to Harry of course. Instead I force myself to nuzzle into his chest and tell him how fabulous his photographs are. We're still talking about them when we arrive back at his flat. 'I just love working with Becks and Luke,' he says, pouring us each a big glass of red. 'In fact, there's something else I want to show you.' I'm ready to crawl into bed and say a fervent good-bye to Friday night, but his jet lag's making him strangely hyper. He rifles through his DVDs, pulling out a black case triumphantly. 'I've hardly shown this to anyone, Anna. I hope you like it.'

It turns out to be a short film that he and Lucas collaborated on a few summers earlier. 'It's a kind of mini romantic comedy,' he says, although I struggle to find any romance or comedy within it. Still, at least I finally get to meet 'The Brazilian'. She's dark and intense, and spends the film walking through London parks, picking up strange men and going on mini dates. 'Love is a dangerous game in which there can be no winners,' she tells one as she moodily feeds ducks. 'Sex has brought us together but it will tear us apart,' she tells another as she mounts him in a toilet cubicle. Jarring electro-chords reach a crescendo as she pulls the chain whilst overacting an orgasm. 'I composed the music,' Harry proudly announces, and I give his knee a pat, unable to muster up an appropriate compliment. At the end of the film she's seen passionately kissing a girl who works in the park café, while all her random encounters line up mournfully next to a hedge. 'She's a lesbian all along!' says Harry gleefully, as though it justifies the whole incomprehensible mess.

'Right, I see,' I tell him, groping for the right response. 'Um, it looks fantastic.' And it sort of does, it's all black and white and brooding, like an incredibly expensive perfume ad. It's just a shame it doesn't make any sense: how the hell does Lucas make a living as a writer? I can't help but ask Harry, framing it in the context of him having 'a very unusual style'.

'Oh, well, he hasn't got much off the ground as yet. This is a bit of a calling card for him.'

Good luck with that, I think, uncharitably thrilled that he's so talentless.

'I thought he had a script that was looking really promising?'

'Yeah, he's got a feature which Becky's dad's probably going to fund as a tax write-off.'

Now it's all falling into place. The talentless little twat has really landed on his feet with her.

'Do you promise you like it?' says Harry eagerly. 'I'd love to do some more directing when I've got a bit of time. I'm thinking of sending it to a few agents.'

'Yeah, you should,' I say, wondering when I stopped telling anyone the truth about anything. But taking in his proud glow I can't face bursting his bubble.

Anyway, what do I know? Perhaps the film really is a work of staggering genius. That's the problem with creative endeavour – it's so hard to be objective about your own efforts. Right now I'm stubbornly insisting on making the wedding event as subversive and sexy as I possibly can, determined to kick Jocasta's light jazz version into touch. I'm capitalizing on the fact that she's spent most of the week out of the office trawling potential schools for Percy with her chinless husband. The imminence of his common entrance means she's getting more and more uptight, leaving her little time to keep me on the leash. She even asked Ruby to postpone her lunch with Dr Fox, so we've moved it to a Tuesday two weeks hence in the hope he'll finally get the message. I only hope my self-belief pays off. The price I'm paying is brought home to me when I run into Doreen in the canteen. She's piling her plate up with chips, and barely looks up to say hello.

'Doreen, I'm so sorry about ... I just needed something a bit different for this issue. You know I loved working with you all ... um, love working with you, I mean.'

'It's fine, Anna. You've always known what you want, haven't you?' She sounds so icy, every vestige of her motherly warmth extinguished.

'Doreen ...' I'm choked, suddenly aware of how much I look for little fragments of my ideal parents in other people. Now I've actually seen her, throwing her off the issue seems far worse than it did when it was just a disembodied conversation. She sweeps off with a majestic imperiousness I've never seen before, and I creep back over to the table I'm sharing with Ruby. Luckily she's a pragmatist.

'Look, Anna, the photos are great. The end justifies the means.' I showed her the proofs this morning, and she was as blown away by them as I was. Now an equally impressed Roger's taken them away to show to Victor. 'Anyway, she's going to have to forgive you, she's got no choice. We'll be back working with her in a few weeks.'

I'm trying to block that bit out of my mind. The last couple of months has been such a whirlwind and I'm not sure I can survive being plunged back into debating Venetian blinds versus curtains. Ruby gives my hand a comforting squeeze.

'What are you up to Saturday?' I impulsively ask her.

'Not sure. Why?'

And before I know it I've invited her to karaoke. She can contribute to the human shield I'm trying to construct between me and Lucas. And you never know, maybe she'll fancy Tom. She recently told me that her ideal man was Kevin Spacey, so she's clearly got eccentric taste in older men.

'What's he like? Is he sexy?'

Now there's a question. 'It's hard to say, because he's not my type. He's funny, which is a definite plus. And he's not weedy, he's a proper bloke.'

248

'What do you mean, a proper bloke?'

'He just gets on with it, you know. He doesn't faff around being tortured about everything.'

'You're not really selling him, Anna.'

'Just see what you think.'

What I don't tell her is that I'm now dreading the whole event, silently cursing myself for letting Susie talk me into it. Don't get me wrong, I love to sing, but there are so many random, tense-making aspects of my life coming together. I wake up on the morning of it to Karen and Greg warbling 'Happy Birthday' through the bedroom door. There's brown toast and tea in bed and a small pile of presents.

'Aren't you going to open them?' says Karen eagerly.

I get ready to arrange my features into the right shape. They mean so well, but their choices of gift tend to be wide of the mark. Like the time I asked for a 'My Little Pony' stable and got a card telling me that they'd sponsored an abandoned donkey on my behalf. Or the Christmas they decided that everyone should pick themselves a book from the Oxfam shop and the money we'd saved would go to Ethiopia: Dan literally cried until New Year's Eve. This year they've given me some earthy brown soap, reminiscent of cow dung, a John Pilger book and a pashmina. Karen's quite keen on buying me clothes she deems fashionable, but she's always at least five years out. I swear she gave me a 'Frankie Says Relax' T-shirt for the millennium Christmas. There's also a twenty-pound Marks and Spencer voucher from Dan and Julia, perfect for replenishing my supply of pop socks.

'Do you like them?' says Karen anxiously, draping the pashmina around my pyjamas.

Inappropriate though they are, I'm struck by how much they want me to love my gifts and the effort that's gone into the wrapping.

'Yeah, they're great,' I say warmly, 'thank you.'

'We got some more good news today,' adds Greg, grinning broadly. 'They're dropping the charges against me!'

'That's fantastic,' I tell him, feeling a surge of relief flood through me. I didn't realize how anxious I was about it till I heard he was in the clear. I give them each a big hug and excuse myself to get dressed.

I'm not meeting Harry until lunchtime, as he's flying back from yet another trip. In a weird way I was quite relieved not to wake up with him this morning. I always feel quite ambivalent about my birthday – the anti-capitalist family message made them something of an anti-climax – and I didn't want him to think it was personal. It's also one of those mornings when the absence of Adam hits me full force. He'd always construct some fancy-schmancy breakfast for me – eggs Benedict with Buck's Fizz perhaps – and then complain I was dropping crumbs on the sheets. He's a brilliant present buyer too, which helped me finally overcome my childhood gift anxiety. I wonder if he's feeling a twinge this morning, or if he's too wrapped up in his relationship with Polly to care? It's so hard to know, and perhaps better that I don't.

*

Harry's outside smoking a roll-up when I arrive, and stubs it out guiltily like I'm his headmistress. He flings his arms round me as he guides me into the restaurant.

'Another year more beautiful,' he declares, and I laugh.

'You've got all the best lines,' I tell him, reaching across the table for the small pile of gifts that he's stacked up. 'All in good time,' he says, pulling them away, and handing me a glass of champagne. 'God, they'll have to be more on the money than my parents',' I tell him, describing their haphazard selection. He laughs.

'Have you invited them tonight?'

'No! Are you insane?'

And then I remember that he's freakishly close to his mum, an ex-model who was widowed very young. He keeps promising to introduce me to her, but it never quite happens.

'You really hate it there, don't you?'

'No I don't, part of me appreciates having this time with them. I mean, it's not something you ever get once you're a grown-up. But I guess I'd appreciate it more if I knew when it was going to be over. I really need to sort something out soon.'

Two glasses of champagne down the line Harry finally allows me to open my gifts. Displaying his usual impeccable taste, he's given me some stylishly dirty underwear and a gorgeous necklace.

'Let's go back and see them in action,' he mutters in my ear as I unwrap the knickers in full view of our waiter. Blushing, I bundle them into my handbag and let him deal with hailing a cab.

We spend a delicious afternoon in bed, and I emerge about five to start reconstructing my 33-year-old face. I peer at it critically in the mirror, preparing to go into battle with every unguent in my armoury. Did I always have those subtle but undeniable creases around my eyes, or are they new in town? Are vitamin injections organic-sounding enough not to count? I never want to have Botox – it seems like the height of vanity – but I can't bear to stand by and watch my face crumple and crevice before my very eyes. Harry appears behind me at the mirror, slinging a lazy arm round my waist and kissing my neck.

'Don't get up.'

'I've got to, Harry. I've got to go back to my parents' and get changed.'

He looks momentarily sullen. 'I thought we were spending the whole day together.'

'We did, and now it's dusk. I'm really sorry, I should've brought my stuff with me.'

'This is stupid,' he says emphatically. 'You're here all the time, you don't want to be stuck living with them. Move in with me.'

'Come on, Harry, you don't mean that. It's such a big step.'

His eyes bore into me. 'I do mean it.'

And I feel almost frozen with the sweetness of his gesture. In that moment I'm suffused with affection, but also aware of the shock factor inherent in moving in with someone. The odd smells they leave in the bathroom and try to mask with Lynx Oriental, my tendency to

252

accidentally leave toenail clippings on the side of the bath. Not to mention all the anticipation and excitement you lose once you're both available on tap.

'Anna?'

Oh no, here we go again. I can't destroy another relationship because I won't throw myself over the edge. I just hope we won't go from *Romeo and Juliet* to *George and Mildred* without passing Go. I snuggle into his chest.

'I'd love to.'

'You realize I'm a novice at this, don't you?' he says, tugging my hair. 'I've never been able to face it before.'

'You'll be a natural,' I reassure him.

It seems churlish to leave after that, so I decide to live with spending my night in the spotlight in a pair of rather ordinary jeans. In the cab my heart's beating like a snare drum.

'Are you really OK about Adam coming?'

'Course,' says Harry, flashing an easy smile. Oh, to be that laid-back.

We're early, giving me time to order a nerve-stiffening vodka. Polly texts to say that she and Adam are running late, which is something of a relief. The thought of the four of us sitting in this velvet-lined box, desperately groping for conversation, is too cringe-making to bear. Mark and Amy turn up first, with another couple of friends from university. I give her a hug, wondering how she copes with big jolly occasions. Can she really zone out from what's going on, or does it hit her in waves and undercut everything? Obviously I don't ask her anything so depressing; instead I treat her to the privilege of picking the first number. 'Are you sure?' she says. 'It is your birthday,' before relenting and choosing 'Electric Dreams'.

'Is Tom still coming?' I ask Mark.

'Oh yeah, he's gone out for dinner first. I thought he was going to ring you and check it was all right to bring someone.'

'Yeah, of course,' I say, feeling slightly put out. 'It's going to be a squeeze though.'

'If it's a hassle I can text and tell him not to come.'

'Don't worry. It'll be fine.'

Our conversation's brought to an abrupt halt by the sight of Amy swaying from side to side with her eyes shut, wailing the chorus of the song. It's like she's stranded in a parallel universe. Harry, a karaoke virgin, subtly covers his ears. 'I'm not sure if I can take a whole night of this,' he whispers.

'Pick yourself a song,' I tell him. 'Once you've done it you'll get the bug.'

He scrolls through the on-screen list. 'There's nothing I like here, it's a load of shit,' he says petulantly. I grab his hands.

'Let's do a duet. How about "Islands in the Stream"? I love Dolly. Or "Don't Go Breaking My Heart". You can be Kiki Dee.'

'I'm all right for now.'

'Oh, OK,' I say, feeling chastened. Just then Polly, Adam and Susie all pile in.

'Happy birthday!' shriek the girls, and hand me a squidgy present. I try to control my shakes as I hug them, locking eyes with Adam over Susie's shoulder. I kiss him hello – one cheek, not two, to tell him my affection's genuine – and hope that the lighting means no one will notice how pale I am. He gives me a half smile.

'Hi, Anna,' he says, refusing to hold my gaze. Polly's self-consciously talking to Susie, watching out of the corner of her eye. It's raining outside and Adam's hair is sticking up in odd clumps. I want to break the ice by teasing him about it, but it feels way too intimate.

'Thanks for coming,' I say, feeling tripped up by the combination of alienation and familiarity. Just then Harry appears.

'Are you going to introduce me?' he says, slightly prickly. Adam pumps Harry's hand up and down, desperately overcompensating for the awkwardness of the situation. I remember in a flash how unsure of himself he is, and how simultaneously endearing and irritating it always was. It's inevitably the faults we share ourselves that grate the most. Luckily the circle of hell is broken up by the arrival of Horst.

'Anna, I am so happy to see you! I bring you a gift.' He's brandishing the best present of the night: *The Best Driving Album … Ever!* It's full of those bands from the seventies with terrible names – Styx, Rainbow, Sad Café – and features all their most anthemic numbers. That's the problem with living with someone; they're privy to all your dirtiest little vices. Horst knows I'll love it, but I'll have to make sure I play it well out of Harry's earshot.

Ruby turns up next, casting a nervous glance around a room filled with strangers.

'Thanks so much for coming!' I tell her. 'Though I've got a horrible feeling Tom's bringing a date.'

'Oh, don't worry about it,' she says, just as Horst comes leaping across the room to offer her a drink. Oh God, how inevitable. As he bears her off, I give her a sympathetic smile, but I'm too busy to rescue her. Spying Becky and Lucas arriving I decide it's time to avail myself of the facilities, and force Polly and Susie to sing 'No Scrubs' by TLC with me. Could we be more embarrassing? The sound of three middle-class north London girls trying to rap along convincingly with three black Americans is almost too painful to describe. The fact that we're doing a peculiar swaying dance only serves to compound the horror. We're in full flow when Tom comes striding through the door with a petite brunette. God, she's pretty. She's got a sleek bob, and is wearing one of those Chinesey dresses, which perfectly defines the hourglass of her curves. Surely she can't be a mum? There's no trace of tummy. She's out-glammed me to the power of ten. I instinctively look for Harry, but he's determinedly ignoring the sorry spectacle of my performance, concentrating intensely on Becky and Lucas. I break away to go and greet Tom.

'Singing and Scrabble, you're one multi-talented lady.'

'What can I say?'

I suddenly panic that his, his what – girlfriend, date – will think I'm flirting.

'Hello, I'm Anna,' I gabble. 'Would you like a glass of champagne? I'm sure there's a bottle going round.'

'Thanks, but I'll be fine with some cranberry juice,' she

says, with a self-deprecating laugh. 'I'm actually allergic to alcohol.' She proffers her hand. 'I'm Louisa by the way.'

Oh, so this is the Louisa he mentioned all those weeks ago. Was he lying when he told me he was still on his own? 'Allergic to alcohol?' I say, trying to keep the disbelief out of my voice. 'That must be great. No hangovers! I always seem to be crawling out of bed with a furry tongue praying for some Nurofen.' That's an attractive image, Anna.

'No, none of that.'

'Great! Well, I'll go and order you a cranberry juice then.'

'Let me give you your card first,' says Tom, thrusting it into my hand, along with a present. The card's got the Teletubbies on it, and he's added an extra '3' to the 'I am 3' badge on the front. 'Very funny,' I say, remembering how I tried to get him to explain to me how he could bear to watch them the day we took Freddie to the hospital. Inside Louisa's scrawled her name under his, which I find unreasonably annoying. It's not her joke after all. I put the present on the embarrassingly large pile that's mounting up, and go off to find her drink.

Harry grabs me as I'm coming past, and pulls me over to Becky and Lucas.

'Hey, I've hardly seen you.'

'It's just all these people,' I say, before submitting myself to Lucas's unwelcome embrace. They've given me a dove grey wash bag, which I'm convinced is a free gift from a first-class flight.

'Are you going to have a go?' I say, pointing at Horst, who is, truth be told, not a great advertisement for karaoke. He's belting out 'The Final Countdown' by Europe, stamping his feet in time with the bass line and shaking his head vigorously. Ruby's laughing her head off.

'Do you want me to?' says hateful Lucas.

'Yes, of course,' I reply primly. 'It's the whole point of the party. But you've got to get Harry up there with you.'

'I was actually a chorister when I was at school,' Lucas tells me. 'I've got a very wide vocal range.'

'I know what would be perfect!' says Becky, dragging them both off to the machine.

I look for Louisa so I can give her her drink. She's standing with Mark and Amy, snuggling into Tom's bear-like embrace. 'So that's Harry, is it?' he asks as I hover on the side of the group.

'That's him,' I say, as a high, reedy noise starts up. Oh my God, Harry and Lucas are attempting the choral intro to 'You Can't Always Get What You Want'. I whoop with laughter and give them a clap, earning myself a stern glare from Lucas who clearly takes his vocal efforts incredibly seriously.

'Harry's really tasty,' says Polly, drunkenly appearing at my elbow.

'I know,' I say, trying to make eye contact with him, but he's concentrating fiercely on channelling Mick Jagger.

'I really want another go,' slurs Polly, 'but there are too many other people!'

'Come on then,' I say, determined to reforge the bond between us. I bossily force her to the front of the queue, handing her the microphone with a flourish.

Before I know it she's belting out the opening bars of 'Nobody Does it Better', pointing shakily at Adam and pouting while she does it. Oh God, I should've known better than to facilitate this. As she hurtles towards the chorus she's reaching maximum volume: windows are surely shattering across the capital. I steal a glance at Adam, convinced he'll be mortified, only to find that he's giving her an indulgent smile. I look back at her, stunned to see the sincerity that shines through the drunken exterior. She's madly in love with him. It's too weird. How did all the pieces of my life get jumbled up in such an unrecognizable way? I don't want to begrudge them their happiness, but I'm really not sure if I can handle this. I go and shut myself in the loo and desperately try to gather my thoughts. I give up on that sharpish, and go in search of someone foolhardy enough to do tequila shots with me. I'm clearly nowhere near drunk enough.

I blunder back through the door to be greeted by the sight of Louisa and Tom swaying along to their very own cover of 'Islands in the Stream'. Not only is Louisa as tight and springy as an elastic band, she can also sing in tune! And she's got a boyfriend who's prepared to sing Dolly Parton with her. I glower at Harry, but he doesn't seem to notice. In fact, why would he: it's such an unreasonable thing to be angry about. I stand there, transfixed. They're holding hands now, injecting their performance with just the right degree of irony.

Tom's voice is as wobbly as it was for 'The Wheels on the Bus' but the fact that he's having so much fun makes his performance oddly charming. When they finish, the entire room gives them a spontaneous round of applause. Who's bloody party is it, anyway? Not Louisa's.

'Who are they?' asks Harry. 'I don't know any of these people.'

'I don't know him that well,' I say for some bizarre reason. 'He's Mark's older brother.'

'He's got a really shit voice.'

'He's just having a laugh, Harry,' I snap, feeling even more irritated by him.

'Just calm down, OK? You're so uptight tonight.'

He strops off to find Becky at the bar, leaving me with Lucas. I try to turn away but he grabs my arm.

'Hey, slow down.'

'Why should I?'

'What's your problem?' he snarls, with a nasty look in his eye. His fingers are welded around my wrist.

'What a stupid question. You're my problem, obviously.' I can feel a flood of rage rising up through my body. 'Why the fuck are you marrying Becky if you can't keep your hands to yourself?'

'Have you ever thought you might be the problem? I know you're probably jealous that she's five years younger than you and she's got a ring on her finger, but it's no reason to try and destroy what we've got.'

'I'm on to you, Lucas. I've seen your dreadful film. You wouldn't have a career if it wasn't for her.'

'Think what you like. She'd be a wreck if she lost me, and your stupid article would be fucked without us giving it some cool.'

I shake him off and storm across the room. The

horrible truth is that he's right. Now the photos are doing the rounds, they've become the centrepiece of the entire supplement. As I'm trying to calm myself down I run into Tom.

'Hey, are you OK? You look stressed.' He looks into my face. 'It's not too much of a car crash, is it?'

Thank God someone appreciates how hard this is. But just as I'm about to respond, Louisa materializes at his elbow like some kind of glamorous munchkin. I've always envied those doll-like women; the fact that they automatically make men feel so butch gives them an unfair advantage.

'Are you having a nice time?' I ask her beadily.

'It's great. I've only ever done it through the Play-Station with the kids.' So she does have children – no wonder they've got so much to talk about. 'But it's far more fun like this.' She takes another dainty sip from her glass, and then suddenly gives way to a violent sneezing fit.

'Are you OK?' says Tom, magicking some tissues out of nowhere.

'Yes, I'll be fine,' she says weakly, sneezing some more. 'I think some vodka might've got into my cranberry juice.'

'Oh no,' I say, hoping I sound sympathetic enough.

Tom runs off to get her some water, grabbing a handful of napkins off the bar. He leads her over to the banquette, where he rubs her back and holds the water glass up to her lips. Horst shakes my gaze away from them.

'Anna, the singing gives me so much pleasure. Perhaps

I will find a rocking band to join up to when my time on the stage is up.'

'That's a brilliant idea, Horst. How's it going with Ruby?'

'She is finding me a drink. I think she is very, very enticing.'

And here she is now, beaming at him. I look around the room, picking out Harry deep in conversation with Lucas. Polly's keeping herself upright by winding her body around Adam's while Mark and Amy slow dance to a Dire Straits song which some fool I don't even recognize has decided to attempt. How in love do you have to be to find Dire Straits romantic? And why the hell am I having the least romantic evening of anyone? Right: I've had enough.

'Horst, I need tequila as a matter of urgency.'

I slam a shot back and march over to the machine. It's my birthday and I'm determined to enjoy it. I page through the songs hazily, suddenly aware of how lethal tequila can be. If Tom can be ironic then so can I: Tight Fit should fit the bill.

'In the jungle,
The quiet jungle,
The lion sleeps tonight.'

Despite the snaky jungle dance I'm doing, I'm not getting much love from my audience. Only Horst seems to be really engaging with my performance, clapping his hands and giving me encouraging thumbs-up signs. As I hit the chorus it occurs to me that I've made a terrible mistake.

'Wimoweh, a-wimoweh, a-wimoweh, a-wimoweh,
A-wimoweh, a-wimoweh, a-wimoweh, a-wimoweh,
We-de-de-de, de-de-de-de-de de, we-um-um-a-way.'

I catch Harry subtly shaking his head while Lucas sniggers into his beer. People are trying to smile encouragingly, but it's clear I'm dying up here.

'Near the village,
The peaceful village,
The lion sleeps tonight . . .'

I'm starting to peter out, not sure I can face the horror of another chorus, but I can't bear to give Lucas the satisfaction of seeing me walk off. Louisa's leaning in close to make Tom hear her, but I somehow manage to catch his eye, giving him a look of quiet humiliation. He jumps up, patting Louisa's shoulder, and grabs the other microphone.

'A wimoweh, a-wimoweh, a-wimoweh, a-wimoweh.'

He's really going for it, his loud, tuneless baritone almost drowning me out. But now there's two of us, the whole thing seems quite funny. I'm laughing, suddenly realizing how seriously I was taking it before. Suddenly everyone's joining in with the 'a-wimowehs' and jiggling around. I'm actually quite disappointed when the song finishes.

'I've got to take Louisa home,' says Tom, putting down the microphone with a flourish. 'We're going to the country tomorrow so she needs some recovery time.'

'Oh, OK,' I say, wondering if they're going for a rural shag-fest. He starts back over to her and I grab his sleeve.

'Tom?'

'Yes?'

'Thanks. I was making a real tit of myself before you turned up.'

'No, you weren't. You were just a bit haphazard.' He grins down at me. 'Glad to have been of service.'

Louisa's got her coat on and is waiting at the door. I wave goodbye, but he's too wrapped up in her to notice, although she affords me a twee little finger wiggle. I re-enter the fray, finally starting to relax. It's gone midnight now and it's only the hardcore massive that are staying the distance. I go and snog Harry back to good humour, determined to enjoy the dying days of the celebrations. Swilling back some water, I find myself muttering a silent prayer that the turmoil of tonight is not a precursor to my moment of truth three weeks hence. If there is a God, let's hope he's no party-pooper. I'm going to need all the help I can get.

24

Waking up alone in Harry's bed is the strangest sensation. I roll over and luxuriate in the space, wondering when his flat's going to start feeling like home. He's away on yet another trip, and I'm trying on my new live-in lover role for size. I've tentatively started moving stuff from Karen and Greg's but I haven't quite made the break. I look at the alarm clock. Only an hour till my summit with Adam, where we're due to thrash out the division of the flat. My tummy's turning over at the very thought, and I'm not quite sure why. Of course I'm anxious in case it's fraught, but there's also a part of me that's strangely excited by the idea of seeing him one to one. I still feel so starved of him, and yet it seems wrong to express it now that he's Polly's.

I agonize over my outfit like it's a first date. Too dressed down and he might think I'm going to seed, too dressed up and he could think I'm trying to score points off Polly. I go totally neutral, jeans and a black top, but I put on a necklace he gave me a couple of years ago. It's not that I want to mess with his head, I just don't want him to forget how much I once mattered.

I watch him through the window of the café, stalker-like. He's making a weird little house out of sugar lumps with a straw poking out of the top as a makeshift chimney. He must be really nervous. He sweeps it flat as I come in, stepping forward to give me an awkward hug. I try to remember how it felt when his hugs were real, but the sensation's started to fade.

'So did you enjoy your party?' he asks, ordering me a one-shot latte. 'Sorry, that is what you wanted, isn't it?'

'Am I that predictable?'

'Wouldn't say that,' he shoots back.

'Yeah, I enjoyed it. It was lovely that everyone came, but it was sort of stressful . . . you know.' I tail off, seeing from his expression that he knows exactly what I mean but that he doesn't want to go there.

'Harry seems nice.' Could we be more bland? I've seen this man naked more times than I've seen myself, and yet we're talking to each other like we've just met at a bus stop.

'Obviously Polly's great,' I say, trying and failing not to sound sarcastic.

'Look, Anna, I'm sorry you felt lied to. We didn't know what to do.'

'I didn't *feel* lied to,' I snap back, 'I *was* lied to.' A flash of rage shoots through me, but then I remember my own leaning tower of untruths and try to cool off. 'Did you always like her, Adam?'

'Of course I liked her, but not like that. I wasn't looking,' he adds defensively.

'What, you're saying you never looked at anyone else in ten years?'

I'm wondering if I should step off now, but I'm suddenly craving his truth. Honesty became such a dangerous commodity by the end of our relationship, and I'm desperate to know how it was for him.

'No, that would be a lie. There was a girl at work I really fancied for a bit . . .'

'What, that Gemma girl? I knew she was after you.'

They'd been seconded to a project together, and I hated the odd times of the evening she chose to call up. Adam insisted I was being paranoid, but I knew in my gut she'd take him off me in a heartbeat.

'Yeah, and maybe I should've told you. But nothing happened, I wouldn't have let it. It's a pay-off, Anna, isn't it? You lose the newness, but you get something better instead.'

He's staring at me quite intently, as I try to process what he's saying. Is he right? Was his solution the right one – the odd furtive wank over a passing fancy, but enduring loyalty to the woman he'd picked? I can't face a philosophical debate about the nature of commitment. It's way too late in the day for that. Instead I reach my hand across the table, stopping just short of making contact with his.

'I still miss you, you know.'

'Me too,' he says, bridging the gap to squeeze my fingers. If Polly could see us she'd hate it, but I can't pull away. 'The most stupid things made me cry, for ages,' he continues. 'When I found your emergency mascara I nearly caused a pile-up.' I used to keep it in the glove compartment for last-minute touch-ups on the way to work. 'There were all these little bits of you, but no you.'

Acrid tears spring to my eyes as I search for the right

thing to say. I want to tell him how many times I longed to come back, to crawl under the duvet and pretend none of it had ever happened. But how the fact that the idea of marrying him still filled me with churning dread meant that I knew I couldn't. That once I'd forced myself out into the cold, like a stiletto-clad Captain Oates, there could be no turning back. Most of all I want to know if he loves Polly like he loved me, but I'm scared of the answer. Either way it'll suck. 'I'm really sorry,' is all I settle for, but I'm sure he reads much more in my face. I know now that understanding someone like we understand each other doesn't just trickle away, but that the fact it doesn't is as much a curse as it is a blessing.

'So,' he says, briskly pulling out a wedge of paperwork, 'shall we talk about it?'

Of course we've made an absolute fortune – the flat's virtually doubled in value – but unless we want to move to Swansea the increase is completely meaningless. Adam generously agrees a fifty per cent split, even though his deposit was way more, pointing out that he never could've bought it if it hadn't been for me. Half the profits won't afford either of us anything remotely as nice: perhaps he's planning to join forces with Polly to cushion the blow?

'Christ no. Not yet. Why, are you going to buy something with Tarzan?'

'Tarzan?'

'He's just so bloody blond,' he says grumpily.

'I thought you said he was nice?'

'I'm sure he is nice.'

I stare at him sulkily. Is this proper 'I'm not over you' jealousy, or just a dick-swinging contest?

'Yes, he is. And he's actually asked me to move in with him.'

'And are you going to?'

'Yes, I am.'

'Congratulations.'

Suddenly the fight's gone right out of me. 'Thanks,' I say in a small voice, feeling like it's another door clanging shut on our relationship.

'Look, Anna, I'm sure he's great, I just didn't think you looked like you were having that much of a laugh maybe.' There's a smile playing round his lips as he holds my gaze. 'You need to have fun otherwise you go into neurotic meltdown.'

'No, we do, we really do,' I say earnestly, regretting what a poor show we put on that night.

'Good,' he says simply. 'Look, I've got to go. I've got loads to do before lunch.'

And I can tell that it's Saturday lunch with Polly. How weird that I'm not invited; we'd always have invited her. The new rules so don't compute. He promises to start getting agents round, and gets up to go.

'I'm really glad we did this,' he says, giving me a farewell hug. 'I'll see you soon, I'm sure.'

'Yeah, great,' I say petulantly. Get a grip, Anna, you dumped him!

I buy myself a huge slice of cake and hole up in Harry's bed with *When Harry Met Sally*. Maybe this Harry's right and men and women can't be friends. If that's the case then me and Adam are doomed. We'll just have stiff little chats at dinner parties, until the hateful moment when he and Polly ask me to be godmother to their first-born son. I decide to disprove the theory by calling up Horst.

'Anna, I am thrilled that you called. There is so much excitement in progress!'

'Why, what's going on?'

'Ruby and I have become lovers. Oh, I should have kept that a secret. But we are very delighted with one another.'

'Really?' I say, wondering if he just means that he's held her hand. Surely she wouldn't go for him – she's so out of his league. And why the hell hasn't she told me?

'Oh yes! It is hugely, hugely thrilling.'

And I stupidly find myself inviting him to crash my night out with the girls, even though I know Polly won't be remotely happy about it. Partly I want to get to the truth of his claims, but is it also that I'm plain terrified of getting up close and personal with her?

Anyway, there's a long Horst-free stretch, as we start with dinner at a super healthy vegetarian restaurant that Susie's insisted on. She catches me peering suspiciously at the aubergines that are painted on the walls, and immediately apologizes.

'It's this sodding diet I'm on. I've got more alternative therapists than Lady Di. Honestly, this nutritionist seems to think that wheat and coffee are only one step up from crack cocaine.'

'But are you feeling better for it?' asks Polly.

'I don't think it's possible to feel good on steroids. Poor Martin must think he's married a monster.'

'Poor Martin,' chime Polly and I, trying not to catch each other's eye.

The restaurant only serves wine by the glass or half bottle, in order to promote limited drinking, and Susie forbids us from ordering three. I'm nervous as hell about what Adam said to Polly, but it seems like he just told her that it went well. I don't know if our conversation was unacceptably intimate, or if its intimacy was inevitable. Either way, nobody wants to dwell on it. Instead I tell them about Lucas's gruesome behaviour at karaoke. Polly insists I've got to tell Harry.

'But then he'll want to know why I didn't tell him in the first place.'

'Why didn't you?' asks Polly simply.

And I lay out for her all the potential devastation and destruction it would've caused, not least to my article, but she's still not convinced.

'Anna, you love him, don't you?'

'Yes,' I immediately reply, secretly struck by the layers that love needs. I do love him, but how much do I truly know him? He'll probably feel like a different man entirely a year hence, once I've done the full tour of his inner machinations.

'But that's the total upside of a relationship. There's someone who's always on your team. You could've negotiated all that shit together.'

But is it that simple? There's always a point where your truths become different, and it's no longer just a case of exposing everything and relying on the other's acceptance. A patronizing part of me revels in her naivety, looks forward to her discovering that even Adam has feet of clay, but another part of me envies it. Since when did I get so cynical? Perhaps I should tell Harry all of it, and guarantee that the next phase of our relationship isn't plagued by secrets.

'It's exciting that you're moving in!' says Susie. 'You must be so glad to be out of your parents'.'

'Yeah, I am, but it's sort of odd too. Like, I accidentally jammed the skylight open last night, and I was really panicking in case I'd broken it. It's hard not to feel like a guest still. I felt more at home at yours in a funny way,' I say to Polly, firmly reminding myself how much I have to be grateful to her for.

'It'll come!' says Susie. 'Remember how much I hated Martin's house?' Well, it was a bungalow in Reading, I think, breathing a sigh of relief that we got her back to civilization. 'You need to mark your patch, make it home.'

'Are you actually suggesting that she pees on the carpet?' says Polly.

'No! I'm just saying she should do something nice for the house, so it feels like she's sharing the space.'

'What are you smiling about?' Polly asks me. 'We need another one of these puny little bottles by the way.'

'I was thinking about Tom actually.'

'Were you indeed.'

'Not like that!'

I've suddenly remembered the photos he showed me on the Scrabble night of some of the urban oases he's

created. Perhaps Harry could have a mini jungle sur-
rounding him when he has his midnight roll-up on the
roof?

The carob brownies turn out to be remarkably tasty,
and before we know it we've polished off four of the
Oompa Loompa-sized wine bottles. 'That means I've had
more than half a bottle!' groans Susie. 'I think I might
actually be a bit drunk.'

'Excellent,' I say, persuading her we should go to a
nearby cocktail bar which has dancing in the basement.

'I'm too old,' she says, and we tell her not to be so
ridiculous.

'Look,' says Polly, 'you're never going to have any fun
again once you've had a baby, so make the most of your
dwindling opportunities.' Once she's persuaded, I break
the news that Horst is joining us.

'Anna, why did you do that?' says an exasperated Polly.
'He's been having the loudest, most German orgasms
through the wall all week. I swear he shouts *schnell, schnell*
when he comes.'

'Have you met her?'

'She always seems to scuttle out before I can get a
handle on her. She's really pretty though.'

'Long blonde hair?'

She nods. It's true! How did he manage it? He's
grinning from ear to ear when I ask him.

'She says that the men she meets are often very false,
while I wear my heart on my shoulder.'

Which is a fair point – what you see is what you get with
Horst. Right now he's doing an odd, jiggling dance to

'Thriller'. Let's just hope he doesn't start moon-walking.

'And your Harry? Are you still lovers of the highest order?'

'Absolutely.'

'So all of us find happiness. My play also brings me great joy. You will come to our première, Anna? The tickets go on sale on Monday and I will hold some back for you.'

Yeah, like there's a grave danger of them selling out. I promise I will, suddenly contemplating the horrific possibility that I'll have to invite Horst to the wedding event. I can't really see him mixing it with the fash pack, but I don't want to hurt Ruby's feelings.

'OK,' says Susie, wobbling over. 'I actually am officially drunk. How did this happen?'

She grabs Horst round the waist and starts twirling him around the dance floor. Soon he's shaking his head and rocking his body, clearing a significant circle round himself. 'I love the music of the nineteen eighties,' he cries, sweat dripping from his whirling form. Susie's right there with him, demanding I get her a tequila slammer.

'Are you sure?' I ask her uncertainly.

'This is my one chance, Anna, I'm going to make the most of it.' Horst has one too, and they decide to slam their drinks off each other's chests.

'Who knew?' says Polly, who's determined to have as little to do with Horst as humanly possible. We retreat to a sofa, where the loud music saves us from the need for a proper heart to heart. She starts to say how sorry she is again, but I cut across her and drag her on to the dance floor. I'm so desperate not to talk about Adam that I'm even prepared to share my rhythm-free shuffling with the world. I take evil pleasure in Horst gyrating next to Polly during 'Hungry Like the Wolf', treating the assembled throng to his snarling wolf impressions during the chorus. We roll out around 2 a.m. and I pour Susie into a taxi.

'You have no idea how much fun I had,' she slurs, arms round my neck. 'Thank you, Anna.'

'That's OK.'

'No really, thank you.'

I kiss her goodbye, writing down her address for the driver in case she forgets it. Oh God, I hope Martin won't think I've corrupted her: I don't think I've ever seen her that drunk.

Not that I'm one to talk considering how ropy I feel in the morning. Determined not to waste the day, I call up Tom to see if he'll take a look at the roof, and see if it's garden-worthy. He's out of London, but promises to try and pop by on his way back into town. 'As long as you don't bring that vodka-hating midget' is what I want to say, but of course I don't. Besides, she was perfectly nice. The fact that she doesn't like vodka is no reason to dislike her.

He turns up when I'm painting my toenails, and I waddle down, duck-footed from the toe dividers, to let him in. He's looking super tanned, and has cut his hair right down close to the scalp. Cranberry girl's obviously making him over. Maybe she's not allergic to alcohol at all. Maybe she's just got a chronic cystitis problem.

'Good hair.'

'Are you mocking me? Belle hacked it with some scissors when I was asleep and I've had to make the best of it.'

Yet another reason not to breed. If anyone did that to my hair, my podgy cheeks would look like a beach ball. Tom, however, looks more defined. It's as though he was hiding behind his messy 'harassed dad' hair, and is only now emerging, sleek as a seal.

'It's loads better, honestly.'

'Coming from a fashion guru like yourself, I'm flattered.'

Is he taking the piss? I'm not quite sure. I make him a cup of tea, watching him assessing the flat from the corner of my eye.

'Sometimes I wish I'd had a man about town moment. I would've loved this kind of place.'

'Yeah, it's great,' I say uncertainly, wondering if he thinks I look like a fish out of water. I gingerly pick my way over to his side. 'They'll dry soon and then I'll show you the roof.' Then I panic that I'm talking to him like he's some kind of random tradesman I've landed on in the *Yellow Pages*. 'So how was the weekend?' I ask, even though part of me doesn't want to know the answer.

'Oh, you know,' he says, with a surprisingly dirty laugh.

'No, I don't.'

'Um ... relaxing.'

There's an awkward pause, which I break by suggesting we head upstairs. Smudged toes never killed a girl. I throw open the hatch, and we clamber on to the roof. I watch him take in the view across the city.

'So what do you think?' I say proudly. Bachelor pad or not, it's an amazing location.

'It's very urban, isn't it? It's going to need tough guy plants that can survive the smog.'

For the first time I notice how yellow and droopy the couple of plants that are already up here look.

'We need big yuccas and cactuses.'

'Manly plants.'

'Exactly.'

And with that, Tom starts lugging around the garden furniture that's up there, stacking the existing pots in the corner. I offer to help, but he's a man on a mission.

'Come on, we're going on a trip.'

He's striding back down the rickety steps, and I hurry after him, losing my footing in my haste. We zoom off in his messy old Volvo.

'Just tell me where we're going.'

'No, Anna, it's a surprise. We need to be quick though.'

'Do we? I'm just going to lie down flat watching *Grey's Anatomy*. Have you got the kids tonight?'

'They're on holiday with their mum. I'm going out for dinner.'

'Oh. Great! It's obviously going swimmingly then.'

'Yeah, well. It was about time I got back into the swing of things. As it were.'

And we're suddenly plunged back into awkwardness. As I'm pondering my unwarranted vitriol towards cranberry girl, Tom's winding his way around the back of the city, finally pulling up off Fleet Street.

'Follow me,' he says, pulling a big bag of keys out of the glove compartment.

And he lets us into a ridiculously trendy hairdresser's. It's like a photography studio, all open plan and mirrored. He leads me up to the upper floor, which opens on to an amazing terrace area. There are trellises at either side, up which vines and honeysuckle grow. Huge pots house big red flowers, bougainvilleas I suspect, while enormous spider plants make you feel you're cosseted away in an urban rainforest. The smell of all the flowers even manages to mask the traffic fumes below. It would almost be worth having a perm just to spend an afternoon here.

'It's amazing, Tom.'

I'm shamed by the memory of how offhand I was about his work at that dinner party. I somehow imagined that he pruned suburban hedges before returning to a sad single bed at his mother's house. Who was I to talk anyway? I was back living in a one-time shrine to Nik Kershaw within a matter of weeks.

'So obviously we're not going to do anything as elaborate, but an adapted version is sort of where I'm going. You like?'

'I like.'

'Come on then, Anna, back in the car.'

I linger for a minute, drinking it in. It feels so peaceful up here, despite the low hum of traffic. I just want to recline on a lounger, sipping something long and cool.

'Do we have to go? Can't I just admire your artistry for a few minutes more?'

'Very funny.'

And he's bouncing down the stairs, a ball of energy. He zooms back out of central London, delivering us to a garden centre in Muswell Hill in double quick time.

'You're a really good driver.'

'What's with all the compliments today? Not that that's really a compliment.'

'Yes it is.'

He gives me a disbelieving grin. 'A good driver, that's sexy. I bet it's the real reason women go for George Clooney.'

But to me it is. Obviously in carbon footprint terms it's no accolade, but there's something very capable about the way he handles his lumbering dad-mobile. Anyway, the fact that I took my test so many times gives skilled driving a certain mystique.

The Volvo fits in a treat in the car park. The whole place is teeming with happy suburban families looking for the deckchairs of their dreams. I feel vaguely alienated by it, until Tom makes me realize that this is just another form of shopping, which is obviously my all-time favourite pastime. He forces me to think about the shapes and colours of the plants in a way I've never considered. When I try to plump for some luscious purple pansies he dismisses me out of hand.

'You have to think of it like an orchestra – all their different notes are making up the symphony. They just won't go.'

'I hate to break it to you, but your trousers don't really go with your T-shirt.'

'Cheeky bitch!' he says, laughing. 'Louisa bought me this T-shirt.'

So much for my make-over theory. I wish I could restyle him; he might look almost hot by the time I'd finished. We load up the car with all our horticultural goodies and whiz back to Harry's. Or should it be mine and Harry's? I try to help him unload the plants, but my weedy little arms are no match for the big terracotta pots he's put them in. He effortlessly scoots them up to the roof, and then flops down on the sofa for a breather.

'So tomorrow I'll turn it into a garden rather than a random load of plants.'

'Thanks so much, Tom,' I say, handing him a cup of tea. 'Is that all right? I figured you wouldn't want a drink because you're driving.'

'Louisa's driving, not me. In fact I ought to go soon.'

'She must be the perfect designated driver. What would actually happen to her if she drank an entire pint of beer? Would she spontaneously combust?' Shut up, Anna.

He considers me for a second. 'I don't think so, no. Why don't you ask her?'

I smile at him, regretting my acidity.

'It's Harry we need to be talking about. I can't construct a garden for someone I know nothing about.'

'What kind of thing do you want to know?'

'What's he like? Is he rational? Is he passionate? Is

280

he going to want something regimented and linear, or something more unstructured?'

What would Harry like? I suddenly have a flashback to his awful film, and panic that he'd have chosen pretentious stone structures punctuated with ugly, angular shrubs. But that's not really what Tom's asking me.

'He can look a bit dreamy from the outside, but inside he's working out exactly what he wants. Then he just goes out and gets it . . . in a good way,' I add hurriedly.

'So he's always got a game plan?'

'Yes,' I say, suddenly wondering what his game plan is for our relationship.

'What else?'

'He's got this innate confidence. He always believes it's going to work out, and it usually does.'

'No wonder you like him so much.'

'What do you mean?'

'I dunno, you just strike me as one of life's worriers. It's quite sweet in a way. It's good you've got someone to tell you what's what.'

'It's not the Victorian age, Tom. Women can actually survive without the protection of a patron.'

'Don't be so chippy!' he says, laughing. 'We can all benefit from someone to balance us out a bit.'

I think about asking him what fabulous qualities Louisa's blessed him with, but I don't want to know. She'll have all that motherly wisdom, combined with her unreasonably taut body. He must think Christmas has come early this year.

I persuade him to come back up to the roof, arming us

with glasses of white wine, so that he can explain his final concept to me. The sun's setting over the city as he describes the clean lines he's going to create.

'It'll be focused, but also very aesthetic. He's obviously very visually creative, but I want it to reflect that clarity of purpose that you're talking about.'

'With plants?'

'Yes, Anna, with plants.'

'Sorry, I don't mean to mock. It sounds amazing.'

We look at the view for a bit, sipping our wine in companionable silence. It's actually such a relief to stop talking: why don't I do it more often? I do miss the moments of quiet that Adam and I used to share. Although the two of us went full circle, eventually reaching the point where they became awkward silences all over again.

'I wish I could cook you supper to say thanks, but . . .'

'Another time maybe.'

'You and Louisa could come over together, once Harry's back.'

'Yeah, that would be great.'

There's the distant sound of a car horn.

'That's probably her now actually. Shit, I promised I'd be ready and I haven't even packed up my stuff.'

He stands aside so I can inelegantly clamber through the hatch. As we're discussing where he's going to leave the keys, I can see Louisa giving another staccato toot on the horn of her sporty little number.

'Oh God, I'm late. I think she's booked somewhere really posh.'

'I don't want to rain on your parade, but are you dressed for it?'

'I'm hopeless at smart. I look like a complete tramp, don't I?'

'At least you're wearing her T-shirt.'

'But I've got soil all over it. I promised her I'd make an effort. I meant to go home and change, but there wasn't time.'

Mainly because I persuaded him to hang around on the roof quaffing wine. 'Stall her,' I tell him, racing over to the Oxfam bag in the corner. I've been desperately trying to clear space in Harry's cupboards for my shoe collection, and now I can put the spoils to good use.

'Darling?' he says, in a tone of voice I've never heard. 'I won't be long. I've just got to finish a couple of things off . . . yes, of course you can come up.'

I'm frantically holding up shirts now, worried she's going to catch him out. He gives a thumbs-up to one of Harry's most garish cast-offs, but I override him, chucking over a muted green one instead.

'I'm really sorry,' he says, pulling the muddy T-shirt over his head. 'I didn't realize we only had a two-hour slot.' A two-hour slot equals super posh – let's hope it's posh in a smart casual kind of a way. God, he's really quite muscular. I stare long and hard into the Oxfam bag, feeling distinctly embarrassed by his semi-naked form. There's no escaping it as I've still got to find him some passable trousers. Harry's matchstick legs are no match for Tom's bulk, but luckily he went through a baggy jeans phase. I throw him some black ones and hope they won't

283

declare themselves as denim quite as obviously as blue ones would. 'OK, I'll buzz the intercom,' says Tom, as he drops his trousers. 'Sorry,' he mouths, but there's no time for modesty. I look away before I see his pants (briefs or boxers – who knows?), struck by the sound of Louisa's dainty high heels picking their way up the long flight of stairs.

'Hang on,' I urgently whisper, spying a splodge of earth on his neck. I grab a cloth and vigorously rub it off, putting a hand on his waist to keep myself steady.

'Will I do?'

I draw back from him to take a good look. He looks straight back at me, a serious expression on his face.

'Yeah, you totally will.'

The green shirt is perfectly showcasing his tan, and the jeans are a bizarrely good fit. I take an awkward leap backward as the door opens: there's no good excuse for standing this close. Louisa's wearing a short black dress with her tippy tappy heels, and looks more than a match for new, improved Tom. She's even managing to carry off fishnets without looking slutty. I'd look like a hooker in that outfit, but she looks like some kind of gamine French actress.

'Louisa, hi! How lovely to see you again. I was just saying how great it would be to have you round for dinner.'

'That would be fantastic,' she says, sounding utterly bored by the idea, 'but tonight we're on a bit of a tight schedule.'

She crosses to Tom and grabs his hand, all ready

to forcibly lead him away. That's the problem with mummies: sometimes they don't know when to switch off. 'Hello, darling, I'm glad to see you've spruced yourself up.' She stands on tiptoes to give him a prim little kiss while I look away. He risks a small smile over her shoulder, obviously thrilled my two-minute turnaround did the business.

'So where is it you're going?'

'Le Gavroche. Tom promises it's his treat.'

Stuffy, French and exorbitant: I bet he'll hate it. Oh well, at least he won't get stung on wine. I walk them down to the front door, giving Louisa an over-enthusiastic hug. I hope she's not starting to think I'm slightly simple. 'Thanks, Anna,' whispers Tom, and I experience a bizarre tingle from the sense of conspiracy. I retreat back upstairs, gathering his muddy clothes from behind the sofa where he hid them. I stick them in the washing machine, struck by the distinctive mixture of soil and aftershave.

I know honesty should be the best policy, but somehow it never quite works out that way for me.

25

There's only a week to go before my article goes to the printers, and I'm steeling myself for the final meeting with Becky and Lucas. Desperate to minimize contact, I task Ruby with fixing it up. I stare at her while she's on the phone, wondering why she's keeping schtum about her bunk-up scenario with Horst. Although I can think of a million reasons why one wouldn't own up to regular sex with Stuttgart's finest export, I can't bear the idea of him suffering yet another rejection – particularly now he's found someone worth pining for. Ruby jauntily hangs up, turning to me with a beaming smile. She's a girl in a happy place.

'Lucas is on a writer's retreat apparently, but she's going to meet you for lunch. She said that she's got something she needs to ask you.'

'Did she tell you what?'

'No, she said she needed to ask you face to face.'

Cold panic spreads through me as I contemplate what that weaselly wanker might've said. The whole scenario's like a perverse game of poker: he must've figured that I might tell Harry when he got back, and decided to get in there first. Before I know it, he'll have rewritten history and turned me into the whore of Harlesden. He's guessed right: my conversation with Polly has left me determined to open up to Harry, but I haven't quite plucked up the courage to drop the bomb.

'A penny for your thoughts,' trills Jocasta, clocking my faraway look. Where does she dredge up her irritating phrases? I wonder if her husband's as grating and anodyne as she is. The long winter nights must fly by, what with all those discussions about how best to expand their collection of Le Creuset kitchenware and whether or not Puglia really is the new Tuscany.

'Were you worrying about the panel? It's such disappointing news about Dr Neil Fox.'

Please God may she never find out that I emailed him direct and told him he was neck and neck with Dave Lee Travis for a place on the panel.

'I know. But with Harry, Caitlin Somers and our shoe guru we should be fine.'

'Yes, Anna, but it's all about accessibility. It's vital that the event connects with the kind of harassed but fashion conscious mum who reads *Casual Chic*. Chic but not too chic, that's the watchword!' Trust her to bring it back to her people: the mothers. 'Let's hope the photos fit the brief. They're arriving this afternoon, aren't they?'

Ah, the photos. Almost certainly the only aspect of the whole production that Jocasta and I will see eye to eye on. She's had to grudgingly fall in with the general consensus that the Becky and Lucas shots are fantastic, so now I just have to hope that the rest of Harry's work proves as universally popular.

*

Becky's somehow managing to look every bit as glamorous for a low-key lunch as she does in Harry's portraits. I arrive to find her intoning earnestly into her BlackBerry, diamond-clad hand wrapped tightly round it. She gives me a stressed wave, and I hover uselessly a few metres from the table. If she and Lucas are in meltdown I don't want to be party to it. She waves me over – a little imperious, a little stressed – and I step forward to accept my fate.

'Sorry, Anna, curtain rings.'

'Curtain rings?'

'Those lovely heavy brass ones are so hard to come by and I'm desperate to lay my hands on some.'

How is it possible to care this much about curtain rings? It suddenly occurs to me that her job might be as silly as mine. Both of them are seemingly artistic, yet entirely lacking in that glorious blaze of creativity inherent in Harry's photos or Tom's luscious gardens. I felt slightly unfaithful when I saw Harry's delight at the glorious enclave Tom had conjured up on the roof. I remembered the semi-clad moment we shared and meanly described him as 'that geeky bloke'. Luckily Harry couldn't even remember who he was.

My insides are coiled up, watchful and expectant, while my perky facade chit-chats away about nothing. How would a girl as happy-go-lucky as Becky approach a situation like this? Is she lulling me into a false sense of security so she can pounce? Or is she as lacking in guile as she appears?

'So I thought the last bit of the piece would be about

the wedding itself.' I'm faltering a bit now. 'Um ... you know, what your concept for it is and how you're executing it.'

'Oh, darling, I feel like I've bored you stiff about it already.'

'No, not at all.'

'Can I be truthful with you, Anna?'

Oh no, there's no need for that. I look at her fearfully, a perfidious rabbit caught in very bright headlights.

'If it was up to me I'd go away and do it on some distant island, just me and Lucas. There aren't that many people I really care about having there with us. But Ma and Pa would never forgive me.'

'Oh,' I say, taken aback. I never imagined that a creature as exotic and prized as her would want to miss her moment in the spotlight.

'Which brings me to what I wanted to ask you.'

Oh God, this is it.

'Would you be one of my bridesmaids?'

'Sorry?'

She repeats the question, smiling expectantly in the face of my blank shock.

'I'm not big on girlfriends, which made school something of an assault course.' She giggles hollowly, and I sense there's a story. It occurs to me what a prison extreme beauty might be – women mistrusting you and men lusting after you in a way that's almost insultingly undiscerning.

'Are you sure?' I say, playing for time. 'I'm a bit over the hill for an organza frock.'

I remember a teary moment I shared with Susie at the outset of the break-up when I pointed out that this summer could've been the one where she and Polly finally did their duty. 'Don't worry,' she said cheerily, 'it'll come, even if we're the oldest bridesmaids in history.' It's shockingly obvious that Becky doesn't have any cheer-leaders to dispense wonky comfort in her hour of need. No wonder she's ended up picking a dud like Lucas.

'No, I really want you to do it. You're completely different from most of the girls I know. Quirky,' she adds, grinning like it's a compliment. 'I know Luke would love it too, and Harry'll be best man of course.'

Naturally there's no escape: I reluctantly agree, vowing to myself that I'll tell Harry the whole truth before the night is out. It's down to him to decide if there's any such thing as cruel to be kind. But tonight's looking fairly action-packed already. Amy's mum is having one of those pointless, painful operations which might possibly buy her a little more time, and I've offered to have Freddie to stay. The dying always cling on to those last months with such fierce insistence, even if their treatment makes the last splutter of life unbearably painful. I wonder if I'd do it myself? Straining furiously to spin out your dwindling time as far as it can reach must make all those moments one inevitably wastes feel like squandered gold.

In preparation for Freddie's royal visit I've bought a secret tub of Ben and Jerry's – I've decided his infant palate needs educating beyond Magnums – and borrowed *The Aristocats* from Tabitha in the office. I think I actually wet myself when Karen took me to see it in 1983: let's hope my bladder control's improved in the intervening years.

I'm chugging through a mountain of emails when Jocasta announces that the proofs have arrived. I hate the way everything has to go through her these days: now I won't have a moment to digest them before they're on show. I rush down to the post room, trying to control the anticipation. 'Harry's an artist, Harry's an artist,' I mutter compulsively, earning me some strange looks from the mail staff. I don't want to pore over them in the hallway, but it's a fatal error. Jocasta's got Roger down for the grand unveiling, and they're waiting expectantly in the boardroom. 'Come with me!' I hiss to Ruby, forcibly dragging her in.

'So, the moment of truth,' says Jocasta, with a nasty smile.

Roger jumps in. 'Can we just hang fire for a moment?' I give him a grateful look. 'Victor should be here any minute.' Great. We all stand around for what seems like an age before Victor greyly materializes next to me.

'Anna,' he says, giving me a strange grimace. The exposure of my lie has turned his already chilly manner down to sub-zero.

'So!' I say brightly, opening the packet with a flourish and spreading the photos out on the table. Oh God: who knew? Arthur's wearing a tight leather shorts and waistcoat combo and aiming a bubble gun at Hilda. She's wearing a bizarre metal hat that even the most ardent Hoxtonite would shy away from, and posing as though she's been shot. The next photos feature Arthur in armour, chasing Hilda with an enormous bow and arrow. This time she's wearing a peculiar puffball wedding dress that wouldn't look out of place in a Cindy Lauper video.

'Goodness me,' says Jocasta, 'neither casual nor chic!'

I'm speechless, searching for a response. 'Harry's got a unique vision, Jocasta. That's why people pay him a fortune to shoot for them.'

'Quite,' says Victor, looking puce. 'Shall we investigate the remainder?'

Could Oliver and Steve's poses actually be worse? He's put monkey ears and tails on them in the first shots, stripped them down to their underpants and photographed them chasing each other around a grim urban playground. You can hardly pick them out in the second shoot: their blurry forms are bouncing up and down on a garish bouncy castle.

'Sometimes the road less travelled proves to be the bumpier path,' says Jocasta, casting me a sorrowful glance.

'These simply aren't suitable,' says Victor, while Roger stares dumbly, mouth flapping like a fish.

'I agree that they push the envelope,' I say, red and flustered, 'but we can always prioritize our third couple over the rest.' I push Becky and Lucas's shots forward, encouraging everyone to remember how pleased they were with them.

'It's almost like a different person took these,' says Victor, and for once I agree with him. 'He'll have to re-shoot them. The level of advertising we've secured makes the page count critical, not to mention the fact that we've sold space on the basis of his involvement.'

'But we're going to press in six days. Shoots like this take weeks to set up, and I know for a fact he's got an editorial for *Elle* all weekend.'

'How fortunate that you've got a personal relationship. I'm sure you'll find the perfect way to convince him. Roger, I'll see you upstairs in fifteen minutes.'

Victor stalks out, radiating vitriol, while Jocasta and Roger wait for my next move.

'They're very directional,' ventures Ruby.

I steel myself, determined to find some of that indomitable grit that my granny has in spades. If I can channel my inner grandmother I know I can turn this around.

'Yes, they are. They're imaginative and original, even if they're not right for *Casual Chic*. But I know Harry can deliver for us.'

'Your level of self-belief has always been one of your most sterling qualities,' says Jocasta.

'Thank you, Jocasta, now I need to get on.'

I tear out of the building and flag down a cab. I'm shaking, dreading the confrontation I'm facing with Harry. I'm struck again by how fragile the bond between us is. Adam and I could fight like cat and dog, but I always knew that the bottom line was that we'd do anything to defend the other from life's traumas. I still feel unreasonably, irrationally protective of him, but I'm not even sure that Harry and I are on the same side. He's beaming at me as I slam in.

'So, what did you think? Were they pleased?'

If I'm going to achieve what I need to, I've got to take my finger off the nuclear button.

'Well, we all love the Becky and Lucas shots, but I'm not sure the others are quite what we were aiming for.'

'What *you* were aiming for? Isn't it about what I'm aiming for?'

'There was a brief, Harry. It is *Casual Chic*, not *Dazed and Confused*.'

'Do they not get it? The old geezers talked about the war, so I wanted to reflect it, all that conflict and jeopardy. And that Oliver guy's left all his responsibilities behind, he's decided to play.'

'Right.'

'You don't get it either, do you?' He gives me a slightly supercilious look. 'I don't want to be patronizing, but I do think there's something very conventional about you sometimes.'

'Conventional?' I feel a surge of anger as I think of all those years I spent longing for convention. For parents who didn't get arrested and clothes that came from actual shops.

'Yes, there's a big part of you that likes ordinary.'

'Oh, spare me the cod psychology, Harry. I knew what we needed, and I thought you did too. You'll have to re-shoot them or else I'll be out of a job this time next week.'

'No chance. If you don't appreciate my work then you don't appreciate me.'

'Well, maybe I don't. I begged you to show me what you'd done and all you let me look at were Becky and

Lucas's shots. And surprise, surprise, you chose not to make your best friends look like total fools.'

'You're very threatened by our friendship, aren't you?'

'No!'

'Don't think I didn't clock how negative you were about the film we made. It's like you're intimidated by the kind of risks we take.'

And before I know it I'm telling him what a load of old bollocks I thought it was, and what a talentless arse Lucas is.

'What's wrong with you, Anna, why are you being so vicious? Lucas really likes you.'

'Likes me? That's one way of putting it.'

I try to calm down. This is too important to tumble out in a stream of rage. I take a deep breath and launch in.

'When we went away for that weekend, I didn't run away because of Freddie. It was because of him. He shoved me up against the wall and stuck his tongue down my throat. It was so horrible.' I'm choked by the relief that confessing instantly brings me. But when I notice Harry's hard, measuring look the feeling instantly subsides.

'It doesn't sound like Lucas to me.'

'Well, it's exactly what happened. You need to tell Becky. There's something very fragile about her, Harry; she might choose to go ahead anyway, but she needs to know what she's getting in to.'

'I'm not going to do that to her.'

'What, you think I'm lying?'

'No, I just think you might be over-reacting.'

'Harry, he mauled me. If I hadn't fought back I don't know how far he would've gone.'

'Why would he do that?'

'Err, dunno, because he's sexually incontinent? I hardly know the guy, you tell me.'

'Well I do, and I know he's not like that. You're very insecure, Anna – you're not trying to make me jealous, are you?'

'How fucking dare you! Of course I'm not.'

'OK, I'm sorry.'

'Sorry's not good enough, Harry. Polly asked me why I hadn't told you, and I know now. It's because you haven't got the maturity to deal with it, to support me rather than doubt me. It says a lot.'

'What are you saying?'

'I'm saying I'm not sure I want to be here any more. I feel like it's all about you – the photos, Lucas's hideous behaviour. You're never going to take care of me, because you'll be too busy taking care of you.'

'That's you all over, isn't it? Needy.'

'Maybe I am needy, maybe I don't sweat self-confidence like you do. But I would've given anything to this if we'd had a real shot. It's not going to work.'

'What, you're dumping me?'

I didn't know I was until the words were out of my mouth, but now I can't see an alternative. It's obviously a professional disaster, but I can't bear to be with someone who believes themselves to be so invulnerable. It's not that he's hiding the chinks in his armour, it's that he doesn't even know they exist. When life starts getting messy he's in for one hell of a shock.

Neither of us speak, we just stand there staring at each other. The silence is broken by the droning cry of the buzzer: Freddie.

'Look, I'll take him to my mum and dad's.'

He presses the intercom. 'No, don't.'

Amy's red-eyed and tense, desperately trying not to communicate her distress to Freddie.

'Now you'll have a lovely time with Anna, so be a good boy.'

I wait for the inevitable howl of protest, but to my amazement he comes and hugs my leg.

'Hullo, Anna. Can we do the funny singing?'

Funny singing? What a nerve, I'm positively tuneful in comparison to Tom. Nevertheless, I'm oddly moved by his reaction to me – it's been a very emotional day. Amy leaves, and I ask Harry again if he wants me to go, but he insists he doesn't. I can see Freddie's uncertainty at this new environment – he's been shunted from pillar to post during this whole ordeal – and I'm hugely relieved I don't have to parcel him off somewhere else. Harry retreats upstairs, and we settle down with *The Aristocats*. As Freddie giggles away, I turn over what's just happened. I've got a cold, sick feeling running through me but I still think this might be the right decision. The core of truth you need at the centre of any relationship isn't there for us – that bit of emotional nakedness which allows the other person to know you in a way that no one else can. But is that just a question of time? I'm such a novice after ten years off the horse. I look down to find Freddie's head in my lap. He's sucking his thumb, squeaking with pleasure at the cats' escapades, while I stroke his soft hair. I feel bizarrely content in this moment, despite the chaos that exists outside of it. Harry comes downstairs, casting a searching look in my direction.

'He's asleep now, look.'

He's right; Freddie's making small snuffling sounds like a piglet. Would it be a disaster if I didn't wake him to brush his teeth? Will one night's coating of Ben and Jerry's leave him with blackened stumps? I decide to risk it, and attempt to carry him through to the spare room.

'Hey, I'll do that,' says Harry, scooping him up and trying to slip him under the covers. He's clumsy about it though, and Freddie starts to whimper.

'Shush,' I say, stroking his sticky face, and making to leave. He grabs hold of me with a vice-like grip.

'Sing me the song.'

'No, Freddie, it's time to go to sleep.'

He asks again, voice starting to wobble, and I reluctantly pipe up. 'The wheels on the bus go round and round, round and round, round and round …' I give Harry an embarrassed smile.

'You sing too,' says Freddie, bossily pointing at him. Freddie's clapping along delightedly, despite my distinctly dodgy vocal performance. I sneak a look at Harry, who's silently observing us.

'OK, darling, that's enough now.'

I tuck the covers around him, wiping some of the

stickiness off his face with the duvet. We sneak out, quietly shutting the door. As soon as we're out, Harry pushes me against the wall.

'Don't do this, Anna. Just don't.'

'I'm not sure if we even know each other, not really.'

'That's ridiculous, of course we do. I love you.'

And then he's kissing my neck, and all my resolve's slipping away. The thought of having to turn my life inside out is so exhausting, admitting defeat all over again, and yet I'm not sure this can ever be right. But suddenly I'm a woman possessed. All the stress and anger comes pouring out of me, and I unleash my inner porn star. Who knew she even existed? I'm magnificent, if I do say so myself. Afterwards we lie next to each other, sweaty and content. 'I love you too,' I whisper and fall asleep.

I wake at an unseemly hour, conscious Freddie needs to be roused for school. I sit up, blinking, to find Harry looking over at me.

'You're up early. Couldn't you sleep?'

'No, Anna, I couldn't,' he says soberly. 'I think you were right last night. It's not working, is it?'

I look at him in disbelief. I feel ambushed, unable to focus on what he's saying. Despite everything I said, I can't bear the idea that he's going to withdraw from me.

'We were both really wound up . . .'

'I know,' he says, aggrieved, 'but you meant the things you said. Not just about us. What you think of Lucas, and the way you feel about all the work I did.'

'Do you honestly not believe me?'

He's out of bed now, pulling on his jeans. 'I don't want to get into it again. And I don't want to be with someone who doesn't feel lucky to be with me.'

'Oh, fuck you, Harry. If you don't trust me then there's no point.'

'No, fuck you, Anna,' he says, with a nasty smile. Has he really stooped as low as a revenge fuck? I'm trying not to raise my voice, conscious that Freddie's downstairs.

'I'd like you to go. It's better for both of us that we found out now. I won't let you down on the panel, but I'm not going to re-shoot my photos. You're lucky to've got them, and you can tell your bosses that from me.'

I feel like I've been punched in the gut, but it doesn't seem like there's much left to say. I wake up Freddie and take him to the builders' café round the corner for a bacon sandwich. Sadly I forget to brush his hair, and there's no way I'm going back, so he goes to school with an odd sort of Mohican. I keep myself chipper till he's safely deposited, and then collapse on a nearby bench for a sob. How did I manage to screw up on this many counts: is there anything left for me to lose?

26

'It's none of my business, Anna, but I really didn't think he was right for you.' I'm in the Polish café with Adam, signing my life away. We've had a reasonable offer, so it's time to say goodbye to yet another piece of my past.

'This week I hate him, but he's not a total arsehole. I did dump him first. At least he's still doing the panel.'

'Whatever.'

I look over at him, profoundly touched by the knowledge that my welfare still matters that much. Maybe we can remain a part of each other's lives without it ripping us apart. My reverie's broken by the waitress slamming down my breakfast so hard that she nearly takes my fingers off.

'Any sauces?' she growls.

'Um, no thank you. We're fine.'

She strops off, and I hold his gaze.

'I want to say sorry properly. I know I said it before, but I didn't really understand what it meant till now. You must've felt so abandoned by me.'

'I couldn't really believe it for a while,' he replies.

'I'm sorry if me leaving made it seem like it was your fault. I was way too critical of you, too self-involved. You were so loyal and kind, and I'll never stop being grateful for it.'

'Do you know what, Anna, you were right to do what you did. We weren't right together any more, but I never would have had the guts to admit it to myself.'

Tears are rolling down my cheeks. Now he accepts that, I know it's truly over.

'I've got no right to ask this, but do you love her like you loved me?'

'No, I love her differently,' he replies. 'There's only ever going to be one you, Anna, you're completely unique. You're not easy, but you're unique.'

It's the perfect answer to a question that's tortured me for months. I suddenly think how much uncertainty he's short-circuited by starting a relationship with someone he knows so well. I feel irrationally jealous, filled with dread at the idea of putting myself out there all over again with an unreadable stranger. Adam's working up to asking me something now, winding his napkin round his hand to control his nerves.

'There's something . . .'

Suddenly it's blindingly obvious to me where this is going.

'I know what you're going to say.'

'Do you?'

'You want to marry her, don't you?'

He looks shocked, not conscious of how much we'll always be able to read each other. 'I do, I want to ask her, but I wanted to ask you first. I didn't want you to hear it from anyone but me.'

And as I look at him I realize it makes perfect sense. He's ready, and their relationship is already cooked. It's been on slow simmer for the last fifteen years without any of us knowing. There's momentary agony, but then it clears. Harry dumping me has turned out to be a bizarre emotional enema. I'm stronger than I thought, and I know I can survive this.

'That's incredible news. You have my total blessing.'

A huge grin spreads across his face, and I'm sure I hear a chorus of self-help witches serenading my maturity. This ship has sailed, and I'm waving it off. I wonder if the plumber's still single? I don't stay much longer – however grown-up I'm being I don't think I can take too much of Adam's premarital bliss. Besides, I've got a professional crisis to resolve. I sent Doreen a huge bunch of flowers yesterday, and I'm following it up with a face to face charm offensive later today. But even if I can get her back on side, I know that I can't just go back down the hag route. These photos need something that will lift them above the ordinary, and I think I've come up with the perfect solution.

Tom's remodelling a palatial garden in Highgate, and is precariously balanced on a ladder which is leaning up against a tree. He leaps down and gives me a big hug.

'Life's never boring for you, is it, Anna?'

'You could say that.'

We sit on the grass, and I give him a potted version of me and Harry's break-up minus the revenge fuck, which still makes me feel slightly sick.

'He was transitional man. At least you've found out early.' He looks at me thoughtfully. 'It's a shocking waste of that garden though, it was really for you. I imagined you lounging around in a deckchair fantasizing about your next pair of high heels.'

'How'd you know I wouldn't have been lying in a deckchair reading Proust in the original French?'

I think about asking how it's going with Louisa, the textbook second wife, but I can't bear to hear about any more romantic reverie. Instead I lay out my plan to him.

'If we could use some of your gardens as a setting it'd really lift the photos. The hags normally go for these awful mauve backdrops like it's a bar mitzvah.'

'I wouldn't start slating them now, Anna, you need them way more than they need you.'

I feel instantly chastened: he's absolutely right. 'I know, I know. I've got three days to sort this out or else I'm completely dead.'

'I'm sure your natural charm will win them round. They're only human: no one could resist you when you're on form.'

Is he flirting with me? 'Yes, well ...' I say, a bit flustered, but he's already moved on. He's thinking through his gardens, asking me about the couples.

'I don't think Harry was completely off track. We need something light and bright for the gay couple and something more classic for the oldies.'

'I really don't want to take advantage of your weekend.'

'It's OK, it'll mean some juggling, but I'll make it work.' He stands up. 'Anyway, Anna, I need to get back to the foliage.'

'Oh,' I say, disappointed. 'I thought I could take you for lunch to say thank you.'

'No time. Weeds wait for no man.'

I kiss him goodbye, and try to force myself to go back to the office but the prospect of seeing Jocasta is too hideous. Instead I head for the Starbucks round the corner from the studios where the hags effect their miraculous make-overs. I sit there honing my copy and dealing with last-minute arrangements, desperate to ensure nothing else goes tits up. Ruby meets me there and we load up with coffee and muffins. The hags love to snack and I'm willing to employ anything in my armoury.

As we walk round to the studios I decide it's time to flush out the truth.

'Why haven't you told me about Horst?'

'Oh . . . I – I don't know, Anna, I just wasn't sure you'd approve and I knew you knew anyway . . .' she tails off, all red and tongue-tied.

'Of course I approve, if you like him. Why would you even care what I think?'

'You're always so sure about people. Who's in and who's out. And he's not a catch in a Harry way.'

I give her a rueful smile. 'You don't want a Harry, take it from me.'

I find Doreen in a dressing room, and theatrically ambush her with the huge bouquet.

'Thank you, Anna,' she says, briefly casting a cold look in my direction. 'They're very pretty.'

She turns her back on me, busying herself with washing her brushes in a noxious-smelling liquid.

'Doreen, I should never have taken the job away from you. I can't tell you how sorry I am.' I can hear how hopelessly clunky and insincere my apology sounds. She cuts right across me.

'It's good of you to come, and obviously we'll be working together again soon, but I know why you're here, news travels fast. And I can't see any way I can help you out.'

'Doreen . . .'

'We need to get on. We've got a mother and daughter through there who've come all the way from Hartlepool.'

She's halfway out the door when I grab her arm.

'Sometimes I think I know way more than I do.' I pause, groping for the right tack to take. 'And I know that right now I need you way more than you need me. But I promise I will find a way to pay you back. I don't deserve your help but I'm begging for it.'

'Begging for it, are you?' she says drily.

'Yes, Doreen, I am. I was hasty, I was thoughtless and I've learnt my lesson. And I've got muffins.'

She breaks into an unexpected grin and soon we're divvying up bakery goods over cups of industrial strength PG Tips. I'm more a camomile tea kind of girl, but it's patently not the moment to argue.

With the photos back on track, I head back to Karen and Greg's feeling faintly reassured. I pick up a bottle of fair-trade wine en route, and challenge a delighted Karen to a game of Scrabble. I'm conscious I've been treating their house like a hotel – or at least a low-rent hostel – for some months, and I don't want to be too much of a sullen adolescent. Karen's a Scrabble maestro. I beg her to let me use the dictionary to scout for obscure words, but she's not having any of it.

'You always used to let me win!'

'Only when you were ten or eleven. You never would've got the knack if you'd lost every single time.'

God, it must've been so boring for her, having to put down 'but' just so me and Dan didn't feel too inadequate. Parenthood involves so many different sizes of sacrifice.

'How long do you think you'll be back for this time, darling?'

'As soon as I've got this event out of the way I'm going to start looking for somewhere.'

'What, on your own?'

'Yes, on my own,' I say, laughing. 'I think I'm old enough to cope.'

'Just as long as you know you can stay as long as you like. It'll always be your home too.'

I think about the prospect of living here indefinitely, permanently pickled in teenage aspic. It's obviously a non-starter, but it's nice to be wanted. I study my terrible tiles, desperate to conjure up an unseen seven letter. My concentration's broken by the shrill shriek of my phone: Harry. I take it outside, sullen but polite.

'Anna, I'm going to get to the point. I talked to Becky about what you said about Lucas, and she was disgusted. None of us know what you were trying to do, but we don't want any part of your event. They'd like you to pull their part of the article, and there's no way I'm doing the panel.'

I go through the whole gamut of responses. I try reasoning with him, screaming at him, pleading with him. Nothing works: he's out and so are they. With one week to go till the event kicks off, I'm back in the depths of crisis. It's like trying to put out the Great Fire of London with a water pistol.

27

I'm holed up in the make-up caravan with Doreen, desperately trying to dissuade her from applying frosted peachy eye-shadow to Hilda's lids. I've already been mortified by Hilda's description of how much Harry bullied them into those awful poses, insisting it was the look I'd specified. How could I have been so doggedly trusting? God knows I'm paying for it now.

Tom gives a hesitant knock on the door. 'Is everyone decent?' He's taken us out to a country pile where he's remodelled a rose garden. We're going to photograph Hilda and Arthur in the centre of it, with the house acting as a backdrop. Meanwhile I'm hoping the lawyers will prove we own the rights to Becky and Lucas's contribution. I'm not letting them off the hook without a fight. 'Any news?' says Tom, knowing I'm on tenterhooks waiting for the verdict. 'No, nothing,' I tell him despondently.

'Bugger!' he says, with a sympathetic grin. 'Horst's here, he's looking for you.'

Ruby's roped him into helping out on the shoot: the photography budget's long since been squandered on Harry's extended moment of madness. 'I'll be out in a sec,' I tell Tom, 'I'm still making calls on the panel.' If I can't find a replacement soon I'm going to be reduced to going back to Dr Fox, cap in hand. I can't rustle up anyone remotely cool in the time available, and the kind of low-rent talent that *Casual Chic* normally attracts won't be blowing away the fashion elite any time soon. Let's hope none of the surviving panel members find out that Harry's dropped out prior to Monday. There's no avoiding the fact that he was my unique selling point.

I pick my way through the mud towards Horst.

'Anna! You appear to be in the bloom of health despite your many troubles.' I fling my arms round him, intensely comforted by his lanky German presence.

'Tell me about your rehearsals. You're on any day now, aren't you?'

Horst goes one better, performing his principal speech for me, complete with extravagant gestures. I'm pleasantly surprised by how much better he's got. His accent's way less overpowering, and he's actually developed comic timing.

'You're going to be brilliant, Horst, I can feel it in my bones.'

'My life has taken an upswing in many directions, and much of it is due to you, Anna. Perhaps there will be a reparation I can make at a later date.'

'Well, this is a pretty good start. We need all the help we can get.'

He gives me a tentative look. 'Anna, do you hear Polly's happy news?'

'I'm really pleased for them, honestly.'

Adam took Polly to Rome for the world's shortest mini break, proposing to her on the roof of the Hotel

Locarno. We always said we'd go, but somehow we never quite made it – which was pretty much the story of our life together. Polly's beyond thrilled and I'm doing a pretty good job of sharing her joy.

Horst is determined to prove just how helpful he can be, scuttling off to get me a welcome cup of coffee. I stare after him, a crazy plan starting to evolve. I outline it to Ruby back in the caravan.

'If we say he's like Czech, or Polish or something, no one from *Casual Chic* will know the difference. He could be a knitwear designer who's so cool that he's still underground. If I'm confident enough about it, I swear they'll buy it. It's all about the illusion.'

She claps her hands with glee. 'I love it! It has to be a better option than Dr Fox.'

'What have we got left to lose? Either it's a catastrophe, or a triumph. There's not much in between.'

Horst is bowled over by the idea. 'For you to trust me with your precious party is a gross, gross honour. And I need to practise my acting at all possible times.'

So with that insane strategy in place, we head down to the rose garden to check on the progress of the shoot. Tom's skilfully manipulating the wildly bog standard photographer we're using, leading Hilda and Arthur round the garden to find the perfect spot. He's too absorbed to notice me, so I simply stand and watch him, struck by what a skilled diplomat he is. They snap roll after roll of film, till I'm worried that Arthur's ancient legs will crumple beneath him.

'That's enough for now,' I say, leading them off to the

caravan for a cup of tea and a sit down while the team set up the next location.

'Never seems to stop, does it, Anna?' says Hilda, grabbing my arm.

'I'm sorry about that,' I say guiltily. 'I really appreciate you taking more time out for this.'

'Time out from what?' she giggles. 'It's not like I've got a career! Anyway, we missed you.' I smile at her affectionately, wishing on so many counts that I'd overcome my paranoia and attended the earlier sessions. 'I want to hear all about what's happening with your young man.'

'Oh, the young man. It's all gone tits up, since you ask.' What on earth possessed me to use such a phrase? Hilda doesn't seem to mind at all though, merrily launching into a stream of questions. Before I know it I'm telling the whole unvarnished truth, right from the top.

'Ooh, he was a right cool Eddie that one. I wish I'd known. I could've told you he'd be trouble.'

'I think I knew myself actually, Hilda. I just didn't want to hear it.'

'So why did you bother yourself with him? You're a lovely looking girl: you could have your pick.'

I love it when people say things like that. It's the kind of statement kindly cab drivers make when they pick you up and you're looking downcast. It's so not true though, not when you take out all the ones who are married, or alcoholic, or commitment-phobic. Or all three.

'I'd never tried a man like that before. You know, a trophy. I guess I didn't appreciate how much polishing was involved.'

Once Arthur's revived we head back out for the next set-up, which Tom's located round the back of the house in the kitchen garden. Arthur and Hilda hold hands amongst the lettuces, the afternoon sun casting a rosy glow over proceedings. Tom strides over to me, hair askew and hands muddy.

'Anna, I really think this is going to work out.'

'What?' I say, oddly excited.

'The photos. I think they'll look really good.'

'Oh. Yes. Thanks so much for this. I'd be totally scuppered without you.'

'You would, wouldn't you?' he says, laughing at me. 'Who knew I could ever be someone's knight in shining armour?'

This is day two of our photography extravaganza. We went back to the hairdresser's roof garden for Oliver and Steve, and followed up with a lush enclave in Hampstead.

'What are you doing tonight?' I ask him. 'Can I at least take you for a drink?'

'Um, I'd love it but I'm not sure there'll be time.'

'Oh, OK.'

I clam up, unreasonably petulant, before my phone starts up. It's our slothful, podgy lawyer calling to tell me that we've got absolutely no rights over Becky and Lucas's contribution.

'Surely if we've put all that work in we must own the material?'

'Sadly not. We would have if you'd got them to sign a release form, but under the circumstances we don't have a leg to stand on.'

A release form: how obvious. But how hard to effect when your subjects are meant to be close personal friends. I turn to Tom, tears springing to my eyes. I can't keep this many spiky, unyielding balls in the air indefinitely.

'Hey,' he says, giving me one of his all-enveloping hugs. 'We can fix this, I know we can.'

We pace around the caravan, throwing out options. Watching how Tom's effortlessly run the shoot I almost consider asking him to try to talk them round, but I know it'll be futile. His phone rings but he dumps the call, face screwed up in problem-solving mode.

'Got it!' he shouts, and then more subdued, 'But I don't know if you'll like it.'

'Try me.'

'Polly and Adam.'

'You're actually suggesting I interview them about how they fell in love? I'm literally the last person on earth who needs to have that conversation.'

'Look, Anna, I know it's hard, but I'm not sure you've got much choice. We've got a day left to pull this off, and I for one am not prepared to let you squander all your hard work.'

I sit in sullen silence, trying to conjure up an alternative personality for myself, a personality in which I'm magnanimous and saintly enough to go through with it.

'Have I ever told you about the first time I picked up the kids from Maggie's new place?'

'No.'

'So Arnold Schwarzenegger comes lumbering to the

314

door – he's all ripped muscles and stubble – and I'm feeling like this putrid shrimp.'

'You're muscly!'

'Not like him I'm not. Anyway, the kids take ages to come downstairs and Joe is kind of surly but Belle flings her arms round his fat neck and asks him if he's going to read her her bedtime story. I felt like I'd been dumped all over again, first Maggie then Belle.'

'That must have been hideous.'

'It was hideous, but eventually I thought, well at least she's happy.' Even as he says this, I see a cloud crossing his face. 'At least she's not hating living with him, and storing up all kinds of pain to screw up the rest of her life. And then I felt OK about it.'

'And your point is?' I say, reaching out to grab his wrist, hoping he'll appreciate that I've heard how much it hurt.

'That humiliation, or rejection, is a temporary feeling. It's possible to rise above it, particularly for someone like you.'

'Someone like me?'

'Someone who appreciates the ridiculousness of life. I don't know, I'm not explaining myself very well, but I know you've got to do this, and I know you'll do it with dignity.'

'Dignity, always dignity,' I declaim theatrically, thinking again of my grandmother. I must go over for supper once my one-woman war is finally over. I go to take my hand away, but he grips it tightly, holding it aloft. 'Courage, Anna,' he says jokily, but with real fervour.

I call Polly en route back to London in Tom's car, his silent presence giving me the strength to ask this agonizing favour. 'Are you sure?' she says doubtfully, and I promise her that I am.

'I don't want actual, gory details but I do want to hear how good it is. I am pleased for you, Pol, I promise you.' She gets a bit teary, and agrees on the spot, promising to strong arm Adam. I think about telling her how much he hates having his photo taken – even holiday snaps were like torture for him – but decide she's not going to appreciate my insider knowledge. I momentarily imagine making them pose for some Harry-style outrages, but obviously I bat that evil thought away.

By the time we get to Harlesden it's almost dark.

'So this is where it all began,' says Tom. 'How are you coping with being back here?'

'It's a lot better than I thought it would be,' I tell him, 'but I know I've got to make a run for it soon.'

'Take it from me, escaping from the parental home is even better the second time round.'

Tom's rented a maisonette in Queen's Park. It sounds like a big step down from the family home, but an ideal venue for all that athletic lovemaking with cranberry girl.

'Do you actually stay at your flat much, or are you mainly at Louisa's?' Why am I asking that? Most of my thoughts should stay locked in my stupid head.

'No, I do stay there. You know, Chicken Tonight and *The Simpsons*. I'm pretty much your typical divorced man.'

I laugh, wondering why I originally thought he was

such an A-grade dullard. As I'm reflecting on his many sterling qualities, Karen flings the front door open and comes down the path. She's wearing a vile tie-dyed tunic and her 'Rats Have Rights' badge.

'Is that you, darling?'

Before I know it Tom's stepping out of the car.

'Are you Mrs Christie? I'm Tom, Anna's friend.'

'Karen Parker. I've never believed in the patriarchal enslavement of marriage.'

Shut up, Karen.

'I'm not too much of a fan either,' laughs Tom.

'How lovely to meet you,' she says. 'I've heard all about what a trooper you've been.'

'I love rats,' says Tom, clocking the badge. 'My daughter's got a white one called Boris.'

That's it. Karen's off, expounding her views on animal experimentation (not a fan) and the government's many other crimes against our furred friends.

'You must come in for a drink, Tom, now you've driven all this way.'

'Well, actually I've got to get going . . .'

'No, no. I love meeting Anna's friends.' Does she? 'Surely you can spare fifteen minutes?'

She pretty much manhandles him inside, pouring him a half of Greg's lethal home brew and plaguing him with questions about his gardening. 'The rape of mother earth is the tragedy of our age,' she tells him earnestly. I feel like I'm going to die of shame, catapulted back to all those years when I avoided bringing boyfriends home at all costs. Still, there's something oddly touching about the warmth of her hospitality. I can see she's really enjoying having him here.

After a good forty-five minutes he insists he's got to leave. Karen gives him a fulsome hug, and I walk him to the door.

'I'm so sorry I won't be able to help you out tomorrow,' he says.

Tom's fixed up a Japanese garden in Kensington for us, but has to get on with his day job.

'No, it's all right, I think I've watched you enough to have a vague idea of how to set it up. Which is not to say I'm looking forward to it.'

'You can do it.'

'Will you come to the event next week? I know it's not really your bag, but it would be weird to not have you there now.' I pause. 'Bring Louisa obviously.'

'We'd love to come. I think she actually reads *Casual Chic*.' That figures. He smiles down at me. 'I've really got to get in the car now. Don't forget, Anna, dignity always dignity.'

He's looking straight at me as he says it, and I'm suddenly overwhelmed by the desire to kiss him. Perhaps it's the phrase making me feel like I'm in some fabulous black and white melodrama, but before I know it I'm leaning upward to lock lips. Sadly he's in an entirely different film. He gently pulls backward, and I topple inelegantly into his chest.

'Sorry, I . . .'

'Hey, it's fine.'

'No, it's not. I'm an idiot, I'm sorry.'

And with that I give way to a sob, stumbling back into the house, slamming the door. How could I have made such a fool of myself? I'm running about ten years behind everyone else's timetable, throwing myself at attached men and living with my parents. 'Tom seems like a very decent chap,' says Karen, coming up the stairs. It's too much for me: I rush into my bedroom and throw myself down on the bed, wrapping myself up tightly in my birthday pashmina. Is there anyone in the world who's a bigger loser than me?

28

That night I barely sleep a wink, plagued with obsessive thoughts about how stupid I've been. Was Tom the point all the time, had I not been too shallow to notice? My whole relationship with Harry seems like some kind of bizarre optical illusion now, and in wasting all that time peering down the periscope I've lost the chance to be with someone proper. Someone who understands that life is painful and difficult, but also that it's worth the effort. It's blindingly obvious to me that I've never really tried before – I've drifted through relationships skimming off the cream and complaining about the milk – but for him I think I could finally grow up. Too bad he's gearing up to have a whole herd of cranberry children with that destiny-stealing dwarf. I keep my phone on all night hoping he'll call, but it remains stubbornly silent until 7 a.m., just when I've finally drifted off to sleep. I blearily snatch it up, to be greeted by the morning trill of Jocasta.

'Hello, Anna, did I wake you?'

'Not at all,' I lie, 'I was getting in the shower.'

'Mummy time is rather unforgiving,' she says with a tinkly laugh, 'and sometimes I forget to reset the clock,' before launching into a grilling about my imaginary Czech knitwear designer. 'I do worry that the panel doesn't have the profile I would've hoped for. If only Dr Neil Fox hadn't been otherwise engaged.'

'I know, shame. But Jan Pzeknik is a total find. Harvey Nichols and Harrods are, as we speak, fighting over who's going to carry him next season. At least they would be if it wasn't quite this early.' Quiet, Anna, keep it lean.

'I see. As you're unable to attend to the final arrangements I'm going to visit the venue and ensure there's plenty of room for Spicy Nights to set up.'

'Spicy Nights?'

'The jazz band, Anna. You do need to stay across the detail.'

Oh God. Let's hope my French DJ can drown them out with wall to wall hip hop. I get her off the phone and try to pull myself together. I can't go to pieces today of all days. As these photos are the replacement for the shots that everyone loved, it's imperative they deliver.

I turn up to meet Polly and Adam with tiny, swollen mole eyes and mad person's hair. Frankly I'm surprised I don't get sectioned en route. At least I'm too wrapped up in misery about Tom to feel overly anguished about the bizarre situation we find ourselves in. I try to recreate the alchemy with the surroundings that Tom had – that instinctive visual sense which lifted the other two shoots way above average – but I'm no artist. Having had him alongside me for the last two days, I feel unreasonably bereft without him. Perhaps it's because it feels like more than a temporary break in transmission now I've inelegantly lunged. He's so bloody honourable; he'll probably tell Louisa, who'll get a restraining order out on me and ensure that we're parted forever. I've got to snap out of my melodramatic reverie and get on with the job in hand.

Polly's fighting off Doreen's best efforts with the sparkly blusher, but submitting to the hair hag's rollers. 'You look amazing,' I tell her, which she does. She's got that blissed-out glow that I'm never going to have, not unless the nunnery I'm destined for has a particularly good drug dealer.

'Thanks, Anna,' she says, giving me a wary smile.

'How many times do I have to tell you I'm pleased?' I say, shaking her shoulders.

'How many times do I have to tell you I'm sorry?' she fires back.

'No more times, Pol. I don't want to be going up the aisle behind you, still hearing it.'

'Would you really be my bridesmaid? I was worried you'd be insulted if I asked.'

'I'd be insulted if you didn't ask.'

Seeing she's liable to dissolve I give her a stern look, knowing full well it'll give Doreen the perfect excuse to give the blusher another try. Besides, there's no time for emotion today, it's all about the work. We shoot roll after roll, and I pray that there'll be hidden gems amongst the inevitable turkeys. If only Tom was here to make it all come together, but there's no trace of him – not a single text or call. Maybe he's disgusted by me, convinced the only reason I've turned 180 degrees is because he's unavailable. I can't bear to have my worst fears confirmed by calling, particularly having sent a long, rambling text last night. Every time I'm tempted, the self-help witches pour poison in my ears about how much men hate needy.

Eventually the job's done, and the three of us head to a nearby restaurant for the dreaded interview. There's a weird moment when we sit down and Polly and I each offer up the seat next to Adam, but I insist they go on the same side. I inhale a gin martini in a single glug and get down to business.

'Look, we're obviously not going to talk about me and Adam's relationship here. I think what we should do is explore what it feels like to fall in love with someone you've known for years.'

'What do you mean?' asks Adam quizzically.

'Well, you've missed out a stage, haven't you? That phase where you can pretend the other person's whoever you want them to be because you don't know them well enough to think different.'

Harry's smug blond face floats past my mind's eye, but I force it aside. Meanwhile Polly's giving Adam a look of total devotion, a look I don't think I ever gave him in the entire ten years we spent together. My looks were always ones of assessment, deliberation – even if I didn't know it at the time. It must've been so exhausting for both of us. She jumps in.

'I feel strange saying this.'

'Just be honest, it's fine.'

'I don't think we have missed out, I think we've made a trade. There's no nasty surprises if you know each other as well as we do.'

'I'm not sure about that,' says Adam. 'Not that I've had any nasty surprises,' he adds hurriedly, 'I just mean that being someone's boyfriend is way different from being their friend. Or their husband,' he says, squeezing her hand.

He's right of course, but he only knows it because he's gone the distance with me, while Polly's never even lived with someone before. You expose your biggest flaws to the person who you share your life with. No wonder we never think our friends' partners are good enough – we're not party to the domestic dragon that lurks beneath the social facade.

'Even so,' Polly counters, 'if we didn't already have all this familiarity we never would've known we wanted to get married so soon.'

But isn't it the memory of that early novelty that keeps you ploughing on through the long haul? When your breasts are leaking milk and your stomach's hanging out over your post-natal support pants, at least you know there was a time when that person prized you as exotic and mysterious. Then again, what do I know? All those truths I've confidently held as self-evident seem to be hitting the skids in rapid succession.

We talk about their wedding plans (surprisingly Polly doesn't fancy getting married in the depths of Harlesden) and their five-year life plan. Although it's unbelievably bizarre, it's nowhere near as corrosively painful as I expected it to be. Perhaps I really am happy for them.

'Oh, Anna, surely you've got enough now,' says Polly,

leaning over and snapping off my Dictaphone. 'Are you worrying about that arrogant wanker? You've looked really down all day.'

And it all comes tumbling out. How Harry seems like a lucky escape, a weird romantic mini break that didn't quite work, but that Tom's absence feels like a gaping wound. And a self-inflicted wound at that.

'Why didn't I bloody notice sooner? I know he had crap dad clothes, but I could've sorted that out. And the rest of him is so unbelievably dear.'

'He did wear a fleece to karaoke,' says Polly sagely.

'That's true; I do hate fleeces more than anything. Even so, I've really screwed up. Sorry, Adam, is this weird? Actually, forget that. You deserve it.'

He laughs at me. 'No, it's fine. Maybe you'd like to tell me about some particularly juicy sexual fantasies you've been having about him.'

'Funnily enough ...'

'No, stop,' he yelps, holding his hands up. 'If you like him this much then you need to go out and get him, simple as that.'

'But he's got cranberry girl now, and if he had any feelings whatsoever he'd have called. Or gone one better and actually kissed me back.'

'Maybe you had halitosis,' says Adam wickedly.

'Don't say that!'

'I'm being stupid, Anna, but I mean what I said. There's obviously a lot of feeling between you. Maybe for once in your life you're going to have to work for something.'

'But he's with someone else now. Perhaps the grown-up thing to do is just accept it and move on. God, I hate that phrase.'

'Maybe,' says Adam thoughtfully. 'Or maybe it's too important for you to sit it out being a martyr.'

'What if he's the love of your life?' adds Polly. 'What if the love of your life actually owns a fleece?'

I think about their advice all the way back to Harlesden, and as it's in the arse end of nowhere that's a lot of thinking time. A cynical part of me thinks about how much they need to justify the pursuit of true love at any cost. But even if they're right, I can't see how I could make my intentions towards Tom any clearer than my clumsy attempt to get intimate. I can't bear the fact that he won't be there for the event. Even if he'd come with a simpering Louisa in tow, his very presence would've made me feel less exposed. Now it'll just be me, flying solo, relying on Horst's dubious acting skills to save me from abject humiliation.

The next forty-eight hours pass in a blur of preparation. Tom sends me a good luck text too bland to stand up to any neurotic over-analysis. I do my best, but 'Good luck for tomorrow, you'll be brilliant!' is the kind of thing you'd send a spotty nephew sitting his GCSEs. He might as well have said 'Best wishes'. I send him one back reiterating my invitation but hear nothing – he's so over me.

The highlight of the two days is the photos coming back. Hilda manages to look both matriarchal and radiant, the beautiful setting giving a gravitas to the pictures: their part of the article will make a fantastic centrepiece to the other two couples. Polly and Adam's shots are nowhere near as polished as Harry's efforts with Becky and Lucas, but they do have a warmth and immediacy that the highly posed photos never had. I'd love it if Victor saw it the same way, but somehow I doubt it. Even so, there's none of that strutting self-regard that Lucas can't help but exude, even when he's in 2D. I feel a sudden stab of concern for Becky, which I squash down by remembering how much trouble her refusal to believe me has caused. Oliver and Steve's are also wonderfully boosted by Tom's amazing locations – if only he was around to share my relief. Jocasta pronounces them 'passable', but I'm too stressed out to rise to the bait. Ruby and I are casting models, shouting at caterers and organizing curious riders for the remaining panel members. The cobbler to the stars wants Smarties and white roses in his dressing room, while Caitlin, our supermodel, insists that no food is left within 100 metres of the judges' table. I decide to treat Horst to a surprise plate of bratwurst while I'm at it: there's no reason why he shouldn't share in the perks.

The night itself creeps up way too fast. I bought a new red dress in the hope that it would give me confidence, but now I'm worried I look like a traffic light. It also feels way too clingy: I swear my stomach's as large as my cleavage. As Karen zips me up I'm taken aback to see she's got tears in her eyes.

'You look so sophisticated, Anna, how did you get so grown up? I never looked like you do, not even when I was in my prime.'

That's true – there are very few evening dresses that are made out of cheesecloth or corduroy – but I'm amazed it matters.

'You're in your prime now! Besides, you've always had your own special look,' I add tactfully.

'I just don't know how you ever learnt to be you when you only had me. To have a job and a life like you do.'

Is that how it looks from the outside? I always thought they despised my refusal to help the dispossessed. I tell her I love her, something I don't think I've articulated for at least five years, but then I have to turn back to the job in hand. I don't want to leave her though, so I stay in the kitchen, putting on my make-up to the accompaniment of her favourite Fairport Convention album. She conducts some woefully unflattering experiments with my eyeliner – apparently she last owned a tube of mascara in the summer of 1976, but the blistering heat dried it up and she never got round to replacing it. When the cab comes I suddenly feel about five, like I want to bunk off school and hang around her ankles listening to *The Archers*, but I know there's no escape. I hug her goodbye, promising I'll give her a much-needed make-up lesson some time soon, and hobble down the path. What on earth possessed me to wear four-inch heels: I'm swaying like an alcoholic and I've only had fennel tea.

I watch London zipping past the window, feeling totally alone. The very familiarity of it adds to my sense of isolation. I know it so well that it's almost like a person, a watchful friend who's witnessed all my different incarnations. How is it that my relationship with bricks and mortar is more enduring than with any of the men I've professed to love?

The church is buzzing with activity when I arrive, a heavy bass line underpinning the frenetic atmosphere. It's emanating from my French DJ's record decks and according to Ruby is antagonizing Jocasta beyond measure.

'Is that Spicy Nights by any chance?' I ask her. A group of balding middle-aged men are cleaning out their trombones and straightening their spotted bow ties.

'The very same,' confirms Ruby. 'Apparently they specialize in Dixie.'

I can't face Jocasta quite yet; instead I seek out Horst in his dressing room. He's pacing the floor striking poses, and throwing out odd statements.

'Hugely fashionable, enchanting hems, most agreeable trimming. Oh, Anna, I am practising my fashion lingo in order to be highly prepared. Ruby has been teaching me colloquialisms to improve my general performance.'

'Maybe pull back a bit on enchanting. Did you get the sausages?'

'They were a very fine example of the genre, Anna. I enjoyed them inordinately.'

Just then Ruby rushes in to tell me that the other panel members have turned up. Leaving her to continue Horst's much-needed tutelage, I dash off to find them. Why are models so relentlessly dull? It's as if they think their looks negate the need for any semblance of a personality. It's no good having a palatial attic if the rest of the house is a hovel. Maybe I'm jealous; whenever anyone tells me I'm beautiful I want to argue the toss, assuming it's just a cynical ploy to get into my pants. 'But look how my nose twists at the end,' I'll say, shoving it at them inelegantly like a truffling pig. We talk about the respective merits of our shoes for a while, before Caitlin launches into an earnest diatribe about how important it is to wash clothes at 30 degrees. She momentarily extracts her Marlboro Light from her perfect mouth and clutches my arm. 'I'd just really like a chance to tell the crowd. It would make such a difference to the polar ice caps if we all did it.' I think about explaining the concept of flight emissions, having just heard about her last three jet-setting holidays, but decide to spare her the science lesson.

At least she's well meaning. The cobbler's some kind of tortured genius, demanding to know the credentials of the other panel members and rewriting my introductory remarks.

'I'm a shoe maker, not a designer. It's all about the craft!' He slams his hand down on the dressing table, making me jump. Oh God, I hope Horst is going to be able to hold his own.

'Is there anything I can get you while you're waiting?'

'Bottle of Glenfiddich should do the trick, darling.'

Great; so I've got a drunken psychopath, a sanctimonious airhead and a fraud. It's all shaping up marvellously. Jocasta corners me as I'm leaving his dressing room.

'I don't want to have to give you a dressing down, Anna, but the noise your friend with the record player is producing is intolerable. Spicy Nights can barely tune up.'

'This is *actually* a fashion party, Jocasta, not a wedding reception in Weybridge.'

I think I've gone a bit too far: now I've thrown down the gauntlet it's going to be a fight to the death. High spots of colour spring to her cheeks, and her intensely lacquered hair starts to wobble menacingly.

'I'm forced to remind you that I'm senior to you, and if you continue to plough your own furrow with no regard for my instructions then the consequences will be severe.'

'I'll take my chances,' I tell her, turning on my heels. I know I'm playing with fire, but I'm not sure I care any more. I've got to stake a claim to a future outside the cloying confines of *Casual Chic*. It's no good hanging around hoping someone's going to rescue me – I'll have to make the break, whatever the cost. Which might well be a decade spent living in penury with Karen and Greg, but so be it. Feeling strangely elated I head off to find the finalists for the design competition. They're much as you'd expect – all angular hair and flat caps, and that's just the girls – but a couple of them are endearingly excited to have made it this far.

Now the guests are starting to arrive, taking in the darkly Gothic interior and pouncing on the champagne. The first tranche seems to largely consist of the kind of PRs I'm constantly fobbing off; vacant girls whose life purpose is trying to persuade people like me to write about their client's waxing strips. Let's hope that at least a smattering of the celebrities I invited deign to turn up. I can see Victor huddled together with a consortium of directors, poised to pounce on the key advertisers as soon as they step through the door. If they step through the door that is: there's still a million ways in which this event could fail.

Stills from the shoots have been blown up across the back wall, and I'm oddly comforted to have a huge version of Polly's face smiling down over proceedings. She, however, is mortified. 'You never told me you were doing that,' she hisses as she comes through the door.

'You look fab,' I tell her, but I know in my heart of hearts that the original photos would've made more of an impact. Maybe Jocasta's right and I have summarily failed to deliver.

I want so much to hang out with my friends, but it's all about working the room. Susie turns up with Martin who, while not wearing an actual fleece, still manages to look completely incongruous. Maybe it's because his beige windcheater looks like it came from a *Howard's Way* wardrobe sale. Even so, they're both looking exceptionally jolly. Susie envelops me in a hug. 'I'm pregnant,' she squeaks, as a big grin erupts across Martin's face. 'We're not meant to tell anyone yet, but it is kind of down to you.' It turns out that her drunken dancing with Horst the other week was the spur she needed to conceive again. 'All this bloody prodding and poking, and one night of proper passion was what it took.' I look away, trying my hardest not to imagine Martin peeling off his windcheater to reveal the delights of his naked form, but it's too late.

'That's so brilliant,' I tell her, excitement mingling with nausea.

Right now it's all about births, marriage and ... well, hopefully no deaths. Although Jocasta does look fairly murderous when she spots the sushi coming out. 'Bit of a mix up,' I tell her, smiling sweetly and tucking into some tempura.

'Fantastic canapés,' says Victor, appearing beside us. 'They're distinctly reminiscent of the night we spent at Nobu.'

Is it a reprimand? I'm not sure, but either way it succeeds in shutting Jocasta up. Besides, the prawn vol-au-vents are proving strangely unpopular with the wheat-hating bulimics who are populating this party. I spot my first celebrity heading through the door – she's only a *Hollyoaks* actress, but it's a start. A few flashbulbs go off, and I allow myself a brief moment of relief.

I go to check on Horst, who is way too nervous to venture into the fray. Ruby and I have styled him as expertly as we can, going for minimal chic. Out goes the heavy metal T-shirt, and in comes a tight, ribbed grey number. He actually looks surprisingly toned now the layers of bad taste have been peeled back. Skinny jeans and silky black Japanese trainers complete the look.

'Do you think sunglasses are a step too far?' says Ruby anxiously. 'I reckon it'll be easier to fake it if they can't see his eyes.'

'Stick them on,' I say, and we stand back to admire our handiwork.

'You look hot!' I tell him, pleasantly surprised.

'Hot like chilli sauce,' says Horst, all too pleased with his newfound command of the English language.

'Look, you're meant to be Czech, don't over egg the pudding with these weird phrases.'

'Over egg what pudding?' he says, puzzled, but with no time to explain I leave him in Ruby's capable hands. I duck backstage to check on the preparations for the show, only to be greeted by the hideous sight of Doreen, blusher brush at the ready, commanding operations.

'Surprise!' she says, giving me a warm hug.

Where the hell is the make-up director I booked? All the quirky, eccentric faces that Ruby and I worked so hard to find are being made to look like they've stepped out of the Littlewoods catalogue, circa 1989. I do my best not to convey my horror, quickly establishing that Jocasta took it upon herself to cancel my team on the basis that they were too expensive.

'Let's try and keep it subtle,' I say. 'Michael, do we need to tong the hair quite as much as you're doing?'

'I'm going for volume, Anna,' he says emphatically, as the bird's nest-headed model he's working on tries to silently communicate her abject distress. Who can blame her: she looks like she's had a bubble perm and then been electrocuted.

'And, Doreen, let's limit the palate a bit more. Maybe pull back on the purple. It's all about nude tones at the moment.'

'Leave it with us, Anna.' She gives me a fond smile. 'You need to learn to trust the professionals.'

Could I trust them any less than I do? But having promised them my undying loyalty I can hardly turn round and read them the riot act. I wish so much that

Tom was here; his innate tact would somehow manage to rescue the situation. I'm depressed beyond measure by how out of step the models will look with the directional designs: we're going to be a laughing stock.

I try my level best not to neck the champagne like it's going out of fashion. Instead I down most of a bottle of Karen's rescue remedy and take deep breaths. As it's pretty much pure brandy it probably has the same net result, but at least I feel drunk in a holistic way. The large atrium is filled to the brim now, the high ceiling ensuring that the music and conversation sound roaringly loud. Does that add up to atmosphere or relentless noise? Either way, the crowd seem to be enjoying themselves and have diversified beyond the world-weary function addicts who turned up first.

Soon it's time to gather the panel at the judges' table and round up the finalists. Initially I succeed in seating Caitlin next to Horst, but then Ned the cobbler has an unexpected shit fit. 'I'm left-handed!' he shouts. 'Left-brained! I need to go in the middle to balance myself out!' Horst stares at him nervously, subtly shifting his chair away. I'm filled with a wave of guilt; is this yet another selfish and disastrous decision I've made? Watching Ned eyeballing Horst, all too eager to cross-question him about his work, I decide it's the perfect time to befriend Spicy Nights.

'I hear you specialize in Dixie!' I tell them enthusiastically. 'Come on, boys, let's hear some. Loud as you can.'

Grinning madly, trombones aloft, they launch into

some ghastly plinky plonky jazz standard. As I duck backstage to hurry up the hags, I see Jocasta clapping her hands wildly and attempting to draw Roger into a strange lopsided jig. She's drunk! Maybe she'll try to mount Victor, or leap on to the stage to try her hand at catwalk modelling. Not that I'm one to talk about clumsy passes. Hit by a wave of sadness I banish Tom from my fevered brain, and start lining up the models. I manage to let down some hair along the way, and smudge off the odd bit of lurid shadow, but it's so not the look I was after.

For some insane reason I decided to compere myself, from a vantage point opposite the judges' table. The music starts out mangled, with Spicy Nights and the DJ struggling for supremacy, but luckily Ruby manages to wrestle the trombones off the band. Seeing the models come out, I'm pleasantly surprised by how good the dresses look, even with the bizarre styling they've been subjected to. I'm put off my stride by the sight of Horst chewing compulsively on his pen and making reams of notes; he's not going to launch into some searing critique of each piece is he? 'Bravo!' he shouts as a particularly outlandish design comes down the catwalk. 'Top hole!' Ned glowers ominously at him, but refrains from an outright attack. When the final dress comes out I'm blown away. It's scrunchy red velvet, with a long train and a headdress: sort of Anne Boleyn but sexy. If anyone ever proposes to me again I'd be thrilled to stand up at the front in that. I force myself out of my reverie, shocked to realize that this is probably the first positive fantasy I've ever had about my wedding day. Tom's crumpled face makes a brief appearance in my mind's eye, but I knock it out the park and concentrate on bringing all the models back on to the runway.

To my delight, the designs get a standing ovation, and then there's a brief pause before the judging kicks off. I go over to their table, but can't seem to manage a private word with Horst. Ned greets me by putting his hand on my arse, before pulling it away with an insincere 'Sorry'. I can see Horst bristling, but I give him a quietening look. Ned hates him enough already, without him leaping in to defend what's left of my virtue.

'Could do with a top-up,' says Ned, gesturing at his whisky glass.

I wonder if we can water it down? I despatch someone to fetch it, and try to focus on Caitlin, but Ned wants my full attention.

'Your mate here doesn't seem too clear on what it is he actually makes.'

'He's Czech, Ned, his English isn't that great.'

'Prague's such a magical place,' Caitlin informs us, earning a tight smile from Horst.

'His English seems all right to me,' says Ned. 'It's more like he's a bit gormless,' he adds in a stage whisper. I want to hit him, but I restrain myself. Luckily I don't think Horst's English quite stretches to gormless. 'What happened to that Harry Langham anyway?'

'I love Harry,' says Caitlin, sounding positively orgasmic at the very thought of him.

'Harry, hmm,' says Horst darkly.

'It's a pity he had to pull out, but unfortunately it

'couldn't be avoided,' I say brightly, trying to distract Ned with the topped-up whisky.

'Yeah, well, it's not exactly what I signed up for.'

'But the show was a triumph, Ned, you must admit.'

'Wasn't it?' squeaks Caitlin. 'I loved all that retro make-up. You must give me the name of your make-up artist.'

'Absolutely,' I say, ducking out to make the final preparations for the judging. If I can just get through this bit, I'm kind of in the clear. I realize I'm shaking; the end's in sight, and yet it still feels so far away too. I've always vowed that I'd never go on holiday alone, but I'm going to have to go and lie down flat somewhere hot after this.

The lights dim, and the first designer joins his model on the catwalk. The dress is an odd tartan confection, a sort of misguided take on Vivienne Westwood. It hitches up on one side with a pin and would be completely unwearable as a wedding dress. I hate it, but I sort of knew the fash pack would admire its brio. It receives a huge round of applause and I start the judging with Caitlin. She recommends it for the final three and we move on to Horst. I've actually provided him with a list of phrases, none of which were 'enchanting hems', so I'm praying he'll stick to the script. He pulls a strange, wistful face.

'For me, fashion is art made flesh.' Oh no, what's he talking about? 'Or indeed fabric! And this is art of the very biggest order. I hold it in very high esteem and also wish for it to be in the final fight.'

Ned tersely backs their choice and we move on to the

next design. It's a fairly trad piece, which I mainly included for contrast, and gets swiftly dismissed. Horst's loving his newfound authority a little too much, sorrowfully telling the student that 'I hope that in the future you will learn to be still braver and let your beating heart sing out through the cloth.'

We whittle it down to three, sending four teary candidates off into the sunset. Ned's been looking increasingly irritated by Horst's extravagant remarks, particularly as the crowd have grown to love him. He keeps dropping references to his years in the business into his own comments, and undermining Horst as much as he can. We're left with the tartan, my beloved red number and a purple puffball monstrosity that Ned's staked his reputation on. Surveying the scene, I realize just how little I know or care about fashion. Whatever made me think that Harry's stupid, pretentious job meant that he had a soul?

The idea is that each judge now picks their two favourite dresses in order of preference. Horst has promised to quietly make his choices and meekly concede if there's a tie, but his red face and prickly body language make me fear the worst. Is it better to leave him till last, or is it too dangerous to give him the casting vote? Unfortunately Ned takes it upon himself to go first before I've had time to refine the order. Horst tries to jump in, but Ned shoves an imperious hand in his face.

'Fashion's a tough business, and it's hard to get the breaks. It takes graft!' He hits the table with his fist, swigging from his glass. Does he actually think he's in

Fame? 'My years in the business,' delivered with a sneering look to Horst, 'have taught me to sniff out talent from a mile off. That's why I KNOW Katie deserves to win. Second choice Mitchell.'

So it's the purple followed by the tartan. My lovely red frock I'm going down the aisle in hasn't even had a look in. At my imaginary wedding! Have I already turned into one of those freakish hermits who has no boyfriend and no job, and sits at home cutting out pictures from *Wedding and Home*, waiting for Johnny Depp to tip up on the doorstep and profess undying love? Caitlin goes next, choosing my red number as her first choice, followed by the purple.

'And I'd just like to ask you all to think seriously about whether you need to use that forty-degree cycle. Clothes wash just as well at thirty, and the polar bears will thank you for it!'

No they won't, seeing as they can't actually speak. They don't even have opposable thumbs. The monkeys might sign their gratitude, but the polar bears are a dead loss.

Horst is next. Much as I hate the purple, I just want him to let it steal the prize and finish this fiasco once and for all. But looking at the red dress's designer – a baby-faced gay guy who's beyond thrilled to have made it this far – I'm suddenly torn. Horst's psyching himself up to speak.

'Let's hear your pearls of wisdom then,' interjects Ned nastily.

Horst flashes him a look of visceral loathing. It's a

whole new side to his character I've never seen before, and I fear it could be dangerous.

'I too have many years of experience in my home country of Czechoslovakia. As a young child I spent much time in my father's leather factory, stitching designs of my own making for my mother.' Please let him stop talking soon. I mime a throat-cutting gesture, but he ploughs on. 'She is dead now, and for her memory I am determined that we choose the person who displays the most talent, not the biggest peacock feathers. For me, the purple is devilish, but ultimately an over-egging of the pudding. Victory to the red!'

So now it's a dead heat. Why didn't he do as he was told? There's palpable tension in the room as I ask the judges if they can try to reach a consensus. It's not quite the *Pop Idol* final, but nor is it far off. Jocasta suddenly lurches over to my side. I swear she actually hiccups.

'Hate to admit it, old girl, but it's a jolly good show.'

'Glad you're having fun,' I tell her, wondering if 'old girl' can ever count as a compliment. No matter. Right now I've got bigger things to worry about. Neither Horst nor Ned are backing down, and their argument is reaching fever pitch. Ned's jabbing his finger at Horst, insisting he gets the casting vote.

'I've Googled you, mate, and there's no sign of you. Where'd you train?'

'In Prague's Institute of Design! I received both a First and a huge distinction.'

'Bollocks. Where'd you put on your last show?'

The crowd are erupting into feverish chatter, clearly

sensing potential scandal. Victor's sat opposite me, his face set in mute horror as the event falls apart in front of his very eyes.

'You will not doubt me!' shouts Horst.

'I do, mate, I do doubt you,' says Ned, looming up out of his chair. Horst stands up, throwing out his arm dramatically as if he's in court.

'I studied under Johann Voysic between 1994 and 1996. He said there had never been a student as exceptional as me. My ability to combine colour with form . . .'

I can't let this go any further. I grab the microphone and cut across Horst.

'Our judges obviously feel very passionate about the designs we've seen tonight. Let's take a short break and give them a chance to make their decision in private.'

There's a low hum of excitement as the assembled throng are herded back through to the party space for an emergency glass of champagne. Thank God I didn't stint on the booze budget. But how long have I got before it becomes obvious there's a full-blown crisis? I stride over to the judges' table.

'Can we all try to calm down here? Talk this through and reach a joint decision? Jan, can you do that for me?'

I'm glaring at Horst, trying to convey how much I need him to come back into line, but he's lost himself in character. Who knew he was so method? I wonder if Caitlin might bat her beautiful eyelashes and flirt one of them into submission, but she's too busy toying with her Marlboro Light packet and whining about not being allowed to smoke inside. With Horst totally intractable, I turn my attention to Ned.

'Can you not see any virtue in Jan's choice? It's a very distinctive piece, you must admit.'

My attention's drawn away for a second as I realize the door's ajar. I swear there's someone lurking in the shadows. Could Victor be lying in wait, looking for the perfect opportunity to fire me?

'So you agree with him, do you?' snarls Ned. 'You got some kind of conspiracy going on here, backing up your bogus mate?'

I'm starting to panic now. He's getting uncomfortably close to the truth, and still no one's showing any sign of backing down.

'You will not call me bogus!' says Horst, standing up and shaking his huge German fist. 'You will not insult my Anna like this!'

'My Anna is it?' says Ned, with a malicious smile. 'I knew there was something up with you two.'

'She is my friend and for this I will not apologize.'

What's he doing? He's mangling fact and fiction in a hideously dangerous way. This needs to end now.

'Jan . . .' I say, putting a hand on his arm. 'Perhaps we should take another look at the merits of Ned's choice. Purple is very next season.'

Horst's eyes blaze. 'He is a foolish, foolish man with no merit at all. I will not bend to his whimsy.'

'I'm a fool, am I?' says Ned, looming up out of his chair.

'Yes, a gross fool,' says Horst, standing his ground.

And before I can do anything, Ned is up and out of his chair, hurling himself at Horst. Caitlin squeals as I try to pull Horst out of the way, but he's all too ready to take Ned on. 'Horst!' I shout, before I can stop myself, but it has no effect. They're squaring up now, ready to aim punches, while Caitlin lurches towards the door . . . and runs straight into Tom. I don't think I've ever been so pleased to see anyone in my whole life. He rushes over to them, using his bulky form to push them apart. 'This stops now,' he says firmly, and Horst immediately starts to deflate.

'Who the fuck are you?' snarls Ned, pulling back.

'It's not important. I'm here to tell you you need to break it up.'

As Ned starts to draw back, I breathe a sigh of relief. But then he suddenly whips back, aiming an unexpected right hook at Horst.

'Ow, Christ!' says Tom, whose lightning attempt to hold him back has landed him with the full force of Ned's blow.

'Tom!' I rush over, trying to stem the flow of blood from his nose. 'What the hell do you think you're doing?' I shout at Ned furiously. But Tom recovers quickly.

'I think technically that's an assault. And obviously I've got quite a few witnesses.'

'Absolutely,' I add determinedly, 'you'll be looking at an ASBO at an absolute minimum.'

Good old Greg, thanks to him I'm something of an expert on the subject. Ned's on the back foot now, spluttering about it being self-defence, but Tom demolishes his argument in a heartbeat.

'I might be willing to skip pressing charges, but only if you agree to be a little more cooperative.'

Ned's artistic integrity takes a sudden nosedive as he considers the consequences. With no time to lose I foist the last of the rescue remedy on a shaken Caitlin, and instruct Ruby to pull the crowd back in. I want to ask Tom, the hero of the hour, a million questions but there's no time. 'I'm most sorry, Anna,' mutters Horst sheepishly as he returns to his seat, but I'm too cross to speak to him right now.

As the guests start to stream back in, Tom pulls me out into the garden. When he asks me if I'm OK I realize I'm shaking like a leaf. 'Hey,' he says, pulling me into him. Friendly or frisky? I hope so much it's the latter, but I can hardly bear the disappointment if it's not. I relax into it for a minute, but then start to break away. 'I'd better get back out there.'

'Hold up,' he says, keeping a determined grip on me. And before I know it we're kissing up against the wall of the church like godless teenagers. I can't believe how right it feels to have his big, bulky body pressing me against the cold stone. I could almost go for a knee trembler right here and now, but obviously that would be highly inappropriate.

'Now I've really got to go,' I say, feeling high on nerves and excitement – and love, I think. He follows me back in, squeezing in on the end of the front row. I cast a glance at my troublesome panel, fervently hoping they've been chastened into silence. I've appointed Caitlin jury foreman and, despite his heavy scowl, Ned refrains from contradicting her when she announces Marco as the winner. Horst risks giving me a tiny thumbs-up under the table, but I'm still too angry to manage anything more friendly than a glower.

The room erupts in applause as tears roll down Marco's callow cheeks. While no one's looking my way, I grab the opportunity to give Tom the biggest snog imaginable, accompanied by Spicy Nights' spirited rendition of 'I Get a Kick Out of You'. Suddenly I'm feeling quite warm towards them.

With the competition over, the party spills back into the main area. The drama's somehow brought the event to life; there's a real sense of bubbling excitement and bonhomie. With everyone well-oiled and content, I decide I'm excused hostess duties. Besides, I've got to cross-question Tom. It emerges that he slipped in during the catwalk show, but lurked at the back so as not to throw me off my stride. Now I finally risk asking him the million-dollar question: is cranberry girl history?

'It just wasn't me, Anna. It might make my life, and Belle and Joe's lives, easier if it was, but it wasn't. Louisa's a fantastic person, but she's not you.'

'When you didn't call, I just thought . . .'

'I wanted to sort it out properly. I didn't want to get into some hideous love triangle.' He says it with a smile, clearly unable to believe he'd ever be worthy of a cat fight. 'It just wasn't right.' He pauses. 'Besides, she had this weird sexy dance she kept doing.'

'A sexy dance? I never dance, just so you know.'

'I can't believe I'm saying this. It's just the kind of thing you fixate on.'

'Tell me.'

'She'd sort of do this sort of wiggle, with her eyes shut and her arms like this.' He's gyrating and pouting: it really isn't very erotic. 'Anyway, I never knew quite what to do with my face. And I kept thinking how much it'd make you laugh. I thought that about lots of things actually.'

I kiss him again, feeling vaguely guilty about (not) dancing on Louisa's grave. But reading between the lines it sounds like what she really wanted was a pinstripe-wearing stockbroker type who was happy to take her to the River Café at regular intervals. Whereas it turns out that what I really want is a shambolic, fleece-wearing single dad who lives in a rented basement. Who knew?

'Anna?'

Oh my God: it's Becky. Hair scraped back, and clad in baggy jeans, she's a million miles from the polished über-babe I last laid eyes on.

'What are you doing here?' I say, too happy to do frosty.

'I know I'm a mess, but I just had to come and find you.'

I draw back warily. Maybe this is my karma from the cranberry girl saga, and she's concealing a knife.

'I just wanted to say how sorry I am, and to say thank you. And to tell you I'll sign anything you want me to sign. Although I doubt you're going to want that story anyway now.'

She tells me how my accusations nagged away at her, however much she tried to deny them. Eventually she followed Lucas on one of his many writing retreats, only to find he'd gone for a dirty weekend with the Brazilian.

'So I changed the locks, and chucked his stuff out on the street. And you know how high up the flat is!'

'What, you literally chucked it?'

'Yeah, I'm not really sure the laptop survived.' She gives me a satisfied smile. 'I think a couple of his master-pieces could be lost forever.'

'Cheers to that,' I say, handing her a glass of champagne. 'Come and meet my friends, I think you'll like them.'

I take her over to Polly and Susie, and soon the four of us are laughing like drains about the whole sorry debacle. We're interrupted by Horst, who's eagerly rewriting history.

'My acting is very polished I believe, in order for me to have convinced the unpleasant man that I was truly a fashion professional.'

Polly raises her eyebrows, clocking my murderous look, but Tom jumps in before I can speak.

'It was fantastic the way you stood up to him. You did really well up there.'

'I thought I knew nothing of dresses, but I believed that Marco was the true winner. I could not stand back and allow the crown to be snatched from his jaws.'

And in a funny way I find myself admiring his mis-placed integrity. Though I suppose it's easy to now I'm in the clear. Roger looks like he's going to weep with relief, and Victor's congratulations verge on effusive. 'Martha wants to have a private word with you too,' he tells me, which triggers a bit of a panic attack. She was clearly a big fan of Harry's, and I'm not sure my more downmarket shoots are going to satisfy her. As I cross the room, I notice that Jocasta's trapped one of the handsome young designers in a corner. Is her gay-dar really that hopeless? She raises a wobbly glass in my direction.

'We should give ourselves a firm pat on the back for tonight's efforts!' she says.

'Yeah, we should,' I say, feeling absurdly warm towards her. 'Even without Dr Neil Fox it's turned out to be a bit of a triumph.'

She leans in conspiratorially, leaking booze fumes. 'I have to admit that ever since Percy popped out, I haven't had many chances to kick my heels. It's rather a hoot to have a night off.'

'It is, isn't it?'

'Enjoy the freedom while you've got it, that's my tip.' She taps her nose conspiratorially. 'I can assure you it doesn't last forever.'

'I plan to,' I tell her, suddenly wondering if it's possible she's been more jealous than smug. But there's no time to stop and reflect: I'm on a mission to track down Martha.

'Anna!' says Martha, enveloping me in an unexpected hug. 'Thank you so much for all you've done.'

'Thank *you*. I'm sorry about the whole Harry thing.'

'Well, this Jan Pzeknik was an inspired alternative. He's obviously got great vision.'

'Yes, quite,' I say, praying there'll be no more

Googling. Anyway, if I resign quickly enough I'll be out the door before he's exposed.

'I've got a proposition to make to you, Anna, but I don't know how you'll feel about it.'

'Try me.'

'How do you feel about New York?'

'Very, very good.' I really do. Every time I go I come back with my own bodyweight in shoes.

'We're going to be staffing a new imprint out there, which is due to hit the stands next spring. Fashion's clearly your thing, so it seems a waste that we've got you stuck on a more domestic title.'

Oh my God, this is it. It's not quite George Clooney at Claridge's, but it's not far off.

'So what do you say? Would you consider relocating? It would need a minimum commitment of two years, but we could offer you an excellent package.'

And I stand there, frozen. An eager acceptance forms in the back of my throat, but then I look across the room at Tom suffering Horst shoving a cocktail sausage in his face. Horst has very firm views on the poor standard of sausage that the English endure, and Tom's clearly making a sterling attempt at feigning interest. I can't believe I'm going to say this.

'Can I think about it?'

29

Every time the bells peal, I feel like my head's splitting in two. Why the hell did I drink so much champagne last night?

'You're so lucky having nine months, hangover free,' I whisper at Susie.

'Yeah, but at least you look elegant. I swear people are going to mistake me for the marquee.'

Polly's done us proud, giving us elegant blue shift dresses rather than hideous mini-meringues, but Susie's enormous bump has necessitated quite a lot of fabric. And here she is now, gliding down the stairs in her fabulous off-white, off the shoulder wedding dress.

'Do I look a twat? Be honest.'

We hug her, we cry, we practise carrying her train. And then we head for the church, where I watch the man I once believed to be the love of my life marry my best friend. And I cry again, but for all the right reasons. 'Are you OK?' whispers Tom, passing me a tissue. How much earth does he have under his fingernails? He's always slightly off-smart. Thank God I didn't go down the fashionista route – having him by my side would've made it so obvious I was a fraud. I grab the tissue gratefully and lean into him.

Polly and Adam have asked everyone to request their

favourite song for the wedding disco, hence the fact that I later find myself dancing to 'Livin' on a Prayer' with Horst. 'God knows it won't be a sexy dance,' I tell Tom as I leave him valiantly discussing the joys of parenthood with Wet Martin.

'How do you enjoy your newfound freedom?' asks Horst, punching the air vigorously as the chorus kicks in.

'I love it,' I tell him, which I do. I've been pleasantly surprised how much work I've picked up since I've gone freelance. I can write about what I want, when I want to and funnily enough it's never the magic of mushrooms. The kind of publications I never thought would give me the time of day seem oddly receptive to my ideas. And the fact that I've got my share of the house means there's no great pressure. Not now I'm living with Tom. New York would've rocked but he couldn't be that far away from the kids, and it turns out I couldn't be that far away from him.

'And do you believe that you will be the next of the ladies to trip up the aisle? I hope extremely that Ruby will one day agree to make this most special journey with me.' Maybe she will. Right now she's smiling at us from the bar, revelling in Horst's unbridled affection for shaggy-haired rockers. If she loves him despite his music taste then her feelings must run pretty deep.

'Marry Tom?' I say. 'It's entirely possible.' I look over to him, an unstoppable grin peeling its way across my face. He looks back, instinctively aware my gaze has turned in his direction, and I immediately stop my embarrassing pogo-ing. He ambles over.

'Sorry, Horst, can I borrow her back?' He pulls me into him.

'It may surprise you to learn this, but that actually was a very sexy dance.'

'Oh really?'

'Yes, really.'

'I aim to please.'

I smile up at him, taking in his weather-beaten face. All his imperfections have started to feel like perfections, just slightly twisted ones. The fact that none of them send me into a neurotic tailspin makes me positively delight in them.

'We should go back soon,' I tell him. 'We've got to pick up the kids by midday.'

Easter at EuroDisney. I can't quite say it's the holiday of my dreams, but I'm starting to adjust to the bizarro version of happy ever after. I even suggested that we take Freddie along for the ride. He's so excited that he's had his Teletubbies backpack filled up and ready to go for a whole fortnight.

'Hold on,' says Tom, 'we can't leave yet. Any minute now my song's going to come on.'

And here it is.

Wimoweh, a-wimoweh, a-wimoweh, a-wimoweh,
A-wimoweh, a-wimoweh, a-wimoweh, a-wimoweh,
We-de-de-de, de-de-de-de-de de, we-um-um-a-way.

'This is your song?'

'No, it's our song.'

'No way, it can't be our song. It's physically impossible for this to be anyone's song.'

'Get used to it, Anna, you're going to be hearing it for the rest of your life.'

And with that he starts up a crazy jungle dance, a dance too seductive for Horst to resist joining in with. And before I know it I'm right in the middle of them, throwing my arms around randomly, wondering if this really might be as good as it gets.

Acknowledgements

For my mother, Stephanie Brann, who is most definitely not Karen, with boundless love and affection. And in loving memory of my father, John Patrick Moran (1952–2000).

For my peerless grandmother, Rosemary Brann. Huge love to my exceptional family – Claudia, Antonia and Andrew and all their lovely appendages (Leyla, Toby, Caitlin, Leo, Felix, Milo and Joe) and spouses. And Lizzie and Annie. And Miller of course.

For Kay, with endless affection. And Ray, who is all about plums. And Kate, Clova and Anne. And also Sophia – thank you for making Hysteria Lane such a haven.

For Warwick. Come home soon – there's no substitute for quality … For Chazza the wolf, thanks for keeping your pants in the cereal cupboard. And Piers and Matthew too, and Charlie the girl – a late addition but a very dear one.

With huge thanks to the Woodward Gentles for the timely loan of their lovely cottage at a particularly spiky moment. And Nina for being there too.

For my Arvon tutor Christopher Wakling, whose initial enthusiasm was invaluable. And for Steve May, who gave such brilliant notes throughout. And with huge thanks to Camilla Hornby at Curtis Brown and Kate Burke at Penguin.

For Lucy Richer, Louise Clayton, Nicola Larder and Olivia Trench, who all gave me fantastic input.

And in memory of Sheila Parsons (1935–2008) who was very much here during the writing.

Loved
this book?

Meet someone who loves
what you love too.

Go to www.penguindating.co.uk
and discover your next chapter.

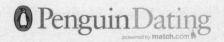

He just wanted a decent book to read ...

Not too much to ask, is it? It was in 1935 when Allen Lane, Managing Director of Bodley Head Publishers, stood on a platform at Exeter railway station looking for something good to read on his journey back to London. His choice was limited to popular magazines and poor-quality paperbacks – the same choice faced every day by the vast majority of readers, few of whom could afford hardbacks. Lane's disappointment and subsequent anger at the range of books generally available led him to found a company – and change the world.

'We believed in the existence in this country of a vast reading public for intelligent books at a low price, and staked everything on it'
Sir Allen Lane, 1902–1970, founder of Penguin Books

The quality paperback had arrived – and not just in bookshops. Lane was adamant that his Penguins should appear in chain stores and tobacconists, and should cost no more than a packet of cigarettes.

Reading habits (and cigarette prices) have changed since 1935, but Penguin still believes in publishing the best books for everybody to enjoy. We still believe that good design costs no more than bad design, and we still believe that quality books published passionately and responsibly make the world a better place.

So wherever you see the little bird – whether it's on a piece of prize-winning literary fiction or a celebrity autobiography, political tour de force or historical masterpiece, a serial-killer thriller, reference book, world classic or a piece of pure escapism – you can bet that it represents the very best that the genre has to offer.

Whatever you like to read – trust Penguin.